A WARTIME

The next twenty days were one long
booze-up. Bombs never stopped Ginger,
who took Jim and Maggie up to London to
dives, beer cellars and night clubs. Maggie saw
and heard things she never knew existed.
It was lovely to see Ginger again, but at the
end of the twenty days, Maggie had had
enough of the comings and goings.
Also, the way her Jim hung around the
girls Ginger brought home upset her.

On the last Saturday night, the party
broke up. Since it was a quiet night with no
raids, Maggie decided to take Pie Shop
for a walk. In the full moonlight the little street
seemed so silent and empty, apart from a
young couple who made love by the park
railings. Maggie crossed the road not wanting
to pass too close to them. She suddenly
heard that deep chuckle—there was no
mistaking it. The moonlight showed them
clearly. She was blond and pretty and her big
bully Jim held her close. Maggie's heart
missed a beat, but she turned and went
in the other direction and was in bed when
Jim came in. It did not hurt as much as she
thought it would; in her heart she had
always known it. But wait until he went back,
she thought. She was not going to sit
at home anymore.

Books by Lena Kennedy

Kitty
Maggie

Published by POCKET BOOKS

Maggie

Lena Kennedy

PUBLISHED BY POCKET BOOKS NEW YORK

POCKET BOOKS, a Simon & Schuster division of
GULF & WESTERN CORPORATION
1230 Avenue of the Americas, New York, N.Y. 10020

Published by arrangement with Paddington Press, Ltd.
Library of Congress Catalog Card Number: 78-21603

ISBN: 0-671-42378-9

First Pocket Books printing April, 1980

20 19 18 17 16 15 14 13 12

POCKET and colophon are trademarks of Simon & Schuster.

Printed in the U.S.A.

For Angela
who encouraged and
inspired me

BOOK ONE

1

Childhood

The back streets of Stepney was where it all began. Maggie could still see her own mean little street, Witton Street, with its houses along each side of the road without a space in between. "Up-and-downers" they called these dwellings in Stepney, with their two rooms up and two rooms down. There was a pub on each corner at one end of the street and the overpowering spire of the Roman Catholic church at the other. The whole of Maggie's youth had been spent in that dim street where the rough stones that made up the road cut into your bare feet and a tumble made a nasty cut or graze, often ending with a trip to the hospital when the dirt infected it. But still the kids played out there. The street teemed with them for there was no room to play in the up-and-downers, especially since there was often ten to a family. But Maggie, she was different: an only child was Maggie amid huge families.

You could always find Maggie during opening hours, sitting on the doorstep of the Barley Mow—the most popular of the two locals which adorned the street. From six in the evening until ten at night, and longer at weekends, in a little plaid dress and black stockings with holes in them, Maggie sat on the wooden doorstep waiting for her beloved father—or Dah, as she called him. In later years she often thought back to those long hours of waiting and she would remember the smell of the fish-and-chip shop round the corner and the oily taste of the ha'p'orth of cracklings—for that was all that Dah, who was Irish and a navvy on the tube, could afford in the week. But Friday and Saturday were gala days when the wages were paid. Then, Maggie had a whole pennyworth. At the fish shop she would order skate, and maybe get a pig's trotter from the man on the barrow who came past at nine o'clock in the evening.

In the cold of winter she would wait in the corridor of the Barley Mow, standing silent and still, while the children played outside. On summer evenings she would watch the flies as they crawled up the pub door. They used to go to sleep in the cracks of the wood, drowsy with the smell of beer, and Maggie would push them along with her finger.

At ten o'clock the men would all begin to come out of the pub. As the large boots covered with white cement passed, Maggie knew it was her Dah and she would tag on behind him. He would stay outside for a while with his mates. Sometimes they talked, other times they argued and even fought. But it was all the same to sleepy Maggie; she just waited until the toil-worn hand grasped hers and she and Dah went home together.

Home was a little up-and-downer three doors from the pub. There was an old brass bed in the corner where Dah slept, with its four ugly brass knobs. If you looked in them, your face seemed alternately long and then fat, and kept changing as you moved. This was a favorite game of Maggie's on the long days alone. She faintly remembered someone who slept with Dah in that bed; must have been her mother, but it all seemed so vague and in the distance.

Because another family lived upstairs, Maggie slept in the same room on an old horse-hair sofa which had arms that wobbled and squeaked. Whenever she turned over the horse hair came out and pricked her legs. In the summer, there was the "red army," but Dah had a cure for them: he drowned everything in paraffin which smelled even worse than the bugs. This was Maggie's bed—the only one she had ever known and she was quite content in it as long as Dah was near.

Dah rose early every morning. Even on Sunday, he would bring her a mug of weak tea and say, "Here ye are, gel, just a wet." On Sundays they never had a proper breakfast until after Mass. Punctually, at ten to ten, they would set off down the street towards the church—Maggie in her best white dress and a little straw hat with an emerald green ribbon, and Dah, with all traces of cement removed from his boots which had plenty of "spit and polish," wearing his best tweed jacket and gray flannels. This was a terrible ordeal for Maggie; she was so conscious of the street, of the eyes that peered from downstairs windows and the looks of the women that hung out of the upstairs, and worse, the conversations of the shawled women who sat on the windowsills.

"There's old Con, off to holy Joe's," they would call out.

"Needs to do a bit of praying, the old bastard," others would retort.

To this, Dah seemed deaf. He just marched on holding Maggie's hand. Nothing and nobody was going to make him late for ten o'clock Mass.

Once they were safely inside the cold church and Maggie had placed her fingers in the cool holy water at the door, a grand feeling of relief came over her and her knees went weak as she knelt beside her Dah. It was a feeling that never left her all her life, even when hard living made her lose her faith—it was always there. It was probably nerves, Maggie used to console herself, but really it was the extreme tension of walking through the street that was the cause.

After Mass, home to eggs and bacon cooked by Dah —that was luxurious living in those hard days. Then off to the Barley Mow and Maggie to her seat on the doorstep.

On Sunday morning the street was teeming with kids, most with their backsides out of their trousers. They played, boys and girls together with a thick rope stretched right across the road. They did skipping and sometimes a game called Tibby Cat which they played with pieces of wood for bats as the two players tried to hit the ball into each other's chalked-up square on the ground. The windows often got broken and there were many rows.

So there was plenty for Maggie to see as she sat out there. As the customers went in and out of the pub they said hello to her, and she was even given the occasional halfpenny.

The one person Maggie dreaded was Mrs. Burns. When she saw her tall figure coming down the street Maggie would shiver in her shoes. There was no reason for this as Liza Burns was really quite a kind-hearted woman. On Sunday mornings she would be coming for her "livener," as she called it, still wearing the sacking apron that was wet at the edges with traces of hearth-stone decorating it. For Liza cleaned doorsteps for two-pence a time; in better class districts in the main road she got fourpence. In this way she had managed to bring up five fatherless children after her husband, Jim, had gone down at sea, as she repeatedly informed the neighbors during the little outbursts of trouble that often broke out. Now in her thirties and still handsome (no widow's cap or shawl for her), her black hair was bound tightly in a bun and never moved while her black button eyes swept the streets as she sailed along —and woe betide anyone who spoke out of turn . . .

"Get your arse off that doorstep, gel," she would say to Maggie. "Tain't natural sitting there like a bloody old woman. Go and play with the kids."

But little Maggie never moved or spoke. She just twisted her long plaits nervously with both hands while tears flooded her blue eyes.

Liza would flounce into the bar and say, "Con, get that kid of yours off the doorstep, she'll grow up daft."

Then Maggie would hear the soft brogue of her Dah as he said, "Now Liza, leave the child be, 'tis better she sits there than runs with hooligans in the street."

"Calling my kids hooligans?" Liza's voice would become shrill and then there would be shouting. But Dah would just retire to the corner, quietly drinking his pint while Liza let off steam.

Little Maggie on the doorstep would listen but never move until Dah put his hard-working hand in hers and they went home to Sunday lunch of boiled bacon and spuds in their jackets.

In comparison to the rest of the kids in the street, Maggie had a good life, so Dah said, as he put huge lumps of fat from the bacon on her plate. A newspaper was their tablecloth in the sparse kitchen which was furnished with only the table and two chairs.

"'Tis not many sees a good Sunday dinner like this, girlie," Dah would say. "Half starved, them poor bloody kids out there. All on the bunghouse they are. *Me,* never had a day's charity in me loife—not while I got a pair of hands to work with."

So there sat little Maggie, trying to swallow the fatty food, and learning the philosophy of working-class life in Stepney from the lips of her beloved Dah.

Goodbye to Dah

As the weeks and months passed Maggie's legs grew too long for the black stockings and the sides of the plaid dress burst out. She had turned thirteen and a half now —almost a young woman. But with her long legs stuck out over the pavement, Maggie still kept up her long vigils.

This was about the time when Jim Burns came home. He was the eldest of Liza Burns's brood and, as they say in the East End, he had been in a "bit of bovver" with the law. Jim had been lucky, for instead of being sent to an approved school, he went to a training ship

as a special concession for a naughty boy whose dad
had died serving his country. Now, with his hair cut
very short and wearing a smart sailor's uniform, he
swaggered down the street. Jim was fifteen, big and
broad-shouldered; the open-air life and good food
aboard the *Arethusa* had matured him. He was Liza's
son all right with the same black button eyes, now
combined with a crooked nose—the result of many
fights on board. He was no beauty, but Jim with his big
shoulders was quite unique in the street where weedy
little boys worked in factories to support the home. So
when Maggie saw Jim her blue eyes stared in admiration and she tried to pull her skirt down to hide the
holes in her stockings.

The etiquette of the street demanded that the first
place Jim visited was the Barley Mow, the family local,
where he stood up to the counter and drank pints of
ale, amidst an admiring audience of little men in checked
caps and white mufflers who felt his muscles and said
how much like his pa he was.

Jim had taken a good look at Maggie as he went in.
"What's that daft gel sitting out there for?" he asked
his ma.

"It's Maggie Riley," she said, "I'm always telling
that boozy old man of hers to shift her. Don't think
she's quite the ticket." They both laughed the same sort
of loud cackle, and Maggie, with her ears very red, got
up and crept round the corner to wait for Dah.

It was past five o'clock and Maggie had lit the fire and
made the tea. Dah would be here soon. He was going
to bring home pease pudding and faggots which she
fancied. Soon she was getting quite hungry. Perhaps
he had gone straight to the pub, though he didn't
usually go until he and Maggie had had their supper.
Better go and look, she thought.

By now it was gone six o'clock and there were quite
a few regulars in the Barley Mow. They seemed to be
whispering together, but when Maggie looked in they

all went silent. A strange feeling stirred Maggie's stomach—perhaps it was because she was hungry.

"Have you seen me Dah?" she asked a man who came out. He looked dismayed. "No, cock," he said and hurried on.

Then Maggie heard them say in the pub: "She don't know. Who's going to tell her? Better ask Liza." Another man left the pub and crossed the road to Liza Burns's house.

Maggie felt frightened; they were talking about her Dah, she felt sure of that.

The huge figure of Liza came on the scene. Wearing the snow-white apron she wore in the evenings, she beckoned from the small doorway of her house. "Come here, Maggie," she called. "I want you."

Maggie went very reluctantly, but Liza, with a white face, said, "Come in and have a warm, love," and ushered Maggie into her back kitchen.

Maggie had never been in anyone else's home before. She looked around the bright little room in surprise. A wooden dresser, filled with clean, shining crockery, stood against the wall; there was a white cloth on the table, and four shock-headed little boys sat playing Ludo. Big brother Jim lounged around the fire, reading the newspaper.

The homely, comfortable scene shocked Maggie; she just stared.

"Move over, Jim, and let Maggie near the fire," Liza said. "You want a cup of tea, Maggie?"

With her hands round the mug of hot tea, Maggie gathered her wits together. What was happening? Where was her Dah?

Her blue eyes asked the silent questions of Liza, who burst out, "Don't get upset, Maggie, your dad's had an accident. He's in the 'orspidal."

"Where is he? I want to see him."

"Tomorrow, my love. You stay with us tonight." Liza put a gentle arm around Maggie. "Now, you have a good cry if you want, love."

But Maggie did not cry. She just sat, looking forlorn.

"Get off to bed, you little sods," screamed Liza turning her attention to the boys who all scooted up the stairs. She wiped her eyes with her apron.

"Gawd, need a wet," she said. "Jim, you look after Maggie." Grabbing her black shawl, she made straight for the Barley Mow.

On either side of the fireplace sat Maggie and Jim. His black, deepset eyes looked sympathetically at Maggie who stared solemnly at the polished grate with its great iron kettle.

"You was fond of your old man, wasn't you Maggie?"

"Of course I am. I love me Dah," she said simply.

"You know he's dead, don't you?" Jim looked directly at Maggie's bowed head.

Maggie remembered for the rest of her days how her heart wept at that moment. She began to scream.

"Cor blimey," said Jim, getting up. "Shut up, Maggie! You'll wake the bloody neighbors." Not knowing what else to do, he sat down beside her and held her to him until she had calmed down. They sat very close together on the chair.

"Don't know why the old gel didn't tell you the truth," he said. "This is how I see it, Maggie: your old man was a bloody hero. He volunteered to go down the tube with the council bloke to look at the gas bottles that was leaking. Both got blown sky high."

Maggie began to cry again.

"Don't take on, gel. You can't bring him back and you're a big gel now."

His hands felt her small breasts and Maggie drew closer. She liked the warm feeling from the pressure of his body.

When Liza came back, Maggie was asleep on Jim's lap.

"You ain't wasted much bloody time," she snapped.

"Well, I told her the truth, Ma."

"Well, that's over anyway," said Liza. "Poor little cow. He never let her out of his sight. She ain't 'alf

gonna miss 'im. Come on, Maggie, off to bed," said
Liza, nudging the girl awake.

As she lay in bed beside Liza in the front room,
Maggie could see the aspidistra and the lace curtains
by the window. Fancy her being here; she could not
believe it. Liza's heavy body moved in her sleep and
she snored lustily. I'm never going to see Dah any more
—she could not believe that either. Then she thought
of Jim and the warmth of his legs as she sat on his lap,
and suddenly a luscious, comfortable feeling possessed
her and she dozed off to sleep.

The funeral was a grand affair. The many Irish men
who had worked with Dah on the tube came in force.
These big, brawny and hard-working navvies carried
the coffin in turn and knelt shoulder to shoulder in the
church in respect of their comrade who had given his
life to progress while building London's underground
railway system.

Maggie was an orphan in all respects; not one relation came forward to claim her. Dah had lost contact
with his relatives in Ireland.

"Poor little bugger," said Liza, "she's got a home
with me. I had respect for old Con. Hard-working man
he was."

So Maggie went to live in Liza's house.

The novelty of living in Liza's spick-and-span home
pleased Maggie. She loved to dust the ornaments and
rearrange the many vases on the mantlepiece. "That's
right, Maggie, make yourself useful, gel," Liza would
say. So when Liza went off cleaning doorsteps, Maggie
tidied the house and called the boys up for school and
handed them their breakfast of one huge "doorstep" of
bread and margarine.

Then Jim would chase them out of the house and
he and Maggie had the place to themselves. When Jim
held her close in the dark passageway, she forgot the
hurt in her heart, and loved Jim with all the unques-
tioning loyalty she had given to her Dah.

"Don't tell Ma, will you Maggie?" Jim would say.

"No," said Maggie. The devil himself would never have got out of Maggie the things Jim did to her.

The news went around the street that Maggie Riley and Jim Burns were courting.

"Better get that boy back in the navy," said Liza. "Seems like he can't leave that girl alone. And she's as dossie as they make 'em. Can't wonder at that, the way she was brought up."

But Jim had no intention of returning to the navy and the navy was not so keen to have Jim either. In spite of his good physique, Jim had been quite unable to learn; anything to do with books Jim could not take in. So in the peacetime navy where studying was important, he was not much use.

He became a working lad and got a casual job in the market. On Saturday nights, he and Maggie went to the pictures, but every other night of the week, while Liza was over at the pub, they made love in the back kitchen.

When Jim was sixteen and a half and Maggie just fifteen, she became pregnant. What a scene there was when Liza found out! She clouted Jim good and proper, but to Maggie she was kind.

"Can't put all the blame on you, Maggie, gel. Got in the family way meself when I was your age. He's like his old man, he is—never got his boots off, when he came on leave, before he had me across the bed."

But Maggie couldn't care two hoots. She gloated because she had landed her Jim. No one else could have him now. He was hers.

"She won't be so bloody pleased with herself when he's married to her," said Liza to her cronies. And to Maggie, "Wait a while for the wedding. Give Jim a chance to save a few bob so we can have a party."

"But I'll be six months by then," protested Maggie.

"Don't make no odds," said Liza, "as long as you get married before it's born."

So little Maggie waddled around the house with her belly getting fatter. She wondered what her Dah would say if he were there.

As time went on, Jim seemed to change. He stayed out late at night and made a lot of flash friends from down the market. These wayward lads who had lived through a depression never held down a regular job. That they would eventually lead Jim into trouble was quite obvious.

Maggie's Wedding

Maggie Riley was only fifteen years and six months when she married her Jim at the local registry office in the town hall. "Better say you're sixteen," said Liza.

So with a long gray dress that Liza had borrowed from a shopkeeper whose doorstep she cleaned, and a white, floppy hat which set off her dark hair, Maggie looked very sweet. The dress was tight across her stomach. Jim was very smart in light-blue Oxford bags and a fancy waistcoat.

After the wedding, there was a big party in the Burns's house and the Barley Mow. All Jim's mates from the market came, and the little back yard was stacked high with crates of beer.

Jim's four impish little brothers—Mick, Ginger and the twins, Lennie and Boy Boy—helped themselves to bottles of beer and scrounged fags from all the company. Then they got so excited that they started to fight between themselves until Liza waded in and beat them all up so they went crying to bed.

It's funny, thought Maggie, but she was not enjoying herself at her own wedding. She supposed you should. The Knees-Up-Mother-Brown which the guests were dancing shook the wooden floorboards and the vibration was just like someone hitting her in the stomach. She felt uneasy. She couldn't find Jim anywhere; he seemed to keep disappearing. She felt lonely and longed to see her Dah again.

Maggie wandered out into the road. Apart from the noise of the party and the crowds in the Barley Mow, the street was unusually quiet. The two street lamps were lit and somehow everything seemed unreal. The yellow light from the gas lamps shone in through the window of Maggie's old home and the two brass knobs were outlined inside. (The young couple that had moved in had taken the bed—bugs and all. It was easy to get a place to live; the hard part was finding the money for the furniture.)

As Maggie stared in through the window, a baby started crying and a man's voice called out, "Shut that flaming kid up! What with that bloody party and that flaming kid, I ain't getting no sleep."

Feeling embarrassed, Maggie walked away and went further down the street towards the church. The tall spire and the white, stone walls shone out eerily in the yellow of the gas lamp. Over the door was a little statue of the Virgin. Maggie held on to the iron railings and looked at the locked door. If only she could get inside, she would feel safe. She remembered how she used to be as a child, but now there was no warm hand to hold or a soft Irish brogue that said: "Come along, Maggie gel, or we'll be late for Mass."

"Oh Dah! Dearest Dah!" cried Maggie out aloud. Suddenly, a shadow crossed over the moon casting a strange, silver light which shone on the church steps —and there was her Dah! He was going up the steps, his hat in his hand, wearing his best Sunday suit. Maggie sank down by the railings sobbing.

That was where Jim found her when he came looking. He pulled her up. "Come on, Maggie," he said. "What are yer doing here? There's a party on." Jim was well boozed. His collar was undone and there was lipstick on his face.

A very subdued bride went back to the wedding party. A strange thing had happened to Maggie. It was many years before she could enter a church alone again. The parish priest tried hard, but nothing would induce her to go up the steps. In the end, knowing she had married into a rough family, he gave up. It was a mystery; all Maggie would say about it was, "I shouldn't have got married in the town hall."

2

The Barves

After the wedding there were a few changes in Liza's house.

"I'll move upstairs with the boys," said Liza to Jim. "You and Maggie can have the parlor."

It could not have been easy for her to part with the precious parlor for Liza had been very proud of that little front room with its lace curtains and the aspidistra placed in an art-pot in front of the window. "Come here when we got married we did, me and my big Jim," she used to say.

Maggie liked dusting the big black vases with red roses painted on them, but most of all she loved the one with dingle dangles on it—long crystals that hung down and glittered with different colors. She would arrange and polish them daily while Liza was off on her doorstep cleaning. She had never seen pretty things like these before. In the house she had shared with Dah, there had just been the bare necessities for living. She loved the little white cloth on the table by the bed and she loved the bed too. Although it was only wrought iron, it was decorated top and bottom with frilly muslin curtains, and there was not one trace of a bug. There were bugs upstairs in the boys' room all right, but none dared to enter Liza's front room.

"It'll do till you get a start of yer own," Liza said, "But don't let them bloody kids go in there."

Maggie often wondered how the rest of the family managed to get into the one room upstairs. It was square and contained three beds. There was no room for anything else and to make them, Maggie had to climb over each bed in turn. Liza slept in one and the four little boys slept two in a bed. Liza had never had a daughter, just boys. "Just my bleeding luck," she used to say.

The blankets and sheets were always clean. Liza was very fussy about washing. The weekly wash was always done on Mondays down at the public baths. There was only a cold water tap outside the house, in the scullery at the back.

The little brothers loved washdays. "Muvver's gone to the barves," they'd be heard to say and they proceeded to play up merry hell for they knew Liza would be gone most of the day and not sitting in the Barley Mow looking to see if they had gone to school.

Maggie hated going to the "barves." Early in the morning, the old-fashioned pram would be piled high, and off she and Liza would go, through the market to reach the huge stone council building with its long, cold corridors and main washroom which was such a boon to the overworked women of the slums.

It was not so much the endless standing and the steam that Maggie disliked; it was more the shouting and swearing of the untidy women. Liza would gossip and jaw all day as she scrubbed the linen and piled it into the heaters to dry. Little Maggie, doing her bit, would hear scraps of the conversation.

"That your daughter-in-law, Liza?"

"Yes, she's Jim's wife."

"Young ain't she?"

"Only fifteen. Got herself in the family way, silly cow."

"Don't they all. Living with you is she?"

"Yes. Got me best front parlor they have."

Maggie longed to run and hide, but there was no-where else to go.

At about four o'clock they emerged: little Maggie tired, wet and bedraggled, and a triumphant Liza parading up the street with her snow-white washing in the pram for all to see.

"Dirty load of sods, some of them," Liza would say, referring to the inhabitants of Witton Street. "Never see them up the barves. Don't know what state their bedclothes are in."

When washday came along on the week the baby was due, Liza shot a quick look at Maggie and said, "Better stop here today, Maggie. Looks like you're gonna drop it any minute."

Maggie's blue eyes widened with fright. "What shall I do if it starts?" she stammered.

"Send Ginger for Granny Goring. That'll be all right, she knows you're due. I told her last week." Then off down the road she went, pushing the pram of washing.

Towards evening Maggie stood at the door to watch the kids playing in the street, keeping her eye on Ginger's red head, afraid to let him out of her sight. When she yelled, "Fetch Gran," he was off like a shot.

Gran was soon toddling up the street with her wide figure, her knots of gray hair and the famous carpet bag which contained the tools of her trade. Gran was not a qualified midwife but she knew her job. Very soon, little Jim was being held up by the legs, while Gran's horny hand banged the life into him and he let out a ferocious yell. "It's a boy, Maggie," she said, "and a fine big one too." Scales were not part of Gran's equipment but she had a good sense of what she was doing. "Weighs about ten pounds, I reckon."

But the tired girl in bed, her hair all over the pillow, had closed her eyes and dropped off to sleep.

All the neighbors were good to her. Although, as they said, there was little to spare in the way of food in the other up-and-downers, they loved to be able to give what little they had. They brought her egg custards to buck her up, and every night a jug of black beer was sent over from the Barley Mow.

"Get that down, gel," said Liza. "Makes milk, that does."

Heroically, Maggie sat up and drank the vile stuff. Then she held little Jim to her breast and he guzzled lustily. There were no bottles for babies in those days; mother's milk was what they thrived on.

"Better get a job, Maggie," said Liza after Maggie's ten days in bed were over.

"A job?" Maggie stared at her, surprised.

"Jim ain't bringing home much, and my doorsteps ain't going to keep the flaming lot of us."

Maggie, who had never had to worry about money, looked embarrassed.

"Don't stand there looking daft, gel," shouted Liza. "All the gels around here have to work. What makes you think you're so different?"

"But the baby . . ." said Maggie timidly.

"He'll be all right," said Liza. "It's the school holidays so Ginger can look after him till I get back, and you can come home and feed him in your dinner hour."

Maggie looked doubtfully at Ginger who sat in the passage taking it all in and grinning. The way he dashed around made her nervous. To leave little Jim, only ten days old, was more than she could bear. But it was no good arguing with Liza; her fate was decided.

"There's a factory up the road," she said. "It makes clothes. I asked the guvnor. You can start Monday."

So Maggie became a working mother and little Jim was wheeled around the streets all morning by Ginger. At lunchtime, Maggie dashed home from the factory to feed him and in the afternoons he was parked outside the Barley Mow while Liza had a drink and gossiped to her cronies.

At first, the factory was a nightmare experience for Maggie; the long line of pale-faced girls who sweated over sewing machines, and the stale odor of rats that overran the factory sickened her. But soon she made friends and they taught her the machine and in a few days she had grown used to it. Half way through the morning, her breasts would begin to ache and the milk would seep through her blouse. The girls would call out: "Yer milk's coming in, Maggie. Hurry home and feed the kid."

Punctually at twelve o'clock, Maggie would be hurrying down the street to where little Jim was sitting outside the pub. Picking him up she would sit on the windowsill of the house and feed him. There was nothing odd about this; in those days it was a common sight to see a woman feeding her baby in the street. After she had changed him, she just had time for a quick cup of tea and a slice of bread and margarine. Then it was back to work until six o'clock.

In an old navy blue skirt and faded blouse that was too small for Liza, Maggie went back and forth six days a week—finishing at four on Saturdays. For this she received the princely sum of eight shillings a week.

Meanwhile, Jim had his casual job in the market. It was so casual that he had three days each week down the races with the boys. He had grown bigger and heavier, and wore loud clothes—a black-and-white dixie scarf tied twice round his neck and a light blue suit with the new style in pants. He was not unkind to Maggie. He crept into bed beside her at eleven o'clock each night after the pub had shut, and his strong arms went around her tired little body and Maggie was too sleepy to protest. So that's how, soon after, Tom was conceived.

The girls at the factory would say: "Blimey, Maggie, if you get any fatter, you won't reach the machine."

As her belly got slowly bigger, Mr. Fox, the little Jewish guvnor said: "We'd better have you pulling out bastings, Maggie, otherwise you might put a tuck in that belly of yours."

When her old navy skirt burst out at the sides, Maggie tried keeping it together with a safety pin until the forelady said: "I've got a remnant at home. I'll bring it in and one of the girls can run it up for you."

There were a lot of smiles when they dressed her

up in her brand new maternity skirt, and someone presented her with a red woolen jumper that had been badly knitted. Maggie looked very nice; the red jumper suited her dark hair as it hung down her back in waves.

All the girls in the factory stood around admiring her until old Mr. Fox rushed up waving his hand. "What's this?" he demanded. "A fashion show? Come on, girls, get those machines going." Laughing and giggling, they all went back to work.

The next day Maggie was absent, but someone had seen Granny Goring hurrying up the street, and the news soon went round that Maggie Burns had had another boy. Baby Jim was just fourteen months old when Tom was born.

"I suppose you'll have to pack up work now, Maggie," said Liza. "I can't manage two of them, me knees is playing up. I expect it's rheumatics."

Liza had housemaid's knee. And doctors cost money and there was none available. So she rubbed her knees with White Horse Oil and went on with her doorstep cleaning.

One day she burst into the house. "I've got a job for you, Maggie, gel," she said. "You can do for Mrs. Malloy twice a week, and take baby Jim with you. Ginger can mind Tom."

Maggie was dismayed. Mrs. Malloy, her father's friend, was a real church-going woman; every morning she was down at Mass with a lace mantilla on her head of bright red hair. She had a greengrocer's shop around the corner over which she lived. Shopkeepers were considered a cut above the stall holders and way above the sphere of folks who dwelt in the little up-and-downers—they had their own class distinction.

"It's only a couple of hours and you'll get a bit of stuff to bring home," said Liza, trying to console Maggie who knew that it was no good trying to argue with her mother-in-law.

So on Mondays and Fridays, she went to do for Mrs. Malloy.

At first, the flame-haired woman had stared at Maggie disapprovingly through her china-blue eyes. "You don't look over strong," she said, red in the face. "Still, having them kids so quick is bound to pull you down.

"I'll pay you sixpence an hour, Maggie. That's good pay around here—you won't get it anywhere else. Better put the baby somewhere, I suppose." Pulling out an empty orange crate, she said, "Wait a bit till I get an old blanket and he can go in here. Give him a crust to chew if he starts."

So with little Jim tucked up in the orange crate, Maggie swept, dusted and scrubbed for Mrs. Malloy. She would make a cup of tea at eleven thirty and then hurry home with her breasts full, almost bursting to feed Tom.

After a while, as Liza had foretold, there were a few bits to take home. One day a few carrots and onions; another, a stale cabbage; and once, a whole bag full of soft bananas. Ginger scoffed them up so quickly that he got diarrhea.

He was not a bad little boy, Ginger. Maggie had grown quite fond of him, and was confident that he would take good care of Tom. In spite of his urchin-like appearance and that mop of red hair that stuck out so wildly, always in need of a trim, he was a happy, generous boy and he loved Maggie; he would willingly do anything for her.

A Spark of Rebellion.

Ginger often came to meet Maggie from work, pushing the old-fashioned pram with the baby sleeping peacefully inside. He would meet Maggie in case there was an apple or something going.

One Friday after he had met her, as they walked home through the market, Maggie stopped to look at the second-hand shoes on one of the stalls. "Could do with a pair of shoes," she said. "These have got holes underneath." In her hand she held the shilling that Mrs.

Malloy had given her. No, she thought, she had better not buy the shoes, Liza would be waiting for her wages.

While Maggie looked at the shoes, little Jim had taken a fancy to a brightly colored rattle off the next stall. He waved the celluloid toy and cooed with joy. Maggie gently loosened his baby fingers from it and put it back on the stall and Jim started to scream blue murder.

Ginger stood nearby holding the pram. "Oh, buy it for him, Maggie," he said. "It's only tuppence."

"I daren't," whispered Maggie. "Yer ma relies on my shilling today."

With a shrug, Ginger walked on with the pram and Jim quietened down after Ginger made faces at him. But when they reached home, without a word, Ginger rushed off to play.

Maggie felt so downhearted as she placed the shilling on the mantlepiece for Liza. It would be nice to have some money of her own to buy the rattle for Jim and a white woolly hat for the baby, she thought. All the clothes they had were what Liza scrounged from the regulars whose doorsteps she cleaned. As Liza had said, Jim did not bring in much. Maggie was not disloyal to him, but sometimes, when he sneaked in late on Fridays, she knew he had gambled away his wages, and she wished he had not.

She would hear Liza's strident voice call out: "That you, Jim?"

Then the bawling match would start.

"No flaming money again, then?"

"All right, Ma, I might have a bit of luck next week."

"Next flaming week? What about this one? Who's going to feed them bloody kids of yours, eh?"

So they would go on and on, shouting and swearing until Maggie bit her fingers to stop herself screaming out in defense of her children.

As she changed the baby on the kitchen table, Maggie wondered how long it would go on. "Getting fed up with this bleeding life," she muttered. Maggie was now seventeen and mother of two. A spark of rebellion was beginning to glimmer.

Little Jim was rolling under the table and Ginger had suddenly reappeared. In Jim's tiny fist, Maggie noticed the brightly colored rattle.

"Where did you get that?" asked Maggie suspiciously.

"Look what I got yer," said Ginger to little Jim who shrieked with joy.

"Where did you get it, Ginger?"

"Nicked it of course." And away he went out the back, over the wall and was lost in the maze of streets.

This was the beginning of Ginger's life of crime. Maggie never knew what to do as little presents used to appear. One day it was a little powder puff inside a pretty crêpe hankie. No one had ever given her pretty things before.

"Oh, Ginger," she said sorrowfully, "you didn't nick it, did you?"

"Of course I did," he said proudly.

Maggie still had the words of Dah in her mind. He had taught her the ten commandments: thou shalt not steal. She looked at the little powder puff, turning it over in her hands. Ginger watched her with a big grin.

"It's no good to me, Ginger," she said. "I ain't got no powder. Give it to Ma."

But Ginger had already darted off. After a while he returned with a small box of Phul-nana face powder.

"Well," said Maggie as his little face looked up at hers seeking the affection he had always been starved of, "you're a case, you are. Come and have a slice of bread and jam."

From then on, Maggie kept "mum," as they say in Stepney. Later on, when things were really bad, she was very glad of the loot that Ginger brought home.

It was shortly afterwards that Jim was in his second bit of trouble. This time it was serious. A man had been beaten up and knifed on the train between Newmarket and Liverpool Street. He was not dead, but likely to die. They had Jim and two of his gang in custody awaiting trial.

To Maggie it was a shock but somehow, as the days leading up to the trial passed, she never felt the miss of Jim—he had left her to forage for herself for too long.

It was Liza who went to pieces. She got drunk twice a day for two weeks. "It's all your fault, lumbering him with those kids," she yelled. "Jim would've had a fine career in the navy."

But Maggie was getting tough. "That's right, Ma. Might have been a captain by now."

She put poor Liza to bed. Liza was always too drunk now to climb the stairs so she slept in the front parlor while Maggie went upstairs with the boys. "Little bitch," Liza muttered drunkenly as Maggie took off her shoes. "Dirty little bitch," she mumbled until her voice slurred off into a heavy sleep.

It was Ginger who was the lifeline in all of this. He played with the baby while Maggie did her best to quieten her mother-in-law and when Maggie came into the kitchen, her face white and drawn with exhaustion, Ginger laughed and said: "Bloody fine captain Jim would be—on a winkle barge." Roaring at his joke, he dashed out, taking his usual short cut over the back yard wall.

Maggie began cutting up the new loaf that Ginger had come by on his way home from school. Little Jim sat in the old armchair crumbling a sticky cake in his fist—he was never forgotten, there was always something for Jim. She was worried. She felt queasy in her stomach and had been sick that morning. If big Jim had left her in the family way again, she would not be surprised. But how the hell was she going to cope with three? Perhaps he would get off, she thought hopefully. But what difference would that make? Jim never brought home any money and if the old girl didn't pull herself together, the doorstep cleaning would be finished. Liza had lost a lot of her regulars already. Maggie's mind was in a whirl. How was she going to get enough money to feed them all? At seventeen and a half, it was quite a load for her young shoulders. Oh well, she thought, I suppose something good will turn up, and she went on slicing the bread and putting margarine on the huge pile of "doorsteps" which would soon disappear when the little boys came home from school.

The day of Jim's trial dawned and Liza, who had sobered up, was sitting waiting for Maggie. She was very solemn in her black coat which normally only came out for weddings and funerals.

"That all you got to wear?" she snapped at Maggie.

"That's all," said Maggie firmly. The old gray skirt which the girls at the factory had made for her was dirty and stained. Over it, Maggie wore a very old-fashioned striped jacket that someone had given her.

"Looks like a bundle of bleeding rags," said Liza. "Them kids don't look too clean either."

Feeling a trifle depressed, Maggie realized that if Jim went to prison she would have plenty of trouble with Liza.

"How do you expect me to look?" she retorted. "I've never got any money to buy clothes."

"Money?" shouted Liza. "How far do you think your bleeding half-crown a week goes?"

Off they went to the court where Jim was being tried. It was a long walk to Old Street. Maggie pushed the pram with the two babies inside while Liza marched along in front.

The trial did not last long. The gray-haired old judge, who had never known a day's hunger in his life, had no patience with these East End people. They made trouble for themselves. So when Jim and his two mates came up, he sentenced them to eighteen months hard labor.

"You hooligans," he said, "are very fortunate not to be here on a charge of murder. Luckily for you, that poor fellow didn't die. Society is not safe while you are lurking in the streets."

Jim and his mates stood in the dock; not a muscle of their faces moved. The women wept and shouted obscene things at the judge while Maggie sat in the corridor as they marched her man away. The little boys pointed at their dad. All Jim gave Maggie was a friendly wink as he passed by.

Outside the court, Liza stormed and carried on while a crowd of sympathizers gathered round. "Never had a bloody chance, he ain't. Snatched up he was, just a schoolboy. She knew what she was at. Crafty, that's what she is. Artful as a wagonload of monkeys—those quiet ones always are."

Maggie knew that it was her whom Liza referred to. It was to be expected for Liza worshiped her Jim. But Maggie's mind was confused as she pushed that heavy It was to be expected for Liza worshiped her Jim. But had left her pregnant once more. Whatever was she going to do?

Mrs. Malloy's face showed her disapproval at Maggie's lateness.

"Sorry I'm late, Mrs. Malloy," Maggie excused herself. She was about to tell her that Jim had been sentenced but instinct told her that this woman would not want to know.

"I brought both the kids," said Maggie. "I couldn't find Ginger."

"All right. Leave them in the front and get on with it. I have my nephew coming to stay so I'm busy this morning."

Maggie obediently put the pram outside the door. She didn't like leaving the babies; now that Tom sat up, he and Jim would torment each other. Jim was cutting his teeth and bit anything he could get hold of, including Tom. Perhaps Ginger will come along, she hoped.

Soon she was down on her knees with a big scrubbing brush, scrubbing the bare boards in the shop. That was the very first view John got of Maggie as he came in. His shadow blocked the doorway and Maggie looked up at this tall, fair, young man laden with bags.

"Hello, Aunt Betsy," he called. "Whose kids are those out there? They seem to be eating each other."

Maggie's eyes stared straight at him. He had never seen eyes so blue or cheeks so red and rosy before.

"Go and see to your children and then you'd better go, Maggie," said Mrs. Malloy.

John's mild gray eyes watched Maggie all the time as she washed her hands and took off her apron. But she was too preoccupied to notice. Miserable old cow, she was thinking, those poor kids stuck out there in the cold. For two pins I'd tell her where to put her job.

Taking the babies, Maggie went home to face her future without Jim. Liza had been brought back drunk and was in bed. Little Ginger was there with his pockets loaded as usual and, for a change, Mick was there too.

Mick was the next one to Jim. He was sixteen and ran round with the newspapers in the evening. He was a small boy for his age, but very independent. He was home very little, usually running in the streets, and Liza could not stand him. "Sly little bugger," she would say. "Makes plenty on them papers he does. Never brings much home."

Mick was standing by the table when Maggie came in. He had a bundle of clothes under his arm.

"I'm sorry about Jim, Maggie," he said.

"It's all right, Mick," said Maggie, "I'll get by."

"Here's a quid, Maggie. You keep it."

"I can't take that, Mick."

"Go on," he said, "you deserve it. You think I don't know how hard it is now the old gel's cracking up?"

Maggie looked uneasy. "Where are you going Mick?"

"I'm getting out. No one will miss me. I'm going in the merchant navy. Ta ta, old gel," he said softly and pointing to the note on the table, he added, "Treat yourself." Then out of the little front door he went. He never came home again.

Tears streamed down Maggie's face and Ginger came and held her hand.

"Have a new dress, Maggie," he said. "Go on."

"No, Ginger, I can't do that. Here, I tell you what. We'll have some fish and chips—a tuppenny and pen'orth all round. Go on, hurry up before I change me bloody mind. And get some lemonade."

The three little brothers dined like lords that night while Liza lay on her back and snored like a pig in the front parlor. In the back kitchen they had a bean feast—fish and taters and lemonade—what luxury! They fed the babies with chips, and with bloated bellies they all went up to bed and Maggie told them stories.

Maggie's stories were always popular. The only ones she knew were those that Dah had told her. They were about leprechauns who carried little bags of gold with them.

"Coo," said Ginger, "wish I could find a leprechaun."

Then Lennie joined in, "Do him in, I would, and nick his bag of gold."

Maggie laughed at them and with them. In spite of all the hardships, Maggie was happy with family life all around her; it was so different from her own lonely childhood.

An Admirer

The next morning, Maggie looked at the fifteen shillings left over from the quid Mick had given her. She wondered what to do with it. It was a small fortune to her. She thought of all the nice things she could buy the kids but some instinct told her that she was going to need it in the future. The way Liza was guzzling up the beer, the rent was not being paid and everything was going to pot. "Better not let Liza get her hands on it," she said out aloud to herself.

Once again, it was the astute young Ginger who told her what to do. "Use yer loaf, Maggie," he said, tapping his ginger head. "Hide it, shove it away till yer need it."

He showed her a "hidey hole," as he called it, and crossed his heart and hoped to die if he told anyone. It was upstairs in a dark corner of the landing where the plaster was cracked and the dingy wallpaper hung down off the wall. Ginger lifted a strip of paper and exposed the hole in the plaster. Wrapping up the money carefully in newspaper, he pushed it in between the laths and placed a piece of loose plaster on top. Smoothing down the paper, he added, "Even the cops wouldn't find it there."

Maggie laughed. Little Ginger was one ray of sunshine in her life. "A proper bloody rogue you are, Ginger. Let's hope the bugs don't eat it. You going to school?" she asked.

"Well, I'm supposed to," he said with a cheeky grin, "but I'd do anything for you, Maggie."

"Take the kids to the park. That old cow Mrs. Malloy don't 'alf moan if they play up."

Whistling cheerfully, he took the pram with the two little boys in it. They loved Ginger and chattered to him like a couple of monkeys as he pushed them down the street.

He's a good boy, thought Maggie as she put on her coarse apron. I hope he keeps out of trouble.

She looked into the front room. Old Liza still lay on her back breathing heavily.

"Cor blimey," said Liza. "Can't move this morning, me leg's all stiff."

Maggie suddenly felt desperately sorry for her. Poor old girl, she was right cut up over Jim, she thought. It must be terrible to be old. I suppose I ought to feel upset about it, but it's funny, I feel good today—must have been the fish and chips last night. She smiled to herself as she went into the tiny scullery at the back, where there was a tap and an old stone sink with a cracked mirror hanging above it.

It was here the family washed. Maggie could never reach to see herself in the mirror because it was hung too high up for her short figure. Jim shaved there so the mirror was high up enough for him to see his face. I'll take that looking-glass down, thought Maggie, it always got on my nerves stuck up there. She stood on a chair to reach and looked at herself as she propped it against the sink. Two bright blue, Irish eyes stared out at her. Maggie took another look. She was quite surprised at how nice she looked this morning. She washed her face and, with a big comb that was used by all the family, she combed the long black hair which hung down to her waist. Tiny pieces of hair curled around her cheeks. After a moment's thought, she went upstairs and got the little powder puff and the box of Phul-nana and plastered her rosy cheeks with it.

As she passed the front room, a pathetic voice called out, "Maggie, gel, do us a favor. When yer get yer wages, bring us 'alf a beer, will yer?"

"Of course I will, Ma," said Maggie kindly, and she trotted off to Mrs. Malloy's.

Madam Malloy was not in a good mood. She looked suspiciously at Maggie with her tidy hair and white powder all over her face. "You took your time getting here this morning," she grumbled. "Leave the upstairs, my nephew is still in bed. You'd better give the downstairs an extra do."

John did not stay in bed. Instead, he sat at the top of the stairs in his dressing gown and pajamas and watched Maggie scrub the long, bare boards in the passage. He sat for a long time watching her bottom as it went backwards and forwards in time with the scrubbing brush. He looked admiringly at her long hair which was tucked up in a knot and at the back of her neck where he caught a glimpse of her snow-white skin. When her eyes smiled at him he nearly fell down the stairs.

John had never wanted anyone like he wanted Maggie. That morning he sat smoking cigarette after cigarette until she faced him and said, "You'd better get off those stairs, 'cause I got to do them."

A nod is as good as a wink to a blind horse, so he moved back up the stairs to his room, wondering all the while why she didn't sound like the rest of them around there.

"Is Maggie Irish, Aunt Betsy?" he asked.

"Well, sort of half Irish," replied his aunt. Then, looking very alarmed she said, "Here, John, don't go looking at Maggie. She's married and into a real rough family. You have to mind your p's and q's down here— it's not what you're used to."

But John fancied Maggie and he had always got his own way. He had lived with various aunts and uncles most of his life, for his parents were in the army out in India. He had been sent to various good boarding schools and on to university. He was now about to go abroad to study further for his career.

He moved up close to her as she washed the dishes in the sink. "Want a fag, Maggie?" he asked.

"I ain't never smoked," she giggled.

"Well, now's your chance." John lit a cigarette and placed it in Maggie's mouth. "Now draw," he said, "like this." He pursed his lips to show her how to blow out the smoke.

Maggie was enjoying the attention from this smart young man and she pursed her red lips.

When John kissed her, he took her by surprise. His lips full on hers, he pressed her against the sink; Maggie tried to push him off, gave up the idea in the end and went off into a world that was unknown to her. Jim's kisses were not like this.

"Here, pack it up," she said as she came up for air. "The old gel might see you."

"Just a taste," said the jubilant John. "I'll see you later, Maggie."

So that was how John and Maggie first became friends. But Maggie was no fool. A little petting and fussing each morning and a cigarette, but that was as far as he got.

"Let me come home with you, Maggie," he pleaded. "Your old man's in the nick, so what are you going to do for a bit of love?"

"I can do without that," said Maggie. "All that brings is bloody trouble." She thought of the baby that would soon be stirring in her womb.

"I'm going to have you, Maggie. I can promise you that."

"Blimey, you'll be lucky, I don't think," said Maggie scornfully.

A couple of weeks went by and Liza did not go out to work. Her leg had gone stiff so she hobbled from the house to the Barley Mow with the aid of a walking-stick.

Maggie had been to see Jim in Pentonville Prison. They talked through a little hole and a policeman listened to everything they said.

"I'm in the family way again, Jim," she whispered.

"Christ, Maggie," he said, "ain't we got enough trouble without you loading us up with kids?"

Maggie felt ashamed, as though she alone were responsible for this last catastrophe.

"I'm two months," she said. It was all she could think of to say.

"Well try and get rid of it then," he snarled.

Maggie sat open-mouthed. "Get rid of it? How do you do that?"

"For gawd's sake, Maggie. Use yer loaf," said Jim. Then he paused and looked at her closely. "What's that all over yer flamin' face?"

"It's powder."

Jim's eyes flashed with rage. "Now don't you start that lark, Maggie my gel. I swear I'll swing for yer if yer does."

Maggie looked hurt. "What lark, Jim?" In the back of her mind was the kissing and cuddling she did with John, and her cheeks flamed a guilty red.

A change came over his face; his lips went narrow and his eyes squinted viciously. "Whoring, that's what. I'm warning yer, Maggie, I'll get you and the bloke if yer lets me down."

But Maggie had already got up and run out. She cried all the way home. Whatever's the matter with me? she thought. Better buck up before the kids see me.

It had begun to get dark and the lamp-lighter passed

her with the long stick he used to switch on the lamps. It was very quiet as she walked through the streets. When John's tall figure stepped out in front of her as she reached the house, Maggie was scared. "Crikey, you made me jump," she said.

"One day, Maggie, I'll make you jump as high as the sky," he said as he looked down at her.

"Don't be daft," she said, trying to get past him.

"I'm taking you for a drink."

"Daft. I don't drink."

"Well, we'll make a start."

"I'll have to get back for the kids."

He stopped in front of her. The yellow of the street lamp shone down on her pretty face.

"Listen, Maggie. The kids are all tucked up in bed and your mother-in-law is in the boozer. And Ginger's got half-a-crown in his pocket to keep an eye on things, so to speak."

"You're joking. I must go, it's getting late," said Maggie.

"Honest. I sat in the back yard until they were asleep."

"Oh, you didn't. Anyone see you?"

"Only Ginger, and he's a very reliable look-out, I can assure you. So my beautiful, you are mine until the pubs shut, and perhaps for a little while afterwards," he added.

Maggie threw her bonnet to the wind—John looked so nice standing there. She took his arm saying, "Come on then. If you're taking me to the pub, hurry up before I change me mind."

John and Maggie strolled arm in arm down the deserted road. Lace curtains moved and eyes looked out as they always did in those little back streets. But John did not know and Maggie did not care; for some reason she felt suddenly carefree.

To Maggie the big public house on the main road was like a palace. It was called the Queen's Arms and

even the name impressed her. She had never been inside one of these gin palaces.

They sat on a red plush seat with lots of lights and
mirrors around them. Maggie liked the mirrors; they
had little babies with bare bottoms on them and a
flower lady doing a dance.

"Ain't they pretty," she said.

John looked at the frosted glass with its nymphs and
cherubs. He thought the mirrors were atrocious and
said so. Maggie looked disappointed.

"Is it true that you've hardly ever left that crummy
little street, Maggie?"

"I used to go to the pictures with Jim," said Maggie,
brightening up.

"My God, it doesn't seem possible, a pretty girl like
you."

The port wine was taking effect and Maggie leaned
her head on John's shoulder. She looked very sweet
tonight in a blue print frock that had cost threepence
at the mission jumble sale. She had washed and starched
it and taken up the hem. It was a forget-me-not blue
and matched her eyes. This hard life had not stopped
Maggie's beauty from developing. With her slim hips
and well-formed bust, she was blooming. John looked
her over and knew he would love her all his life.

A woman started to play the piano and all the customers sang loudly. The men wore checked caps and
the women had hats with feathers; some wore fur coats
and long, gold earrings. Maggie was most impressed
but John said, "Costers, they are. Plenty of money
down here, Maggie. I don't suppose they have ever paid
taxes in their lives—most of them are on the fiddle.
They even have their own royal family," he added dryly.

Maggie looked up at him quickly. Was he mocking
her?

"That's right, the pearly king and queen, and all the
little princes and princesses."

Maggie began to giggle. Of course she remembered
them. The small Cockney king in his flat cap covered
with pearly buttons with his queen, that large woman

in a feathered hat and an intricate costume literally covered with pearly buttons. She had often puzzled about how long it must have taken to sew them on as she watched them lead the carnival procession through the market.

John is so knowledgeable, pondered Maggie. She thought of poor old Jim in the nick. Jim, who never had two halfpennies to rub together, had done the dirty work for these costers. She looked down at her hands —no diamond rings, a jumble-sale dress, and scrubbing to feed his kids.

"Don't look so solemn, Maggie." John had caught her looking thoughtful. She could not explain the injustice of it all, not to him. She swallowed the port wine and held out her glass for another one.

"You're going it, old girl," he said, but nevertheless he filled her glass for her.

Outside there was a jellied-eel stall. These Maggie had to try having stared so often at the bits of snake in jelly wondering what they tasted like. John had a passion for them and consumed three bowls of eels to Maggie's one. In every dark doorway they stopped to kiss and cuddle. The port wine made her feel lovely and warm. She snuggled close up to him.

"Maggie, let's go home. I can't stand it any longer, I must have you, darling. Please, Maggie."

A cold breeze seemed to sweep over Maggie and Jim's mean face floated in front of her.

Maggie tried to pull away but the young, virile body of John held her in a vice-like grip. "Don't do that," she said, as his hands felt her body. Then panic seized her and up came her knee and her teeth sank into his lips. Breaking free she ran down the road as though the devil were after her. Dear John was not a swearing man but the language he hurled after Maggie was really worthy of the street.

As she neared the house, Ginger's red hair glowed in the light of the street lamp he was sitting under.

"The coppers chasing you, Maggie?" he asked.

"Don't be so cheeky," said the breathless, disheveled

Maggie. "Come on, don't wake the old girl up." Hand in hand they crept up the narrow stairs to bed.

The babies were sleeping peacefully and the two little brothers in the same bed snored. Since Mick had gone little Jim slept with Ginger, so Maggie had only the baby in her bed. As she undressed in the moonlight dreaming of the love she nearly had, Ginger's voice came over from the corner.

"You know, Maggie," he said, "when I get old enough I'm going to get a gel with a figure like yours."

"Oh you naughty boy. Stop looking," said Maggie. Covering herself up she quickly dived into bed.

Maggie felt bad in the morning; the port wine and her early pregnancy had really turned her stomach. As she retched and vomited in the sink, Liza thumped down the passage banging her stick.

"Blimey, don't tell me you're in the club again, gel. Gawd knows what it'll be like with another mouth to feed—it's bloody starvation now.

"What time did you come in last night?" asked Liza aggressively. "You took long enough to get back from Pentonville."

"Got on the wrong bus," said Maggie at last.

"Silly bloody cow."

Maggie was too ill to care. But as she splashed cold water on her face, Maggie was worrying about how to get to work on time and how to face John after the business of last night.

"Better not be late," Maggie said to Liza. "She's a real tartar if I'm even a bit late."

Maggie need not have bothered. At that moment a little boy knocked at the door with a note which said: Please accept one shilling in lieu of notice. I do not require your daughter-in-law anymore.

Old Liza looked at it and then gave it to Ginger to read. "What's her game?" asked Liza. "Sacked yer. What for? I'll soon find out." On went the old black shawl and she stumped towards the shop.

"That's torn it," said Ginger. "What are you going to do, Maggie?"

"I suppose old Malloy had her spies out last night. I don't care. To hell with the lot of them," said Maggie.

Liza shouted and raved at Mrs. Malloy. She called her a hennaed whore while John sulked in his room; he was not pleased that his aunt had sent his Maggie away.

The Bunghouse

Liza did not return until the shilling from Mrs. Malloy had disappeared in the Barley Mow. Then, in a sad but slightly blurred way, Liza said, "I told her off, Maggie. No one around here is going to give you a bad name, gel, not while I'm alive they ain't."

Maggie was a little puzzled. She still found it hard to understand the philosophy of this family. It didn't seem to matter what you did so long as you weren't found out.

"I've been thinking it over, gel, and there's really only one thing to do, and that's the bunghouse for you, me gel. You can't keep working now there's another kid coming. The bloody government put my Jim away, so let's see what they're going to do about his kids."

Maggie looked shocked. She knew how proud Liza was. She was always shouting about how she never lived on charity. It must have taken a lot for her to agree to the bunghouse.

That afternoon, they set out for the relief office. Maggie had the babies in the pram and Ginger and his two little brothers tagged along behind her while Liza followed up the rear.

In the dreary office with its walls painted half green and half gray with a black line between the two colors —Maggie thought it was very depressing—the people crowded round as each one was served in turn. A sorry lot they were—ragged children and tired-looking women.

Soon Maggie's turn came. A hatchet-faced woman asked her all kinds of personal questions.

"Where is your husband?" she asked in a loud voice.

"He's away," replied Maggie softly.

"Away? If you mean he's in prison, then say so. We'll give you relief tickets to buy bread, meat and coal. If you start work or your circumstances change, let us know immediately."

To Liza she said: "So you're unable to clean doorsteps because your knees are bad?"

"That's right."

"Have you been to the doctor?"

"If someone gives me the bleeding 'alf crown to pay 'im, I might go," said Liza.

"Can't your daughter-in-law help you while you're sick?"

"Let's see you go to work with two kids in a pram and another in the oven," retorted Liza. Maggie flushed and looked around to see who was listening.

Eventually they got the relief tickets—a whole fifteen shillings worth.

"By the way, Mrs. Burns," said old hatchet-face, "we'll want to visit your home to see if you have anything of value."

Outside the office, Liza handed her tickets to Maggie. "Here you are, gel, you'll never get me in the shop changing those things. You'd better take over." So Liza let go of the reins.

It was Ginger who came to Maggie's aid once more. "I'll show you how to change them, Maggie," he said. "Me mate's muvver always has these."

"Wish I had a threepenny bit," said Liza diving into her pocket. "Just enough for a half . . . that would do me."

Maggie felt guilty.

"Take no notice," said Ginger. "She does all right. Always got money for beer she does. Puts her book over the counter."

"What do you mean?" asked Maggie.

"She got a pension when the old man got killed in

the war. She puts the book over the bar and has the booze on tick." He was a bright lad, our Ginger, never missed a trick.

"Don't matter," said Maggie. "We got our own tickets now."

"I'll show yer how to fiddle 'em," said the enterprising Ginger.

They went down to the shops and Maggie, who had never done the shopping, had a great time with Ginger.

First they went to the butcher's and Maggie stood coyly by while Ginger negotiated with a plump man in a straw hat.

"If you ain't got no money, hoppit, Ginger," he said. "Don't you go nicking anything." He looked at them suspiciously.

Ginger stood with his hands behind his back, his mop of red hair sticking out on end and his bare feet spread wide apart.

"We was thinking of having a nice bit of scrag, Mr. Robinson."

"Oh you was, was you? And how much would you like to pay, may I ask?" The butcher's belly, wrapped in the striped apron, wobbled as he laughed at the boy's audacity.

"Me sister, Maggie, has tickets here provided by His Majesty's government to feed us poor kids," Ginger said haughtily.

Mr. Robinson looked at sweet little Maggie. He admired her rosy cheeks and dark hair. "So that's how the land lies, is it?"

Into the shopping bag went a nice shoulder of lamb and plenty of scrag for a stew. For all this, Maggie gave the butcher two shilling tickets. To Ginger it was a real novelty to act like a millionaire but to most of the people in Stepney it was a disgrace to be on the bunghouse and the shopkeepers took advantage of it and threw all the old rubbish on the "mumpers," as they were called. In the baker's a couple of stale cakes were thrown in for the kids and Maggie thanked the lady kindly. They went home with real food in the bag, a novelty in that house for Liza had always managed to spend more on beer than on food if she ever got down to the market.

Later, the little brothers were sent to get fourteen pounds of coal and Maggie lit the fire to cook a big Irish stew.

That night there was a warm fire and everyone had full bellies. After a hot bowl of stew, Liza said to Maggie, "You ain't such a bad gel, Maggie. My Jim could've done a lot worse."

Praise from her mother-in-law was praise indeed for Maggie.

Lying in bed, she thought of the little baby that had started to form inside her. She did not want any more kids. What did Jim say? Get rid of it. She wondered how you did things like that. There was still the money that Mick had given her—perhaps she could buy some pills or something. She would try and find out.

In the morning Liza was up early. She had got out her bucket and scrubbing brush.

"No good giving in," she said. "Got to get back to work some time."

Maggie watched her as she bent down, grunting and groaning. She felt so sorry for her. "Give us the bucket," she said, "I'll go."

"Will yer, Maggie?" Liza looked relieved. "It's just me regulars I'm worried about. Don't want to lose them."

So Maggie went off doorstep-cleaning. She hated it when she knocked on the door to ask if they wanted their doorsteps cleaned. They looked at her as though she were something the cat brought in. But she knew she had to do it. And because she was not earning much she did not tell the woman at the relief office that she was working.

3

The Pawn Shop

It was on one of these mornings when she was doorstep-cleaning that she met Sarah Bernstein and started what became a long friendship. Sarah was very fat, but a better natured girl than Sarah could not be found anywhere. She was twenty-five years old and not married. She kept a shop which belonged to her two brothers for whom she also kept house. They were so good to her that Sarah did not want for anything except a man.

The Bernsteins' shop was known as the in-and-out shop. It was a strange, long and dusty place you could walk into, examine the goods and walk out again. There were long rails of second-hand clothes—unredeemed pledges, they were marked—and in the back was a pawn shop where parcels lay all over the place. There were also a few pieces of jewelry and a couple of clocks.

But Sarah, who was very lazy, just sat knitting on a little stool, looking out of the door. No incident happened without Sarah holding a running commentary on it.

That morning, as Maggie went by with her bucket, Sarah called out to her: "What's up, Maggie? The old gel snuffed it?"

Maggie, who was fed up and a little weary, stopped to talk. "Want yer doorstep cleaned, Sarah?"

"Yes, you can do it, love—not that I care what color it is."

With her fat legs astride, Sarah watched little Maggie as her small hands held the scrubbing brush. "You got nice-shaped hands, ain't you," she said enviously. "Shame yer got to spoil them with all that scrubbing." She examined her own white, podgy ones which glittered with rings. "Mine's not so bad," she said. Very vain was Sarah. Always smartly dressed with gold rings in her ears, Sarah was not that much older than Maggie but she was so fat and ungainly she could easily be taken for a middle-aged woman.

"Tell yer what, Maggie," she said, "when yer done that, pop in and put the kettle on and we'll have a nice cup of tea."

Lazy, fat cow, thought Maggie. Still, I could do with a rest.

When Maggie went through the dingy shop to the back kitchen, the mess and confusion amazed her. She had never seen so many cooking pots before. They were all dirty and stacked up waiting to be washed. There was dust and dirt everywhere.

"Sorry about the mess, Maggie," said Sarah who had waddled in behind her. "It's that old gel Maudie Evans. She gets soaked up with gin and don't turn up on Mondays."

But Maggie was slowly sorting out the mess, trying to find two clean cups. "Might as well wash this lot while the kettle's boiling," she said.

"There's hot water in that tap," said Sarah hopefully.

Maggie had never seen hot water coming out of a tap before. "Hot water! I don't believe it."

"Abe got it done for me to see if I'd wash up more often. But I don't like bloody housework," she said wistfully.

Maggie was already busy mixing the soap and hot

water. Washing up was no trouble for her. Sarah sat comfortably drinking the tea Maggie had made, eating chocolate cake and surveying the clean, shining, well-washed pots. Maggie knew she had found a friend.

"I think you're marvelous," said Sarah. "Listen, Maggie. I'm not short of a few bob—the boys look after me. So why don't yer come in and help me every day? I'll look after yer. What about ten bob. That do yer?"

Maggie was slow in answering. Sarah thought it was because the money was not enough.

"All right, twelve bob a week, Maggie. You can come and go as yer like as long as yer keeps it a bit tidy."

Maggie's blue eyes twinkled. "Sounds like a fortune to me," she said. "Of course I'll come, but one thing bothers me . . ."

"What's that, love?" inquired Sarah looking at her over the tops of her gold spectacles. Her nose was long but her brown eyes bright and lively. Maggie was sure Sarah could see quite well without those spectacles, and that it was just vanity that made her hang on to them even though they made a red bump in the middle of her nose. It was difficult for Maggie not to laugh when Sarah stared soberly over the top of them.

"Yer got some troubles, have yer?"

"No," said Maggie, "not exactly troubles, but we got relief tickets from the bunghouse, and they said if I started working I had to tell them."

This really roused Sarah. "Tell them, Maggie? You'll do no such thing. You keep stumm, gel." She held her hand to her mouth. "And don't tell no one yer business. It makes me sick, it does, when I see them poor kids around here."

So Maggie learned another lesson in the art of silence.

"I'll come in the morning, then go and see to the kids and come back when Ginger comes out of school," said Maggie.

"That's fine," said Sarah, "and I won't overwork yer, love."

So Maggie Burns started to do for the Jews. It was a turning point, that job with Sarah. Things became much easier and the shop was so funny, Maggie looked forward to going to work.

On Mondays, as soon as the shop opened, in they came—women in caps and shawls with little ragged children. For an hour or so Sarah was busy looking very important with her spectacles clapped right on her nose. She stood behind a square opening at the back of the dark shop and each customer would carry a bundle there. All of them wanted to borrow money on these few possessions. There would be a kid with Dad's best trousers. "Muvver only wants a couple of bob to get her through the week," he would say. "That's all she's bleeding likely to get," was Sarah's comment as she examined the goods, "the arse is nearly out of these." Maggie in the kitchen would start giggling.

Then a poor woman would bring a bundle—all sheets and household goods and worn-out clothes. "Take these out," Sarah would say, holding a pair of baggy bloomers. "Can't give clean money on dirty drawers."

And so it went on. The rest of the week was quiet until Friday evening. Then in would come rushing the little boy anxious to get his dad's pants before he found out they were in the pawn. Sarah would stare closely at the ticket, rummage in a load of parcels and give him the trousers. Ten minutes later, the boy's mum would come in shouting and raving because they were the wrong pair. While she and Sarah had a flaming row, Maggie would sort out the missing trousers.

After the irate mother had gone, Sarah's face would be like a beetroot. "Gawd, don't they get on yer nerves? Thanks, Maggie. Don't know what I'd do without yer." And Maggie would wonder what she would have done if she hadn't met Sarah.

There was always time for a cup and a jaw as far as Sarah was concerned and whenever anything happened in the street she would call out to Maggie. "Maggie, just come and see Mrs. So-and-so belting that kid. Why, the spiteful old bitch. Leave him alone!" she would scream and then the sparks would fly.

"You shut up, you fat Jew cow," was the usual retort back, but Sarah hurled insult after insult until there was a move to fight. Then Sarah would be in like a shot, shutting the door and saying, "Quick, get the cops, Maggie." She would be like a bag of jelly until the next day when she would be back in the doorway as brazen as ever. Maggie used to laugh all the time at Sarah.

More people pinched goods from the shop than paid honest money for them but Sarah, nosing out in the street, never saw them. It puzzled Maggie how she managed to keep open. That was until one day when the two brothers, Abe and Bernie, arrived and the door to the kitchen was shut and a seedy little man was let in at the back door. Maggie heard them bargaining and caught the glint of diamonds when the kitchen door came ajar. It did not need much imagination to guess what went on in there. The pawn shop was merely a front for the real business.

Things were much better at home now. The kids were well fed and Maggie gave Liza threepence every morning to have a half of beer, and Ginger a shilling to mind the kids for her. Every day she sorted among the unredeemed pledges in the shop for clothes for the family. "It's all right, love," Sarah would say, "take them and give me a bit off at the weekend."

Liza was beginning to drink more and more and made no attempt to work but she did keep her eye on the young boys until the pub opened in the morning. She had one obsession: the relief officer. She was always watching for him. She came in half tiddly one day and screamed, "Maggie, get them flaming vases off the mantelpiece. He ain't having them—belonged to me mother, they did."

"He won't come," said Maggie.

"Oh yes he will. Come all of a sudden, they do."

Liza would not be content until the vases were all packed away in a suitcase and lugged upstairs under Maggie's bed for safety. The little front parlor looked bare and empty without them.

Liza's other concern was big Jim who had now been gone for three months. She had been to visit him, but Maggie had not, not since that first time. Liza was never interested in her other boys, she was always waiting for her Jim to come home.

Goodbye John

Maggie had been with Sarah a few weeks when, from her watching post, Sarah called out, "Come here, love. Ever seen one of those?"

Maggie looked. It was a taxi and stood parked outside Mrs. Malloy's at the corner. "No, what is it?" she said.

"It's an automobile," said Sarah, very pleased with herself. "Bernie's got one."

Maggie looked at the high shuddering thing on wheels and was not impressed. Then John came out loaded with bags.

As Maggie turned away quickly, Sarah's fat elbow dug into her ribs. "Go on, don't be shy, Maggie, gel. It's your boyfriend going away for Christmas."

Maggie looked astonished. "How do you know, Sarah?" she gasped.

"They all knows round here, Maggie. Some old crony of Betsy Malloy saw you in the boozer. Don't look so worried, love—we was all on your side. Smashing fella, ain't he? Fancy him meself, I do."

"It wasn't like that," said Maggie, getting a bit uneasy.

"Come on, let's go and have a cup of tea," said Sarah, "and you can tell me all about it. Never had a bit of the other, I ain't, but I do like to hear about those that does."

There was no peace until Maggie had told her, word for word, all that went on between her and John.

"Mean to say that after all that you never done it?" Sarah was terribly disappointed but then, cheering up a little, she said, "Kneed him did yer? I bet it didn't half hurt."

Maggie became impatient. She did not understand this fat girl whose mind dwelt on other people's sex lives.

"Why didn't yer do it, Maggie?" she persisted.

"Because I was afraid of Jim. Also I was in the family way."

"You're joking, Maggie. Mean to say you're having another one?" Sarah's eyes almost popped out of her glasses. "You ain't going to leave are you?"

"No, I'm going to try and get rid of it."

"Oh, I see." Sarah looked thoughtful and waddled out to see if the taxi had gone.

"He's gone," she said, looking suggestively at Maggie's stomach. "You might never see him again, Maggie."

"It's nothing to do with him, Sarah. Jim left me in the family way," said Maggie, exasperated.

"Sorry, Maggie," said Sarah. "If you say it's so, it's so with me, but if it had been me, I'd have enjoyed myself. You know, I was betrothed once. The rabbi found him. He was a bloody old bag of bones, and what with me being a bit awkward . . ." she stared down at her fat thighs, "and him being past it, we never got anywhere. So I called it off. I ain't like them Yiddish gels that marries for business. If I get married I want a real man. Otherwise I'll do without."

Maggie smiled at her. It was always the same, she could never be angry with Sarah for long.

"Better get home for the kids' dinner. See you later, Sarah."

On the way home she began to think of John. The last bit of the story she never told Sarah—how all the next week John had hung around sending notes with Ginger. At first, Maggie had ignored the messages and when she saw his tall figure standing at the corner of the street, she avoided him.

One day, very pleased with himself, Ginger rattled the money in his pocket and said: "I'm making quite a few bob out of him, Maggie."

She was furious. "Why, you horrible little villain," she said.

"Well, why don't yer answer his letters?" asked the incorrigible Ginger.

So Maggie sat down to write a letter. There was no such thing as a pen in the house but Ginger found a stub of pencil. Now Maggie had been a bit slow at school and could not get things down on paper, but with much concentration she wrote: Please John don't try to see me, I am a married woman so there could not be anyfing between us. Maggie.

Maggie was really proud of her letter until Ginger said: "It's not 'anyfing,' it's 'anything,' Maggie."

Maggie, near to tears, tore the note up.

"Why don't yer see him, Maggie?" said Ginger. "I'll hang around in case he bashes yer up."

"Fat lot of good you would be," said Maggie. "Tell him I'll see him in the park tomorrow afternoon."

"In the daylight?" asked Ginger looking surprised.

"That's right," said Maggie. "Now hoppit."

The next afternoon when she had come back from Sarah's, Maggie put the children in the pram. "I'm going to take them to the park," she told Liza.

The park was actually an old graveyard surrounding a church, but it was the only bit of grass for miles around so a visit there was considered a great treat.

Maggie knew she looked a sight, but she did not care. The fact that her heels were worn down and her skirt was stained and dusty did not bother her. Once and for all she must get this over with before Jim found out. Tagging along behind her was Ginger but she pretended not to notice him.

John was already in the park, sitting on a seat. His head was bent down and the sun shone on his fair hair. But the determined Maggie, pushing the old-fashioned pram, saw only someone who needed putting in his place.

"Hello," she said.

John looked up and she was shocked to see him so unhappy. He looked at the pram full of kids and at the untidy girl of his dreams. He seemed to be a bit disillusioned but still he got up to greet her and started to talk to baby Jim who even at that age loved conversation, and in his baby talk, pointed down the road to show everyone that Uncle Ginger was lurking behind. John looked in the direction of the chubby baby's hand and said to Maggie, "You came well protected. Why didn't you bring that old battle axe of a mother-in-law with you too?"

Maggie's Irish temper flared up. "Look here, John Malloy," said a red-faced Maggie, "I don't know who you think you are but it doesn't impress me. Stop sending notes to my house, or when my Jim comes home he'll make mincemeat out of you." Turning the old pram, Maggie marched off. So that was the end of that budding love affair.

For the next few weeks life settled down. Maggie was earning and Liza was getting her beer money, so everyone was happy.

Ginger had recently "acquired" a tall, dilapidated, old bike and Boy Boy never left it alone. He would sit in the back yard polishing it and ride proudly around the street with his thin little legs scarcely reaching the pedals. For some strange reason he had this name. Maggie used to think they must have run out of names by the time Boy Boy came along, but it seemed that Liza had thought that he was going to be a girl and had not thought of any boys' names beforehand. So the baby was called Boy Boy and the name stuck to him all his life.

Boy Boy's twin brother, Lennie, had joined forces with Ginger to form a companionship that lasted many years. This friendship bothered Maggie. Ginger had recently got a gang together and now the two boys stayed out late and came in filthy dirty; they played truant more than usual; and little things were often appearing out of the blue—a wireless was one, and toys for baby Jim and Tom were others. One day Maggie asked, "What are you up to, Ginger?"

"We got a gang, we have," little Lennie said. "We do all the posh houses." Ginger aimed a kick at him.

Maggie was scared. Every time a policeman came down the street she shivered in her shoes. But who could she tell? No one. Liza was always half cut and did not look well lately, and big brother Jim was missing. So Maggie coped only as she knew how and she protected them.

The first brush she had with the law was rather funny. She was standing at the front door waiting for the boys to come home from school, when down the road belted Ginger, his long hair blowing in the wind, and carrying what looked like a tray. He dashed past Maggie, fell over in the dark passage dropping what he was carrying, and ran out of the back door and over the wall on his usual escape route. Maggie looked down and at her feet was a big tray of stick-jaw. Stick-jaw was the name given to a sticky mess of toffee, containing nuts and shredded coconut, which was sold by Mr. Pugh from his stall in the market. With a tray of stick-jaw at her feet lifted from a market stall by Ginger, Maggie could hear the menacing sound of a copper's footsteps approaching. So Maggie, without a moment's hesitation, pushed the tray with her foot until it slid under the dusty old doormat.

P.C. Murphy came lumbering along—a heavily-built man in his early forties who was very partial to a pretty face.

"Was that young Ginger who just ran in, Maggie?" he asked while he stood panting from the exertion of the chase.

"He ain't come in here," said Maggie. "What's he been up to?"

P.C. Murphy drew a deep breath and puffed out his cheeks. Maggie could see the tobacco stains on his drooping mustache. He should be easy, thought Maggie, I remember when he used to drink with Dah.

"What ain't he been up to, Maggie? Nicks things right under me nose he does now, love."

"He never brings anything here," said Maggie. "I wouldn't allow it."

"I know, gel, but it's a bad lot you married into. Never mind, I'll get him soon."

So off he went. Maggie breathed a sigh of relief and felt very pleased with herself.

When she went up to the crowded little bedroom that night, she saw that the stick-jaw had been retrieved and all the boys slept with sticky faces. Baby Tom clutched a piece of it in his sticky little fist as he slept. Maggie removed the evidence and empty stick-jaw tray with the pieces of coconut matting still adhering to it. She wiped Tom's hands and face and covered up the two silent brothers, wondering where it was all going to end.

As she slipped in beside Tom, her mind went on to the little one inside her. So far, there had been no sign of life. It did seem wicked not to want it and perhaps it would be a little girl. Then, looking at the crowded bedroom, she wondered where she would put her and how she would manage to feed her. All these questions went on and on—there was no answer until sleep came and Maggie's mind was at rest.

Maudie Evans

Things had improved at the in-and-out shop.

Just before Christmas, Sarah said, "Do me a favor. Come round and help me—we're going to have a bit of company for the holidays. Would you like to come?"

"Of course I will," said the warm, generous Maggie. "Love to help."

"Don't suppose you got a black dress, have you?" asked Sarah.

"No, duck. This is me one and only," said Maggie, briskly polishing the best furniture.

Sarah loved smart clothes and one of the few occasions when she left the shelter of the shop was to go to the dressmaker's which was somewhere in Whitechapel. In spite of her size, Sarah had nice, tailored coats and dresses, and elaborately beaded dresses for the evening.

"Look after the shop in the morning, love, and I'll go up to Whitechapel to get a dress for the holidays. Wait a bit. Give me the tape measure and I'll measure you up and see if I can't get a smart dress made for you. It's a bloody shame you don't get nothing for yourself with all the Burnses to fend for. Smashing figure you got too."

The next morning, in her best hat and coat, Sarah waddled off to this unknown region called Whitechapel. Maggie liked minding the shop—it made her feel important. Sometimes Ginger came poking about. "Hoppit!" she would say. "You ain't going to do any nicking while I'm here."

"Only looking, Maggie," he would say and then disappear.

Over the road outside her house sat Maudie Evans, well soaked with gin, as usual. A little dried-up woman of thirty, Maudie had a pale, faded face and eyes that looked as though they were sewn up with red cotton.

When Maggie had asked Sarah about getting some pills, she had looked scared.

"Don't tell anyone I told yer, but Maudie Evans is always having a miss. Don't know what she does, but be careful, love."

So that morning Maggie called her over. Maudie came at once hoping there might be an errand to run. "Want me, Maggie?"

Maggie went straight to the point. "Where can I get some pills, Maudie?"

Maudie's face came alive with interest. "Yer mean to bring it off, Maggie!"

"Of course I do. I've enough kids to last me."

"That's what I say, Maggie. Keeps yer poor, they does. After my Teddy was born I said no more for me, and I ain't either. Got rid of six, I have," she said with pride.

"One will do me," said Maggie a bit disgusted. "Where do I get the pills?"

"I'll get 'em for yer, Maggie, if you get the money."

"How much?" asked Maggie.

"Well, it's ten bob for the pills and half a bottle of gin to work them through yer."

The gin was probably for her, thought Maggie, but nevertheless she had to do as she said. She had the fifteen shillings that was hidden in the wall. It had come in handy after all.

"I'll bring the money over tomorrow. Thanks, Maudie," said Maggie.

"You're welcome. Why should we be lumbered with a lot of kids? That's what I say."

The next day Maggie took the money to Maudie. It was a smelly house was Maudie's. All the conversation was of Maudie describing the numerous miscarriages she had had. Maggie was beginning to feel quite sick and faint as Maudie's voice droned on. "They is very good, these pills," she was saying. "But of course they don't always work. Then you have to try something else. This is what I do . . ." Going to the cupboard she produced a dreadful-looking thing. It was just a long, black, rubber douche, but to Maggie it was a ghastly sight. She chucked the money on to the dirty beige oilcloth on the table and ran out in case she vomited in Maudie's room.

Sarah thought it all very funny when Maggie told her. "My gawd, gel. I wonder where she stuffs that thing." Sarah's mind was as crude as ever.

Promptly at lunchtime, Maudie arrived with the pills in a plain box and a bottle with just a drop of gin left in the bottom. "Had a little snort, Maggie," she said. "It was cold walking all the way back from the market."

Maggie hated gin, so she did not care. "Here's half-a-crown for your trouble, Maudie. But keep your mouth shut. Don't want my mother-in-law to know."

That evening when the boys were all in bed, Maggie got out the box. "Take three first, and three two hours later," the label read. Well, here goes, thought Maggie. She swallowed the pills and washed them down with the gin. She sat for a while. Nothing different happened. Better go up to bed, she thought.

It was the middle of the night when it started—this terrible pain. Gritting her teeth, Maggie crept downstairs to the outside lavatory in the back yard, and there she remained until the morning. Then, white and exhausted, she crept back to bed.

"Don't go to school, Ginger," she begged. "Mind the kids and send Boy Boy to tell Sarah I'm not well." So she lay in bed until the pain that tormented her had subsided, leaving her weak and trembling.

When Maggie got up and made a cup of tea at four o'clock, still nothing definite had happened. The child in her womb was as strong as ever.

"Tell you what," Maggie said to Sarah the next day, "I'd sooner have a baby than go through all that."

"Don't worry, love. You tried, and it might be a little girl. And you won't lose your job—I'm too fond of you for that," said Sarah consolingly.

The following Saturday was Sarah's party. It was a new world to Maggie. The place upstairs was shiny and polished like most of the shop; there was a long room, ideal for a long table laid with "nosh," as Sarah called it.

Maggie, in a smart black dress and white, frilly apron, went around with coffee and all kinds of sweetmeats. She had never seen so many fat, well-dressed people in her life. The heavy atmosphere and the smell of perfume excited her. Here was rich living. She thought it must be wonderful to have money. The diamond rings and pearl necklaces dazzled her and she noticed how they talked out aloud while eating all the time. Maggie had several glasses of red wine as she served it and Sarah, elaborate in a purple, beaded dress shouted to her guests, "This is me gel. Ain't she a beauty?" Maggie, quite unused to attention, felt like a film star.

They were just turning out of the Barley Mow as Maggie tripped gaily home in her smart black dress. She had lit up the long Russian cigarette that Bernie had given her. For the first time in months Maggie felt gay and carefree. She burst indoors. The little boys sat playing endless games of Ludo. "I've been to a smashing party," she said as she unrolled her apron and the little sweet cakes she had brought home tumbled out onto the table.

They all sat about the fire that burned low in the old-fashioned grate, and played a game which Maggie had invented. It went like this: "One day I will buy, or one day I will have . . ." Sometimes it was lovely dresses Maggie bought, and Ginger had everything from a car to a yacht. It was a lovely, silly game and the boys enjoyed playing it.

"Tell you what," said Maggie when they had finished playing, "it'll be Christmas soon and we'll have a party and a Christmas tree too."

"Smashing!" said Ginger. "We could all decorate it."

It's funny, thought Maggie to herself as she undressed for bed, I don't miss Jim a bit. Perhaps I never loved him. I wonder what it would be like to really love someone. There I go soppy. Ain't I got enough bovver with all these boys without thinking on things like that?

4

Christmas 1931

"Bovver" was a good word for Maggie's life, looking back through the years. Nineteen thirty-two was one of the worst years of her life, so much happened that year. But it was still 1931 and at nearly eighteen, you feel on top of the world even if you have got two kids and one on the way.

Next week it was Christmas. As far as the Burns family was concerned, Christmas did not mean much. They usually got tickets for a party at the Salvation Army and Daddy Burt's Mission and put on a Christmas dinner but otherwise it was pretty flat. Naturally there was more boozing and plenty more fights but generally the street went on as usual. Maggie recalled the Christmas times she spent with her Dah: midnight Mass on Christmas Eve; the candlelight and the singing; the fresh feeling in the air when you came out on the street early in the morning, and the little tree with a paper fairy on the top.

"Ginger!" she called. He was out in the back yard with his boys. "Come with me down the market," she said. He looked at her with that straight, saucy look he had.

"Why? What yer going to buy us, Maggie?"

"A Christmas tree," she said.

"Whoopee!" Ginger careered around the kitchen

57

shouting. "Come on, boys, we're going with Maggie to get a Christmas tree."

The performance of getting that tree! They all crowded around the stalls while the proprietor held up each tree as he auctioned them off. "Here you are, Madam, a fine tree. To you, a shilling."

When the Burnses arrived he got nervous. He kept one eye on the little group of boys, but especially Ginger as though he were expecting him to dash off with the prime of his stock at any minute.

"What you after, Maggie?" he asked, almost pitifully.

"Just a nice little tree," said Maggie.

"No," said Ginger, "we want a big one. We got money."

"My life," the stallkeeper said sarcastically, "a visit from Rothschild I got." But he could not beat Ginger who prowled around the stall, hands behind his back, examining each tree.

Then Ginger picked on the biggest and best specimen. "Give you a bob for that," he said, planting his feet firmly on the ground right in front of the tree he wanted.

"You won't," said the stallkeeper. "Worth a dollar, that one is."

"Please yourself," said Ginger, "I got plenty of time."

The stallkeeper appealed to Maggie. "Here you are, love. There's a nice one here you can have for a tanner."

Maggie was getting worried when suddenly the hoarse voice of the exasperated man shouted, "All right, Ginger. Sod yer! Take the bloody thing and give us yer bob.

"Get rich quick like this, I will," was the parting shot as little Ginger and the crowd of four marched jubilantly off with the great Christmas tree.

"Blimey, where we going to put it?" asked Maggie as they reached the small house. "And we ain't got nothing to put on it."

"Shove it in the washhouse, fellas." Ginger was giving orders. "Stop worrying, Maggie, we're going to fill that right up for you."

Maggie's heart missed a beat. Oh dear, what trouble had she started now? They'd be nicking toys all over the place. Still, not to worry, soon it would be Christmas.

The huge Christmas tree was installed in the wash-house—a brick-built addition to the house containing a sink and a big round copper. The tree was planted in a bucket and put up on the copper. It looked magnificent with its branches reaching up to the ceiling.

All the next day there was scuffling out in the passage and little feet scampered in and out. These were the kids from the street. Some had permission to view the tree from Ginger who was naturally in charge of operations. Some came to bring the loot—a sugar mouse, a piece of tinsel and various other items—to fill up the tree. By six o'clock it stood in all its glory and a scarlet-faced Ginger called to Maggie. "Come and see, Maggie. Ain't it beautiful?"

Maggie was surprised. It looked very fine. "But Ginger," she said dubiously, "you ain't nicked all this stuff, have you?"

"No, course not, Maggie. Me and the boys all got together. They're all coming to the party."

Maggie was astounded. "How many?" she asked, pulling baby Tom away from the tree. He had just eaten the head off the sugar mouse.

"Dunno, yet," said Ginger. "If they don't bring no stuff, they can't come."

Hoping for the best, Maggie said, "When I get me wages, I'll get you some lemonade."

"Thanks, Maggie, you're a real old darling."

"Get away, don't give me all the old blarney." They really had a good understanding, she and Ginger.

When Maggie left work at six o'clock on Christmas Eve, Sarah said, "Here you are, my love. That's your wages and there's a quid for you for Christmas."

"I can't take that, Sarah," protested Maggie.

"Yes you can. Abe said to give it to you, and he's got plenty. The half-a-crown's for the kids."

The market was very busy on Christmas Eve. Most people were doing their shopping at the last minute in the hope of getting cheap bargains. The gas flares that lit the stalls shone out creating glowing heat. It was nice and warm down there. Maggie wandered around the stalls, getting little toys for the babies and a white blouse for Liza—it was a luxury to have money to spend. Then she got a piece of belly of pork for dinner and oranges for the kids. There were a lot of people with too much drink in them and, as Maggie passed, the men tried to talk to her and reach out for her neat little figure. But she was so busy selecting things for the party, she hardly noticed them. From Sarah's shop she had paid off three brand-new shirts for the brothers and was looking forward to seeing them all dressed up.

When she got home she wrapped up each little parcel and put their names on them. After all the festivities that evening she crept up and put each parcel at the foot of their beds. There was great excitement in the morning when each little boy tried on his checked shirt. They were the latest fashion—lumberjack shirts.

"Cor, fanks, Maggie," they said, over and over again.

The roast belly of pork and baked potatoes were a great success—even Liza agreed. They had even managed to come by a Christmas pudding.

It was not possible to buy a cheap Christmas pudding in those days; you either made the traditional plum pudding, in a pudding cloth, that took ages on the coal stove and was usually a great success, or you went without. Enterprising young Ginger said to Maggie on Christmas Eve: "If you go up the Salvation Army and get in the queue, you'll get a Christmas pudding given you. It's for poor people on the relief but they won't let kids queue up."

Maggie looked dismayed; she hated refusing him anything. "I ain't got time to do that," she said. "Never mind, perhaps I'll ask Liza how to make a pud."

But two hours later, in came Ginger blue with the

cold. "Got it," he said, waving a cloth-covered basin. "Told the man about me poor old mother who's got a bad leg and can't queue up."

Everyone laughed—even Liza looked amused. "You are a caution," said Maggie as tears rolled down her face with laughter.

That same day Ginger had organized a big scrumping expedition to the market after the stalls had been cleared away. Piles of rotting vegetables and fruit were left behind and Ginger, with a big sack, systematically cleared up anything that was edible. The sack was dragged home to the back yard where they sorted out the bruised apples and oranges, and the big spuds were put in the oven at the side of the grate with the best of the chestnuts on top. It was going to be quite a do, with potatoes in their jackets and hot chestnuts. If anyone had told Maggie about a public health and hygiene inspector, she would have laughed for she had never heard of him. However, she did say, "Blimey, Ginger, take that rotten cabbage out. It don't 'alf stink."

On Christmas Day Ginger's friends began to arrive shortly after dinner. There were many scrapes at the front door when uninvited guests tried to come in. Lots of little boys swarmed all over the kitchen and back yard. They sat on the back wall, sang very rowdy songs and dashed in and out of the house with handfuls of chestnuts. Others sat on the floor of the washhouse admiring the brightly lit Christmas tree with its silver balls and candles all alight. Ginger, his face as red and glowing as his hair, was king of all he surveyed. Maggie poured the lemonade and tried to organize a game but the boys had their own idea of a party.

Meanwhile, Liza was busy gossiping over her pint of ale in the pub. "Blimey, it's a bloody madhouse at home. Our Maggie's no better than a kid herself."

At the party was one little tiny girl with fair hair and a washed-out pink dress. Her name was Rose.

"Come here, darling," said Maggie, when little Jim and Tom joined the throng of wrestlers on the floor. "Sit on my lap or you might get hurt."

Rose sat quietly sucking her thumb and looking at the glistening tree, her eyes fixed on the fairy doll at the top. "That a fair-ry," she mumbled in a whisper to Maggie.

"Of course it is, dear." Maggie cuddled her up. Little girls were sweet. Perhaps the next one would be a girl. She hoped so.

"She's Johnny Robinson's little sister," explained the twins together. 'She's got to get the fairy doll, otherwise he's gonna start somefink."

"Oh, is he?" said Maggie looking at the tall boy scoffing the lemonade out of the bottle. Little Lennie came closer. With his hand over his mouth he whispered, "He's the one that nicked it. See?"

This code of the back streets Maggie was beginning to accept. "So that's for Rose, is it? Won't that be nice." She fussed over the little girl who felt warm and content.

The highlight of the evening was the share-out of the tree. Ginger had an old felt hat which held the names of the lucky winners of the prizes from the tree. There was much whispering and there was definitely a fiddle going on. Those not lucky enough to get a toy, got a sweet or a glass ball.

Soon the tree was stripped bare and all the little boys and Rose went home. Maggie surveyed the debris and said, "We'll clear up in the morning, Ginger."

"It was a smashing party, wasn't it, Maggie?" said Ginger. "Oh!" he said suddenly, "I must go and see how me dog is." He rushed out .

Maggie followed him apprehensively and there, under the copper in a cardboard box, was a black curly-haired puppy.

"Where did you get it?" asked Maggie.

"Well, some boy didn't have nothing to bring to the party, so he gave me this," said Ginger picking up the tiny dog.

Maggie stared horrified. Had those poor little kids, in some way or another, paid to come to the party? Her head ached, she could not think any more.

Stroking the puppy she said, "He's lovely. What's his name?"

"Pie Shop," said Ginger.

"That's funny. What you call him that for?"

"He was born in the pie shop, that's why."

Maggie sighed. "Come to bed now, Ginger, and bring that pup with you. He might start howling and keep Liza awake."

So Maggie got another addition to her already over-crowded family, and Pie Shop went upstairs to bed.

A New Year

The New Year brought the freezing, snowy weather and the younger children got colds. Times seemed to be getting bad again. There were a lot of men out of work and people hung around all day on the street corners. Coals were hard to get as there was trouble in the mines, and Maggie and Ginger prowled about with the pram trying to get coals or wood to keep them all warm. Once they were lucky and got a load of tarry blocks from the men digging the road. These huge wood blocks, covered with tar, previously made up the road.

Maggie had quickened with her third child and did not feel well.

"It's funny," she said to Sarah, "I never felt like this before. Don't seem to have any go in me."

"I bet that's a girl, Maggie," said Sarah. "You want a little girl with all them bleeding boys yer got to cope with."

Sarah was not herself lately. She had been a bag of nerves ever since that Saturday morning when they went marching by. There had been about twenty young boys, all dressed alike, in black. A man led them, a smart, slim man in his thirties with a thin, trimmed mustache. As they marched they held their hands up high and shouted slogans. As she cleaned the shop, Maggie took little notice; there was always someone marching through the market—the Boys' Brigade, old soldiers. She went on sweeping without a second look, but the effect on Sarah was startling; as white as death and shivering, she called in a hoarse voice. "Come here, Maggie, for gawd's sake. They're here, they've come."

Maggie looked at the marchers and saw Ginger with his gang, tailing along at the end. Ginger was swinging his arms and thoroughly enjoying himself. Maggie ran to Sarah who had collapsed in a heap.

"Oh, me gawd," Sarah gasped.

"What's up, Sarah? It's only the Boys' Brigade, ain't it?"

"No! No! Maggie. It's them. They've come to murder us. The Nazis, they're here."

"Don't get so upset," said Maggie as she tried to pacify the frightened, fat girl who shivered and shook like a jelly. "I'll murder that bloody Ginger when I get him," muttered Maggie.

Then Sarah shouted hysterically, "They've started!"

Police whistles were going and people were screaming. When Maggie went to the door she saw the stallholders pelting the marchers with refuse. The police with their truncheons were restoring the peace.

Don't know what's going on, thought Maggie. But she felt sure that Ginger was responsible.

When she did get her hands on him he was a picture of innocence. "What's going on, Ginger?" said Maggie. "What's all them boys dressed up for? They frightened the wits out of Sarah."

Ginger put his hands in his pockets in a very superior manner, and said, "That's because she's a Jew."

"What the hell's that to do with it?"

"Well, yer see, Maggie, he's going to do up all the Jews. That's why the blokes on the stalls threw spuds at them."

"Why? What have they done?" demanded the outraged Maggie. "And who the bloody hell is *he* anyway?"

"His name's Mosley and he's a great friend of another bloke called Hitler and *he* started on the Jews already," the clever boy Ginger informed her. "I might join them when I'm thirteen—get a nice smart shirt free."

Maggie flew at him and grabbed his hair, shaking his head back and forth.

"Turn it up, Maggie," yelled tough boy Ginger.

"If I catch you getting mixed up with that lot, I'll get a stick and beat the daylight out of yer."

Ginger rubbed his sore head. "Yer wouldn't do that, Maggie?" he asked. "Yer see, it's like this: you can either be a Blackshirt or a Communist so when we have the revolution you know what side to be on."

"What a lot of nonsense," said Maggie. "You stay out of trouble, young Ginger. I've enough on me plate."

He never stopped out of trouble, but he did stay out of politics after that.

Poor Sarah remained a bag of nerves. "What would I do without you, Maggie gel?" she would say and stayed in the shop. She wouldn't even go down to get the bagels from the Yiddish bakers. She always liked that daily trip when she could collect all the gossip from the women who gathered there. But now Maggie went for her. "Leave the dusting and go to the baker's, love," Sarah would say.

On one of these trips, Maggie passed a corner shop that had been a barber's when she and Dah had passed by there. Until recently it had been empty but now it was freshly painted and the door stood wide open. Maggie looked in. On the wall was a picture of a man with a mustache, and all around, inside the shop, lounged these young boys in black shirts. So Sarah had been right; they had come. Poor old Sarah—let them start! thought Maggie to herself and she stared aggressively at the loungers. She was rewarded with wolf-whistles. Whatever is the matter with people? wondered Maggie. What do they want to stir up trouble for? Should have thought they've got enough to put up with down here, what with the dirt and the bugs and the freezing cold weather without coals. It was all a Chinese puzzle to Maggie.

Looking back, Maggie remembered that 1932 had been a strange year. The weather in January and February had been the coldest ever and the kids seemed to be under her feet all the time. Then there had been this great fight. A fight was not uncommon in the street but this one beat them all, and scared Maggie out of wits.

It started in the house opposite which was an up-and-downer just like Maggie's—the only difference being the occupants. It was number ten, where a bookie named Mr. Karlow lived. A street bookie made a good living in a poor street—it seemed that money could always be found for the gee-gees. On every street corner there were bookies and there was a great rivalry among them all as to who had what territory. He was a smart little man, Mr. Karlow. He wore a checked cap and lurked furtively in his doorway while people came, every bit as furtively, and handed him their bets. His sons, with several hangers-on, watched out for the coppers. At the glimpse of a policeman Mr. Karlow sent them all running for cover. His wife and daughters never mixed with poor families like the Burnses; they wore smart clothes and had lots of furniture, even a piano.

It was on a Saturday night that it happened. Mr. Karlow took his wife up west on Saturday nights on the proceeds of the week's takings. This Saturday, his daughter-in-law, Susie, who was expecting a baby, was indoors with his youngest daughter, Fanny, for company. Fanny, who was only seventeen, was a big, tough girl. The daughter-in-law, who was from Yorkshire, was taking a bath in the kitchen when four men arrived in a car. They carried choppers and knives. They beat in the door and broke all the windows. Maggie heard the screams and went to the front room window to look. Fanny stood and fought the men in the passage, her face covered with blood. Susie, who was still in the bath, put on an overall and tried to run past them but they stripped off the overall and threw her naked into the gutter. She screamed hysterically but no one came forward to help. All the neighbors stood on the other side of the street—kids and all—and watched as Fanny fell unconscious in the passage. The men then went all over the house breaking up the furniture with their axes.

Maggie saw a man who looked as though he was coming home from work. He ran to Susie lying in the gutter and took his coat off and helped her to a neighbor's house. Apart from that, no one moved. Maggie could see Ginger's head moving about in the crowds. She tried to call him but found that she was so afraid that her voice had left her.

Suddenly the crowds parted as the four men came running out of the house. At the same time, down the road in a taxi came Mr. Karlow and his sons—the underground must have given them "the wire," as it was called. They met with a terrific crash. They tore at each other with their hands and feet and the choppers went into action. The blood and screams sickened Maggie but she did not move from her grandstand view in the window. Then there was a loud explosion and old Mr. Karlow lay shot dead on his own doorstep. Those that were able went running down the road. It was then that the coppers appeared—a little band of well-washed heroes who marched shoulder to shoulder to stop a fight that was all over. They proceeded to lay their truncheons into the onlookers.

Maggie never forgot that fight—she even had nightmares over it. The Karlows buried their pa in great style and then moved to another district.

Maggie was getting near her time now so she went to see Granny Goring in the next street. Gran sat on the windowsill with her carpet bag behind the front door—always on call was Gran, never looking a day older though no one knew how old she actually was. Maggie stepped into the clean, bare, little room where all Granny Goring's business took place. Gran felt Maggie's tummy with expert hands. "Due in four weeks," she said.

"That's right," said Maggie. "I'm not very big this time—perhaps it's a girl."

Granny stared at Maggie very seriously. Her eyes looked big through the thick lenses of her spectacles. "I think yer better book up at the 'orspidal this time, dear. You've had these children a bit quickly, you know."

Maggie could not believe what she heard. Hospital? No one in the street went to the hospital unless they were going to die. "I can't go to the hospital, Gran," she gasped. "What about the kids?"

"Now don't get upset, Maggie. It ain't like it used to be. Got special wards now, called maternity wards for cases like yours."

"What's wrong with me?" asked Maggie anxiously.

"It don't seem to be lying right. It might turn later on, but you're only a gel, Maggie, and it don't seem right you should have such a bad time. Why, up there, they give you gas and you don't feel a thing."

"Oh, is *that* all," said Maggie. "Well, Granny, *you* can book me up 'cause I ain't going to no hospital."

"It's up to you, Maggie," said Gran. "I'll see you in four weeks then."

The Great Fire

After the shock of nearly going to the hospital, Maggie was to get another shock the very next day.

She was sitting in the kitchen knitting while the babies were in bed. As usual, Ginger and Lennie were out raking in the streets. Boy Boy was painting his precious bike in the washhouse, so things seemed very silent. A feeling that she was quite unused to came over her: she felt creepy and nervous.

"You there, Boy Boy?"

"Yes, Mag."

"Go and find Ginger," she said. "It's getting late."

"I can't go yet. In a minute I'll go."

"Oh, all right," said Maggie impatiently, "I'll go meself in a minute."

Then, in through the back door came Ginger's dog. He had grown quite big and now followed Ginger on his adventures.

"Hello, Pie Shop. Where's Ginger?" asked Maggie. The little dog crept under the table, tail between his legs.

What's up with him? wondered Maggie. He don't leave Ginger as a rule. Something's frightening him—perhaps I'd better go and see.

Maggie slipped her arms into her coat, and it was just then that she heard the fire engines. I bet that's where they are, she thought. They're looking at the fire. Better go and get them.

Outside, the streets were lit up by the flames. People ran past her.

"It's the brewery stables on fire!" they shouted to her as they ran.

Oh, my God, thought Maggie, those beautiful horses. She loved to take the kids to watch the brewers' drays in Mile End Road, each one drawn by two beautiful gray shires.

The main road was crowded with people who watched as men risked their lives to save the horses. They ran into the flames and came out leading the frightened, rearing animals. It was a most impressive sight.

"Some boys done that," said a woman in a black shawl standing next to her. "They got out. Lucky they weren't burned alive—little devils."

Maggie's mind was in a whirl. Where were Lennie and Ginger? She looked around the crowd but there was no sign of the familiar untidy red hair.

She must get home, she thought. Hurrying along she knew somehow that at last Ginger had come a cropper. It had to be. So when she saw the big shape of P. C. Murphy on the doorstep she was not surprised.

"Have to tell Liza," he said. "She's responsible for

them, Maggie, although we know she leaves it all to you."

A shouting, swearing Liza was dragged out of the pub and Maggie walked with her to the police station to see the five little boys—Ginger and his gang—who had been caught in the stables. They stood in a line, all black and sooty from the fire. Some, like little Lennie, cried, but Ginger just stood with his head held high.

There were several serious charges against them. The police had found them hiding out in the stables and over one hundred pounds' worth of loot had been found.

When Maggie had a minute alone with Ginger, he said, "Did Pie Shop come home?"

"Yes, he did," Maggie reassured him.

"Look after him, Maggie. They're bound to do me for this."

"Tell them yer won't do it again," said poor little Maggie.

He grinned. "Don't be daft. They know that I will. I told the other silly sods not to smoke. I hope the horses got out all right."

So Maggie lost her one pal—the boy who had helped to make life bearable for her. They sent him and Lennie to an approved school for two years and the house seemed dead and cold without them. Boy Boy was the only survivor.

Boy Boy was a quiet, withdrawn boy, but for the next few weeks he looked after baby Jim and Tom while Maggie went to Sarah's. The little dog, Pie Shop, attached himself to Maggie and followed her everywhere.

"I don't think I'll be able to stick it out to the end," Maggie said to Sarah. "Don't feel too good—never felt like this with the others."

"Don't worry, Maggie," said the gloomy Sarah, "let the bloody work go. Can't stand much more meself."

The previous week the Blackshirts had written,

"Down with the Jews," in whitewash on the blank wall at the side of the shop. This had really upset Sarah and although Maggie had thrown soapy water up the wall, it was not easily erased.

"Think I'll go and stay with Abe up in Leeds," said Sarah.

Maggie looked sad at the thought of losing Sarah, but to see her fat friend going to pieces worried her more.

"Go up and have a nice holiday," she said. "I'll keep me eye on the shop."

"No. I'll shut up the damn place. Don't make no money now."

So Sarah left for Leeds and Maggie went home to wait for the baby.

The house was like a morgue without Ginger and Lennie. Liza was morbid. She just sat staring into the fire, her hands grasping her walking-stick. She would remain in this position all morning until the pubs opened, then off she went to her seat in the open doorway where she sat watching the road—always looking for her Jim to come walking along. He had been gone nearly eight months now. It was a strange set-up; no one actually wrote to Jim but every now and again messages would arrive from his pals who had been released on parole. Liza awaited any stranger who might be bringing a message from Jim. She had said very little about Ginger getting into trouble, but Maggie knew her pride was hurt after she had worked so hard to bring up her five sons alone. Three were locked away and one had walked out without saying goodbye. It must be heartbreaking, thought Maggie.

Poor old Boy Boy. With his white face and long nose he was the least attractive of Liza's children and was the last to go. And Liza did not like him. His perpetual sniffing got on her nerves. "Blow yer nose," she would yell at him.

"Ain't my fault, Ma. Teacher said I got sinus trouble. You ought to take me up the clinic."

"Clinic be blowed. A good dose of licorice powder is what you need."

It was vile stuff, the licorice powder, but it was used to cure all ills. Poor little Boy Boy. Maggie used to feel sorry for him when Liza grasped his nose and forced it down him. Maggie tried to be extra kind to him and bought him sweets and once, a box of paints and a book. He sat for hours painting, and was very good at it too. But Maggie missed the reliable Ginger who had looked after the babies so well.

Sarah had shut the shop, as she had said she would and gone to Leeds on holiday with her married brother. The pawn shop was missed more than Sarah. "When's that fat cow coming back?" people would ask Maggie. "Got a parcel in there and can't get it out."

Maggie missed Sarah a lot—not only money-wise but also because she was the only friend and confidante that Maggie had.

The weather was getting warmer so Maggie would spend time sitting on the windowsill watching the kids play. The corner boys were there in full force with their flat caps and chokers, all standing idle for there was no work about. Sometimes they played a game that consisted of throwing halfpennies up the wall and calling heads or tails, until the police came in sight—then they would all scarper, for the existing law forbade gambling. At other times the Salvation Army band would come along and form a ring and the rest of the street would join in with their singing. Then along would come some poor old fellow walking in the middle of the road singing, his cap in his hand, hoping as he watched each window that a penny might be dropped in it. There was never a dull moment in the street. Often, a poor derelict alcoholic, full of meths, would fall down in the road, and along would come the police with a canvas stretcher on wheels and he would be carted off with all the kids walking along behind. It was a bright, varied pattern of life. While kids skipped and played marbles, the enormous tribe of dogs fought or mated to an appreciative audience.

As Maggie sat on the windowsill waiting for the birth of her third child, she would half close her eyes and daydream. Her dreams were not of the dingy gray brick dwellings all around her, but of a house of her own. Maggie had never been to the country but in her mind she saw green fields and tall trees with a little house standing alone in a beautiful garden. She could not recollect ever having seen this house but it was always there in her mind. She could see herself cutting flowers and putting them on the table just like Betsy Malloy did. In one room there were pink satin chairs and gold cushions like those in the window of the big shop up on the main road. She was sharing the house with someone, but not Jim. He was a cross between John and Ramon Navarro whom she had seen at the talkies once when Ginger and she had gone to the local flicks.

In the middle of one of these daydreams her pains started. She went indoors and made a cup of tea. Liza, half whoozy as usual, looked at her and said, "Ain't you well, Maggie?"

"No. I think my pains have started. When Boy Boy comes in from school, I'll send for Gran."

Liza gave her a strange look and said, "Look here, gel, you can't have that kid upstairs. You'd better go back in the front room."

Maggie, who had been thinking about what to do with Boy Boy and the little ones and the new baby's sleeping quarters, was glad of the offer.

"Thanks, Ma," she said. "But where are you going to sleep? You can't climb the stairs."

"I'll be all right. I'll kip in the chair tonight and in the morning I'll get Boy Boy and his mates to bring Mick's old bed down to the kitchen. That'll do me. Can't have old Granny Goring poking her nose in up there—it's a pigsty with all the kids."

Maggie marveled at Liza. It was not kindness that made her give up her room, it was pride. It was not the first time she had come across this trait in her mother-in-law. In this poor district, there still existed this working-class pride which was hard to define.

Boy Boy was not like Ginger who would have dashed off for Granny without a word. When he heard what he had to do he whined and sniffed a good bit. "Oh, do I have to go now, Maggie? Me bike's not working, I got the wheel off."

"It's not far, Boy Boy—only around the corner," Maggie said painfully.

But Liza reached over and gave the boy a crack with her walking stick. "Get going, you lazy sod," she yelled.

"Go yer bloody self," he replied and ran out holding his shoulder where the stick had caught him.

Maggie, now almost rolling in pain, was worried in case he wouldn't go to Gran's, but Liza was quite unconcerned.

"He'll go." she said simply. "He knows I'll take the skin off his back if he don't."

Maggie was terribly tensed up. She held her back and prayed for Gran to come. This time she was afraid but she did not understand why.

When Gran appeared at the door in her white apron, Maggie collapsed on the bed.

"Relax, my girl," Gran said as she busied herself making preparations. "Anyone would think this was your first."

Three hours later, near evening, Gran's face was red and perspiring. She rushed out to Liza who was on the doorstep. "Stay with her, Liza. I'm going for the doctor," said Gran as she hurried off.

Maggie lay white and still as Liza looked in. She was thoroughly exhausted by the long labor. Suddenly, she raised her face, convulsed and started to scream.

"Oh my gawd," said Liza as she rushed in and held her still.

When the doctor arrived, he sent for an ambulance, and Maggie, still screaming, was driven off to the dreaded hospital. The neighbors stood, arms akimbo, looking on at this unusual sight.

"Has 'em too quick, she does," they muttered. "Not a bad gel, young Maggie. Hope she'll be all right."

Liza went down to the Barley Mow to drown her sorrows. I wish my Jim was home, she thought.

The Hospital

When Maggie awoke the sun was shining through the window. Where was she? Above her was a high, white ceiling with no damp marks. As she turned her head, in the distance she saw some yellow flowers. They looked lovely. I wonder what they're called, she thought. Then at last, her mind grasped the fact that she was in the hospital. She tried to sit up but a voice said, "Don't try to sit up yet, Mrs. Burns. You have had rather a bad time."

Maggie looked solemnly at the white-clad sister who gave her a cool drink. "I lost the baby, then," she said sadly.

"No, of course you didn't. We don't allow that sort of caper here." This lovely apparition in the white cap smiled, showing a set of perfect white teeth. Maggie smiled too and was not afraid any more.

"You had a little girl. She's had oxygen because it was a delayed birth. But she's sweet. I'll bring her to you soon."

Maggie was so happy—a little girl. Perhaps Jim would be pleased. Her mind wandered. What day is it? Is it Friday? Of course, it was Good Friday and a holy holiday. Suddenly, a strange feeling came over her and once again, Dah was very close. She reached out a hand to touch him. "Sorry I have been wicked, Dah," she whispered. "Thank God for my little girl, will you?"

The nurse brought the little white bundle and placed it in Maggie's arms. Maggie looked down at the tiny face. It was like a little flower and fair, so fair. Her hair was pale gold like the morning sun. This is a special child, thought Maggie, born on this holy day. What should she call her? Mary would be nice, but there were so many Marys in the street. She thought of the singing and the candles of High Mass at Easter when Dah was alive. *Ave Maria,* the voices rang out high and the sweet music went straight to Heaven. Maria, that was the name she was looking for.

When the priest came visiting, Maggie said, "Please Father, will you baptize my child?"

"There's no hurry, Maggie. Wait until you are well and bring her to the church."

"Please, Father," begged Maggie, her blue eyes looking up at him, "do it before I go home. If I go home first, she won't be done."

He was a young priest and did not know Maggie's history. "Why?" he asked. "You're a Catholic, aren't you?"

Maggie shook her head. "I don't go now." Tears rolled down her face.

The priest consulted the hospital staff. They told him something they never told Maggie. The baby had leukemia.

So Maggie had her way. The priest blessed them both and said, "I'll visit you at home, dear."

The nurses all loved Maggie and, when she left the hospital, little Maria was wrapped in a lovely white shawl which they bought with money they had collected.

It was no different in the little house. The kids looked dirty but seemed to have been taken care of. The house needed a good clean. Most pathetic of all was Pie Shop who was a bag of bones having been continuously driven out by Liza. He was so pleased to see Maggie and howled and groveled at her feet.

"Poor Pie Shop," said Maggie. "Look, we got a new baby. You help me look after her."

Pie Shop wagged his tail and never left Maggie's side again, if he could help it. He followed her everywhere she went and sat beside the pram when she went inside the shops.

After a few weeks, the problem of money cropped up

again. Boy Boy got an early-morning job on the milk cart and conscientiously would never miss school and so was not available to mind the kids. The three shillings a week rent had not been paid for ages and a notice to quit had been pushed under the door. Maggie was at her wit's end and Liza was no help.

"What can I do? I'm only good for the scrap-heap," Liza would moan as she sat despondently in the kitchen when she did not have threepence for a half of beer. "Can't go over without buying a drink. Come to something, ain't it, when you can't have a half of beer?"

Maggie found it so depressing she could have screamed. The baby was a fretful little thing and needed constant attention. "Spoiling that kid, you are," Liza would keep on. "Let 'er cry, I say. It expands the lungs." But Maggie loved this little girl and was happy holding her.

Jim was a fine, strong boy now and the welfare officer had got him into the local school where he went with Boy Boy every day. Maggie would watch them as they went off up the road with their little parcels of lunch and a halfpenny for sweets.

With them out of the way, Maggie was able to look for a job in the mornings. "I'll give you a tanner a day if you mind the babies," she said to Liza.

Maggie got a morning cleaning job in the Barley Mow. She now scrubbed the doorstep she once used to sit on as a little girl. Maria was put in the pram outside the house and Liza sat in the passage to keep an eye on her and Tom. But as soon as weary Maggie came back across the road, Liza would hold out her hand for the tanner and went directly over the road to her usual seat.

This went on all summer until the school broke up for the holidays. Then Boy Boy got the job of minding the babies and he did it very badly too. Jim was hooked out of the canal just in time and Tom was lost for a day and brought back by a copper. He was very proud of that.

Still the baby grizzled, but she was so pretty—all golden curls and a lily-white face. "Looks puny to me," said Liza. But Maggie was not listening, she felt she could not stand any more.

One cold day in early autumn as she was scrubbing in the Barley Mow, Maggie looked across the road and saw little Maria sitting up and whimpering. Liza took no notice. As Maggie went to comfort her, she saw that Maria's hands were blue with cold. Liza slept warmly by the fire, and did not wake until Maggie shook her.

"Why didn't you bring the baby in? She's been crying a long time."

"I dozed off," said Liza. "Me old leg plays me up when it's cold."

So Maggie and Liza had a big row and Maggie cried and Liza got drunk. The next morning the baby had a nasty cough and by the evening a high temperature had developed. The doctor came. Maggie went to ask the missus at the pub to lend her half-a-crown for the doctor. He had asked for his money on the spot—in this district he never got paid once the patient was better.

"Bronchitis," he said. "Keep her warm and a kettle steaming in the room."

So Maria, in the old pram that had served so many, was placed by the fire and Maggie sat night after night watching over her baby until her head dropped down on the pram and she slept a sleep of exhaustion.

It was Liza who noticed it first. In the cold light of morning, she woke to hear the pitiful sound of air rattling in the throat of the dying child.

"Maggie! Wake up!" she said loudly. "Christ! I think she's gorn."

Liza dragged the screaming mother from the dead child and took her over the road to a neighbor until she had calmed down.

Maggie sat stunned. In this strange kitchen it was all a bad dream. A warm, furry body pressed against her and a paw was placed on her lap.

"Oh, Pie Shop," she sobbed. "Whatever did I do to deserve to lose my darling girl?"

She buried her face in his rough old coat and he was a great comfort to her. There was no human to understand the heartbreak of it all.

Of course, there was no money to bury the child with—even the undertaker did not work on credit. So, from a house in the street came two solemn women, their hands in their apron pockets. They presented Liza with some money and a list of names. These poor people in the street had very little but what they had they had given. Each contributor's name had been added to the list and beside that was the amount they had given: Mrs. Johns 3d; Mrs. Woods 6d; and so on. From houses that scarcely saw a good meal on the table, three pounds and two shillings had been collected for the funeral.

After the little white coffin had been buried in the old church yard, a change came over Maggie. The life had gone from her and she drooped and faded like a flower without sun and air.

"Buck up, Maggie," Liza would say as Maggie sat staring into the fire. "Come and have a beer, it'll do you good."

The little boys would say, "Give us our dinner, Mum. We're hungry."

But Maggie just fished into her purse for money to buy fish and chips and went on staring into the grate. Something was on her mind and it was not anything she could share. The well-meaning doctor had tried to console her for her loss.

"It's God's will, Mrs. Burns. Your little girl would not have reached school age and the loss would have hurt far more then."

Maggie looked at him in wonder. "Not go to school? Why?"

"Your little girl had a rare blood disease. The hospital discovered it when she was born. I think that in the circumstances you should have been told."

Maggie could not believe this at first. Then her own common sense told her that the child had not been as strong as the other children. In a blinding flash she remembered Maudie Evans and the pills.

Even though the weeks passed, the ache in her heart did not. There was no one in whom she could confide —no one with sense who would reassure her by saying: "It was nothing to do with the pills." So she sat and brooded until even Liza got so worried that she went down the road to ask the doctor to try and get Jim home.

5

Jim's Return

It was Saturday night and the street had settled down to its usual activity. The Barley Mow was full of singing, swearing and laughter. Maggie stared resentfully out of the front room window. Her face was pale and there were dark rings under her eyes. The kids were in bed and Maggie was alone. With so much on her mind she hated the street at that moment and, if it had not been for the two little boys upstairs, she would have taken her coat and run as far away as she could.

Then, a big heavy figure came walking down the street. It seemed familiar. As she looked again, she saw it was her Jim. Maggie wanted to get up and run to greet him but as he was passing the Barley Mow, Liza spotted him. Maggie saw the light from the pub come out across the road and the shadows of Liza and Jim as they stood in the doorway. Then the light went out, the door shut and Jim was inside. Maggie just sat waiting, without feeling. She simply felt numb. She did not know whether she was glad or sorry he was home.

When the pub had shut, a well-boozed Liza and Jim appeared in the house.

"Maggie!" screamed Liza. "Go upstairs and get me flaming vases down. My Jim's home."

But Maggie never moved or answered. She just sat staring at the big, well-built, well-scrubbed-looking man who was the father of her children.

"Hello, Maggie, gel. No welcome for yer old man?"

Maggie's blue eyes, wide and blank, did not move and she did not speak. Liza started to shout drunkenly. "Told yer, didn't I? Gorn bloody daft, she has. A right life she has led me, I can't tell you, Jim," and she started to cry.

But Jim took Maggie gently from the room and shut the door behind him. "Now, Maggie, gel," he said. "Let's hear from you." He folded his long arms around her and kissed her full on the lips. The effect on Maggie was startling. The last one and a half years disappeared; she belonged again.

Afterwards, they lay in bed in the front parlor. Maggie's face was tear-stained as she let all the grief inside her come out. Jim, kinder and gentler, had changed. He had grown up. Prison makes or breaks you, as the saying goes, but the hard labor and the fresh air had built him up; they made up for the lack of food and exercise in his adolescence.

"Listen, my love," said Jim. "I know what a brick you've been. Nothing much went on here that I didn't get to know. I'm sorry about our little girl but we're young and healthy enough to have some more. There's nothing to worry over, gel—your Jim's a new man. I've even got a job to go to."

Maggie cuddled up to him and felt safe as all the worry and grief left her.

"Let's go up and look at the boys," he said.

They crept upstairs and stood hand in hand looking at the boys who slept cuddled closely in the same bed. "Reminds me of when Mick and me slept in that bed," Jim said.

Suddenly, from under the bed rushed a shaggy body and something grabbed Jim's trouser leg. "Blimey! What's that?"

"Let go, Pie Shop," said Maggie. "He lives here."

Pie Shop obediently let go and crept under the bed again. "That's Ginger's dog," said Maggie. "He looks after the kids for me."

"I'll take you to see Ginger and Lennie, Maggie," said Jim. "I don't suppose anyone has been to see them."

"I couldn't leave the kids," said Maggie anxiously.

"I know, love. But I remember how I used to long to see someone from home."

Liza was happy now that Jim was home, and the kids followed their father everywhere. The happy atmosphere returned to Maggie's home and she was contented. Jim had got a regular job on the docks. It was difficult to find a job anyway and to get in the docks was considered to have landed yourself in easy street. Notice had been brought to the plight of this family after the baby died, and the prison officials had pulled strings to get Jim a job there. Maggie got up each morning to see him off to work with his lunch packed in a case. The tearaway Jim Burns went off until six o'clock at night and he was happier than he had ever been. Maggie dusted and polished the little house and took the kids to school.

"Don't want you working for no bloody Jews," said Jim. "You're my missus and I got a regular job." Maggie was so proud of her Jim.

Maggie was expecting again and the baby was due in the summer. Jim was still sticking to his job. He was always going on about the union, and had been made a shop steward. To Maggie, this was not important. He earned two pounds, ten shillings a week and gave her thirty shillings. On that she managed quite comfortably; admittedly, there was none to spare but, having been used to nothing, Maggie was happy.

At this moment, they were at war with the landlord although he was terrified of big bully Jim. Maggie would stand in the passage and try not to giggle when, on

Saturday mornings, Jim paid the rent. The landlord, as they called him (he was really just the rent collector), was a nervous little man whose life was forever in danger. The rent of this dilapidated house was three shillings a week and now it was paid regularly.

In the past, Maggie would hide in the lavatory when the man called and Ginger would say, "No one in, and we ain't got no money." The little man would stand and chatter angrily, just like a monkey, until a rude word from Ginger sent him on his way. Then he had resorted to putting notices under the door, giving them so long to get out. The first thing Jim did when he came home was to take the bundle of notices and, as the little man put out his hand to rat-tat on the door, Jim pulled it open quickly and caught the landlord off his guard—he was opening and shutting his mouth like a goldfish.

"These yours?" demanded Jim, shoving the papers under his nose.

"Well . . . Mrs. Burns . . ." he stuttered.

"Take these and stick 'em up your arse," said Jim, "and don't rat-tat at my door either."

Maggie was thrilled—her Jim would show him. From then on, each Saturday the landlord knocked very politely on the door. Jim would pay the three shillings but sometimes delayed the little man for half an hour while he informed him of the rights of man and what would happen to the landlords come the revolution. Maggie often thought it was a shame really because the poor man—Hoppy, as they nicknamed him—was doing a very lousy job. But he represented those who forced them to live like that, so it served him right.

She always remembered when the Coombs were evicted. Mrs. Coombs was a cripple who lived at No. 7 and was married to a German. They put her out in the street with all her bits and pieces around her. Maggie could see her now, sitting in a basketwork chair with her children gathered around her. When night time came, the evicted family all held hands and they went, pushing Mrs. Coombs in her chair, down to the workhouse. Someone put bits of sacking over the things in the gutter. A life-time of gatherings, their home was now just a pathetic pile of rain-soaked rubbish by morning.

How often Maggie had dreaded the time when she might be evicted. But now her Jim was home there was nothing to worry about.

So Maggie urged him to make the landlord do the place up. At first, Jim looked amazed. The idea of interior decoration had not reached the working classes yet.

"Do what?" asked Jim.

"Repair and paint it. They ain't never done nothing as far as I can remember. Look, there's all bugs squashed on the wall upstairs and even the front room looks horrible."

"Well, Maggie," said Jim, who never cared what color the walls were, "if he's responsible for it, he's got to do it. I'll see to that."

So once more, poor old Hoppy was put through the treadmill. Eventually, he sent two old men who stripped off the wallpaper and distempered the walls in every room in a horrible, bright, sickly pink color.

"Oh, my gawd," said Maggie, "I can't stand it, it's driving me crazy."

"What's the matter with it?" asked Jim. "It's clean anyway, only I think a nice battleship gray would have looked better." They lay in bed and laughed over it together.

A week later, Maggie, who was trotting down to the market, looked at the shuttered windows of the in-and-out shop and wondered if it had been sold. Then she saw the side doors were open and stopped to look.

Suddenly, out bounced Sarah. "Maggie! Me lovely Maggie!" Two fat arms gave Maggie such a big hug. "Come in, Maggie, and have a cup of tea."

They went through the dark shop full of dust and cobwebs. Sarah was bursting with all the news she had to tell. The kitchen was unusually bright and clean.

"Brought a girl back with me," said Sarah as Maggie's eyes wandered over the polished sink and shining crocks. "She's a lovely worker and needed a home. Things is bad up north, yer know. Her name is Louie. She's gone down the baker's. She'll be back in a minute."

Maggie, putting on the kettle, surveyed Sarah. She was quite changed. Her hair was cut and set in a smart style called the shingle and there were gay earrings in her ears and beads to match around her neck. She looked very nice. Her black dress set off the beads to perfection.

"Well my, aren't we smart. You have changed, Sarah."

"Don't look like you have," said Sarah. "Still in the pudding club, Maggie?"

Maggie looked a little sad but said, "Well, my love, someone's got to keep up the population . . . you ain't doing much towards it." They giggled like two young girls.

"That's what I want to tell you, Maggie. Pour out the tea, love, so we can have a natter before the girl comes back. I'll tell you why I was such a long time up there. My brother Abe went to visit America. My life, Maggie, what a place! I should love to go to America."

To Maggie, America was a country full of cowboys like you saw at the pictures.

"Well," continued Sarah, "they had a little hotel up in Leeds, so Abe said, 'Sarah, I'd like to take the wife and kids with me to America, so will you look after things up here for me?'

"Well, Maggie, did I have a good time. Plenty of men and lots of sailors. It was funny—they would come in and say, 'I would like a room for me and my wife.' 'Of course,' I says with a larf." She went off into gulps of laughter.

"Well," said Maggie, "what's the joke?"

"This bird was everybody's bloody wife. So I'd put a couple of quid on the bill for meself."

But Maggie could not see the joke and fat Sarah's sides went in and out with laughter. "They thought a lot of me, them girls did. Always buying me presents, they was. Look, one gave the beads and earrings."

"I'm disappointed," said Maggie. "Thought you was going to say you got engaged or something."

Sarah came closer. Maggie could smell the strong perfume. "I did it," whispered Sarah.

"Did what?" asked Maggie.

"Had a bit of the other," said Sarah triumphantly.

Maggie didn't know whether she ought to laugh, so she kept silent. Sarah was determined that Maggie should share all the details of her love affair.

"He was smashing, at first. Think he was Irish—a great big fella. I fell for him on sight. Said he liked his women well upholstered. I had had plenty to drink, he liked whisky and I could always get a bottle cheap."

"Well?" asked Maggie. "Did he propose?"

"Propose? Me eye!" said Sarah. "Took what he wanted, the sod, and didn't even say goodbye. Never paid his bloody bill either."

At last, Maggie exploded. She laughed until tears ran down her face.

"Tell you what, Maggie," said Sarah. "It's taught me a lesson. No one else gets me till they've paid for it, because it ain't worth the trouble. All that pushing and shoving; knocked all the bleeding breath out of me, he did."

They were still giggling when Louie returned. Maggie took to Louie on sight. She was small, with brown, bobbed hair and mottled, red skin. There was something nice and fresh about her. She would never be a beauty but she had a vivid personality. She came from a mining village in the north, from a large family which was always poor, but it made Louie dependable. She could cook and scrub with whole-hearted energy, singing merrily all day. To lazy fat Sarah who never liked work, she was a great asset.

Many mornings were spent at Sarah's. The three of them swapped stories while Maggie helped to get the pawn shop organized and Louie cleaned up and cooked the dinner. Maggie thought they were some of her happiest days.

Once the shutters came down, the fun started. The little kids would come along with the parcels and there were many arguments over the long-lost parcels which were all in a heap under the counter. Some old girl would say, "It's been here bloody long enough. Interest? Blimey, I think you ought to pay me."

Sarah, as antagonistic as ever, would stand and argue until Maggie interrupted with a tactful remark. "Well, Mrs. Brown, take it home and if it don't fit yer, we'll give you yer money back."

So peace would be restored by Maggie for a while.

Once a week, Maggie and Sarah went to the Empire. Maggie loved the vaudeville and looked forward to Fridays when, dressed in their best, she and Sarah would walk through the market to the Empire. In Sarah's shop there was a big, colored advertisement for the Empire, so Sarah got two free tickets each week. "You can have them this week," Sarah would offer. "Maybe Jim will take you."

Only once had Jim taken Maggie out since he had come out of prison, and that was when they went to see Ginger and Lennie. The "bruvvers" were at an approved school somewhere near Southend. It was a bright spring day and they had decided to take the boys with them. Getting on the train made Maggie nervous but the green fields that rushed past them, the cows and the houses with gardens were so exciting. "Just like a kid," Jim said as he watched her excitement.

Maggie was dressed in her navy costume that reached the ankles and a navy silk hat which formed a halo around her face, and a white lace jumper. Jim was really proud of her.

The school had a sports day in a big green field where they served muffins and cake. It was good to see her old pal Ginger again. He looked at her shyly. He was nothing like the old ruffian she used to know. He had grown very tall and his red hair was cut short and plastered down; it shone like burnished gold. There was Lennie beside him as usual, almost as tall but fair and slim.

"Hello, Maggie," said Ginger. "Don't you look smart."

Then little Jim and Tom rushed at their old friend. The family group sat on the grass as the boys romped together.

"Don't Ginger look fine," said Maggie.

"Well," said Jim, "one thing I say about getting into trouble—they teach yer more than you ever get at a council school. Look at me, didn't know nothing till I went on the *Arethusa* and in the nick. What with the lousy food we had at home and the bloody damp, it wasn't so bad inside."

Places we sleep don't improve our health, thought Maggie as she looked at her little boys playing, but she didn't want them to get their education that way.

"Times is going to be different for our boys," said Jim. "That's what we're fighting for." Maggie said she hoped so.

Ginger won in the school races and he soon lost his shyness.

"How's Pie Shop?" he asked.

"He's fine," said Maggie. "You'll see him when you come home."

Ginger shook his head. "I'm not coming home, Maggie."

"Why not, Ginger?"

"I couldn't live like that after this," he said, looking across the green fields towards the gray school buildings.

"You like it here?" asked Maggie.

"At first I found it hard but being clean and never hungry is a much better way to live. There's always someone ready to listen. Back home it was a kick up the backside and out in the street to play."

"Will Lennie go with you?"

"Of course he will," said Ginger. He was so confident of the love and trust his brother had for him. "It's

the old lady I'm worried about—in case she won't
sign for us to go."

"Go where?" Maggie asked curiously.

"Australia, that's where. Somefink to do with a
scheme for young boys to emigrate out there."

"What are you going to do in a strange country,
young boys like you?"

"We're going to learn farming. It looks like a smashing country—we've seen films of it."

Maggie looked admiringly at this fine young boy
with his bright blue eyes alight with the thrill of it all
and the great adventures he anticipated. He was actually going to another country. Ginger will make it, she
thought.

Jim returned from watching the sports, looking very
serious. "Did Ginger tell you he's going to Australia?"

"Yes," said Maggie.

Jim sat down on the grass beside her, looking thoughtful. "I reckon it will be the best thing for them. There's
not much for them here in this country. The bloody
capitalists are killing it."

Maggie did not know what a capitalist was but she
wondered what Liza would have to say.

Liza's reaction was strange. To Maggie, it was un-
believable.

A pleasant young man came to visit them a few
weeks later. "I have called on behalf of the government," he said. "Your sons would like to join our
scheme to send young lads to learn farming in Australia."

Holding grimly on to her stick, Liza said, "Oh, I suppose now that I've struggled to bring them up without
a father and they might bring me a bit of money, you
want to take them to some God-forsaken country and
I'll never see them again."

"No, certainly not, Mrs. Burns. It's only for a few
years and you will receive an ample allowance."

"Well, that's different," said Liza. "Let's get down
to business."

Maggie was disgusted, being the mother of two sons

herself. She did not think Liza would put up a fight to keep them but nor did she think that she would change her mind just for a few quid. Maggie thought that she would never understand the people of her mother-in-law's type, though there were plenty of them in the street. It all seemed on the surface; there was no inner feeling about anything. Perhaps it wasn't Liza's fault, she thought. It was a hard life she lived and a very narrow one. Maggie only knew that Liza was as fond of Jim as she was of her fine sailor husband. The other boys she scarcely noticed. When Mick walked out, Maggie thought Liza would be upset but there was not one sign of emotion. Boy Boy was still at home but he was only there for her to take a whack at. That was all she had time for. It was very puzzling, thought Maggie.

Not long after, Al was born. He was a fine, bonny boy who was no trouble at all. This time, Maggie had gone voluntarily to the new East End Maternity Hospital because Jim had insisted. "That's what we pay our rates and taxes for," he said, "so as they can build these places."

If Jim said so, it was so, thought Maggie. He knew everything, her Jim, as she told everyone. He could read books and stand up to the king if necessary. Sarah thought Jim was a mean-looking bully but she kept quiet as she was too fond of Maggie to hurt her feelings.

The "bruvvers" had been out in Australia for some time and Maggie got nice letters and snapshots from Ginger. They seemed happy enough. They always sent their love to Pie Shop, and Maggie would let him sniff the letter when his old tail would wave about with joy. "See, he knows," she would say to the children.

A simple girl was Maggie. At twenty-one, she still laughed as gaily as ever and was just as slim. Jim often looked at her and thought how pretty she was.

He, on the other hand, had changed quite a lot in the last two years. He had become heavier and his hairline was receding. There was continuous trouble down at the docks—always lock-outs and lay-offs. Jim was as argumentative as ever and had joined the Communist Party as well as the union. He drank very heavily and, as time went on, money got short again. Most of Jim's leisure time was spent in the Barley Mow; Maggie would marvel at the men's behavior as they stood for hours swilling beer. All Jim's pocket money was spent by Sunday night and he was broke all week.

He and Maggie began to quarrel. It was usually over money and then he began not to come home from work in the evenings. "Sorry, got a union meeting," he would say. Then Friday would come and there was not much left of Jim's wages for Maggie.

"It's no good, Jim. I'll have to get a job. Can't feed the kids without money."

"You ain't going to work for no bloody Jews."

"I thought you liked them," retorted Maggie. "That mate of yours who does all the shouting on the bridge is a Jew."

"There's Jews and Jews," said Jim obstinately. "That fat friend of yours, her brother's got pots of money. It's them what's destroying the economy of this country."

"Oh, you're potty," said Maggie. As a final parting shot as he went to meet his very important friends, she shouted after him: "Big head!"

Jim thought the world of his friend Tom Tucker. Tuck was as small as Jim was big. He knew it all. Whatever the argument, Tom could settle it. While others wore the flat caps and chokers, he wore a felt hat with a brim and a white collar and tie. It was Tuck who had rowed Jim into politics. He was all for the rights of man but what he did for a living was a mystery. As Maggie said, he was a Jew but no one was sure of this because Tuck never mixed with the rest of the Jews but spent his time at various meetings—either speaking on the rights of man or stirring up the crowd against the Fascists who held their meetings in the same place.

"He's going to get you into trouble, he is," said Maggie to Jim one particularly wild Saturday night when both sides had fought in the street and the police had carted Jim down to the station. He was only fined but received a warning not to come back.

"As if I ain't got enough trouble," said Maggie to Sarah as they went down to the Empire together. Maggie still enjoyed her Friday nights out on the free ticket. With its bright lights and red plush seats, the Empire really took her out of the dreary world she lived in and for two hours a week she could lose herself watching the turns which made her laugh and the lovely girls who danced in a row. But sometimes it was difficult to get Sarah to go. She had never really recovered from her fear of the Blackshirts and when they passed the meeting place where the black-shirted boys hung about, her nails dug into Maggie's arm and her fat legs almost went from under her.

The boys were getting very big and Maggie was finding it difficult to get clothes for them. She would sort through the second-hand stalls and find a variety of garments none of which matched so the little Burnses were not exactly the best-dressed kids at school.

The climax came one day when little Jim had no shoes for school. It had begun to get cold so Maggie, endeavoring to cope as usual, bought a pair of button-up boots at the second-hand stall. They were really old-fashioned and much too big for Jim. They had pointed toes and buttoned up the sides.

"I can't wear them, Mum," said six-year-old Jim, his blue eyes full of tears.

"You ain't got nothing else and it's raining," said his mother.

Little Tom, with his bent nose which had got broken and never grown straight, said in his gruff voice: "He can't, Mum. They'll take the mickey out of us. We always got old clothes on."

Maggie, who was not used to rebellion in the boys, said, "Now get off to school and be thankful you're nice and warm."

So the little procession left the house and Maggie watched them go up the street.

There was Jim, tall for his age, with a mop of dark curls but a rather odd-looking figure. He was wearing an old pair of brown trousers that reached the knee—they had once been Ginger's—a Norfolk tweed shooting jacket that was too big and a cap on his curls that was out of date with its wide checks and ear flaps. He certainly looked a queer little figure.

Then there was Tom in wide-cut flannels and a big red jersey with a roll neck. He looked like a miniature prize-fighter. The two boys proceeded slowly along. It was the boots they were worried about. Tom stared at them and looked to see if anyone was watching, and Jim, in great difficulty, looked forlorn as he steered himself in the direction of school.

To reach the school they had to pass the dock gates and there outside was their dad, about to deliver one of his famous speeches to the men who had been locked out. The boys stood hand in hand waiting to cross the road as big Jim, standing on the platform, opened his mouth to let the pearls of wisdom come out. Nothing came, for the little knot of men had turned to stare at these two kids.

"Cor blimey, look at those poor kids," a coarse voice said. "The big one looks like Puss-in-bloody boots."

There were roars of laughter until suddenly they all realized that they were big Jim's kids.

Big bully Jim rushed in drunker than ever that evening. "Maggie!" he yelled. "What the hell do yer mean showing me up at work in front of me mates?"

"Me?" asked Maggie incredulously.

"Yes. Sending them kids to school like that. Proper bloody pantomime they looked with all that second-hand gear."

Out flared the Irish temper that Maggie usually hid. "Well, buy them some togs," she screamed, "instead of putting yer money in the booze."

This was too much for Jim. He did what he had never yet done, he clouted Maggie. When the china pot hit him on the head and blood streamed down his face he was really upset. He rushed over the road to his old mates in the Barley Mow.

"Look!" he was shouting. "She's done for me. The cow hit me over the head with a bloody basin."

Maggie watched out of the window as Tuck escorted him up to the hospital, and giggled like a girl at big Jim holding his head as Tuck trotted along beside him. They put two stitches in his head and he walked about looking very sorry for himself for a few days. But on Friday he came straight home.

"Here's an extra couple of quid, Maggie," he said. "For gawd's sake, get them kids dressed up proper."

Maggie said to Sarah later, "He's not so bad, my Jim."

"Not if yer knows how to train 'em," roared Sarah, seeing the funny side as usual.

The Funeral

In 1936, Liza died. She had been very quiet during the last two years, going from the house to the pub and back again every day. She had taken to drinking gin instead of beer. "It keeps the cold out," she would say.

One evening she never went out for her trip to the Barley Mow. Maggie came into the house and Liza, with a half a bottle of gin beside her, was sleeping her last sleep.

Jim was very upset. In his rough way he thought a lot of his mother. But the biggest surprise was that Liza had left a will—a real legal document. It was signed, sealed and witnessed by the local doctor.

I want to be buried in style, no new-fangled motor-cars.
Black horses and a hearse and all my family to follow me.
 Any money over is for my Jim.
 Signed, Liza Burns.

They were more than surprised at the amount of insurance money Liza had—nearly two hundred pounds. Maggie felt sick when she remembered how tight the money had been while Jim was away. Liza had paid her life insurance religiously no matter who went hungry.

"She was a funny woman," said Maggie to Sarah.

"You should worry. There's bound to be a bit left over after the funeral," said the practical Sarah.

For the first time ever, the whole of the Burns family was rigged out. Jim was in a black suit and Maggie in a black astrakhan coat while the little boys all wore gray jerseys, long black pants and new shoes.

Liza was put down in the style she wished for. Little Jim remembered for a long time after, the excitement of that day; Granny's funeral, with the coal-black horses outside the door, all the flowers in the passage and the neighbors popping in and out. But everyone remembered the slap-up tea and the grand booze-up afterwards. It was Maggie who had made that suggestion for she was so happy that the house was now hers and her family's since Liza was dead and all her boys had left.

Even Boy Boy had found his right course in life; after sniffing his way through the council school to the grammar school, he was now at an engineering college up in the Midlands. When Maggie saw him at his mother's funeral he seemed like a stranger—a tall, pale-faced boy with large, horn-rimmed spectacles. He did not stay long. In fact, he was most anxious to leave when the boozey Jim wanted to try on his spectacles.

At last, Maggie was the mistress of her own home. This dreary little place was not much of a home but Maggie was full of ideas.

"Let's have a real parlor," she said to Jim.

"Blimey, Maggie, what are you? A bleeding capitalist?"

"No, Jim, I'm not joking. We'll take Liza's bed upstairs and chuck out all the old ones."

This seemed sacrilegious to Jim. "Gawd, Maggie," he said, "the old girl will turn in her grave if you start mucking about with her bed."

"Don't be daft, Jim. We got to live comfortable now the kids are growing up. Don't want them to have your sort of life, do you?"

"No, I suppose you're right, gel. What do you want to do?"

"Well, with the money over from the funeral, I thought we would get a piano . . . on the H.P., of course."

"A piano? What do we want a piano for? And who's going to play it?"

"Don't matter. Everyone has a piano in their parlor now."

"Well they're bloody mad," said Jim. "And what did you say? H.P. Never in my life, Maggie. What we can't afford, we won't have."

"Oh, Jim," said Maggie beginning to weep with disappointment.

"Look here, gel, there's a big depression on now and there could be a war. It's got to come. How'll yer get on then, eh, gel?"

He was on his soapbox again so Maggie ignored him, thinking how lovely it would be to have a piano.

Maggie did get her parlor and Liza's old bed was carted upstairs. The only trouble they had was with Pie Shop. He had always slept under Maggie's bed and he resented all the moving and cleaning up that was going on. He bit Jim in the leg though not badly, it was just a slight nip. That was nothing unusual since Jim and the dog were always in combat.

After the fuss was over they papered the parlor together hiding the pink distemper the landlord had arranged. Maggie loved the wallpaper, it had nice red roses all over it. But the aggravation as Jim put it up went on for a week. He would lose his temper and go out to the pub, leaving strips of wallpaper hanging down from the wall. It did get finished eventually and, as a final touch to her own front room, Maggie got some pink curtains from Sarah.

It was years before it was furnished because Jim boozed away what was left of the insurance money. But he did buy a "grammy phone," as Maggie called it. This was a second-hand monstrosity in a big polished box. To get it to work you turned a handle. The little boys had great fun with it but they drove Maggie mad as there was only one record which they played over and over again; it had *Sheik of Araby* on one side and *I'll Take You Home Again, Kathleen* on the other. The gramophone looked nice in the parlor though Maggie would still have liked a piano.

6

Sarah's Lodger

In 1937 things seemed to pick up. There was more money around and the men found it easier to get work. The corners of the streets seemed empty, but there was still a lot of trouble about at weekends. Blackshirts and Communists marched and made speeches and all the young lads followed them. Jim, as foolish as ever, fought all and sundry for the cause. As Maggie told Sarah, "Gawd knows what this cause is he raves about. It's getting on my nerves."

"Things is bad," whispered Sarah. "They say we're going to have a war."

Sarah never opened the shop these days. The shutters remained up and she lived over the top with all the doors bolted and barred. She spent her time experimenting with various slimming diets and face creams. When Maggie went to visit her she would peep through the curtains. "That you, Maggie? I'll throw down the key."

"What's up, Sarah?" Maggie asked one day.

"It's all right, love. It's nothing you would understand."

A young man was in bed in the back room upstairs.

He was a dark, foreign man who never spoke a word of English.

"Take him some hot soup, Maggie. The poor devil," said Sarah.

"Who is he?" asked Maggie.

"Oh, my life, Maggie," said Sarah, "that you should ask me such a thing." She waved her hands as she always did in a moment's stress.

"He's not English, is he?" Maggie asked.

Sarah came closer and in a hoarse whisper said, "He's come from Germany. But you must not tell anyone."

Now Germany could have been Pentonville where Jim had been as far as Maggie was concerned. "What's he here for?" she asked.

Sarah's big moon face shone very white. "Yer don't know about Hitler?" she whispered, looking furtively around the shop. Maggie shook her head.

"It's terrible," said Sarah, "he's going to kill all the Jews."

"Don't be daft," said Maggie. "How can he do that?"

"It's true, love," said Sarah; tears were running down her face. "You won't believe what they've done to that poor sod upstairs."

"Don't cry, Sarah," said Maggie. "Cheer up, love. Can't be as bad as all that. I'll make a cup of tea."

From that day on Maggie noticed a change in Sarah even after the young man had gone. She would only emerge to go to the Empire on Fridays.

"You'll get as fat as a pig if you don't get no exercise," said Maggie, one day.

"My life, Maggie. I lost three pounds only last week," responded Sarah.

Their friendship was as solid as ever. Bernie, Sarah's second brother, now lived in Stamford Hill with Louie, the girl Sarah had brought from Leeds. They had two lovely children. Sarah was most upset over this and would not speak to Bernie, so she needed Maggie more than ever.

Back on the Breadline

Towards the end of the year Jim's mates brought him home from work. He was badly beaten up. There had been a fight and the other chap was in the hospital. Jim sat by the fire with his head in a bandage looking very sorry for himself. This time he was really scared. The young fellow he had fought with was in a bad way having fallen down into the hold of the ship when Jim struck him. His mates had beaten Jim up but this would not save him from being done for murder if the other man died.

Because she could not help herself and had seen it coming, Maggie nagged and nagged continuously until Jim got up and lumbered across the road to get sympathy from his mates.

At the end of the week, the man recovered consciousness and refused to charge Jim but the Dock Board sent Jim his cards and the union did nothing about it. So once again, Maggie was back on the bread line and Jim sat morose and sullen around the kitchen fire.

Jim did try to get another job but he was blacklisted as a trouble-maker, the employers said. He was out of work for six months, queuing at the labor exchange. The little house was sad and dreary again. Maggie could no longer go to the Empire and she had pawned her black, astrakhan coat.

Once again, Sarah came to the rescue.

"Why don't yer get a job, Maggie? If yer so hard up, yer should."

"You know Jim won't let me do housework for other people and what else can I do?"

Sarah shrugged her shoulders. She would like to have made a rude comment about Maggie's Jim but she kept silent.

"Why don't yer go and see Bernie?" she said at last.

"Why?" asked Maggie, "I thought you didn't talk to Bernie."

"I don't," said Sarah. "Getting that shiksa in the family way. Fine disgrace he brought on me. Don't say I told yer, but he just bought that factory up the road. They're going to make uniforms. I bet there'll be a war."

"Will he give me a job?" asked Maggie.

"Of course he will. He thought a lot of you, Maggie. I expect if you'd let him have it, he wouldn't have gone off with Louie."

Maggie, who always laughed at Sarah's crude mind, imagined herself with the nineteen-stone Bernie, and could not stop laughing.

Bernie was so pleased to see her when she called at the factory. "Why, it's little Maggie," he said. His head was like a polished billiard ball and his stomach stuck out in front. He smoked a cigar and looked prosperous.

"How's Louie?" asked Maggie.

"She's fine," he replied, "and a lovely son and daughter we got now." He loved Louie.

"Of course, I got just the job for you, Maggie," he said. "We got a big contract and I want a nice reliable gel to look after the staff—you know, give out the work and see to the complaints. It'll give me more time to go out and do business."

So Maggie became a forelady. At first, there were strong objections from Jim. "What sort of a ponce do you take me for?" he said. "Me old woman going out to work to keep me?"

Maggie, whose wages were better than what Jim had got at the docks, was not going to give this job up. "All women work now," she said. "If you had any sense you'd shut up and do a bit to help in the house. I'm getting better wages than you ever did."

So Jim helped in the home and got the kids ready for school. Everyone was happy, except for Pie Shop; he strongly objected to Jim being home all day instead of Maggie. Each morning he and Jim had a couple of rounds; while Jim swept the bedroom Pie Shop would dart out and attack the broom while Jim did his best to shake the dog off.

When Maggie came home one evening she said, "Where's Pie Shop?"

A pathetic whine told her he was tied up in the back yard.

"Oh, poor little thing!" she cried, releasing him quickly.

"Either that bloody dog goes or I do," said Jim.

"Don't be so soft," said Maggie, kissing old Pie Shop on the nose. "All he wants is to be friends."

From then on, Pie Shop left the house with Maggie in the morning, and hung around the factory all day and returned with her in the evening.

The Crisis

Maggie liked her job and was very good at it. She gave out the work and sorted out the little problems that cropped up. The girls all liked her. Her slim shape trotted here and there and she could certainly handle the guvnor. He was like a babe in arms when Maggie turned her charms on him.

It was September and there was a lot of excitement in the air. They called it the "Crisis." All the girls in the factory were talking of Hitler and Mr. Chamberlain. To Maggie, it meant nothing; she was fed up with Jim and his politics and did not want to be bothered.

"Ain't you worried, Maggie?" some young girl asked.

"Worried?" said Maggie, "about what?"

"The war," the girl said, "and old Hitler."

"Not his sort. Got enough to do looking after my kids. Can't worry about some old bloke I don't even know."

"But Maggie," the girl went on, "what about your kids? He's going to drop bombs on us."

"Go on," said Maggie. "And what are we going to do while he does that?"

"Leave her be," the others said. "She don't care. She's not a worrier."

So Maggie, busily earning money and even putting

some in the bank, was quite unconcerned about the tension that was felt all around her.

The boys were getting on at school, and the teacher had told Maggie that little Jim was exceptionally clever. Maggie went back and forth to work making great plans for the future. She even thought about moving to a nice place where there were trees and green fields. It would be so nice for the kids to have somewhere to play—they were always in trouble in this damn street.

Jim was getting on all right at home—his early training at the naval school helped. The house was as clean and bright as a battleship. He had painted the other rooms and Maggie was proud of her passage with its lace curtains and the freshly painted stairs.

One September evening, she was walking home through the market. I'll get some kippers, she thought. It's been quite a day with all the girls doing their nuts because that funny old man with the umbrella has been to see Hitler and there was not going to be a war after all. Hope they don't stop making the uniforms, she pondered. I might lose me job.

The man at the fish stall said, "Good news, eh, Maggie?"

"Three pairs of kippers," said Maggie. "Service me well, 'cause old Hitler ain't going to get you after all."

"I don't know about that," the fishmonger said, his face serious under the straw boater he always wore. "It ain't going to be easy to stop a bloke like that . . . never know what he's got up his sleeve."

"I should worry," said Maggie, trotting off with her parcel of fish.

Jim had been a bit quiet that week and Maggie had looked at him in the morning and asked, "You got a cold, Jim?"

"Of course I ain't," said Jim. "I'm getting fed up with all this housework. Like a flaming pansy, I am, stuck here with me apron on."

"Shut up, Jim. The lolly's coming in. What yer grumbling about?"

"Grumbling about? I'm browned off, that's what.

There's going to be a war. The country's in great danger and what am I doing about it, eh?"

He stuck out his chin in an aggressive manner, so Maggie said, "Get off the soapbox, Jim. Anyway, they've got a prime minister, the job's not vacant." She fled out of the room, banging the door as she went.

Coming home that evening, her conscience pricked her. Poor old Jim. Perhaps they might go up the pictures tonight.

In the kitchen sat Jim. Beside him was Tuck. On seeing Maggie, Tuck sidled out. She could smell the whisky fumes as she walked in and saw the empty bottle on the table.

"Thought so. Seeing that little rat, I might have known." But Jim said nothing.

"What's up?" she asked. He looked pale.

"I'm sorry, gel," he said simply.

"Sorry for what? Spit it out!"

"I've joined the navy," he said.

"Well, I'm blowed." Maggie sank down into the old armchair by the fire. It was the same one in which she and Jim had done their courting.

"Whatever you do that for, you silly fool? There ain't going to be a war. It's all over. That Mr. Chamberlain said so on the wireless."

"I know, Maggie," Jim whispered sheepishly. "But I joined this morning and I can't get back out of it now. Tuck and me volunteered because we wanted to go in the navy and we thought if we was called up we would be put in the army."

It was after Christmas when Jim got his papers. Maggie was as decent as she could be. The last year had been good to her and she dreaded what the change of circumstances might bring.

Jim was over in the Barley Mow bidding goodbye to his friends and neighbors. He seemed to have got used to the idea and was now acting like a bloody war hero.

"You'll be all right, Maggie. There's no babies to

worry you. Al's five and you got your job and a good allowance coming."

In his way Jim tried to console her. "There ain't no war so unless I get drunk and fall overboard, I'll come back home to you."

But it was no good. That house in the country was going further away from her and there was a strange feeling inside her. It was as though this was only the beginning.

She went outside and sat on the windowsill. The singing from the pub echoed across the street and sent her memory back down the years to her wedding when, so lonely and unhappy, she had shut out the sound of revelry and gone down to the church railings where Jim had found her. Then she thought of 1937, the year of the Coronation. That was a happy day, one of the best memories she had. She looked along the street and in her mind she saw the laughing, happy kids sitting at a long table the length of the street itself, all wearing paper hats. Then there were the celebrations in the evening when an old piano was brought out into the road and they all danced. Maggie had waltzed with Jim; they had never danced together before. It had not been so bad to her, the street.

The sound of Jim shouting from the direction of the pub broke her train of thought. "Come on, Maggie," he was saying. "Come over and have a drink, it's me last night."

So Maggie joined him and, after the pub had closed, all the neighbors came in with more booze and they drank until morning. How they managed to get Jim and Tuck on the train was a mystery to Maggie. Well Maggie, gel, she thought, as she cleared up the debris, you're on your own again. Better pull your socks up.

To keep her mind occupied, Maggie dived head first into her job and Bernie, who was expanding the business all the time, was very pleased with her. Each day she assumed more responsibility.

"What do they keep making these uniforms for if they ain't going to have a war?" asked Maggie.

"Don't let 'em kid yer," said Bernie. "There's going to be a big bust-up soon, with all the big countries. We got to beat that bastard. He's going to kill all the Jews."

Maggie was sorry about the Jews, but what about her Jim?

She now went to the pictures with Sarah, as well as the Empire on Fridays. It was Sarah who said, "Get some smart clothes, Maggie, and use a bit of make up." And it was Sarah who persuaded her to get her hair cut and set.

This nearly ruined Jim's first leave. Maggie's lovely hair was her crowning glory so when he came home and Maggie met him at the door, he roared like an enraged bull. "Gawd, Maggie. Where's yer hair gone? What the hell is that on yer mouth?"

It did settle down after a few days but the argument went on and on until little Jim said to Tom, "Like it better when the old man's not here. Don't you, Tom?" And Tom agreed.

Jim looked smashing in his uniform, and Maggie was glad when they made up their quarrel. She would walk down the market holding his arm so that all the girls from the factory looked out of the window at them.

Jim liked it in the navy. He was stationed at Portsmouth and he and Tuck scoured the town on Saturday nights. Tuck started the fights and Jim finished them. Then there were the girls. Up until then Jim had not had much time to mix with women. He married Maggie when he was seventeen and he never looked in another direction. But down in Portsmouth the young single girls gave Jim the eye with his smart uniform and broad shoulders. And he loved it. With Maggie miles away, he and Tuck made the most of it.

The War Begins

Time was eating into 1939 and spring was near at hand. On Saturday, Maggie went out with Sarah. With plenty of sweets and comics the boys were happy enough on their own and Pie Shop was in charge. Pie Shop had developed from being a scraggy-looking mongrel to a well-groomed, well-behaved dog. Maggie used to say, "Why, he's like a human being. I just say, 'Mind the kids, Pie Shop,' and he sits there and won't move."

Sometimes when Maggie came in from her nights out with Sarah she was a bit flushed and giggly.

"Mum's been on the booze," Tom would say. "Don't you think so, Jim?"

"Looks a bit tiddly," agreed Jim. "Don't say nothing to the old man, Tom."

"Scouts' honor," Tom would say.

It was true that Sarah and Maggie had taken to going and having a port when they came out of the pictures. Sometimes they had two.

"Makes me sleep," Maggie would say to excuse herself.

"Makes up for not eating," Sarah would add. "Some of them diets is awful."

A good thing came out of Jim being at Portsmouth. He got lodgings for them all in Southsea so for the first time in their lives, the family had a holiday. As they sat in the train, the excited little boys jumped up and down and held bets as to who would be the first to spot the sea. It was Al who won because Jim and Tom were fighting at the time, pointing his little finger, unable to shout aloud with excitement, as the Solent came into view; a long, silver strip of sand with the blue line of sea behind it.

It was a lovely holiday. The landlady gave eye to the boys when Jim took Maggie around the pubs in the evenings to show his mates how smart and pretty she was. During the day they sat on the sand together while the boys played. Sometimes Jim went into the water with them which was the one thing they could not persuade Maggie to do. But Jim and Maggie kissed and cuddled on the beach and the boys buried them in the sand.

One afternoon as they sat hand-in-hand, across the bay came the sound of guns.

"What's they?" asked Maggie, looking scared.

"It's nothing to be afraid of," said Jim. "It's target practice. They're trying out the big guns."

The sound vibrated the place where they sat and the boys stopped playing and stared out to sea.

"Is there going to be a war, Jim?" asked Maggie.

For once Jim did not shout or argue with her. He looked straight into her eyes and said, "Yes, me love, there is. And this is my last leave. Next week I go overseas."

The world stopped still for a moment.

"You're sure, Jim?"

"They can't help themselves. He's taken us on long enough."

Maggie always remembered those last few days. The house where they were staying had a lovely pear tree in the garden and it grew up in a mass of white blossoms and peeped in through their bedroom window. Somehow Maggie always remembered the scent of that tree on the last night. The navy had made Jim kind and gentle. It was a different experience for Maggie; she had never slept with any man but Jim.

"I don't want to leave you lumbered with kids, Maggie," he said and explained how the navy had told him how not to have them.

Maggie listened and said, "It's all right, Jim. I don't mind kids."

"No love," said Jim firmly. "We'll use this. Then it will be certain." So Maggie gave in and gave Jim her best.

When they said goodbye at the station, they were closer than they had ever been. In their final embrace as they parted, Maggie whispered, "Come back safely, my love." Then she returned to London with their three sons.

That September Sunday morning in 1939 when the sirens blew, Maggie was sitting peeling the potatoes for

Sunday lunch. The boys were playing out in the street. She had just finished reading a letter from Jim. It had been posted in Gibraltar, in a thin envelope with a foreign stamp, and she had felt terribly nervous about reading it.

Jim seemed cheerful enough but his words at the end worried her: "Get yourself and the kids out of London, Maggie. Never mind about the house because when it starts they're going to bomb the hell out of London."

Go away? thought Maggie. How can I walk out on me job? The thirty bob a week from the navy won't keep us. Although Maggie had heard people talking about "evacuation," she had never taken much notice of what was said.

It was while she was engrossed in these thoughts that the shrill voice of the warning sounded and echoed all over the street. As did every other Londoner, Maggie ran out into the street followed by Pie Shop who barked his head off.

The boys. Where were they? "Jimmy! Tommy! Al!" she called and they came running up to her. Maggie stood with her arms around the boys wondering what to do. People ran past her. "Come on, Maggie," they shouted. "We're going down the tube."

It was then that the all-clear went. It had been a false alarm.

Holding her children close to her, Maggie knew that she must do as Jim had suggested and send them away. If she were at work what would they do in an air raid?

They all went round to Sarah's with Pie Shop trailing along behind. Sarah was frantically packing her bags.

"I'm going back up to Abe's, Maggie. Oh, my gawd. I'd die of fright here waiting to be bombed."

Maggie's voice was choked. "I'm going to miss you, Sarah."

"Well, come with me, you and the kids," said the generous Sarah. "We'll find a place to hide."

"No," said Maggie. "I'll just get the kids evacuated like they've said."

One of the finest things Maggie ever did was to send her boys away. She was passionately devoted to her family. They compensated her for that lonely childhood; all the hard work and the worry was all for them. Each boy had his own individual personality. There was tall, good-looking Jim who was bright and alert; clever and tough Tom with his face already disfigured but the love for his mum clear and strong; and little Al, a big baby, greedy for sweets and always first on Jim's side and then on Tom's. Maggie used to wonder about Al. A handful of sweets and Al would tell all. There was a time when Tom started stealing and brought home a little car. It was Al who told, and Tom was dragged to the shop to return the goods. "I'll have no nicking," said Maggie. "And no bad language, either."

She often thought of Ginger and how they had depended on what he stole for food, and she had felt ashamed when she covered up for him. But he had got caught in the end. Oh well, she would think, my kids ain't going to no approved schools.

When she lined the boys up on that fateful morning before taking them to the school where the evacuation of the children had begun, they looked neat and smart, and Maggie was proud of them.

"Be good boys for me," she said. "And stay together, no matter what anyone says."

"Yes, Mum," they all said.

"I rely on you, Jim, to see that you all keep together."

The boys had their tickets and large cards with their names written on them hung around their necks. Each had a little suitcase and a gas mask in a case.

As the long line of children moved off from the school, Maggie stood with all the other mums and waved as they went. In the long, unhappy years of the war, that was the saddest moment of all. Women and men cried; even Pie Shop set up a terrific howling. But the boys were looking forward to the ride on the train; to them, tomorrow was another day.

When Maggie returned to the house an empty feeling surrounded it. Better go to work, thought Maggie. Otherwise I'll get the creeps.

At work it was not much better. Red-eyed women whose husbands had been called up and those who, like Maggie, had sent their children away, tried hard to work. But as the long line of machines whirled the khaki material along, their thoughts wandered to those they loved.

"Bloody depressing morning," Maggie said to Bernie.

"Louie won't let the kids go," he said. "She says if we go, it'll be all together. Funny gel, she is. But I'm getting a good shelter put up in the garden."

It's all right for her, thought Maggie. She ain't got to work, she's got that fat so-and-so to keep her.

That afternoon, the first submarine was sunk. Young Marjorie's husband was aboard so from then on it was pandemonium in the factory; women got up and went home. "It's no good, Maggie, we can't work," they said.

Maggie took Marjorie into the office and gave her a cup of tea. She looked at this slip of a girl who was not yet eighteen sobbing her heart out.

"It's going to be all right, Marjorie," Maggie said. "No news is good news and they know where it's gone down."

A wise, aged face looked at Maggie. "He's not alive, you know. He's dead."

"Don't be silly, Marjorie. You don't know."

"Yes, I do. I knew this morning, my Bill's dead."

She was right. Maggie could not forget about it. Would she know if something happened to Jim? Somehow she had never thought about it. It seemed to her that, like a bad penny, he would always turn up somewhere. Perhaps we're not so close, Jim and I. Maybe I never loved him.

On her way home she stopped outside the Barley Mow and she looked over the road at her own house

with the curtains still drawn and Pie Shop waiting, chin
on paws, outside.

"My gawd," said Maggie, "I need a drink." She
dived into the pub. "A large port," she said, and sat
down in the same corner that Liza had spent most of
her life in.

It was a protesting Pie Shop who brought her down
to earth. He pushed open the pub door with his nose
and his bright eyes looked shocked: Maggie not bothering about his dinner after he had waited all day for it.
He sat down and stared up at her. Maggie patted his
shaggy head.

"Sorry, mate," she said. "I forgot I still got you to
worry about."

And they went home together.

The next few days she waited anxiously for news
from the boys. A card from the school came through
the door to say that the children had been safely bil-
leted in Worcestershire. It seemed like the other side
of the world to Maggie. In fact, she had never heard
of it.

Soon after, little Jim's carefully-worded letter arrived
and Maggie felt much better.

Dear Mum,
We got here safe and we all stopped together like you
said.
It is nice here and everso posh. We miss you.
      Lots of love, Jim, Tom, and Al.

Maggie kissed the letter. "I love 'em," she said out
aloud. Then she found a pen and sat down to laboriously write a letter back to them.

7

Evacuation

In the village of Edgeley in Worcestershire, there had never been so much excitement. When the evacuees got off the train, the whole village had come out to greet them. Outside the village school the farm trucks drove off with their loads of humanity to billets that had been found in the outlying districts. Those who had not yet been found a home sat outside on the grass verge; tired little faces, grubby with the soot of the train. Harassed officials rushed here and there trying to sort out the problems and get all the children settled by nightfall.

Three little boys stood close together; the eldest, in the middle, had his arms around his brothers. They had been there a long time.

"I'll take the fair boy," said a middle-aged lady to the vicar.

"It's no good," replied the vicar. "They won't let us part them, I've been trying all day. It's not easy in these small cottages to house three boys. I'll try again." He walked over to try to persuade Jim to let his brother go with the kind lady.

"No!" said Jim, shaking his curly head. "Mum said we got to stay together."

114

Along the road came a great limousine. It slowed down and the peaked-capped chauffeur hooted his horn to clear the road. In the back sat Morris Bloom watching the children. His eye caught the strange situation of the small boy who argued with the vicar.

"Pull up," he said to his driver. Calling the vicar over he asked, "What's the matter, Mr. Hurst?"

"It's a bit difficult with these three brothers, Mr. Bloom. They won't be separated."

"Put them in here," said Morris.

The vicar, who had plans of his own for evacuees to the big house on the hill, said: "These are boys from the East End, Mr. Bloom."

"I never asked where they came from. I just said put them in here." He moved along the seat to make room for them.

So Jim, Tom and Al stayed together and got the very best billet—Mr. Bloom was a South African millionaire.

Tom and Al in the front seat examined the great car. "Smashing, ain't it," they said to Fred Smith, the chauffeur. He looked at them and smiled. Jim, next to Morris Bloom in the back, sat up straight and said, "Thank you, sir. I promised my mother we would not be parted and thanks to you we're still together."

"Stop worrying, lad," said a kind, warm voice. "We'll all have a good time. It's better up here and there's fishing and lots of things to do."

Morris Bloom's wife, Jante, was not so pleased when she saw the newcomers.

"Oh dear, Morris. Why didn't you wait? There's a nice lot of boys from a good school coming tomorrow."

"These will do fine," said Morris. "Mrs. Smith!" he roared. "Come and get these boys and wash and feed them."

Dolly Smith was Fred's wife. Her short, stumpy figure and fresh complexion did not make her a beauty but, if beauty is as beauty does, then Dolly was perfect. She cared for Maggie's boys as though they were her own and Aunt Dolly, as they called her, was never to be forgotten.

Jim, Tom and Al spent the next four and a half years living in the big Abbey of Edgelev Hill. It had once been a monastery and, before Morris Bloom had bought it, many great families had resided there. Morris had done well in gold and diamonds and in the beginning the abbey was just an investment. But now he had left South Africa and made the abbey his home. He had no regrets. He loved the beautiful countryside and the wide rivers. Fishing had become his leisure-time occupation.

He and his wife never had any children so when the boys arrived, Morris felt young again. He took them walking in the woods and canoeing in the great lake in the park. Every day there was something fresh to do with "the lads," as he called them. But Jante showed her feelings by packing her bags and visiting friends in Scotland until, in her words, "Morris gets over those damned evacuees."

The local taxi-driver who pointed out places of interest to visitors to Edgeley would stop at the top of the road to look down on the abbey as it lay in the midst of the green woodland of the valley. "There goes the owner with the little evacuee boys," he would say. Then across the wide straight of the meadow that led to the river would go the heavy lumbering shape of Morris in his straw boater, carrying a bag of fishing rods. Running all around, the three little brothers, tearing over the vast expanse of green, would shout with happiness at all the space they had.

Down on the river bank they would light a fire and Morris would show them how to cook the fish on a stick. It was great fun and the war seemed a long, long way away. On the way home they would all sing as they walked against the thin, blue shadow of the Cotswolds. Morris sang Dutch sea songs in a deep voice and the boys taught him their street songs.

In a pony cart they often rode with Morris to the

village. Once he took them in the big car to Oxford, to
see the university. Another time, they went to Stratford-
upon-Avon where Shakespeare was born. It was Jim
who benefited mostly from these trips. Tom was more
partial to the woods and the shooting trips while Al
liked the village with its cream cakes. Each boy had
something he liked, and each gave Morris his own refreshing love and the straightforward candor of the
back streets. This meant a lot to Morris and he was
like a boy again.

Aunt Dolly cooked, cleaned and sewed for them and
tucked them up in clean white sheets at night with a
goodnight kiss. After a few weeks they did not miss
Maggie but Jim wrote regularly to say what a good time
they were having.

By September the blitz was at its worst but the boys
had never heard a bomb drop. Morris received a letter
from Jante saying it was time he pulled his socks up
and went to London to do something for the war effort.

It was November when Morris finally left the boys.
"I'll be back in the spring," he said. "Be good boys."

Maggie worked hard through the winter putting a little
away each week so she could pay her fare up to Edgeley
and take the boys some presents. It was early spring
when she made the trip.

She felt very tired as the train pulled into the quiet
country station. It had been hell on earth the last few
weeks in London and she was glad that she had had
the courage to let her boys go. After such a long time
she could not wait to see them and she wondered how
they would look. She was nicely dressed in a black,
tailored suit with pearl studs in her ears. Her black hair
curled about her face and she had grown thinner and
there were dark lines around her blue eyes.

It was a long walk from the station to the abbey and
her feet ached in the new, high-heeled shoes. As she
walked up the drive, she saw them in the garden of the
lodge where Fred and Dolly Smith lived. They were
playing cricket on the lawn. It was quite warm and the

boys were wearing spotless white shirts. They were running and jumping and Fred was batting. When they saw Maggie they left their game and tore down the drive to meet her, nearly bowling her over in their excitement. Maggie was thrilled; they looked so healthy and fit. She had never seen them look so well.

They all had tea with Aunt Dolly who explained that the big house was closed for the time being and the boys were staying with her and Fred. They loved them, she said, what well-behaved boys they were. Maggie was proud, but towards the end of the day she became depressed; the boys seemed to have grown away from her. It was, "Can I do this, Aunt Dolly?" and "May I have some cake, Aunt Dolly?" until Maggie felt like screaming. They told her stories of Morris and how he took them here and there and that he was coming back soon. There was a strange feeling inside her. Was she jealous of Dolly? She sat in Dolly's spotless kitchen nibbling pastry and home-made cakes. The table was laid with fine cups and saucers. Maggie looked at Dolly as she poured the tea. A vision of clean, dainty homeliness. Maggie felt resentful. The woman had so much love to give and was stealing her boys from her.

She pulled Al on to her lap while he was busily helping himself to the cream sponge on the table. "Want to come home with Mum?" she asked.

"No," said Al with his mouth full of jam and cream. "Morris is going to take us on the boat when he comes back."

Jim and Tom sat up at the table, very clean and well behaved.

"You won't make us go home, will you, Mum?" said Jim. His eyes which were so like Maggie's were wide open with astonishment. Tom got off his chair and came to her side.

"You're all right in London, Mum. You go down the shelter, don't you?"

"Of course I do," said Maggie. "Old Hitler ain't gonna get me."

Everyone started to laugh. But the conversation

lagged after that. Dolly seemed to go quiet, so after tea Maggie said goodbye to the boys.

In an old motorbike and sidecar, Fred took Maggie to the station. As they were waiting on the platform he looked soberly at Maggie and said, "Do you mean it about taking the boys home?"

Maggie shrugged her shoulders, a habit she had when unhappy. "I miss them," she said.

For a moment, Fred's kind, cheerful-looking face seemed sad. "I hope you won't," he said. "Dolly has grown fond of those boys and I'm likely to be called up if the war enters another year. It's a lonely place up here and the boys would be such good company for her."

What about me? thought Maggie, but she did not reply.

The train came puffing up and Fred shook her hand. "The master thinks the world of them. Not a week passes when he don't send them something and he's got the vicar to help Jim with his schooling. I think you would be very silly to take them home now."

As the train pulled out the tears began to fall. An old gentleman in the seat facing her pretended not to notice and hid behind his newspaper.

At Reading Station she left the slow local train to wait for a fast connection to London. It was nine o'clock and the station was crowded with service men and laughing young girls who had escorted them to the train after an early Saturday night in town.

London's Burning

It was cold and misty on the platform. The lights were dim because of the blackout and, as Maggie watched the train going out on the opposite side full of men in uniform, she thought of her Jim and wondered where he was.

I'll write to him and ask if I can have the boys home. There's a lot of kids down the tube, she thought. I've

seen them sitting around. Families together having a
sing-song. That's what I'll do. I'll get them home and
give up me job and we'll all go down the tube.

With these plans in mind, Maggie began to cheer up.
Poor old Pie Shop would have to stop at home on his
own, but he was used to the noise by now; he had been
in enough raids.

When the blitz had first begun the neighbors had
called out, "Come on, Maggie, we're going down the
street shelters." So Maggie, clapping a lead on Pie Shop
who objected strongly, left the house for the end of the
street where the shelter had been built. At the entrance,
a burly figure in a tin hat barred the way.

"Where are you going with that dog?" he demanded.

"Down the shelter," said Maggie.

"No you ain't. Dogs ain't allowed. He's supposed to
have been put to sleep. Yer not supposed to have dogs
with the war on."

"Well, if he ain't going down, no more am I," said
Maggie as she turned back toward the house.

After that the old kitchen table served as a shelter
for her and Pie Shop. Maggie put a mattress under it
and Pie Shop would get in and warm up the bed for her,
while Maggie went across the road and had a few
ports to give her a bit of Dutch courage.

Sitting hunched up on a platform seat trying to keep
warm, Maggie thought about old Pie Shop tucked up in
her bed. He's a dear old thing. I wouldn't 'alf miss him,
she thought. Then back came the old depression. He's
the only one I've got left, she sobbed to herself, and
tears began to fall again.

She got up. "Where's that blooming train?" she muttered as she went to the booking office to find out.
There were a lot of people there, all asking for trains
to London. The officials were sorry, there was a big
raid going on and the line was blocked. They suggested
that the passengers make themselves comfortable in the
waiting room. They were likely to be there all night.

Most of the passengers, including Maggie, went outside and looked toward London. There was a red glow

in the sky. The roar of the fighters overhead and the crash of the anti-aircraft guns told them that London was being defended. There was a strange feeling of comradeship in those Londoners who spent the night in the waiting room at Reading while the docks and the East End were being bombed to the ground.

"Don't worry, ladies," said a florid little man as he passed his flask around. "Reckon we're in the best place."

It was a sad journey through London the next morning. The buses made great diversions to avoid the badly blitzed roads. In Mile End Road the shops were still burning, as was Bernie's factory. In the side streets people raked in the debris for their belongings.

The greatest shock of all came when Maggie reached the street. It was roped off. Policemen and tin-hatted demolition men were all over the place. One side of the Barley Mow had disappeared and Nos. 2 and 3 had vanished in the ashes.

"Let me through," said Maggie.

"You can't, lady. Not till it's cleared."

"But my dog . . ." said Maggie.

"To hell with yer dog," the man said. "There're babies buried alive down there."

Feeling terribly ashamed, Maggie turned and walked away. But Pie Shop had heard her voice and he came up whining and growling with his tail between his legs. He jumped into her arms and Maggie cuddled him. "I won't leave you any more, love," she said.

All the rest of the street had been evacuated to the school. In there Maggie sat with Pie Shop on her lap, watching the flow of people as they came in, red-eyed and distraught, covered with soot and plaster, carrying their little bundles and their cold and hungry children and even small babies. They all sat hopeless, waiting for someone to tell them what to do next. The young fellow whose wife and babies were still buried sat head in hands alone at one end of the room.

Oh, my gawd, thought Maggie, those boys are going to stop where they are.

By the time evening had come round again, some semblance of order had been restored and those whose homes were only blasted were allowed to return home. A still, creepy feeling had descended on the street; it seemed different somehow.

So Maggie and Pie Shop went home. They passed what was left of the Barley Mow. Two walls stood up stiff and stark in the twilight while the remains of the bar had collapsed into the cellar. In her mind's eye, Maggie saw Liza waving her stick and demanding to know what they had done with the long wooden bench she had spent most of her life sitting on. Oh! I mustn't think things like that, she thought to herself, but it ain't 'alf creepy. What's it like indoors, she wondered looking across at her little house.

The mess of fallen plaster and broken glass was indescribable. It was midnight before Maggie had managed to clear one room and put the old kitchen table back in position. By then the bombs were dropping again. With a bottle of port inside her and the dog beside her under the blanket, Maggie slept through it all.

This became the procedure for the next few weeks while the blitz was at its height—a bottle of port and under the table to bed.

There was no work since Bernie's factory had burned to the ground. Sometimes, Maggie did not wake until lunchtime. Pie Shop could find his own way in and out as the back door had been blown off.

After a couple of weeks Maggie began to feel very ill, sick and faint and she could not pull herself together until she started a new bottle of port in the evenings.

Once she met Bernie in the street who said: "What's up, Maggie? My life, you look terrible. Better come and stay with Louie."

"Can't leave Pie Shop," hiccuped Maggie.

"Lay off the bottle, girlie, or you'll become a wino," said Bernie.

"Can't sleep without it," said Maggie.

"Well, get some work to do," he said. "Go and volunteer for something. I'm an air-raid warden." He proudly indicated the canvas bag he carried and the tin hat on top of his head.

He's right, thought Maggie. I must pull myself together.

An amusing incident had happened that night when Maggie, drunk, suddenly remembered that the mat that kept the light from the door was not in position. Pulling on her skirt and being half whoozy from the bottle of booze she had drunk, she fixed it back to front. Bending down to place the mat in position she heard a Cockney voice say, "Full moon tonight, Maggie."

Putting her hand over the draughty spot, Maggie fled indoors very quickly.

Better pull yourself together, Maggie, my girl, she thought again as she touched the pillow and, cuddling old Pie Shop close, she slept through one of the worst raids ever.

The sun shone down on her in the morning. As she tried to pull her head from the pillow someone was tickling her feet. A voice said, "Blimey, Sleeping Beauty." Jim was home.

"What the hell you been up to, Maggie?" he asked. "You look terrible lying down there with that dirty, scruffy mongrel."

"Oh, Jim." cried Maggie. "You're home!"

"I ain't the devil haunting yer, gel. It's yer old man in the flesh." He pulled her up on her feet. "Look at the bloody place, Maggie. This is a fine welcome, I must say."

Maggie was doused with cold water from the tap and they sat down to drink a strong cup of tea.

"I thought you was the last one to take to the bottle. Port?" he said as he surveyed the empty bottle.

"It's been terrible here, Jim," whispered Maggie.

"Yes, and it ain't been no picnic for me either."

"I'm sorry, Jim."

"Never mind, gel. Get yourself together. Got a tin of bully beef in me bag. We'll have some chips with it."

From that day Maggie never looked at port wine again. The little house soon became ship-shape, now her Jim was home.

Then came another surprise. One evening, as they walked home from the market together, a tall figure stood on the doorstep.

"Who's that?" demanded Maggie, drawing up closer to Jim. The figure had an odd-looking hat on. As Jim went forward to investigate, a shout echoed all down the street: "It's Ginger! It's Ginger come home!"

In the front parlor they looked Ginger over. He was so tall and sunburned and his hair shone like burnished copper. The dare-devil Ginger had grown into a handsome man. The Australian army uniform with its big bush hat suited him.

"It's good to see you again, Ginger," said Maggie.

He hugged and kissed her. "It's fine to see you, our Maggie."

The next twenty days was one long booze-up. Bombs never stopped Ginger, who took Jim and Maggie up to London to dives, beer cellars and night clubs. Maggie saw and heard things she never knew existed. Ginger was bursting with vitality and had a wallet full of notes to help him. He brought girls home by the dozen and his friends treated the house like a hotel. It was lovely to see Ginger again but at the end of the twenty days, Maggie had had enough of the comings and goings. Also, the way her Jim hung around the girls Ginger brought home upset her.

On the last Saturday night, the party broke up; Ginger was off to join his regiment. Jim went with his brother to the station and since it was a quiet night with no raids, Maggie decided to take Pie Shop for a walk. In the full moonlight the little street seemed so silent and empty, apart from a young couple who made love by the park railings. Maggie crossed the road not liking to pass too close to them. She suddenly heard that deep chuckle—there was no mistaking it. The moonlight showed them clearly. She was blond and pretty and her big bully Jim held her close. Maggie's heart missed a beat but she turned and went in the other direction and was in bed when Jim came in. It did not hurt as much as she thought it would; in her heart she had always known it. But wait until he went back, she thought. She was not going to sit at home anymore.

"Goodnight, Maggie," said Jim as he got into bed. But she never answered; there did not seem to be any need. Jim seemed as remote as Pie Shop snoring away under the bed.

During the night, Maggie tossed restlessly and talked in her sleep. "Wouldn't have minded if I hadn't seen them," she was saying.

"For gawd's sake, Maggie, stop it," said Jim. "Do you have to keep nattering all night? I've got to be back early tomorrow."

When Jim had gone back to camp and Ginger was on the high seas on his way to the Middle East, Maggie sat down to catch up on the letters she had received.

There was one from Sarah in very large, bold handwriting. As Maggie read it she laughed. "Having a smashing time," wrote Sarah. "Plenty of fellers up here. Why don't you come up and stay, Maggie? Abe's now bought a hotel in the country so we don't hear the air raids and we got lots of Frenchmen staying here." Maggie had a good idea of Sarah's "smashing time," and thought she would rather stay in London.

There was a letter from little Jim. They were still having a wonderful time. Morris had been back to see them and they had had a party. Uncle Fred was going into the army next week.

"Don't seem as anyone wants us," said Maggie sadly looking at Pie Shop who was at her feet as always. He looked up at her and his pink tongue lolled out as he seemed to smile at her. The windows were boarded up in the kitchen and there were holes in the ceiling; they gave the house a forlorn air.

Maggie drank her tea and stared all around. Miserable hole, she thought. Got to get out or I'll go mad. Better get a job. Slipping on her mac, she went out.

In the Mile End Road there was still that air of quiet desolation. The stalls were all tied down with their canvas covers and people emerged slowly from the tube, sleepy-eyed and carrying their possessions with them. Outside the labor exchange, a big colored poster with a large hand pointing outward said: "We want you. Help the war effort. Nurses and ward orderlies badly needed."

"That's it," said Maggie. "I'll do night work up the hospital. That'll keep me off the booze."

The woman who recruited her was nice and pleasant. "You are used to domestic work, my dear, so they'll be pleased to have you."

The matron at the hospital was all teeth and smiles. "I'm sure you'll like it, dear. We can't all run away, some of us have to stay put and keep the services going."

The job consisted of two nights on duty and one night off. The duty started at five o'clock in the evening and went on until seven o'clock the next morning. Still, everyone seemed so very nice and Maggie looked forward to starting her war effort.

War Work

On Monday evening, Maggie told Pie Shop to go to bed and mind the house. Then she stepped out a little nervously for her new career.

The matron seemed so different. She no longer showed her teeth in a wide smile; her mouth was set grimly in a tight line. "Oh, yes. Maggie Burns. I'd better get you some aprons to wear." Off she marched down the shining corridor to a big store cupboard.

Trailing along behind, Maggie was a bit worried, wondering what she had done to upset the old girl. Maggie had yet to learn the two faces of hospital life: one for on duty and another for off.

The matron pushed and pulled Maggie into a stiff, starched uniform which almost cut her throat, a white apron and a little white hat which almost scalped her when she put it on. Matron twisted Maggie's hair into a tight knot. "Better get some of this hair cut off," she said. "Must look nice and tidy." Maggie was beginning to wish she had not come.

Then off down the corridor they marched again until they came to B Ward—Male. Matron handed Maggie over like a parcel of goods to the staff nurse—a big Scotch lassie who stared aggressively down at Maggie through thick spectacles.

"Get all them flowers out, gel," she said. "Then fill up all the water jugs and get yerself moving. The warning will be going soon and we got to get the up-patients down to the shelter."

So Maggie began trotting in and out, scared to look at the white, tidy beds from which the occupants called out, "Who's the new bird, Alec?" The staff nurse never replied but her vivid blue eyes gleamed with amusement behind the thick spectacles.

By seven o'clock the beds were made and the ward was tidy. Maggie's legs ached so much she thought they would drop off. Then the warning went and those who were able to get up were wrapped in blankets, escorted to the lift, and taken down to the shelter for the night. In the ward, all the beds with very old men and very sick patients in them were pushed to the center. Then, for the first time since Maggie had come on duty, two chairs were produced and Nurse Alec and Maggie sat down.

With a sigh, Alec spread her sturdy legs wide and, looking at the beds in the middle of the room, said, "Now they'll start. See if they don't."

"Start what?" asked Maggie.

"Shitting the bed, of course," said Alec. "They always do."

Maggie started to giggle but not for long. An old gray head poked up out of the blankets: "Nurse! Bed pan," he shouted.

As the bombs dropped the two women staggered around with piles of dirty sheets. By daylight Maggie was exhausted. Then there was the porridge to make and breakfast to serve, bottles to give and bowls for washing. Maggie got into a shocking muddle; there were wash bowls and bottles mixed up on the lockers and the plates of porridge as well. The patients who came back from the shelter helped her to get tidy before the day nurse came on.

Nurse Alec seemed tireless and just plodded on with a zombie-like indifference to all around her. "You'll have to move a bit quicker than you do," she said to Maggie. "If that day nurse catches the patients helping you, you'll be for it."

Maggie was too tired to respond and dragged her weary feet to the door, passing the fresh, white-clad day staff as they came in. Alec, her cloak held around her by one big, capable hand, handed the report cards to the spick-and-span sister with the other. Then she walked beside Maggie down the corridor. Suddenly, to Maggie's surprise Alec started to swear in a low voice. Words Maggie had heard but never uttered poured out of Alec's mouth one after the other.

"Ah, now I feel better," Alec said. Then she put her arm around Maggie's waist. "Cheer up, lass. It's not so bad, you get used to it. I'm away to sleep. See you tomorrow."

Maggie dragged herself home, too weary to care about anything. After his long vigil all night, Pie Shop looked most disconcerted when Maggie got into bed as if to say: What, overtime as well?

Maggie was to report for duty at five o'clock that same day. After a few hours sleep she woke feeling stiff and cold. I feel terrible, she thought as she sat by the fire and drank some hot tea. Thought I'd woken up and found meself dead. I suppose it's no good giving in. Might get a worse job next time, like bashing munitions boxes. I think I'd hate that.

After a while, she got ready and called Pie Shop to come in. But for some reason, he stood at the corner of the street wagging his tail in defiance.

"Come here!" called Maggie. "You little devil. Wait till I get you."

But Pie Shop had hopped round the corner to hide.

"All right then, stay out in the blitz. I don't care," she said and closed the front door. She started up the road towards the hospital. Pie Shop sneaked along behind her as she went. Every time she stopped, so did he.

"Drat that damn dog," said Maggie. "He's going to follow me to work."

At the gates as Maggie was signing in, Pie Shop tried to dodge past the porter who chased him out again. The last she saw was his hairy old face looking through the gate at her. Oh, dear, she thought, that dog's more trouble than all the kids.

That second evening on the ward was much better. Alec told her how to "save yerself a trot," as she called it. "Don't waste yer energy, gel, 'cause before the night's over, you'll need it."

There was a very bad raid but it did not last as long as they used to. The gunners and the fighter planes were getting them before they got to London. Maggie and Alec sat and gossiped. Alec had her knitting and they sat and chatted like two old ladies at a vicar's tea party.

"Given the old ones a sleeping pill tonight. With a bit of luck, they'll sleep. Couldn't stand another night like last night. You're nought but a damned lavatory attendant here. I'll be glad when I get my transfer. It's a military hospital for me."

Maggie began to like Alec. There was something about her, she had a kind of straightforward approach to life.

There were several young patients in the ward as well as the old men. One young man had both arms held up by a pulley; they were stretched high above his head. Maggie had smiled sympathetically at him and he said, "Hello, little black beauty." He woke in the night asking for a bottle. Alec was busy with another patient and said, "Get him a bottle, Maggie." Maggie went off to get the bottle and on her return stood beside the bed holding the bottle with a funny expression on her face.

"Give it to him," called Alec. "Don't stand cuddling it or he'll do it in the bed."

But Maggie, staring at the man's arms, was wondering what to do next. Alec rushed over, pulled back the bedclothes and popped the bottle in.

"What's up with yer, gel? Ain't you ever seen one of them before?"

Afterwards they laughed together and Alec said, "How long's your old man been away, Maggie?"

"Not long. Went back a week ago."

"Well, that's not so bad. I'm married to a boy in the Guards. Been out east a year now. I'll be an old hag by the time he gets back."

One of Maggie's duties was taking the dressing buckets to be emptied. It was a long trip in the lift down to the basement where a big Irish man resided. His name was Mick O'Reilly. He was very cheerful, always a bit boozey but a very pleasant man. On her way down with the buckets, Maggie was thinking of Pie Shop, wondering where he was. Imagine her surprise when, on reaching the boiler room, she saw Pie Shop sound asleep with O'Reilly by the huge furnace.

"Why, you old rogue," said Maggie.

O'Reilly roused himself at the sound of her voice. "That yer dog?" he asked.

"How'd he get in?" asked Maggie.

"Well, he howled so much and wouldn't go away, so when the gate man left, I let him in. He's a nice dog. Company for me." He patted old Pie Shop who crept up close to him as if to say, "Don't let her take me away from this nice warm fire."

"You can keep him," said Maggie. "He's not a dog, he's a human. Tries to run my life for me, he does."

Pie Shop knew he was forgiven, and he settled back to sleep beside the furnace where he spent his nights while Maggie worked at the hospital. Sometimes he got home before Maggie and other times, when O'Reilly had something nice for breakfast, he stayed later.

After a few weeks, the regular pattern of life at the hospital began to suit Maggie. She liked the safe feeling she got as she left behind the gloom of the empty streets for the warm white walls inside.

There were some bad nights, like the one when they had to go down on casualty. A pale, tired, elderly sister had come up during a raid and said, "I'll take over here. You two are needed in casualty."

It took a long time to forget that night. There was a direct hit on a street shelter. She remembered vividly the screams of the injured being brought in and the buckets overflowing with blood-stained dressings while she washed the little children and picked plaster from the cuts that covered their bodies. Worst of all was seeing those who had not survived sewn up in the white shrouds. But at the end of the long night Maggie felt pleased when matron said, "For an untrained girl, Maggie, you're marvelous. Hope we don't lose you. You're the type we badly need, someone who can turn their hand to anything."

Summer progressed into autumn and the days passed so quickly. Better go and see the boys again, thought Maggie. They'll be forgetting they've got a mum.

Boys Will Be Boys

Back in Edgeley, the boys were doing fine. There had been a bit of trouble last year but Morris, who was home, had handled the affair quite amicably. "After all," he said, "boys will be boys."

It happened this way. Young Jim, now nearly thirteen, had got a yen for reading. He had been studying with the vicar who had introduced him to the world of classics. Previously Jim had only read comics—not much else had been available. But once he had become interested in history, he took to it like a duck to water. He spent much of his time in a corner of Morris's library, lost in a world of the knights of the Round

Table and the lives of the rebel rousers, like Wat Tyler and Jack Straw.

This left the two younger boys alone to amuse themselves. Jim had always had a steadying influence on Tom; and Al did what Tom did.

First, there were raids on the village shops. While Al talked sweet nothings to the old lady, Tom filled up his pockets. Then they were banned from the boy scouts because of a big fight there one night. Poor Aunt Dolly did her best; when people complained, she said sharply, "Oh, of course you must blame the poor little London boys." So the villagers kept quiet, hoping to get more co-operation when Morris came home. One morning, the two boys went off on what, according to Al, was called a "safari." They went deep into the woods and got lost. Jim upstairs with his nose in a book never missed them and Aunt Dolly had gone on her once-a-week visit to the town. At midday they were very tired. Al was almost crying but Tom, as sturdy as ever, climbed the highest tree to find the right direction. In the distance he saw the roof of a big house. "This way, Al," he called.

They pushed their way through the thick undergrowth until eventually they came out into a big park almost like the one at the abbey. It was a strange house with tall chimneys and big windows with green wooden shutters.

"Wonder where we are," said Tom.

They climbed up the side of the doorway and peered in through the fanlight above the door.

"It's empty," they both declared.

"Don't it look smashing," said Al.

"Let's go in," said Tom.

They went around the back where Tom's penknife levered open a small window. Before long they were sliding along the long, polished stair rail and looking through the keyholes of the locked rooms. Inside, they saw the white sheets that covered the furniture.

"I bet there's ghosts in here," said Tom.

"Let's go," said Al looking nervous.

"Gawd, look at that!" said Tom, noticing a portrait at the end of the long gallery. They went up to get a closer look and Lady Jennifer Crowley stared down haughtily at them.

"Ain't it beautiful," said Tom as he looked at the crinoline lady with her blonde curls. "You know what, Al," he continued, "that's very valuable, that is."

Al, chewing away as usual, looked up and said, "Let's nick it."

"Don't be daft. Couldn't get it down, it's too heavy."

"Well, let's take it out of the frame, like that bloke did at the pictures," suggested Al.

So, perched on his brother's shoulder, Al laboriously cut out the picture with Tom's penknife, robbing the lady of the nice pink rose upon her hair. After much effort, they at last got the canvas onto the floor.

"We might be as rich as Morris if we manage to flog this," said Tom, feeling self-important as he strolled about the gallery, hands in his trouser pockets.

After they had rolled up the heavy canvas and, with much difficulty, climbed out of the small window they had entered by, they set off along the road carrying the canvas between them.

The storm that had been threatening all day broke, and the rain pelted down on them. A lorry driver slowed down to give them a lift.

"Where are you going?" he asked, staring in amazement at the rain-soaked boys and the long roll of canvas they carried.

"To Edgeley," replied Tom.

"You won't get there that way," said the driver. "You're going in the wrong direction."

Wearily, they turned to walk back.

"Let's dump this, Tom," said Al. "It ain't 'alf gettin' heavy."

"What? And lose all that money?" said Tom. "Come on, let's go in the woods and get out of the rain."

It had become very dark. They stood the canvas up—it made a smashing tent—and crawled under it and went to sleep.

At eight o'clock Dolly informed the police and a search party went out to find the missing evacuees.

It was almost dawn when the sergeant spotted the tent in the woods and found the two boys, like two young puppies, close together, sound asleep. He woke them up and then had a closer look at the tent. Imagine his surprise when the late Lady Crowley stared out irritably from the canvas.

The police did not make a charge and the owner of the house was abroad. Morris tried hard not to laugh about it and he told Jim that in the future he had to keep his nose out of books and give an eye to his brothers. So all was forgiven and Morris gave a super Christmas party for all the evacuee children in the district.

Another guest had recently arrived. Her name was Anne-Marie. She was Jante's niece and at school in England. She was the same age as Al and her long braids of corn-colored hair hung down to her waist. She had a turned-up nose and freckles. In spite of her innocent look, Anne-Marie was a real tomboy. She could climb the highest tree and play football like a boy. And she twisted Uncle Morris round her little finger.

As soon as she arrived, she took a fancy to Al, stuffed him with sweets and fussed and kissed him in front of everyone. Al loved it. He gawped at her, a wide grin on his face and his fringe of blond hair hanging in his eyes. Tom was most put out but Anne-Marie settled him by punching him on the nose. She rode a pony astride like a soldier—it was her riding that Al admired most of all. Anne-Marie was determined to teach Al to ride but the pony bolted with him and threw him off onto the road. He was in bed for several days and Anne-Marie sat beside him to read to him and play Ludo. She was so possessive of him that even Al began to long for the weeks when she would be back at school.

So Maggie's boys were growing into manhood in this hothouse atmosphere, protected, guarded and fussed over. They never thought of their own home; to them, this was home with Aunt Dolly and Uncle Morris.

When Maggie visited them again, they talked of all the recent happenings, of Tom and his fishing rods, of Al and his riding lessons, and Jim, gentleman Jim, wore a collar and tie and used long words in his conversation. He was getting very good looking and was the apple of Morris's eye.

On her journey home in the train, Maggie wondered what big Jim would say. I don't know how they are going to settle down in our little house after the war, she thought, but it looks like it's going on forever, so it's no good worrying.

8

First of the Last

Maggie Burns was very popular at the hospital. As she stepped out in her brisk manner along the polished corridors, from all sides it was: "Morning, Maggie. How's tricks?" Maggie, with a sunny smile, would say, "Fine."

The secret of her popularity was in the empty bucket she carried—one bottle of Scotch whiskey. Sometimes she had nylon stockings for Alec. She and Maggie had become close friends and they took trips up west together on their nights off. The biggest problem for the poorly-paid nurses was getting nice clothes to wear off-duty, and now there was the added problem of clothing coupons.

One evening, on a trip to the basement, Maggie had found that O'Reilly was no longer there but instead, a big man with a greasy cap and a boilersuit greeted her. Pie Shop was snoring in his usual place.

"I'm Sam," the man said. "O'Reilly's gone in the fire brigade. He got fed up sitting down here all night.

"Your dog likes me," he added. "I used to breed 'em. Had a stall down the 'Row' Sunday mornings."

Sam, a true East-Ender, spoke the same language as Maggie, and they became friends.

It began with stockings. "Do the girls upstairs want some stockings?" Sam asked.

"No coupons?" asked Maggie, always eager to strike a bargain.

"No, of course not. Sell half-a-dozen and you get one pair for yourself." The stockings went like hotcakes.

Then it was discovered that Sam could get almost anything—even whisky for the staff party. If anyone had told her that it was wrong or that she was destroying the war effort, Maggie would have been amazed. "Paid good money for them, ain't they?" she would say. It was too complicated for her to understand, and anyway it increased her popularity and that pleased her. Cardigans and dresses found their way to the staff and the sisters were some of her best customers.

Sam would say, "Got your cut, Maggie?"

"I'd sooner have the money, Sam," Maggie would say and she would then put this into her savings.

"I'll put a bit away for a rainy day. I know what it's like to be real skint. Won't let it happen again," she would say.

With the regular food at the hospital, she began to put on weight. With no worries, she began to bloom. She was nearing thirty and still good looking. She reddened her lips with lipstick and wore an uplift bra.

Many of the women who worked at the hospital had affairs but so far Maggie had not indulged. There were lots of dates with men on their nights off—it was for a good feed and a drink but they ran home when their escorts got suggestive.

It had been six months since Maggie had had a letter from Jim. The last one had been posted in Singapore. The newspapers reported that there was a bit of a flare-up there; something to do with the Japs.

"Oh, Jim will turn up like a bad penny," Maggie said to herself consolingly, and continued to have a good time.

There were plenty of parties; there was always a birthday or someone leaving for battle stations. The whiskey acquired from Sam was a great help. Medical students found their way into the kitchens for a crafty cup of tea and Maggie, who made the tea, was often chased around the table. But she took it all in good part and on bad nights she kept them all cheery with her lively humor.

There was one dark man who said very little but once, when someone asked his name and he replied, "Klause," Maggie said, "That's funny. Who's he? Santa Klause?"

This caused much amusement. Klause's black eyes stared straight at Maggie and in a low voice, he said, "I've got a big Christmas present for you, beautiful Maggie."

"Oh!" exclaimed Maggie and ran out of the kitchen.

For quite a long time it was a standing hospital joke. Everyone said, "Did Blackie give you his Christmas present yet, Maggie?"

One weekend they were off duty. It was not often that they got Saturday off so it was a big occasion and Alec's blonde friend, Lucille, threw a party at her flat. Maggie was invited and she got her hair done and wore a new red dress.

"We've got a nice boyfriend for you," Alec and her friend said when she arrived, and from behind the tall, blonde Lucille popped Klause. Maggie was about to make for the door but they joined hands and prevented her, dancing around her singing taunting songs.

"Oh, well." said Maggie to herself, "serves me right. I shouldn't have come. Better face the music." So she joined in the fun.

It was the usual sort of party with a record player no one listened to and people sitting and drinking neat gin or whisky. They were laid out in every little corner available. and shouting and arguing or making love.

Klause was excellent company. With a bottle to themselves, he and Maggie retired to a corner and in a soft, cultured voice he talked of the hospital and how much he had looked forward to meeting her alone. For some reason (it could have been the gin), Maggie wanted to fuss him, to put her hand in his curly hair as she

did with little Jim. After another drink, she gave way
to her impulse and rumpled his black curls, and he
kissed her. From then on the party was far away.
Maggie had never been kissed like this before and she
liked it very much. She heard his soft voice saying, "I
know they call me Blackie but it's only in fun. Actually,
I'm Dutch, but my ancestors came from the Caribbean."

But Maggie was not listening. She pouted her red
lips to be kissed again. She heard laughing voices that
said, "Wow! Look at Maggie." But Maggie simply did
not care what they said anymore. She snuggled up to
her boyfriend and they sang songs in between long,
passionate kisses, until the party broke up.

Far away in the clouds, they traveled home in the
crowded taxi and a carefree Maggie handed Klause
her latch key to open the door. And they entered the
little front room that Liza had been so proud of. It
was Maggie who held Klause's hand and guided him in
and left the world behind.

In the morning, a chink of light came through the
shutters and Maggie awoke feeling ghastly, as though
someone was sitting on her head. From the street came
the sound of people walking.

Oh, dear. What day is it? I have to go to work.

With this thought in mind, she sat up in bed.
"Crikey!" she exclaimed. In the armchair at the side
of the fireplace was Klause, snoring away. His curly
hair was all rumpled and the light of day shone on his
profile and his coffee-colored skin. Memories of last
night returned in a flash. Blimey! Must have been drunk.
Better get him out of here. She got up and shook him.
"Here, wake up! You've got to get out of here quick."

"Beautiful Maggie," he muttered, opening his eyes.

"Cor blimey," said Maggie. "Never mind the compli-
ments, you've got to move out quick, mate, before the
neighbors see you. My Jim'll have my guts for garters."

He never understood a word she said but allowed
himself to be propelled down the passage and pushed
out into the street.

"Oh, dear," she said as she made a cup of tea. "No more parties for me."

She turned on the fire and sat and dreamed. Maggie felt no remorse; in fact, inside her she felt a quiet peace. It reminded her of a feeling she had got when she used to go to Mass. Oh dear, she thought, I must not have thoughts like that. It's wicked and if my Jim ever found out he'd kill me. "It's the first time and the last. I ain't making a fool of myself any more," said Maggie out aloud.

Consequences

On Sunday evening she was back on duty and very subdued. Alec was bursting to know all the news and whispered, "How did you get on with Blackie?"

"Don't ask me, Alec," returned Maggie despondently. "I made a bloody fool of myself."

"So did we all. Don't let it worry you," replied Alec. But it did worry her. How will I face him? she kept thinking.

Fortunately she did not have to. That night Hitler launched his first attack of buzz bombs and the hospital went mad. The East-Enders who had been enjoying the break in the bombing got caught in the houses, in the pubs and in the dance halls. It was a terrible night. Everyone was worked off their feet and Maggie, who was there until midday, walked to the gate tired and sickened by the sights she had seen.

Then a letter was handed to her. She read it when she got home, heavy-eyed with lack of sleep. The words swam before her eyes: See you on Friday, 8 o'clock. The pub on the corner. It was signed "K."

Her indignation was roused. So that was his game, was it? He even knows my night off, she thought. Thinks it's going to be a regular thing, does he? Wait till I see him, he'll soon find out he's backed a loser.

So Maggie lulled herself to sleep thinking just what she would say to retrieve her honor.

Friday morning came along too quickly and she felt a bit apprehensive. Strange, she thought, no letter from Jim for so long. Perhaps I'd better not go tonight. Got a feeling he's on his way home.

By the time the evening came, she had changed her mind. Got to get it over, she thought. So she went off up to the main road to meet Klause.

He was sitting all alone at the bar and she felt a little flutter in her heart as she looked at him. He was so sweet, and she would never forget his lovemaking. Now don't be silly, she told herself, get it over quick.

He looked sad when Maggie said firmly: "Now look here, it's all over between us. I am a married woman with kids and I can't afford this hanky panky."

He half smiled at the strange way she explained her reasons for coming. "Sit down, Maggie," he said in his best bedside manner. "I understand."

So she sat down and sipped the drink he had bought her.

"It's all right, my love," he said. "Perhaps we both got carried away but I think your need was as great as mine, Maggie. But as you say, let us part friends and forget it."

Maggie had expected him to be difficult and was a bit disappointed. He squeezed her hand. "Don't lose that lovely smile, Maggie," he begged. "I'll always remember you."

They sat side by side with nothing to say.

Meanwhile, down Witton Street came the tall shape of Jim. He walked with the true rolling gait of a sailor. He knocked hard at the front door. "Maggie! Where are you?" he yelled.

There was no reply, just the barking and whining of Pie Shop, who recognized Jim's voice and was in a confused state, not knowing whether to be pleased or sorry.

"Shut up, you scruffy sod!" Jim yelled through the letter box. "Where's me missus?"

Then over the road to the Barley Mow went Jim. The outside was all boarded up but they were still open for business as usual. The old neighbors were pleased to see Jim.

"Maggie's working up the hospital," they said. "Won't be home till the morning."

"No, she ain't," said one little nosey parker. "Just saw her up the White Hart."

"Who with?" demanded big Jim.

The old boy, remembering whom she was with, tried to back out of the door, but Jim had him by the scruff of the neck. "We'll both go and see," he said.

Maggie had been watching the door, when suddenly it burst open and in was pushed a white-faced old man, followed by big Jim roaring like a charging bull at what he saw. Before Maggie got over the shock of seeing him, he was upon them. He grabbed poor Klause, held him against the wall and smashed punch after punch into his face. Then, with one big heave, Jim hurled him over the bar and sent him crashing down amid broken glasses and bottles. Maggie ran screaming for the door but Jim caught her by the hair and proceeded to kick and punch her all the way down the road.

By the time they had reached home, she had lost consciousness. She came round to find herself lying on the floor in the kitchen. Her stockings were in shreds and her dress was blood-stained and ruined. She pulled herself to her feet to look in the mirror. Her face was unrecognizable.

"Oh, my God!" she sobbed. "How could you do that to me, Jim?"

Jim sat in an armchair, a bottle of whisky by his side. His face was a deep red, almost purple, and his eyes were narrow and vicious. "Whore!" he snarled. "Bleeding whore!"

A hard feeling crept into her heart. She would beat him. Why should she be afraid? "Whore or not, Jim Burns," she retorted, "take a good look. You have seen the last of me. I'll not live with you again."

"A black man, a dirty, bloody, black man."

"If you don't mind, he was no dirty, bloody, black man, but a student doctor at the hospital, and all I did was to take a drink from him," Maggie defiantly defended her lover.

Jim squinted suspiciously at her. "You liar!" he snorted. "And I don't suppose he's the only one you're knocking it off with."

Maggie moved towards him, mustering what little dignity she had left. "Before you condemn me, Jim Burns, look at your own life. What makes you think I never knew about all them little floosies *you* consoled yourself with? And from now on I shall do likewise."

"Don't you dare leave this house," Jim yelled. "I'll swing for you if you do."

"You might do that anyway," she retorted, "after what you did to that young fellow, and I'll be glad to see the back of you."

Suddenly, Jim started to blubber. In his drunken mind was the thought that he might have killed the other man and he was scared.

Maggie climbed stiffly up the stairs and started to pack. When she came down he had finished the bottle and gone off into a drunken sleep. He looked slovenly with his mouth wide open and saliva dribbling down his chin. Maggie sniffed at the disgusting smell and went out of the door.

Outside on the step was Pie Shop, very pathetic and groveling at her feet. Jim had aimed a hefty kick at him before so he had run off into the street. "I can't take you with me, love," said Maggie as she bent down to pat him. But as she walked along the road towards the taxi rank, he trailed along behind her. "Go to Sam," she shouted as she climbed into the taxi.

She knew there would only be one place where she would be welcome—with Louie. Louie had lost her big fat Bernie. He never married her but no widow grieved more than she when a direct hit on the shelter he was so proud of took him away from her.

When Maggie arrived at Stamford Hill, Louie was in bed in her shelter. She always took the children down there, raid or no raid. You always knew where to find them after nine o'clock at night. As the shelter door slid open and Louie's little boy helped her down, Maggie was shocked to see how Louie had aged in the last two months. But when she and the children saw Maggie's face, they all cried together, "Whatever happened to you, Maggie?"

"Jim did it," said Maggie. "Can I stay with you for a while?"

"Of course you can. Put the kettle on, Tina," said Louie to her lovely sad-eyed daughter. "Make Maggie a cup of tea."

Facing the Music

In Louie's comfortably furnished sitting room, after the children had gone to school, Maggie and Louie sat drinking coffee. It was a pleasant room with highly polished furniture, shining brass and silverware. Louie was very houseproud, never going far from home and always busy.

Since Bernie had been killed she stayed at home more than ever, a duster in her hand as she went around polishing the nice things he had bought her, as though they were even more precious to her than before. Memories were in each little glass ornament, and the candelabrum that held the Sabbath Eve candle stood next to his photograph, his rotund figure and pleasant smile forever with her.

As Maggie sipped the delicious coffee she looked around the room and was filled with nostalgia for her own little home, with its faded wallpaper and cheap lino on the floor; that was all she had. If she never went home again, how would the boys get on when the war was over? She would not like to put them in an orphanage. She put her hand to her head and hunched up her knees, staring so forlornly into the fire that Louie said, "Cheer up, Maggie. It's no good moping, you get used to these upsets no matter how they hurt."

Maggie felt she could not burden Louie with her

troubles when poor Louie had so many of her own with two fatherless children to bring up.

"I wish I had your courage, Louie," she said. "I feel this morning as if my whole life has folded up on me. I don't know which way to turn."

"Give yourself a few days to get over it. Come on, let's get these cups washed up."

Louie's stout figure went out into the kitchen and Maggie followed her. She dried the dainty cups and saucers as Louie washed them.

Suddenly Louie said, "Do you truly love your Jim, Maggie?"

Maggie was silent for a while, then she replied, "You know, Louie, I'm not sure. How do you define this thing called love?"

As she stacked the saucers and plates in the tidy dresser, Louie said solemnly, "There's no half measures about it, either you do or you don't. How would you feel if you were me and were never going to see him again?"

Maggie was silent, thinking how free she had felt after he had gone into the navy and how happy she had been at the hospital.

"I never missed him," she said. "I only thought of him when I was alone."

"You're a strange girl, Maggie," said Louie. "I expect it's because you never had a chance to choose. He got you in the family way and that was that."

"It's the boys I miss most," Maggie replied. "I can get along without Jim, but I could not survive without my sons."

"You're lucky," said Louie. "Someone is bringing them up for you. It's a good job my Bernie left me comfortable, but then I suppose money is not everything," she added bitterly.

But Maggie never answered. She was engrossed in thought, thinking how desolate she had been out in the empty street on her wedding night while Jim was having a good time with the girls. "You were a fool, Maggie Riley," she said to herself. "He never wanted you and nor did you want him. It's just that we had to make the best of a bad bargain and now there are those lovely boys to be considered."

Suddenly a terrible thought entered her mind as she recalled that night to remember with Klause. Could it be possible? Blimey! Knowing your luck, it might be, she thought.

"Whatever is the matter?" asked Louie who had watched her expression change.

"It's nothing, Louie," said Maggie. "But I have decided to go home today."

"It's your own decision to make, love," said Louie. "But you're always welcome here. My Bernie thought a lot of you, and so do I."

Maggie pushed her own street door open. It was on the latch and swung open with a protesting squeak and the house seemed very quiet. There was a light in the kitchen and the familiar smell of damp walls and cracked plaster reached her nostrils. She crept in. It was funny; it felt as though she had been away for ages instead of one night. Her heart beat a little faster at the thought of meeting Jim. The pubs were shut. It was past ten o'clock. He might be drunk but, praying that her courage would not fail her, she swiftly made the last few steps down the dark passageway to the door of the kitchen. Jim sat by the empty grate, his head in his hands. He looked terrible and the room was a shocking mess. Chairs lay broken where he had thrown them and smashed crockery littered the table and the floor. She paused at the door. He looked up, eyes red and bleary from the alcohol and lack of sleep.

"What the hell do you want?" he croaked. Even his voice had lost its power. Then he put his face in his hands and started to blubber.

"I've come home, Jim," said Maggie in a soft voice. "Let's try to get together, if only for the boys' sake."

He pulled her roughly to him. His tears fell on her blouse as his head rested on her shoulder. "How could you do that to me, Maggie?" he wept. "After all I've been through on my last voyage. Lost two ships I did. Sat on a raft for two days, with those Jap bastards taking pot shots at me. Now I'm beginning to wish they had bloody well got me."

Maggie stroked his hair. Proper sorry for himself, she was thinking. In her mind, these Japs and shootings did not register as they should have done. Perhaps because she never read a book and seldom listened to the radio, her world was so small. As this big, war-torn man unburdened himself, she felt embarrassed. "Come on, love," she said. "I'll make a nice cup of tea and we'll go to bed."

Jim's violent lovemaking that night was almost more than her still bruised body could endure.

Whatever's the matter you? she asked herself. Jim and you are back together, what more do you want? But there was something missing, she did not know what it was but that something never came back again.

In the morning, Maggie went down to make the tea and the house seemed empty. What was missing? Then, with a sinking feeling, she realized it was Pie Shop. She knew he would not have stayed at Sam's for this long. "Did you see Pie Shop?" she asked Jim.

"No, I ain't," he replied. "And the less I see of that scruffy old mat the better I'd like it."

But Maggie went down to the main road to look for the dog. She waited at the hospital gate. Still no sign of him. She was about to return home when down the road came Sam, his face white and drawn, looking worried. As soon as he got near, Maggie knew something had happened to Pie Shop.

"He followed me everywhere," Sam said pitifully. "I was on my way home and Pie Shop was with me. For some reason he darted across the road and a bus got him. I'm so sorry, Maggie. I got fond of the old fellow."

Tears ran down Maggie's face, tears that had been bottled up these last few days and now fell thick and fast. She could think of nothing else.

Back home even Jim tried to console her. "Don't

keep crying," he said. "He was only a dog and he was getting old anyway. Better that he went like that than got ill and died in pain."

But her sorrow over Pie Shop was deep; they had shared so much together, she and that poor old dog.

"He must have been about twelve years old," Jim said. "Ginger was only a boy when he got him and he's fighting for his country now."

Maggie soon began to see reason and Jim said, "I'll take you to see the boys tomorrow. I've still got fourteen days of my leave left, let's enjoy ourselves. After my last trip, I don't care if I never see the bloody sea again."

A Day in the Country

The boys were very pleased to see their sailor dad, and their mum, as usual, looked smart wearing a blue-and-white spotted dress, white shoes and gloves to match and a white hat with a brim which hid the bruises on her forehead and the tired look in her eyes. Dolly had packed a picnic basket and they were all going to spend a day by the river. It was a lovely day and Mum and Dad did not argue, they just walked hand-in-hand through the meadow land that led down to the clean, fast-flowing, fish-filled river. Young Jim and his brother Tom ran on ahead from them, carrying the basket and precious fishing rods, anxious to show off to their dad their progress in the art of fly-fishing.

The air had a feeling of spring in it and a fresh breeze caught at the little, white, frothy pools in the wide river and sent them hurling to the bank. In the sunlight, silver shadows glided past—fish just ready and waiting to be hooked.

The elder boys set up their rods, but big Jim and Maggie with Al trailing along behind walked towards a little wood on the crest of the hill. A blackbird sang to his mate and the wood was ablaze with golden primroses: bright, yellow patches of them everywhere, poking their heads up through last year's fallen leaves. Here and there were mossy banks covered with bluebells.

Maggie could not believe that a fairyland such as this existed. She ran round and round the glade with Al as skittish as a young pony. She must pick some primroses to take home, she thought, her dark hair flying in the breeze. She picked the wild flowers, and laughed and played with her youngest son.

Jim stood with his back to the great oak tree watching her as he held the white hat she had thrown carelessly aside. A strange feeling of peace and tranquility held him; it was as though an unseen hand touched him and a gentle voice said: "Stop worrying, it will be all right." That continuous nagging in his brain, that feeling of not wanting to go back to sea, left him. He knew he would come home again, and his confidence was returned to him by the sweet country air and remained with him through those last dangerous days of the war.

The two elder boys came running towards him. "Come on Dad, we'll show you a pool where we can swim."

It was a great day and the first the family had had together since the war began. They all had a wonderful time.

Maggie sat close to Jim in the carriage coming home. Her cheeks glowed with the fresh air and she held a bunch of primroses in her lap.

"Don't the boys look fine, Jim," she said. "Sometimes I wonder how they'll settle down when they come home after having all that space to play in."

"Don't worry, love," said Jim. "You know, Maggie, I had a feeling today. I believe I'm going to come through the war, and then I'll buy you a big house in the country and we'll have a lot more kids. Like that, will you?"

"Not 'alf," said Maggie snuggling closer to her Jim.

9

Putting Tuck in his Place

On the last few days of his leave big Jim was his usual boisterous self and the war news was good. There was talk of an invasion of France by Britain and her Allies. The East End swarmed with G.I.s like bees in a hive. Wherever you looked, there were more and more of them. Big Jim had a good time drinking with these generous Yanks, giving them the benefit of his years of active service and making them buy the beer. He seemed more like the old pre-war Jim than he had been for a long time.

"He seems to have got over it all right," said Maggie to herself. "But I haven't. It will take me a long time."

She had seen some girls from the hospital and they had looked straight through her, and she had been terribly hurt. I don't blame them after what Jim did to little Klause, she thought. He's lucky he never got an assault charge. So she commiserated with herself, knowing she would never go back to work in the hospital again, not after all they knew, and that she could not face Klause again.

Maggie was not sorry when Jim went back. She was beginning to feel the strain as if he were watching every movement she made.

She went with him to the West End to see him off and walked back through Piccadilly. The excitement in the air thrilled her. When she saw the girls laughing and talking with men in uniforms of all nationalities, she felt as though she wanted to join in. Then, in her usual manner, she pulled herself up sharply and said to herself, You get back down the East End where you belong. All the girls up here are on the game anyway.

During the next few weeks she kept busy cleaning the house and writing to the boys, and also to Sarah who seemed to be having a full sex life up north now that the Yanks were there.

So far Maggie had made no attempt to get another job; she seemed to be waiting for something to happen. For a whole month she did very little and did not feel very well. She felt very tired and had a pain in her side. Then eventually she gave in and faced up to what was wrong with her; she was pregnant again. Looking at herself in the mirror, a doubt suddenly appeared in her mind. Don't be silly, she dismissed herself. The way old Jim was at it on his leave, it must be his. Still, I don't think I will mention it till I'm sure.

It was a warm summer and the days dragged endlessly by. Maggie missed the old dog and felt fed up. Just my luck, she bemoaned her fate. Just my luck if it turns out black. The days turned into months and her tummy grew bigger. There was nothing to do now but wait and hope for the best.

One evening, she sat outside the house—it seemed creepy indoors sometimes, too many ghosts of the past in there. She sat looking very bored, her hands resting on her stomach which had already begun to show her pregnancy. It was not like it used to be down the street, no children playing, no dogs fighting. All the houses on the other side were boarded up; they were so badly blasted that they were not fit to live in and their occupants had moved elsewhere. The Barley Mow was still there, of course, but much quieter, the lights dim and

the windows boarded up. But inside the regulars still
stood swilling beer.

A dapper little man in naval uniform came out of the
pub and crossed the road to where Maggie sat.

"Hallo Maggie," he said. "Remember me?"

"Why, it's Tuck, I should never have recognized you
in that uniform."

"I'm in the special branch of the service now," he
said. "How's Jim?"

"Went back four months ago," said Maggie dismally.

"You haven't altered, Maggie," he said, looking at
her closely.

"No," said Maggie, bitterly patting her tummy.
"Same old Maggie and same old Jim. Come and have
a cup of tea, Tuck. I'm real browned off."

While she made the tea, he settled himself in Jim's
big wooden armchair. As he took off his peaked cap,
she noticed that his hair was now iron gray. He was
very smart and he seemed to have lost that hang-dog
look he used to have.

Maggie poured the tea from the blue enamel teapot
that had been with them for a long time.

"You and Jim joined up together," she said, "And
you're an officer and poor old Jim's still an A.B."

"We were out in Singapore together after we lost
our first ship, but I went on a training course and I
haven't seen him since."

"What sort of job?" Maggie asked.

"I can't explain Maggie," said Tuck. "You wouldn't
understand."

For some reason or other this upset her; she was sure
he was having a go at her. Who did he think he was?

"Well you're right there," she returned sharply. "I
don't know and I'm too bloody old to learn."

"Now don't get upset. I didn't mean to insult you,"
he said, getting up and going over to her.

"Well, you did," said Maggie aggressively. "You used
my Jim, got him in that party so that he lost his job."

Tuck scratched his head in an exasperated manner.

"Don't let's quarrel," he pleaded. "Jim was a loyal friend and they are not easy to find."

Maggie pushed a cup of tea towards him. "Well don't try to be superior, Tom Tucker," she said, "because if you have changed sides my Jim has not."

He smiled a little at Maggie's contradictory statements. "Sit down love," he urged. "Let's talk."

The twinkle had returned to her eyes, now she had said her piece, and she sat facing him sipping her tea.

He was thinking how attractive she was even in a loose print dress and with a bulge in her stomach. Her eyes were such a vivid blue as they flashed with temper. It was a pity she married so young, there were a lot of undiscovered elements in Maggie, a kind of still, deep-green pool with uncharted rocks underneath.

"Well Maggie," he began. "I never told any of you, but my parents came from Russia. So, speaking the language well, I got this job as a courier. Nothing has changed, my dear. I am gaining valuable experience to use after the war."

"Oh! is that all?" said Maggie looking bored. "Then fancy wasting your time down here with us."

"I lived near here in worse conditions than you have known, as a matter of fact," he said bitterly. "It was Cable Street. My mother died there. I would wait outside the one room we owned while my mother entertained the seamen. Then she would give me money to buy bread so that we could stay alive."

Maggie's big eyes stared wide open. "You mean she was a prostitute?"

"That's right," he said. "I learned very young the heartbreak that roamed the East End and the soul-destroying poverty. Can you wonder at me wanting to improve things for the working man? As Karl Marx tells us, let all working men unite, there would be no more war and much less poverty."

Maggie could not believe her ears. Never since she knew him had he ever shown his feelings like that.

"I'll cook some supper," she said. "We'll have egg and chips. I got our rations today."

"I would like to stay, Maggie," he replied. "Seeing as I'm letting my hair down tonight, you might as well hear the rest."

She put a little blue-checked cloth on the table and together they had a meal of fried eggs and crispy chips—a real luxury in war time.

"The boys used to love egg and chips. It seems funny cooking for two again. I wonder what it will be like after the war when I will have a big family to think about again."

"It's pleasant to have a lady's company," said Tuck courteously. "It's not often it happens to me."

"Why didn't you get married?" she asked. "Was it because of your ma?"

"I suppose it was," said Tuck sadly. "But when she died, the old man who had deserted her long before turned up conscience-stricken but much too late. He was married to some Jewish bitch of a woman, and for a while I lived with them. He sent me to school, and negotiated with the rabbi to catch up with the religion my mother had discarded. And Maggie, what I saw and heard in that house, turned me from marriage, and religion. The profession that poverty forced on my mother was noble in comparison to what went on in this so-called upper class. I ran away to the East End, where I made many friends and became a Communist."

Maggie had begun to feel sorry for him. "Never mind, Tuck," she said. "None of us gets what we expect from life. It's all mapped out. I suppose it's no good running away."

Tuck put his hand on hers. "There's something about you, Maggie," he said softly. "The way you face up to life. I have never heard you complain and we all know you have had it tough."

"Get away." said Maggie, back to normal. "Don't start soft soaping me. Won't get you anywhere."

"I know it won't," he said picking up his hat. "It's been a pleasant evening, Maggie. We'll all meet when the war is over. Here's my card with a telephone number if you want me ring me anytime."

"Me?" said Maggie aghast. "I don't know how to telephone."

"Well now's the time to learn. You'll be the death of me, Maggie. Time someone took you in hand."

"No thanks," said Maggie. "I'll wait for my Jim, and I still think you have got the wrong uniform on," she said defiantly as she closed the door on him.

D-Day

Once she had closed the door on Jim's old friend Tuck, Maggie went back into the kitchen and started to clear the table. "Blimey," she said, "I thought I was never going to get rid of him."

Then, suddenly realizing she was talking out aloud to herself and how empty the house was, she said, "Crikey! that's bad. It wasn't so hard when I had old Pie Shop; I could hold a silent conversation with him. I have a good mind to pack up and go and stay with Louie until the baby is born."

By the time the morning came her decision was made. She packed a suitcase, turned off the water and gas at the mains and gave a note to the air raid warden to say that she was going to be away.

The side streets seemed to be empty of people. Strange, she thought, where is everybody? As she moved towards the main road she saw that to her astonishment everybody who could had gathered there. The Mile End Road was lined on both sides with cheering people while down it went an army, going out of London towards France: an endless procession of lorries, full of figures in khaki who waved and sang songs as the population of the East End cheered them on. Children threw sweets to them and young girls, kisses and flowers. A stallholder ran alongside the tanks, handing up parcels of fruit, and the general salute from all sides was to stick two fingers up—not a rude gesture but Churchill's victory sign. It was a most impressive sight.

Maggie, holding her suitcase, stood bewildered. Was the war over? What was happening?

"Is the war over?" she asked a bystander.

"No, we are only just starting it. Look at that bloody lot, girl! All ours. Wait till old Hitler gets a look at that lot. We're invading France and we'll give the old bastard a bashing." He went running off crazy with excitement.

It was quite impossible to get a bus, so Maggie went into a small café in the main road and sat in the window to watch this splendid military display. It wound slowly along the road. There would be a small break in the procession to let the traffic through and then another long line of army vehicles.

Strange thoughts went through her mind as she watched the tanks that were passing with stern-faced officers in the turrets and smiling-faced young men sitting on top. All the tanks had a white star on them. It looked like the Star of David on the synagogue. No! it wasn't—it had a circle around it. How little she knew! Perhaps old Tuck was right; time she started to look ahead. Those soldiers looked younger than ever. Why, her young Jim was fifteen; if this war went on much longer they might take him. A terribly frightened feeling was inside her. Oh God! don't get morbid, she told herself; but the face of little blond Lennie floated in front of her; he had been killed in Africa after only being out there a few weeks. She recalled the broken-hearted letter from Ginger, who had seen his favorite brother killed by a sniper's bullet. Never had much of a life that boy; straight from approved school to the army. Her youngest son, Al, reminded her of Lennie. And so her mind wandered as the anti-tank guns and the motor bikes of the dispatch riders thundered by until the road was clear and the pattern of life went on again. But the East-Enders remembered that morning; it compensated them for the many dreary years of war, rationing, bombs, shelter living—a little ray of hope.

Even Louie was excited that day and she was pleased to see Maggie. "Of course you can stay here, love," she said. "I'll go with you to book up at the local hospital. About six months, aren't you?"

She put her arms excitedly around Maggie. "We nearly got them beat, love," she said. "See that army? I went with my neighbors to watch them go down Lea Bridge. Makes you feel proud, doesn't it. See all them American tanks? They have got pots of money, they have. I wish my Bernie was here to see it."

Maggie did not know why, but she could not get excited about it though she wished she could. Men, women and children had died and more were going to die. What for? She wished she were patriotic, but the reason for it all escaped her. Perhaps she ought to read the newspaper and improve her mind somehow. The little body inside her kicked out lustily. "All right, mate," said Maggie. "Don't be in such a hurry to get here, it's not such a great place."

The next three months passed quickly for Maggie. It was pleasant at Louie's house. She had a small garden and they sat out in the afternoons drinking tea and chatting with the neighbors. Louie was more friendly with her neighbors now Bernie was gone; there was nothing to hide and two children growing up and going to school brought her out in a social sense more than ever before. Maggie and Louie were invited out to play cards in the evening and then joined a sewing circle where they sat all evening sewing for the refugees. Maggie found it a warm and comfortable life, so different to what she was accustomed to. Everyone was fond of her and Louie, who was now studying the Jewish faith, was popular too. These large women, whose hearts were just as big, gossiped of weddings and barmitzvahs, but often there was great sadness, when news of a relation who had gone to a concentration camp reached them. Their sorrow, like their joy, was loud and intense. Maggie loved them, they were so alive. Here among them she felt warm and comfortable as she waited for her baby to arrive.

Towards the end of August, the afternoons got chilly as a kind of forewarning of the severe winter that lay ahead. Louie and Maggie were in the sitting room, cutting up old dresses and turning them into trousers for little refugee boys. Louie sat at the machine, a relic from Bernie's East End factory, and Maggie was sewing on buttons to finish them off neatly.

A letter lay on the table. It was from Jim. Maggie had just finished reading it and was looking a little sad. It was a lovely letter, quite unlike the ones he usually wrote. He was in Hospital Alex. A bullet had smashed his kneecap, but he was making good progress. He had received all her mail together and had just learned of her pregnancy. "I am pleased old girl," he wrote. "Perhaps you will have a little girl when I come home, to make up for the one I never saw. It won't be long now. I will make it up to you, love, for all these lonely years."

A lump came in her throat and she was trying not to cry.

"Now don't start crying, Maggie," said Louie. "You are a very lucky girl—at least you and Jim have a future together to look forward to. He's a rough old fellow your Jim, but he loves you." Her mild gray eyes wandered over to Bernie's photo as she spoke.

Maggie looked at her sorrowfully. "I'm not like you Louie," she replied. "It seems you are always with Bernie, even though he's dead."

"Of course you are!" retorted the generous Louie. "Look how you have waited all these years for your Jim."

Then, because she had to tell someone, Maggie poured out the troubles deep in her heart.

"So I'm not even sure it is Jim's child," she ended.

Louie looked very shocked. "Don't be silly, love, of course it is."

But Maggie shook her head.

"That time I got a good hiding from Jim, I never told you the truth. I did spend that night with a doctor."

"Well, who's to know?" said the practical Louie. "What the eye don't see, the heart don't grieve for."

"But suppose it turns out black?" whispered Maggie.

"Why? Could it?" said Louie, becoming almost as worried as Maggie.

"Well, he might be brown, almost a coffee color," she replied.

"Oh! dearie me," exclaimed Louie. "Did you like him?"

"I'm not sure, but I certainly enjoyed it. I was so drunk that night, that might have been the reason. He didn't want me. In fact, he was quite anxious to see the back of me."

Louie nodded wisely. "That's men for you," she said.

"How would you know, Louie?" asked Maggie. "You never looked at anyone else, besides your Bernie."

"That's what you think," said Louie. "Up where I come from the boys don't waste no time, in courting. It's down in the hay as soon as you're old enough."

Maggie smiled; she was always amused by the low drawl in Louie's voice when she spoke of the mining village she had been raised in.

"Also," pointed out Louie, "if your memory is still good, I got in the family way almost as soon as I got here. I remember it all right. That old fat Sarah threw me out, and I did not know where to go. God knows what would have happened to me if good old Bernie hadn't chosen to protect me. Then only by living with him did I learn to love him."

Maggie looked sympathetically at her. Sweet, generous Louie, she deserved her comfortable life and her lovely children.

"Listen, Maggie," she was saying. "Forget what you have told me, and I swear before God your secret is safe with me. I do so hope you will be lucky and have the sweet little girl you and Jim want so badly. But if not and things go wrong, I'll take care of your baby, no matter if it's black or red, white and blue."

Maggie put her arms around Louie, "I don't deserve such a friend as you."

The Birth of Little Joe

The birth was any day now and Maggie looked and felt very well. She was so happy with Louie and her children; they always seemed to be laughing. They had done plenty of giggling that morning, and Maggie was still laughing when her pains began.

It happened like this. Early that morning a newspaper had come through the letter box and Maggie still in her dressing gown had picked it up. Louie had called out from the kitchen, "That's no good to you, it's a Yiddisher paper. I always take it as Bernie did."

But Maggie had opened it and was staring at a picture on the middle page. Then she started to laugh.

"What's tickling you?" called Louie.

"Come and see," said Maggie. They both gazed at the fat figure of Sarah. Beside her was an American soldier, every bit as wide as her. Together they took up the whole picture and underneath was written: A beautiful English bride for our Allies. Sarah Bernstein married Joseph Rosenburg at North Street Registry Office this morning. She is one of the first English girls to become an American bride since our allies entered the war.

"Oh my gawd!" shrieked Louie. "They must have met in the blackout."

But Maggie, looking closer, felt Sarah looked very happy and very smart with her spray of orchids and a hat all flowers and veiling. "I'm glad she's got a man at last," she said. "I was very fond of her. She was good to me when Jim was in the nick."

"A man!" retorted Louie dryly. "It wasn't for the want of trying." Louie was still bitter over Sarah's attitude to her and Bernie. "Still, I suppose, you could call her my sister-in-law. Better send her a telegram of congratulations, Maggie."

Maggie looked at Sarah and wished her every happiness. Suddenly, she said, "Oh dear, Louie, I think I had better get on my way." Joe had begun to arrive.

That evening in the white hospital bed, she looked at her newborn son. She felt so proud of him—nearly ten pounds in weight. It was such a wonderful feeling to hold her own child close again. "No one's going to hurt you, little son," said Maggie as she cuddled him close. "After all that pain and worry when I carried you, you're worth it. I'll protect you with my life no matter who your father is." She stroked his black curly hair and gazed into the long, almond-shaped eyes that looked dark blue. But he had a deep creamy skin. She stared intently at him. He don't look like none of the others, but at least he's not black. Thank God for that. Perhaps he was like her mother; she may have been very dark and they do say boys look like their maternal grandmothers. "But never mind, my precious love," she cooed at him, "you're Mummy's lovely baby and you're all mine."

The nurse came to take the baby back to his cot.

"Isn't he sweet?" she said. "But he's not like you. Perhaps he's like his dad."

Maggie thought of Jim's pink, florid skin and his light mousy hair, and her hopes were dashed to the ground for a moment. Then, giving the pillow a good punch, "To hell with them all," she muttered. "Who can prove who his father is?"

There was much excitement at Louie's when Maggie brought Joe home. If he had been a royal baby, there could not have been more fuss. Louie brought out the old pram, so that her little girl could take Joe riding, and the good neighbors came with presents and bottles of wine to drink his health.

"I think you are going to be lucky, little Joe," Maggie would say as she fussed him and tried not to think of

little Maria, that little girl who lay in her pram facing
the cold wind while Maggie scrubbed saloon bar floors
to get a few shillings for food. "I was a fool then. Not
now, little Joe. I have got money in the bank of my
own and if Jim don't like it, he can lump it. I'll take
care of you, my love."

When Louie first saw the baby, Maggie's eyes had
asked that certain question, but all Louie said was,
"He's lovely. Nothing to worry over there, Maggie,
anyway, he might go fair, some babies do."

In their hearts both of them knew, and little Joe
was more loved and better taken care of than a hundred
well-born, legitimate babies.

"Can I be his godmother?" asked Louie.

"You're not a Jewess yet," joked Maggie, "I never
had the boys christened and I am not quite sure what
religion this one's going to be yet. Think I'll let him
grow up and choose for himself."

There's no beating our Maggie, thought Louie; always a joke and a laugh. "I'll certainly miss you when
you've gone home," she said. "Leave little Joe with me
and see how things settle down with you and Jim," she
suggested.

"No!" said Maggie firmly. "Joe stays with me."

10

Time to Go Home

Back in the village of Edgeley, young Jim was reading a letter out loud to his two brothers as they sat around the laden breakfast table. Dolly listened, her eyes red with weeping. She had just been reading her letter from Fred, from the Japanese prisoner-of-war camp.

"We got another brother," declared Al. "It's a shame, I thought we were going to have a sister."

"Who wants a rotten sister," shouted Tom.

"Shut up while I read this letter," said Jim.

"Behave boys," said Dolly mildly. "Let Jim read your mother's letter."

Jim continued in a very exaggerated voice, carefully sounding his aitches and assuming a slow drawl, the way that Morris did.

"Pouf," snarled Tom giving him a kick under the table, but Jim loftily ignored it and carried on reading Maggie's letter.

"Won't be long before your dad comes home now," Dolly told them.

There was a jealous feeling inside her. That Mrs. Burns, she now had another little one in her nest and soon would be robbing her of these fine boys that Dolly had begun to regard as her own. Life did not seem fair. She had prayed so long for a child of her own and now that those Japs had her Fred his health was destroyed. Perhaps it would never happen now. With a sigh she put these morbid thoughts from her mind. Oh! please God, as long as he comes home I don't care about anything else. But she did care. Before her stretched the endless years when the evacuee children would be gone.

Al did not like to see Aunt Dolly sad. He was her favorite and Al loved her.

"Come for a walk with us?" he said. "We are going to find some conkers."

"No, darling." She rumpled his fair hair and kissed him. "I'll be busy this morning, you run off and I'll make you a nice cake."

So they went running down the drive, Tom and Al, with Jim strolling tall and surly after them. Autumn had spread a mantle of gold around the countryside, and the tall horsechestnut trees on the other side of the park had begun to shed their prickly fruit. The trees were too tall for them to climb, so Tom and Al threw sticks up to knock the conkers down.

Jim sat on the trunk of a fallen tree, much too grown up to join in. He produced some fancy cigarettes and an elegant lighter, with an air of great superiority.

This always got Tom in a temper. "Give us a fag," he yelled at Jim.

"Unfortunately, that was the last one," said Lord Jim, slipping the packet quickly back into his pocket.

"Liar," yelled Tom. "Come on, Al, let's do him."

Jim was off like a greyhound, and half way across the field Tom brought him down with a rugby tackle, and then the disgruntled Jim was sat upon, while his brothers divided the spoils.

This fighting went on most of the time outside the house, while indoors, Jim being Morris's blue-eyed boy usually got his own way. But Morris had left for South Africa the week before. He was back in high finance again now that the war had taken a turn for the better. In the hope of being on the winning side, all the big business men were starting to plan for the future.

Morris's wife Jante had paid them a flying visit, all spick-and-span in her war services uniform. She looked at the boys with hostile eyes; she had never liked them and squinted crossly at them as they came in hot, tired and dirty from play. "It's time your mother took you home," she said.

They all stood in a row, silent and downcast with nothing to say to her. The dislike was mutual. Aunt Dolly and Uncle Morris were all that mattered in their small world.

"Write to her," Jante said to Dolly, "and tell her to come and get them. It's quite safe in London now."

Dolly silently nodded her head and was very glad when Jante flew out again on her war work. Dolly had no intention of writing to Maggie. Why, she would sooner cut off her right hand than send those lovely boys away. She would wait to see what Morris said, he was too fond of them to shove them off like that.

"Come, darlings," said Aunt Dolly. "Have a wash. We've got rabbit pie for dinner."

In the evening when the still of the night descends upon the countryside, creating a deep silence, just the occasional hoot of an owl breaks the stillness. It was then, with the flowered curtains drawn, that they sat before a blazing fire—three young boys, freshly bathed, in striped pajamas and blue dressing gowns. It was a cozy scene far away from the war and the heavily blitzed cities. Jim was studying as usual; and Tom and Al played cards.

Dolly held her head bent over her knitting. The firelight glowed showing up her pale, ash-blonde hair and her fresh country complexion. Her face was sad; she was thinking of Fred far away in the prison camp. Was he cold or hungry? How did she know if he was still living? In his last letter he had said he had been very ill. She let her knitting fall into her lap and her gaze wandered over her cozy sitting room. The oak beams in the ceiling and the tiny leaded windows. It was very old, this lodge. Fred had been so proud of this home when they came here after they were married. Those horse brasses around the fireplace—she remembered when he brought them home from the market for her. A tear escaped down her cheek.

"What's the matter, Aunt Dolly?" asked Tom. "You're crying."

"No, darling," said Dolly. He was a rough diamond, Tom, but always there when you needed him. "I am all right, love," said Dolly. "But I can't help thinking of Uncle Fred tonight."

With one accord they rose, and came towards her crowding round as if to protect her. "Let's play I-Spy," they said. "That makes you laugh."

"All right." She put her arms around them. "I spy with my little eye . . ." she called out, but her heart was heavy. What was she going to do when their mother came and took her darling boys away?

Later, they climbed the narrow stairway to bed, to that little room with a sloping ceiling, containing three clean white beds each with a stone hot water bottle awaiting them.

"I don't want to go home," said Al.

"Who says yer going home?" said Tom.

But Jim, who knew it all, said, "We will have to go home, when the war is over and that will be quite soon."

"I am going to stay with Aunt Dolly," yelled Al defiantly.

"Don't be daft," insisted Jim. "You have to go to your own parents when there is no war."

"I am not going," shouted Al and dived under the bedclothes as though the blankets would protect him.

"Of course," said Jim with a very superior air, "I will probably be away at school, so I won't have to go home and I will just come back here for my holidays."

" 'ark at him, don't he swank," cried Tom.

"I beg your pardon," said Jim. "Morris has already informed me that if I pass my exams he will see about a good school for me, and I expect I will get an allowance as well," he added.

"Belt up, big head," said Tom. "I am going home. Mum will need me and I'm going to no bloody school. I am going to get a job and buy meself a smart suit. Fed up with these short pants old Dolly sticks me in."

Dolly, lying in bed next door listened to them and smiled. They made her life bright and cheery. Whatever would she do when they went home? Morris would be home for Christmas, she would talk to him about it, and if Maggie did not want little Al, perhaps she would let Dolly adopt him. She closed her eyes and slept, little knowing that fate had already decided.

Morris Bloom never came back home to Edgeley. Two days before Christmas he was among the passengers on that ill-fated plane that disappeared over the Atlantic with several war correspondents and statesmen on board. The world lost a kind, generous soul when Morris left it and it was a very sad Christmas for the boys who had looked forward so much to Morris's homecoming. He had spread warmth and love around them and now it was over, gone forever.

Maggie came to see them and brought them Christmas presents, and talked incessantly of their new brother. Jim seemed to have taken Morris's death to heart. But Maggie, feeling on top of the world since the birth of Joe and looking fat and well, did not seem to notice. But Dolly did and she wondered what it would do to him, he was of a funny age, and she was not sorry when that chatterbox of a woman had returned to London and left her and the boys to mourn Morris alone.

In the New Year, after sending a brief note to Maggie telling her to collect them at the station, Jante came and packed the boys off home. Aunt Dolly was going to stay with relations in Dorset for a "rest," as Jante put it politely. Many tears were shed, but the pale-faced Dolly was the saddest of them all.

The boys had made many friends in those four years and many came to say goodbye. One was little Anne-Marie all dressed in black for Uncle Morris. She was going home with Jante to South Africa. "I'll come back when I grow up," she said, kissing Al very passionately, in her lovely incorrigible manner. "And we will get married," she whispered in his ear. Al stood looking soppy, holding the box of candy that she had given him. Even the sour-faced Jante was forced to smile at this scene from *Romeo and Juliet*. But as the old saying goes, "Out of the mouths of babes and sucklings, comes forth wisdom."

Home Again

In January 1945, Maggie went home to clean up the little house. Louie was taking care of baby Joe a few days to give her time to be ready for the boys at the weekend.

As she turned the key in the lock a strange feeling came over her. It was all nearly over and here she was back in the same spot. She was not sure whether she was pleased or sorry. Still it will be nice to have the boys home again, she thought, as she swept up the loose plaster that seemed to be everywhere. Better light the fire, the blankets will need airing.

Soon bits of the house began to shine again, the grate was polished and in it a fire was blazing. "No place like home," she sang cheerfully as she washed the crockery on the dresser. The rest of the room looked dull and dingy, but a nice tin of paint and some wallpaper would soon liven it up. The old energetic Maggie was soon back in action, polishing the furniture, and washing the curtains. She looked around very pleased with it when she had finished.

I just can't believe that it is nearly over. She took a look at herself in the mirror. The face that looked back at her was rosy and plump, the war had not done her much harm. But what about Jim? He's going to find me a hard nut to crack. I've learned that much out of this damn war.

On Saturday morning Maggie went to meet her boys. The three of them were very solemn and Jim, in particular, was very silent.

"We are going in a taxi," Maggie said as she greeted them.

"Ain't we going home?" said Al glumly.

"We are going to get your little brother Joe first, so that we can all be together again." This brought little response.

"Why so glum?" asked Maggie. "Aren't you pleased to see your mum?"

Tom put his arm through hers, but Jim said, "I suppose you know what happened to Morris."

"Of course I do, dear, but you must try to forget it. Your dad will be home soon, and things will be back to normal again."

Jim stared frigidly at her. "Didn't expect *you* to understand," he said and retired into his shell again. She did not like the emphasis he made on the "you." It hurt, but she chose to ignore it as this was his first day home.

They brightened up a bit at Louie's who gave them cakes and lemonade and brought little Joe to meet his brothers. Al held him for a while then handed him back, saying he smelled funny, but Jim and Tom just stared from a distance at him.

"How's he got so brown?" asked Jim. "It's winter and we've not had that much sun."

"Oh, he's dark-skinned," said Maggie. "Some babies are."

After a while the little family bundled into another taxi and this time headed for their home down in Stepney.

"Are we rich now, Mum?" asked Al.

Maggie laughed. "Why should we be rich?"

"All this traveling in taxis."

"Oh! let's say we're comfortable," said Maggie. "It sounds nice."

"We are poor and working class," broke in the supercilious Jim. "We live in a slum, so let's face it."

"Well, Well!" said Maggie. "Listen to the Prime Minister." The other boys laughed, but Jim remained silent, a crease across his brow as though all the troubles of the world were on his shoulders.

Once they got home, Maggie soon had Tom and Al trotting in and out, fetching nappies off the line and hot water to bathe the baby. They were having fun, enjoying the novelty, but Jim just sat staring distastefully at little Joe.

After several weeks, they had begun to settle as a family again. The two younger boys spent most of their time playing out in the street and Jim spent his in the public library. Joe was cross and fretful having been spoiled at Louie's. When they were all home the small kitchen seemed a mass of arms and legs; no matter how hard Maggie tried, it was impossible to keep the place tidy. Books, comics and sweet wrappers littered the rooms and every five minutes they wanted money for this and that, and there was all the extra washing and the baby to cope with. In the evening when she finally sat down she was heard to remark, "Blimey, didn't know how well off I was when they was evacuated."

11

Mutiny and Court Martial

Nearly every morning there was a fight upstairs in the boys' bedroom. Plaster fell down onto the table, into the butter and the sugar. The floorboards creaked as the boys kicked and thumped and wrestled with tremendous vigor. Tom and Jim would fight while Al egged them on but got in an occasional blow himself.

One morning Maggie could stand it no longer. She grabbed the copper stick and rushed upstairs and proceeded to beat them until they quit. "What the hell are you trying to do?" she shouted. "Knock the bloody house down? Give over unless you want to drive me mad."

Tom looked sullen and Jim, holding a bloody nose, stared at her aggressively.

"I hope you behaved better than this at Aunt Dolly's," she remarked.

"It's him what starts it," said Al, pointing an accusing finger at Jim.

"I don't care who starts it," she informed them sharply, "but in future it's me who's going to finish it."

She stood looking at them in dismay. They had only been back home a few weeks and Tom and Al had begun to look like street urchins. Both needed hair cuts, their ears were dirty and so were their nails.

"Look at you," she said in disgust. "Go and get cleaned up, you look filthy."

"We can't," exclaimed Al. "We ain't got no bath-room."

"Well, what's the matter with the kitchen sink and a bar of soap? Get moving." She waved the stick in a threatening manner, and Tom and Al scooted out very quickly. But still Jim sat on the bed, holding a handker-chief to his nose. Maggie stood looking at him lost for words. To hide her confusion she started to straighten up the beds. Her temper had subsided and tears were not far away. She wanted so much to comfort Jim, to touch that lovely mop of curls. He was her first born and had always been her favorite but now there was this barrier between them. She wished for the first time that big Jim would come home; he would know how to handle this moody youngster on the verge of manhood.

"Look here, young Jim." She spoke rather timidly. "Why don't you go out and look for a job?"

"If you think I am going into one of those East End sweatshops, you are very much mistaken," he replied icily.

Maggie was trying hard to keep her temper. "Well, we all have to pull our weight. Those high-flown books and words ain't going to get you much pocket money."

His blue eyes, so like her own, blazed angrily. "If you think I am going to spend my life in this pigsty, you had better think again, dear Mother."

It was that last sarcastic phrase which upset her. Her temper boiled over. "Get your arse off that bed!" she screamed. "The East End is where you were born and that's where you belong. So like the rest of us, if you want to eat, you have to work."

She flounced out of the room. "Dolly made a fine layabout of you."

Down in the kitchen Joe was screaming for his bot-tle. The front door was open and Al kicked a muddy football into the passage.

"Go over the green and play," Maggie yelled at him, "and find Tom. Don't want him raking the streets all day."

Later in the day when she returned from taking Joe out, she surveyed with distaste the table that was littered with bread crumbs, a pot of jam and a half-eaten loaf. Al had been stuffing himself in her absence and was now reading his comics.

"Tom come home?" asked Maggie.

"Ain't seen him," mumbled Al, his mouth full of sweets.

"Where's Jim?" she asked.

"Still in bed," mumbled Al.

"Oh dear!" she sighed. "What a family.

"Get this mess off the table," she told Al.

"I can't," he said. "I'm reading."

With one swipe she knocked him off the chair. He dashed out of the house yelling, "I hate you! I want to go back to Aunt Dolly's."

Maggie was rather disconcerted at this unexpected rebellion in Al. What am I going to do with them? she asked herself.

"Go and find Tom for me, Jim," she called up the stairs. "He's been out all day."

"Find him yourself," called back sulky Jim.

A hand clenched in temper, trying to restrain the impulse to clout Jim as she had done Al. She turned her attention to the baby instead and got him ready for bed.

Al sneaked in at about five o'clock looking as though he expected another blow, and dashed upstairs to join Jim in the bedroom. So far Jim had not appeared or eaten anything all day and where was Tom? She put her hand to her head, almost at the end of her tether. Something had to be done; they certainly were not going to beat her.

In the time between light and dark, just before the blackout blinds came down, London always stood breathless, waiting for nightfall. There was this feeling of apprehension in the air; even though the war was nearly over, it was still there. As Maggie stood at the street door, this sensation came over her; she was looking for Tom who had not arrived home yet. "It's no good, I had better go and look for him."

Still in her overall, she walked to the corner of the street and on the other side of the street a short distance away, she saw Tom and with him a man, short and thick set in a long overcoat and cap. Her heart skipped a beat. Whatever was Tom up to? She went quickly towards them but as she did so, the man placed his hand familiarly on Tom's shoulder and went off in the opposite direction. Tom turned and ran towards home and came face to face with a very warlike mum.

She stared at him speechless. He had two black eyes and his face was all red and blotchy as though someone had used it as a punchball. He took one scared look at her, then ran over the road and headed for home like a scared rabbit. Maggie ran after him calling out, "Where you been? What the hell's happened to your face?" But he got in first and dashed straight upstairs to join the other culprits and by the time she got there a heavy chest of drawers had been pushed against the door. From inside she could hear whispers as she listened at the keyhole.

Then her temper exploded. She rushed at the door shouting and screaming, and swearing like an Irish navvy. She pushed at the door, but desperately they held their position and Maggie really went to town.

"Come out you flaming so-'n-so's. I'll murder you when I get hold of you," she screamed as she battered the door with her fists.

Suddenly a voice from downstairs called out, "What's this? We got a mutiny on board?"

Maggie turned, ran down the stairs and threw herself hysterically at Jim. He picked her up and sat on the stairs nursing her like a baby.

A blond head appeared from the bedroom. "It's Dad," whispered Al.

"I'll give you dad," shouted Jim. "I want you all

downstairs in five minutes and a good explanation, or off comes me belt."

After Jim had calmed Maggie down and she had made a cup of tea, the boys came down one by one. Their dad sat in his armchair, a grim expression upon his face. First came Al, his face all sticky with sweets and that lock of fair hair hanging in his eyes. Then Tom holding his hand to his eye, and after them the tall languid Jim who slid gracefully into a chair.

"Who gave you permission to sit?" roared his dad. Jim jumped up as though one end of him was alight.

"Now," big Jim said as he lined them up, "I want to hear from each one of you in turn, and if another one opens his mouth he gets this." He waved a big fist in front of them. "Who's first?"

"We couldn't come out because she was going to murder us," piped up little Al.

"And why was she after you?" Jim demanded in a soft voice.

"I didn't do nothing," said Al, "I was only getting myself some bread and jam, 'cause she don't give us no dinner."

Jim caught hold of his ear. "You're a greedy little sod!" he shouted. "Tomorrow you get up at eight, wash yourself and go to school."

"Yes, Dad," said Al, pink in the face with fright.

"And what's your grievance?" he turned to Tom.

"Honest," stuttered Tom, "I run because I thought she was going to slosh me."

"Well, it looks like someone's sloshed you," said his dad. "How did your face get in that state? and who's this bloke you been 'obnobbing with?"

"I was going to tell Mum about it," whispered Tom.

A dangerous glint came in his dad's eyes. "Well now, you can tell me," he said.

"He's called Dixi. He's a boxer. He runs the paper boys down on the island."

"What bloody island?" demanded Jim, getting closer to Tom.

"Down the Mile End Road, you know, Dad."

"Well, what's he want with you?" asked Jim.

"He likes me," said Tom. "He's going to give me a job and take me down the gym and teach me to box," he said proudly.

"Well, who hit yer then?" said Jim trying not to laugh.

"I was fighting some boy on the island," said Tom.

"Don't look like you won," laughed Jim. "All right, apologize to yer ma and I'll go and see this mate of yours."

"Sorry, Mum," said Tom hanging his head.

Then Dad turned his attention to young Jim. "And what about you, little Lord Fauntleroy?" he inquired.

Young Jim, with an expression on his face almost identical to the one on his dad's, looked straight at him. "I've no complaints," he said in a most superior manner.

"Well, I bloody well have," said Jim. "How come you stop in bed all day? Fifteen-year-olds ought to help support the home, not ponce on it."

Young Jim flushed a deep red at the coarse expression his father used. "I have no intention of becoming a peasant, and spending my life in this hole."

Big Jim rushed at him and caught him by the collar and shook him like a rat. "You can get all that hoity-toity nonsense out of your head, because tomorrow you go with me to the labor exchange to get a job. I'll decide who's to be a peasant and I'm bloody sure you're not going to be a ponce. Now say you're sorry to both of us."

Jim, with a white, set face, said sorry but never looked at them.

"Now you can sit down," his father said, pushing Jim into a chair.

Maggie sat watching all this. He was really masterful, her Jim. She was so glad to see him now those boys were really getting out of hand.

Once the court martial was over, he ordered them off to bed. "I want you up bright and early in the morning."

"Now, Maggie, my love, perhaps you can find time to say you are pleased to see the old man." He pulled her on his lap and his rough mouth covered hers. "No talking," he said. "Let's go to bed."

They went hand in hand into the front room where little Joe lay sleeping peacefully in his cot with just the top of his head showing under the white blanket.

"Cor blimey!" said Jim, "all that trouble with those others, I forgot about our little new one."

"Don't wake him," said Maggie. "See him in the morning."

That terrible fear inside her—she could not face it tonight. He grunted as he climbed into bed. "Still a bit painful, me old leg. Not that it'll stop me doing what I am about to do," and his great arms folded around her.

During the night Maggie lay unable to sleep while Jim snored beside her. She thought of young Jim and was glad that he had his father at home. There was no half measures about big Jim, he would soon settle those boys down, and Maggie was grateful. But her mother's instinct told her that young Jim was hurt and needed more careful handling. Then, there was the big problem to face tomorrow—little Joe.

Morning came too soon. Daylight came through the shutters and the clatter of the milk cart and the chink of the bottles woke her. Little Joe turned restlessly in his cot. He would soon be yelling for his bottle. She had better get up. She looked more closely at Jim as he slept, his hair that had always been thin, seemed to have almost disappeared except for a few strands on top. She stroked the top of his head. Forgive me, dear, for this extra burden I am about to place on you, but if you don't want Joe, you can't have me.

She went into the kitchen and made the tea, gave Joe his bottle and changed him. All the time a silent prayer was going on inside her: "Please God, let it be all right. I know I am wicked to lie but I will not let my baby be called a bastard." To well-versed religious people this might seem a strange sort of prayer, but within Maggie the training of her youth still lay dormant, and God was an almost real person who answered every prayer.

The boys were bumping about upstairs and the house had come to life. Maggie poured Jim's tea and took it into him. Well, here goes, she thought as she opened wide the shutters.

Jim sat up to drink his tea and little Joe cooed and gurgled in his cot. "Bring him over Maggie," said Jim.

She handed little Joe to him and waited for the explosion. Jim poked his finger gently at him and said, "He's not like the others."

"I think he's like me," said Maggie hopefully as he handed little Joe back to her.

"Well," said Jim, "let's have some breakfast and we'll get them boys sorted out."

Maggie was relieved but uneasy. There was a hurt look in Jim's eyes that had never been there before.

Civvy Street

People turned to look at big Jim Burns with his slight limp and his sailor's uniform as he went down the Mile End Road with his three sons. There was no denying that those boys belonged to him. Each one, in his own particular way, resembled him and Jim was very proud of them. He held Al by the hand and Tom and Jim stepped out smartly in front of him. For the last four years he had been forced to leave his family, and now they were very precious to him and he was going to see that they got a square deal. That's what he was supposed to be fighting for, so that he could live in peace with his family, and no one was going to stop him.

The East End was coming back to life again. People were out strolling and the shops and stalls were busy. Old friends passed by and said, "Hello Jim, pleased to see you home safe." Inside him was a deep hurt, but he was not going to let any bloody wog spoil things for him. Before he tackled Maggie he would get the boys settled down. A fresh spring breeze was blowing and as he passed familiar places he felt that life had been good to him. "Could have copped it, like me father did, but you're home safe and sound, Jim Burns, and by dingo, I'll let them know I'm back."

They came to a tall building. Outside he read: Department of Juvenile Welfare. "Here we are, boys," he said, and they disappeared through the door.

Inside, at an untidy desk, sat Mr. Jenkins. Poor man, he would have been retired but for the war; he suffered from so many ailments. When this big hulk of a sailor blew in, followed by three boys, he was not at his best. It was quite a shock when the man bellowed in his ear. "Hallo. You the bloke in charge?"

Mr. Jenkins felt his rheumatic twinge starting. It always made him irritable.

"What is it you want, my good man?" he inquired looking over the top of his spectacles.

"Don't good man me," yelled Jim. "I want to see the boss of this place. I ain't come to see no office boys."

Mr. Jenkins turned purple, then a sort of scarlet, and he looked as if he was going to explode, when the back door opened and a fat man said, "This way, Sir."

"That's better," said Jim. "If you are the boss you're just the bloke I came to see."

"Be seated," said the fat man. With a benevolent air, he pointed to a row of chairs. The three boys sat down looking very scared. Then he indicated to Jim to sit near him at the desk.

Mr. McKenzie was used to handling angry parents. In his black coat and striped trousers he was a real old type of civil servant.

"Well, what can I do for you?"

"I have three sons," said Jim. "I had to leave them for four years while I served my country. Now I want the best I can get for them and my navy pension ain't gonna pay for posh schools, but I reckon I have earned the right to have a say in their future."

"I could not agree with you more," said Mr. McKenzie. "I wish all parents thought the same."

"Well," said Jim. "That tall one, he's the eldest. He's a smart boy, and will learn quickly, but I don't hold in a boy his age not bringin' a bit of money in. He's got to help in the home—we had to at fifteen."

"Very wise," said Mr. McKenzie, his eyes beginning to twinkle. "Might I suggest we get him a position where there is a scheme of further education. It's not easy at the moment, but the city firms will soon pick up again and I will do my best for you."

"Good," said Jim. "Now there's Tom."

Mr. McKenzie's eyes rested on Tom's battered face.

"He's still school age," said Jim, "But in three weeks he will be fourteen, don't seem no sense in him finishing the term. Besides, it's wasted on Tom. He will never learn."

Tom burst out, "I want to be a boxer."

Mr. McKenzie laughed. "Been getting in a bit of practice I see."

Soon they were all laughing and Mr. McKenzie was told all about Morris and gave Jim a cigar, and they talked of the navy.

A very triumphant Jim walked out of there. At least he had done what he could for them and it never cost a light, just a matter of knowing how to handle people. Jim was to work in the city and attend commercial college twice a week. Tom could do his paper round, as long as he did not do too many hours, and train for boxing. And Al was to go to the grammar school. Dad had obtained all they wanted. They thought him very clever. Even young Jim cheered up.

"Now," said big Jim to Tom, "this mate of yours, better sort him out."

"He's on the island. I'll take you," said Tom very anxiously.

"No you won't," said Jim. "Here's the money. You can all go up the flicks, I'll see him meself."

Once he had got rid of the boys, Jim went for a drink. His leg had begun to ache but he felt very pleased with himself. He'd let them know he was back in civvy street. He sat enjoying his glass of beer. It was not such a bad morning's work, after all. Then he began to think of Maggie. He had not expected to come home and find a cuckoo in the nest, he pondered gloomily. Not much mistaking that little one; if he ain't got a touch of the flaming tar brush my name ain't Jim Burns. But what could he do? He never wanted to fall out with Maggie, he had such great plans in his head for their future. It's not like Maggie to lie to me. If she tells me the truth, I'll forget it, after all, someone's got to look after the poor little bastard and one more mouth to feed won't make that much difference.

So this big, uneducated man sat trying to cope with this age-old problem. Because he loved her, he was ready to take care of another man's child but this feeling of hurt pride had to be settled first.

Over the road was the famous island that Tom talked so much about. There, surrounded by placards containing the latest war news of Japan, was Tom's friend Dixi. Jim looked through the window of the pub at him. Peculiar looking blighter, thought Jim. Short, thickset, dark swarthy skin and a nose that was completely flattened and seemed to spread the width of his face. He wore a greasy cap held up by two cauliflower ears. Looks punchy, thought Jim. I seem to know him from somewhere. I'll go over in a minute.

But there was no need to, for the short figure was crossing over the road and heading for the bar. That's a bit of a coincidence, thought Jim. Dixi ordered a drink and at the same time, took off his long overcoat. Jim was surprised to see he wore a smart suit underneath.

"Hello," said Jim.

"Hello, Jim," said Dixi. "Long time no see."

Jim held out his hand. "Do I know you?"

"Of course you do, but I'm a bit bashed about since then." Dixi rubbed his hand over his face ruefully. "I'm Tommy Spinks," he said. "You and our Ned was in the nick together."

"Well, I'm blowed," said Jim. "Of course I do, you was his little brother. How is he?"

"Got killed at Dunkirk," said Dixi sadly.

"Oh, I am sorry," said Jim. "Do you still live in that little house behind the market?"

"No, Jim," said Dixi quietly. "It got blitzed. Lost the old man and the old lady that night. I am all alone now."

Jim's sympathy was overwhelming. He remembered when he was Al's age, always being round Spink's house—his mum had made smashing bread pudding. Soon they were talking together of the days of pre-war Stepney.

"I came down here especially to see you."

"To see me, Jim? What for?"

"My son thinks you're the greatest. He wants me to let you teach him to box."

Dixi's beady black eyes sparkled and his voice rang out. "You mean young Tom? Why didn't I think of that before; he's the dead spit of you and can he use his dukes. Honest to God I never saw such style in a youngster before."

Jim fancied himself as a boxer and was proud of Tom's ability to take care of himself.

"He's a bit of a street rake, it won't hurt him to learn to use his fists," said Dixi who had become very excited telling Jim of the fight he had witnessed between Tom and another boy on the island.

"Mate," he said, "I ain't short of money, let's have the kid to work with me and I'll take him to the gym. I still do a bit of sparring down there. The fight game will pick up now."

Jim, a bit wary, said, "Don't want him chucked out on the scrap heap when he gets punchy."

Dixie looked down sadly; he knew Jim meant him. But there was a strange gleam in his eye as he looked up again and turned to the photographs of the former boxers which were all round the walls of the bar.

"It's a great game, Jim," he said. "I'm not sorry."

"Well, keep it dark," said Jim. "Don't want the wife to know. She's a bit prejudiced about fighting."

"Don't I know it, mate," answered Dixi. "Why, my old lady was always clouting me when she found I had been sparring down the gym. And she had a heftier punch than any of them sparring partners." They both began to laugh.

Jim was beginning to like Dixi. He was a warm and lovable character, in spite of his bashed-in appearance. They sat on, talking of the brothers they had lost. From beer they went to whisky, until at three o'clock they parted outside, shaking hands several times. When Dixi went over the road to his paperstand, he had a glazed expression on his face and was very unsteady on his legs.

The Battle of the Babe

The burly shape of Jim swayed from side to side as he progressed towards home. Maggie saw him coming down the street. I knew it, she thought, he was waiting till he was full of booze. Never had the courage to face me without a drink. "Jim Burns, this time I'm ready for you," she said aloud. All the morning she had been making preparations for her flight. Behind the street door was a suitcase, containing her own and Joe's clothing and her savings book tucked carefully away underneath. Deep down in her heart she knew he would not let her go; he would make her eat dirt, in future humble pie was to be her diet. The fighting ancestors of Maggie rose up within her: she was ready to do battle for her babe.

Jim lurched against the pram as he came in. "Get that black bastard out of the way," he yelled.

Without a word, Maggie let down the brake on the pram and pushed Jim inside. "Take back those words, Jim," she said firmly. "That child is no bastard. He's our son, the same as the others."

He stared at her, red-eyed with drink. "Don't give me that. Caught yer with yer fancy black man didn't I?"

She stood squarely in front of him, her small figure poised like a cat ready to spring. "I don't care what your warped mind thinks. From someone who's toured all the brothels from here to Timbuktu, I can't expect much else."

He looked astounded. Why, the bitch. She was trying to put him in the wrong. You could never tell with women.

"Look here, Maggie," he said. "That kid's as dark as bloody Hades. Can't possibly be mine."

"That don't make him no bastard," she said. "For all I know my family were dark skinned."

This really got Jim going. "There's bleeding dwarfs and bloody leprechauns out there in the bog where your old man came from, but, by Christ, I have never seen a black Irish man, and I've seen all colors in my life, so don't try taking me on, Maggie Burns."

They had reached deadlock: both stood and stared at each other. Then Maggie darted down the passage to grab her coat from the hallstand, and her tears began to fall.

"All right, Jim Burns," she sobbed. "I'll take him where he's wanted. I'll not stop here and have him called a bastard."

His big hand reached out and caught her hair. As he did so he became aware of how soft it was. "No you don't," he said. "I'll say who goes and who stays. You just open up and tell the truth."

Her sobs were coming thick and fast. "What do you want me to say? That you're a brute and a bully and deny your own child?"

Jim let go of her hair. He was flummoxed. Maggie sat, her hand over her face, convulsive hiccups of grief came through them. Jim had been drunk when he came in, but now he was perfectly sober. He leaned on the mantleshelf thinking, Well here's a pretty kettle of fish. She won't admit it, so what shall I do?

Maggie was sobbing almost hysterically, her black hair hung down in a tangle, her shoulders bowed. It was more than Jim could stand.

"Don't cry, love," he said and picked her up in his arms. "You will break my heart. I have longed so much to come home and be with my family again. I don't care, Maggie. The kid's ours if you say so. I'll never mention it again."

Her arms crept round his neck. "I'll be a good wife to you Jim," she whispered.

"I'll see you bloody are, 'cause I won't let you out of my sight any more."

They stood close together in the dingy little kitchen; for the rest of their lives that moment lived with them.

"Go and wash your face, Maggie. We'll go across the road and celebrate."

She went out the door and young Jim was sitting on the stairs. She wondered how long he had been there.

"Where's the other two?" she asked.

"Upstairs," said Jim, and Maggie caught a strange look on his face. For a moment it looked something like disdain. She began to wonder if he had heard them quarreling and whether he had understood what it was all about.

"Mind the baby," she said sharply. "Dad and I are going for a drink."

So what? she thought as she rinsed her face under the tap. I got my own way and I am damn sure I ain't letting you worry me, little Jim.

Young Jim sat surly and pale faced. Maggie looked at him defiantly: let's hope your world will be better, young Jim, and that you've got the guts to cope with it. Then, with her arm through big Jim's, she went proudly down to the Barley Mow.

BOOK
TWO

1

The Fifties

The years after the war seemed to fly past
and Jim and Maggie settled down to the steady pattern
of life. The older boys were now young men and Joe
at sixteen was a good-looking lad, with shiny black
curls and deep brown eyes. He was so loving and gentle,
he compensated Maggie for all those unhappy past
years. Jim treated him with a sort of amused tolerance,
and called him Josephine when Maggie was not around.
As Maggie got older her temper got more fiery and
easier to arouse, and woe betide anyone who frowned
on little Joe; she was like a tigress protecting her cub.
The rest of the family were very wary and never upset
Joe. They had ceased to tease him and fought the other
boys who called him a "black bastard"—this was what
they called you down in Stepney if you had a black
face; it had nothing to do with your father.

In the last few years the character of the street had
changed; now it had a desolate air. A long wooden fence
stretched the whole length of what was once the opposite side of the street. Huge posters announced that
demolition men were working behind the fence and
strange sounds came over it, accompanied by clouds
of dust.

Maggie hated the barricade and the tall blocks of flats that were creeping up behind it. "Never get me up there," she would say staring up at the tall block with its rows and rows of windows.

"It's slum clearance," stated big Jim. "Good thing. It will get rid of all the bugs."

Jim in his late forties was still a fine figure of a man, but each day the wound in his leg troubled him more. There were pain lines about his eyes, he walked slowly and used a stick. But, with the same happy-go-lucky spirit, he still took life in his stride. He admitted he had not made a success of it; in the last few years he had had many jobs, and none of them for long. Maggie had got work in the shirt factory where Liza had got her her very first job, for she knew that in spite of Jim's bluster about not accepting less than union rates, he was not fit. Many sleepless nights he spent with that bad leg of his.

"Perhaps you ought to go for treatment," Maggie would suggest.

"Talk sense, gel," he would reply. "Take the bloody leg off they will, if I let them mess about it."

Each day Maggie's nimble fingers would run the shirt pieces through the factory machine. It was boring, all this running up, but it earned good money. Her mind ticked over like a computer as she pushed the material quickly through the machine. Old Jim gets more like Liza every day, she thought. Life's funny; you think it's going to be so different, but it goes on the same damn pattern all the time. If it were not for little Joe, I think I'd hop off. Don't get much sense or money out of the other boys.

When the hooter went at five o'clock a disillusioned Maggie put the cover on her machine, called "goodnight" to the rest of the workers, and set off home down the street just as she had done thirty years ago when Jim was a baby and she had rushed home in her lunchtime to feed him from her breasts. Got it a bit easier, the girls today, what with bottles and family allowances. It was work or starve in those days. Then with a slight giggle she thought, and you are still working, Maggie, old gel.

She looked at the street door of the house as she entered. It was painted red with white panels. Maggie did not like it, the color scheme had been young Jim's idea—he was full of them. Time he thought about getting some more money, or spending less. With these thoughts buzzing in her head, she hurried inside.

Big Jim, between jobs, was dozing in a chair and Al lounged in another, his face a filthy shade of black with oil from the engineers he was supposed to work at. He always had plenty of oil on his face—not from the amount of work done, but as evidence that he had attended.

"You're home early." Maggie shot him a shrewd glance. "You sure you went back dinnertime?"

"Of course I did," lied Al staring wide-eyed at the television. It was blaring out. She rushed forward and turned it down.

"What the hell you looking at *Children's Hour* for? Noddy? Big Ears? Go and wash your own."

He did not move. He just waited until she had gone out to put the kettle on, then turned the television up again.

From the scullery, preparing the meal, she called out, "Where's Joe?"

"Up holy Joe's as usual," growled big Jim.

For some reason unknown to herself, Maggie had had Joe brought up a Catholic and he attended the Catholic school. He was always out at meetings and choir practice. The rest of the family held him to ridicule but sweet-tempered Joe never let it worry him. Maggie was proud of Joe, with his faith and ability to amuse himself. He was in many ways so like her father.

The church was no longer at the end of the street. After years of collection, Father Kelly had obtained a new church and a modern school down on the main road. The old buildings stood like derelict skeletons. The little Virgin reached out her hand to empty pews.

Maggie peeled potatoes and cooked some chops in

the cramped scullery, thinking how nice Joe had looked in his navy suit when he had his first Communion. She wished she could go back in her life to when she had respected the peace and beauty of her faith, but it was too late now.

Big Jim and Al still lazed in front of the telly. Young Jim had now joined them looking very smart in the black suit he wore at the office. He had a bored expression on his pale face.

Soon she had laid the table and served the meal. They sat around eating. There was no conversation, just the clatter of knives and forks. They still all had their eyes glued to the television. Maggie did not eat, she just sat with a cup of tea waiting for Tom. She never knew when Tom would arrive. She placed Joe's and his tea in the oven. Don't like the company he keeps. Think I'll have a word with him about coming home so late.

Afterwards she washed the dishes while Jim went back over the pub and young Jim and Al each went off to their own particular haunts. This was the pattern night after night. "Like a bloody donkey I am," she grumbled as she stacked the plates. It would have been nice to have had a daughter, don't think they're as lazy as boys. Still, it's no use complaining. At least I've still got little Joe. Never sorry about Joe. The only sensible thing I've done in my life was having Joe, she told herself as she sat in the old armchair that had been there since she first came over the road the night Dah had died.

Putting her feet up on another chair, she surveyed her slim legs in their cheap laddered stockings and the old slippers with the backs trodden down. "Look at me! Used to take pride in myself. Never buy a new dress these days. What's happening to me?" I'd better pull my socks up, but I feel too damn tired for anything these days.

Slowly her eyes closed and she dozed off. Then a strange thing happened. It was as though she was between sleeping and waking. She tried hard to shake off the feeling, but her body was a dead weight. She could not move a muscle. Then the ghosts of the past appeared. First came Liza stumping down the passage grumbling and swearing; then the sound of children laughing, and Ginger ran in followed by Lennie, fair and flushed and just that little way behind Ginger as he always had been. Oh dear, a policeman at the door. She could not move. The boys will be caught. Little Marie was crying fretfully in her pram. Why didn't someone go to her? Maggie fought desperately to move her limbs. Then the shaggy head of Pie Shop was pushed against her, his face in her lap with bright eyes staring affectionately up at her. Slowly, with a struggle, she put out her hand to pat him. As she did she awoke feeling depressed. She started to cry.

"Gawd, what happened to me?" she exclaimed aloud in a frightened voice that seemed to ring through the empty house. If they were ghosts, why was Ginger there? He still lived. She felt cold and creepy, and longed for someone to come home.

Jim came in when the pub closed. He looked at her and said, "What's up, Maggie? You look like you've seen a ghost."

"Perhaps I have," returned Maggie gloomily.

Little Joe had returned and was eating his supper. His nose was in a book. Maggie pushed the curls from his eyes with an affectionate gesture.

"Go to bed, darling," she said. "Don't strain your eyes there."

Joe picked up his book and went immediately. No answering back from Joe.

Jim had sidled off to bed and when Maggie went into the front room, he was lying on his back snoring like an old badger. He looked just like Liza lying there.

Maggie lay beside him tossing restlessly. She could not shake off this queer feeling that hung over her.

A taxi drew up outside and the sound of drunken voices drifted in. That's Tom. Sounds like he's been drinking. They'll punch hell out of him tomorrow in that boxing ring. The boy might as well quit as be used as a punch ball. She dozed fitfully until the dawn light came through the window. It was not like her to lie awake. Perhaps she needed a holiday. Something was wrong with her. Jim moved uneasily and snorted and muttered in his sleep.

"Jim," she whispered. "You awake?"

"No," he retorted. "But what do you want?"

"I was thinking we could have a holiday together this year."

"Cor blimey, gel," said the astonished Jim. "Did you wake me up in the middle of the night to ask me to go to Southend in the summer? You must be going off your bleeding rocker."

"I don't mean Southend," continued his spouse. "I mean a real holiday."

"Christ!" said Jim turning on his side irritably. "I'll get me bloody skis and take yer to the winter sports in a minute."

"Don't laugh at me, Jim," pleaded Maggie. "I was lying here thinking of that lovely holiday we had before you went abroad."

Jim softened a bit as he heard her pleading voice. "All right, love. It was nice. But now I have got a hopping leg and we ain't got no money." He winced as he spoke. "So give over, gel, and let's get some sleep."

"Sorry, Jim," said Maggie. But there were tears in her eyes and a strange hard lump in her throat and she was not sure why.

The next day was Saturday. The boys disappeared after breakfast and big Jim went with Tom down to the gym where he was to try to get a fight for the night. This was the usual procedure on Saturday: big Jim hung about the pubs until after the fight, then he came home while Tom went up west with his flash pals.

As a boy Tom had been a sensation in the ring, but as he got older others who were better had come up and now he was finished as a professional. At first it had been very good and big Jim had loved the pats on the back and the free booze. But in recent years Tom had been too busy with his gambling friends to train, and started taking beatings.

Maggie was quite used to being on her own on Saturdays. Sometimes she and Joe would go to the pictures, but now the school had a club and Joe liked to go there.

This Saturday she did not want to be alone so she waited outside the club for Joe. The sound of music and young people enjoying themselves was better than an empty house.

A young priest came out. "Why don't you come inside?" he asked.

"No thanks, Father," replied Maggie respectfully. "I'm waiting for Joe."

He looked at her curiously. "Joseph Burns?" he inquired.

Oh, no! thought Maggie. Now he'll want to know. They all do.

"I won't wait," she said and turned abruptly towards home.

As she walked she realized why she did not mix with anyone but her own family. There was always this curiosity about Joe, and she would sooner be hung, drawn and quartered than satisfy that nosy lot.

Joe caught her up half way down the road. "Hello Mum. Why didn't you come in? Father O'Mally told me you were outside. All the other mums were in there."

Maggie hugged him tight. "Next week I might," she said.

"We're learning to dance and I put the records on," he informed her with pride.

After Joe was in bed, she stood looking out of the window at the old familiar street and the lamp post just outside that shed a yellow glow. It was very quiet tonight.

Big Jim was very late, the pubs had been shut ages. Where could he have got to? She wished Tom and Jim were at home. Al had just slid in very secretly and gone straight up to bed. But where was her Jim?

Then came that fatal knock in the night, like a kick in the stomach. It echoed through the house and Maggie stood still, afraid to open the door. With trembling hands she lifted the latch and a young policeman stood on the doorstep. His silver buttons shone out in the dark.

"Are you Mrs. Burns?" he asked. "Will you please come with me? Your husband has had an accident."

Her knees went weak. Not her Jim? Surely he meant young Tom?

"No, madam. James Burns, a man of middle age."

The storm broke over her head. She had known something was wrong. Slipping her arms into her coat she went without a word.

The hospital ward where she had worked during the war now seemed a strange and far away place. There were the same flowered screens about the beds and the same solemn-faced sister escorted her. There was her Jim lying in the narrow white bed, his head bandaged and an awry grin on his face as if to say: Well, this is it and I'm ready.

All night she sat watching him. He never even regained consciousness.

In the gray light of dawn Tom and Jim led her from the ward and took her home in a taxi. Maggie wished she could cry but tears would not come; she just stared sadly, her blue eyes bright with unshed tears.

The boys were very good. Jim and Tom did all the necessary business and Joe and Al accompanied her everywhere. The coroner had said that Jim had had heart failure, fallen and injured his head. It could have happened wherever he was. In a way, Maggie was relieved at the verdict; she alone knew how ill Jim had really been and that he would not give in to that bad leg.

The heartbreak was not saying goodbye, for him to go like that after they had grown so close in the last years. She lay in her lonely bed that night, thinking. Where are you, Jim? My big, lovely Jim with such a zest for living. You were not in the body I saw at the hospital, that was just an empty shell. You had gone. I felt that you had, but where, my love? I wish I was good and able to pray, then I might find you again.

The boys looked worried when they saw her solemn face the next morning, and how silent she was. They were loyal and clung together as a family.

"Who shall we ask to the funeral, Mum?" a pale-looking young Jim asked.

"Not many relations left," said Maggie. "Only Boy Boy. And you better let Tuck know."

"Who's Tuck?" asked Jim.

"He was your father's best friend," replied Maggie. "Here's the telephone number. Go and ring him up."

The Funeral

On the morning of the funeral, Maggie felt quite lost, as though this was all happening to someone else. Tuck had just arrived, a dapper man in a bowler hat and driving a big car. Al could not resist going out and looking over the super shiny Vauxhall, inspecting it from bonnet to boot.

"Come and have a look, Joe," he called. "Ain't it a smasher? Bet he's got plenty of money."

The next one to arrive was Uncle Bob, Jim's brother from the Midlands. This was Boy Boy who was now a fat, pompous, middle-aged man with a large boring wife who just murmured sympathetically and said little else.

Big Jim's friends from the East End lined the street and the little house was full of floral tributes as Jim Burns took his last ride from the street where he had been born, married and raised a family. Not yet forty-eight when he passed on, his big shape would be seen no more nor would his hearty laugh ring out across the Barley Mow. It was over. His wife sat dry-eyed as the funeral cortège moved off.

There was quite a lot of tension in the car as they returned from the cemetery. Tuck felt it as he sat between Tom and Jim, and Maggie, sitting facing them, very silent and sad, also wondered why. But Al knew what it was all about and was enjoying the discomfort as he cast side-long glances first at Jim, and then down towards Tom's feet. The reason was that Tom was wearing his dad's best Sunday boots and brother Jim was very cut up over it.

Earlier, as they dressed for the funeral and were putting on their dark suits, Tom had no shoes to put on. He was always buying flash-colored shoes and had nothing suitable to wear with a dark suit. Poor old Jim left nothing of value but reposing under the dresser were his Sunday shoes, nearly the same size as Tom's.

"I'll put Dad's shoes on," declared Tom.

"No, you won't. It wouldn't be right," said Jim.

Tom laughed. "Don't be a fool, he ain't coming back," he replied rather coarsely. Jim's face went white with anger at this insult to his father. They might have started to fight then and there but Al for once was the peacemaker.

"Turn it up," he cried. "Can't upset Mum today."

So it blew over and Tom stood arrayed in his dad's best shoes, his eyes wet with tears as he took the last look at the coffin.

When they got back home the table was laid with the best cups and saucers and plates of sandwiches. On the dresser were several bottles of whisky and sherry. The neighbors came in to offer their condolences, had a cup of tea or a drink, and left. Uncle Bob did not stay long for he had a long drive ahead of him. Soon only Tuck, Maggie and the boys were left, and the last whisky bottle was nearly empty. Tom and Jim stood on opposite sides of the room looking very flushed and Al, sloshed, sprawled in the armchair.

"Couldn't help laughing," giggled Al. "Old Tom had Dad's shoes on and they were too big."

"Didn't take him long to step into the old man's shoes," sneered Jim.

Then it began. Like a charging buffalo Tom rushed at Jim head down, pinning him against the wall. Al staggered into the affray, fists swinging. Maggie and Tuck looked on astounded, too startled to move. Then, gallantly, Tuck got up and tried to part the combatants. The table tipped over, the chair went flying—a real bar-room brawl was in progress. Quickly and silently Maggie rose, went straight to the back door, produced a mop and joined in. Soon Jim and Tom parted and went dashing out of the house in opposite directions. Al ran upstairs yelling that Maggie had hurt his head. Joe stood and stared, his brown eyes wide with terror, at the mess and the confusion.

It was at that moment Maggie put her hand up to her face and burst into tears. For the first time since Jim had died tears came. They had a hard dry feeling. The unshed tears burst out and she cried and cried unable to stop. Tuck held her close in his arms until she was calm again. Then he went around picking up the broken pieces of china and straightening the furniture.

Little Joe watched this man he had never seen before, who comforted his mum and was so kind and gentle to her. He was not his father, he was quite sure of that but neither was that big jolly man who had been so good to him. He was never going to see him again. It did not seem possible. Parents are funny, decided Joe. Because you are only young they think you do not know anything that goes on. His lovely white-skinned mum, how he adored her! He wished it was himself in there giving her solace, putting his arms around her.

When Maggie had finally stopped crying and Tuck was pouring her a drink, Joe moved towards the passage.

"Where are you off to, darling?" called his mum as he made for the front door.

"Up to the church," he replied, "to light a candle for Dad."

Maggie watched him leave, affection shining in her tear-washed eyes.

"He's an angel," she told Tuck. "So different to the other boys."

Tuck thought so too but made no comment.

"I've had trouble with them ever since they were evacuated," said Maggie morosely. "Al I can manage, but Jim and Tom seem to hate each other. A childless woman she was that had them for four years, spoilt them rotten she did."

Tuck tried hard to console her but thought sadly how ungrateful she was. This other woman, who had taken care of those boys, deserved more than reproach.

"I shouldn't worry so much. Tom's a rough diamond like big Jim was as a youth. I should know; took plenty beatings from Jim when we were out boozing together."

Maggie smiled at the memory of her lovely robust Jim.

"Young Jim's like you, Maggie," continued Tuck. "He's got your ways, an urge to improve himself."

"Lot of bloody good it did me," retorted Maggie, a flash of her old personality returning.

"Getting married so young held you back," urged Tuck. "There's still plenty of time to learn."

"Jim's always spouting politics, same as his dad," she complained. "Does annoy me. Got a nice job in the city but all he cares about is trying to change the world."

"Well, it's his world, let him find out for himself."

"It's all right for you, Tuck. You have money and education behind you. What have my sons got? Nothing!"

"They are young, Maggie. They'll get their opportunities—everyone does." Wise and kind, his gray eyes scrutinized her. "It's not going to be easy for you as a widow with this family. I want you to know that you can rely on me to help for the sake of my old pal."

Her eyes filled with tears again. "I'll get by," she said sharply.

"Will you let me take Jim off your hands?" pleaded Tuck. "I'm in the Labor Party now and I've a small constituency in Bridgnorth. I could do with a secretary and you did say he'd had commercial training. Please

Maggie. I have no son of my own. I promise you, Jim won't regret it. And it's time he left home."

Maggie eyed him shrewdly. He did seem prosperous but she had never really trusted him. Would be nice to get Jim started . . .

"It's a bit awkward. He might not agree."

She seemed undecided as she spoke. But Tuck knew the battle was won. Maggie was relieved of the moody, gloomy Jim, her biggest headache.

"I'll leave a note for him to meet me uptown tomorrow."

In a crisp, business-like manner, Tuck sat pad on knee, white hands holding a gold fountain pen as he wrote to Jim. Maggie looked closely at him and saw that the skin of his face was drawn tight. There were hollows at the sides of his cheeks and lines about his eyes. Not a very happy man, she thought. I wonder why he never got married.

Putting the sealed envelope on the mantelpiece, he kissed her on the cheek and left abruptly.

She felt all alone in the house. A scared feeling came over her. She got up and started to tidy around the room. She stooped to pick up a picture the boys had knocked down, and smiling up at her from the frame was the face of big Jim in his Jack Tar's uniform, taken outside a bar in Cairo. She smiled at him and, placing it in the center of the mantelpiece said, "You know, Jim, you've not left me. I think you're still here in this home where you were born and where we shared so much. I feel you're still here." She glanced over the old kitchen, a soft light in her eyes. "That's it, mate. That's why I couldn't find you at the hospital. You were still here and I'll stop and look after you, me old darling."

She picked up a vase of fallen daffodils. "Here you are, my love. A bit of the old countryside that we saw so little of."

She placed them next to his photo and from that moment Maggie was happy, ready to go on.

Tom was the first to come home. He stood in the

doorway, disheveled and very penitent. He stood waiting for her outburst but it never came.

"Want a cup of coffee?" said Maggie brightly.

"I'm sorry, Mum." And he fled upstairs where Al, under the influence of the whisky, slept like a log.

Soon after came Jim, his white face bearing marks of the battle, two black eyes. He came and sat facing her, looking so humble. He wanted to say something but aloofness and false pride would not allow him to utter a word.

"There's a letter for you," said Maggie sweetly.

He looked surprised but took down the letter and started to read it. A smile lit up his features as he read. "Crikey! That bloke was an M.P. Fancy our dad having friends like that. He wants me to be his secretary. Oh, Mum! What a break." He rushed over, put his arms about her and gave her a hug. Maggie felt warm and comfortable inside. This was the first time her son had shown her any affection since he had come home from evacuation. He read the letter many times.

"Bridgnorth. That's socialist. The border of North Wales. Ain't it smashing? Goodnight, Mum," he said and up the stairs he went, quite his old self again. His Dad's death was forgotten for a time. There was a new life to look forward to, a chance to get away.

Maggie tucked little Joe up that night, kissed him, and murmured,

"Goodnight, my love," and went to her lonely bed.

Back in Action

Monday morning bright and early, Maggie presented herself at the factory. The boss was surprised but very pleased to see her, she was quick and thorough and one of his best machinists. Around her girls whispered. "She soon got over it," someone was heard to remark. "Might have been bleeding glad to get rid of him," another sniggered.

Maggie, her nimble fingers gathering up the striped

shirt material and sending it whirling through the machine, paid no attention to them. A black skirt and jumper were the only things different about her. There were no flags flying half mast for her Jim. She was here to earn money. Couldn't live on a widow's pension. She did not want any sympathy, she just wanted to be left alone. Must get Jim some new underwear, she thought to herself.

Today she felt good, alert and ready to work and take care of the family. No time to stand and stare and no good walking about with a long face, she told herself, that lot of old cows will only talk behind my back. So, to the amazement of all concerned, Maggie went on as usual.

That evening when she got home the empty chair by the fire greeted her sadly. But going over to the mantelpiece she said, "Hello, Jim. Had a good day, mate?" She felt better immediately.

With regular money the weeks and months passed quickly enough. Jim had departed for Bridgnorth and had written several letters to say how happy he was with Old Tuck. Tom had improved now that Jim was not there to aggravate him. But Maggie still worried over him. He stayed in bed all day and was out most of the night. He had plenty of money and was very generous with it.

"What sort of job is it?" she inquired while he stood over the sink shaving, getting ready for work.

"I'm working for a mate in a club up west," he replied.

"Glad you gave up your boxing, anyway," said Maggie.

Tom's rugged face crinkled into a grin. Being a bouncer in a gaming house was not far removed from the ring but his mum did not realize that.

To Tom his mum was quite a gel; look how she refused to let losing the old man get her down. They had been very fond of each other. Funny about Joe though. Wonder what the mystery there is. And she's still a little beauty. Better keep my eye on her. Don't want no damn stepfather nestling in.

"Hurry up, Tom," Maggie called. "I want to use the sink."

One day, dreamed Tom, I'll make it good. Then I'll look after you, little mum. You shall have anything you want.

Tom loved his mum but Maggie's passion was little Joe. She fussed and loved him more than ever now she was alone with no big Jim to rely on.

"Tell you what, little Joe," she said one night as she tucked him up in bed, "this year you and I will have that holiday, the seaside, cockles and ice-cream."

"Where will we go, Mother?" Joe asked seriously.

"You choose, love," she replied. "I don't know one seaside from the other. Only ever been there once, when your dad was in the navy."

Little Joe's eyes looked up at her, appealingly. In the half light of dusk they looked a lustrous brown.

"Tell me, Mum. Was he really my dad?"

A tug at her heart strings. How dearly she would have loved to tell him the truth but fear held her silent.

"Don't be silly, Joe. Of course he was," she replied sharply.

"But, Mum, I'm colored."

She bit her lip in anxiety. "What a lot of nonsense. Who said so?" she questioned him.

"Christine won't mix with me. She says her mum says she's to keep away from the colored boys."

Joe's pathetic tone of voice tore at Maggie's heart. Silently she prayed: please God, don't let my courage fail me, and she tucked the blankets about him impatiently.

"Well, they must be bloody blind," she declared, "because you ain't no colored boy. Now get to sleep."

Joe's dark lashes descended, hiding his eyes, and Maggie's heart ached for him. She knew she had failed her favorite son.

Al started courting a loud-mouthed, big-bosomed girl from the same street. At first it amused Maggie. He was so funny at times. He would come in late perished with the cold after leaning on the fence over the road for a couple of hours with this girl.

He came in one night cold and shivering.

"For gawd's sake," said Maggie, "do your courting where it's not so draughty."

This upset Al. "You've been spying on me," he declared with the air of a Shakespearean actor.

"Can't help seeing you. Only got to look out the window." Maggie informed him bluntly.

He was most offended and went about, hands in pockets, shoulders hunched, his long face full of misery and without a civil word for his mother. But he was never seen over the road again.

Oh dear, thought Maggie, I always put my foot in it, don't I. Still, not sorry to see the back of that slovenly-looking girl. Even Al could do better than that. First Joe, then Al. Who am I about to offend next?

On Saturday morning while Maggie was busy with her weekly chores, there came a knock on the door. Rather irritably, she went to open it. On the doorstep stood a young priest.

"May I come in, Mrs. Burns?" he asked.

She realized it was Father O'Mally, the school priest and young Joe's friend and confidant. "Come in and you are very welcome," she said. She put on her most charming manner, but all the time she was thinking, I wonder what Joe's been up to. She escorted him into the tiny front room, his pale face looked earnestly at her.

"We are very fond of Joe at school," he began. "So I have come on behalf of my superiors to make a proposition to you with regard to Joe."

Maggie's eyes stared straight in his. "What's Joe done?" she demanded.

Father O'Mally smiled. "Nothing at all, his conduct is exemplary. But now that you are a widow we can offer you a special grant paid for by the church."

"What makes you think we need charity?" asked Maggie.

"It's a scholarship, Mrs. Burns. If your son were not such a clever boy we would not be interested. I hope you will not let pride stand in the way of that young lad's future."

Father O'Mally had begun to look very unhappy. So Maggie relented and came half way. "You want him to be a priest. Is that what you mean?"

"No, that comes later, then the decision is his own to make. He will be educated up to university level. There are many corridors that will be open to him."

"I won't stand in his way. I'm an ignorant woman but I'd like my sons to do good."

"Good, that's wise." He breathed a sigh of relief. He was beginning to be worried by this fiery little woman who seemed to have a mind of her own. Now the last step, he wondered how she would react to that.

"It's a boarding school. I feel I must tell you that as Joe does not wish to leave you. It's entirely up to you whether he takes the exam next year. But should you agree I'll tutor him and we are all sure he will pass."

Tears sprang into her eyes. She could not part with Joe.

"It's a very nice school in Kent and he will be home at holiday time," the cajoling voice went on.

"I must talk with Joe. I'll send a note tomorrow," she said sharply.

"I do hope you will give it careful consideration, Mrs. Burns," said the priest as he left.

Her head was spinning. How could she get on without her youngest son? The prospect really depressed her.

The rest of the day she wandered about the house trying to finish jobs already started. She was so close to Joe, her life would be empty without him. He had not been so happy at school since Jim's death. He seemed to have something on his mind. Perhaps it would be a good thing, a change of environment. What did the priest say? University standard? He might even turn out to be a doctor like his father. No, she dare not look back. Must think of the future. She turned this new problem over and over in her head. At last she decided. I'll ask Joe if he wants to go.

Joe came in for tea, tired and grubby. He had been playing football. After he had eaten his tea, she said quietly, "Father O'Mally has been to see me, Joe."

He rushed to her. "Oh, Mum! What did he say? You will let me go?" He looked anxiously at her.

"Do you want to go all that much, Joe?" she asked in a surprised tone.

"Oh, Mum, I hate to leave you but it would be a tremendous chance for me." His voice rose excitedly, then looking down at the floor, he said, "Besides, there are lots of boys there like me, Mum."

"Like you?" she asked. "Why so much like you?"

"Oh, you know what I mean, Mum." He looked reproachfully at her.

Oh, so little Joe had been got at again. She might have known he would tell the priest what had been bothering him. There was a sinking feeling in the pit of her stomach. A battle had been lost.

"All right, darling," she said. "I expect you will get that scholarship. I'll have to try to get on without you."

Just then Al arrived, his hair all over the place and lipstick all over his shirt, and Maggie, as usual, vented her feelings on her wayward son.

"Go and wash!" she yelled. "Scruffy-looking sod. Don't you dare sit at the table like that."

"What's up with her?" was Al's comment to Joe.

Joe only stared down silently at his plate to avoid the tears in his eyes being discovered.

2

The Shopping Spree

Joe won his scholarship and just before his term started Maggie took him up to town to buy a school uniform. She had never been into the big shops up in London and she was like a scared, excited child. The sight of the huge counter displays, the smart dresses and crowds of people hurrying by confused her. Joe was on top of the world and hung on to his mum's arm, repeatedly telling her all the things they had to have at the new school. Her little store of money soon disappeared. They would not have that holiday together but little Joe seemed to be so happy, it was worth all the worry and expense.

Her eye caught a counter laden with lovely underwear, frilly nighties, taffeta underslips. She stood looking at the dainty wear. A feeling of rebellion came over her. On another counter a lovely lavender blouse was on display, long sleeves and a deep frill down the front, the kind of material you could see through.

"Isn't it lovely, Joe?" she whispered.

"Buy it for yourself, Mum," urged Joe.

"Oh, no, it's too expensive," she replied. But she still stood looking. "Shall I?" she whispered, her eyes alight with anticipation like a small child in a candy shop.

Joe's brown eyes stared sadly up at her. "Please, Mum, buy it for yourself. I wish I could buy all these pretty things for you."

She looked in her purse. Three pounds left. How much was it? Two pounds and fifteen shillings. "Still got five bob left for your fare home. I'll have it."

Jubilantly she walked from the big store. Among these crowds of shoppers there was none so pleased with their purchases as Maggie, with the lavender blouse held carefully in a white paper bag. They sat close together on the bus, Joe dreaming of the new school with its long, green playing fields and himself all in white, and his mum thrilled to bits with her new blouse.

She wore it when she took Joe to the station. It made her old suit look quite smart and Joe was proud of his pretty little mum as he waved goodbye.

When the train steamed out Maggie stood for a long time on the platform after the carriage had disappeared, blinded with tears.

She came out of Charing Cross Station and walked toward the bus stop. It was early evening and the West End had begun to come to life: bright lights in the shop windows, colored neon signs overhead. There was nothing to hurry home for. She walked aimlessly from one brilliantly lit shop window to another, admiring all the beautiful wares on display, not even noticing the direction she was taking.

Soon she found herself in Shaftesbury Avenue. She lingered for a while looking up at the theater posters displaying the spangled and sequined half-naked bodies of dancers. This was a world she knew little about, a fascinating dreamland. Taxis sped hither and thither with well-dressed men and women, long evening dresses, white shirt fronts and the glint of diamonds. Maggie just stood looking, wondering if she would ever get enough courage to enter the red plush palace with swing doors.

Suddenly a man came dashing from the foyer, waving frantically and whistling for a taxi. Maggie, looking up in the air, wondered what had struck her as his hefty body collided with her slim one. She spun around and went down on her back, handbag spinning off in one direction, her hat in another. She was so shocked she just sat there. The gentleman was most apologetic as he helped her to her feet. A crowd had gathered and stood gawping while Maggie retrieved her handbag and pushed her hat back on her head.

"Are you hurt?" he inquired. She shook her head and he looked at her rather strangely. "Let me get you a taxi," he insisted.

Still rather stunned, she allowed him to help her into the waiting cab. Taking out his wallet, he asked, "Where do you live?"

"Witton Street, Stepney," Maggie said automatically.

"I knew it was you!" he burst out and hopped quickly into the taxi and took a seat beside her. "What the hell are you doing up here, Maggie Burns?"

She stared at him incredulously. His wide smile showed a line of perfect white teeth. Then he burst out laughing. "Sitting on your backside in a West End street? What's become of you, Maggie?"

Then the penny dropped. "It's John Malloy!" This heavy well-dressed man was nothing like the boy lover of her youth. Her eyes opened very wide as she stared at him. "I'd never have known you," she declared.

"But I knew you, Maggie. In all these years you have hardly changed at all."

"Who are you kidding?" said Maggie. "I've had two more sons since then."

John was scrutinizing her very closely. The same black, shiny curls and blue eyes. "I've never forgotten those blue eyes, Maggie."

She blushed, unable to answer. It was such a long time since any one had admired her.

"I must say, you are better dressed. Such a poor little devil you were in those old days."

"I remember," she giggled. "My first date with you was in a threepenny jumble-sale dress."

"And I still feel the blow I got down below. It's a wonder you didn't rupture me, you vixen."

Together they began to laugh and talk of the old days; of when Jim was in the nick and John was the ardent lover. They felt the years slip away and both, for a brief time, became young again. The taxi slowly traveled along the long Mile End Road. Maggie's cheeks flushed with excitement as they spoke of Sarah and the old in-and-out shop.

"It took me a long time to get over losing you," said John. "I went to Canada to study rock structure. Now I'm a Fellow of the Geographical Society."

"Have you been back long?"

"No, not long. I'm working on a project here in London, and I might stay."

The taxi drew up outside the house. "Maggie, it's been so nice meeting you. Let's meet again for a drink. I'll come around on Friday evening for you."

Before she could reply, he gave her a friendly peck on the cheek, got back in the taxi and went quickly on his way.

Feeling very happy she put the key in the door and went into the house. Tom was indoors looking at the telly.

"Hello," Maggie greeted him gaily. "Nice to find you home."

"I'd thought I'd stay in tonight seeing as Joe was not here."

He's not such a bad boy, decided his mum. It was a nice thought to stay in with me tonight. Tom was looking at her flushed face and her starry eyes.

"You been on the booze?" was his loud comment.

"Of course I haven't. Went to see Joe off," she returned indignantly.

"Well, what's all the smiles and grins for?" questioned Tom.

"Well, if you must know, I met an old friend up in town. Used to know him thirty years ago."

Tom's face dropped a mile. "You wouldn't start doing that, Mum?"

"Doing what?" she called out as she made some tea.

"Messing about. You know what I mean."

Maggie's face turned from red to scarlet. She rushed in. "Yes, young Tom, I do know what you mean and who the hell do you think you are talking to me like that?"

"Sorry, Mum, but it makes my blood boil when I see old women running around and if it's yer mum it must be bloody awful."

"Well, I ain't old for a start and if I decide to run around it will be my own business."

Tom, now very embarrassed, kept quiet, but resolved he would punch the first bloke he caught hanging around his mum.

Maggie's Boyfriend

On Monday morning Maggie was back at work. The long line of machines whirred continuously. The buzz of conversation from the women that worked them went back and forth across the belt that drove the long line of machines. Characters were torn to shreds and complete life stories were recounted as they sat and slaved at the shirtmaking, hour after hour, day after day.

Today Maggie was silent. She usually liked to hear what was going on, but this morning she was miles away. I can't get over old John Malloy. Fancy recognizing me after all that time. He's still good-looking. Perhaps I'd better not go on Friday. Don't seem right, Jim only dead a few months. But still the little flutter of excitement inside would not go however hard she tried.

These bloody bright-colored shirts will give me migraine. What the hell do men want colors like that for? Look more like girls than boys. She pushed the jazzy material along. I bet Al would like one, she thought, sort of thing he goes mad about. I might treat him. He's been a bit fed up lately, looks so washed out, red-eyed and white-faced. I wonder what he gets up to?

* * *

Tom had suddenly become like a clinging vine. That evening after tea, he put his feet up and stared at the television.

"Ain't you going out, Tom?"

"No, Mum. I thought I'd stay in and keep you company."

Too good to last, thought Maggie. "What's happened to your friend with the night club?"

"He's in the nick," said Tom. "Coppers raided the club."

"Well, fancy that. Who you working for now, Tom?"

"No one," he said. "Living on me savings. Thought I'd have a rest."

Maggie shrugged her shoulders and sat down to write letters, thinking how hard his poor old dad had tried to get a job, limping on his bad leg from factory to warehouse. It's their world, I suppose. Better let them get on with it.

She wrote to Joe and Jim and then to Sarah in America and Ginger in Australia. All these years they had corresponded regularly with her. Ginger now had a sheep farm near Perth, and several children. He was always begging her to visit them. She had only to decide and travel expenses would be provided. She would love to see the irresponsible Ginger again, now that he was a responsible citizen. Also there were continuous requests from Sarah to come and visit her in East Hartford, Connecticut. In her letters she never seemed to have altered even though she now had a loving husband and two children. Sometimes the urge to be free, that always dwelt somewhere in Maggie's mind, came to the fore. I bet I'd have a good time out there with Sarah. Never get a chance to go though. Take me to the rest of me life to save the fare. Maggie would then dismiss it from her mind.

The letters were all sealed ready for posting when Al came slouching in, his hands in his trouser pockets, his fair hair falling over his face. He stood in the doorway and stared vacantly at them.

"You look bloody awful," said Maggie seeing his

dead-white face and red-rimmed eyes. He muttered
something, then slowly climbed the stairs to bed.

"Don't he look terrible, Tom," Maggie said. "Do you
think he's been drinking?"

"He always looks stupid to me, drunk or sober," was
Tom's sharp answer.

Maggie stood looking up the stairs after Al. She was
really worried. He had been behaving so strangely lately. He had always been a bit secretive, but now he was
positively sly. He had brought a friend home a week ago,
a strange, thin, white-faced boy, with long sideboards
of hair on his face; he wore a faded blue shirt and he
smelled.

"This is me mate. Met down Soho," said Al as he
introduced him.

The youth, who was called Stan, never opened his
mouth except to consume the food that Maggie put before them. It seemed as though he had not eaten for
quite a while.

"Where the devil did you dig him up?" she asked
when, after a good feed and not one word of thanks,
the boy had gone.

"Do you mind," said Al. "He's a very posh fella.
Got a big house up Hampstead. His parents have a
barfroom and all."

Al had had this obsession with bathrooms ever since
he left Aunt Dolly's.

"Well, it's a pity he don't use it more often," snapped
Maggie.

This put Al up on his high horse and for the last few
weeks he had very little to say to her. Seeing him come
in in such a state really worried her. Something was
wrong, but she could not exactly identify what it was.
Tom did not care and now there was no Jim to keep
the others in order. Perhaps it was better to let Al sort
it out himself. She held her hand to her head. These
damn boys were more trouble now than when they
were small kids.

"You want some cocoa, Tom?"

He still sat, legs up on the sofa. "If you like, Mum."

Maggie sipped her cocoa and looked at big Jim's photograph on the mantelpiece. The little kitchen was still the same, very few improvements had been made. There were the same wooden chairs and square table, faded wallpaper and that atrocious old grate that had to be black leaded every Saturday. Perhaps they'll pull it down soon and we'll get a council house. I'll leave all this lot behind and get some modern furniture. The boys might like to bring their friends home then. Tom seemed to be reading her thoughts.

"This is a proper dump, you know, Mum. All me mates got nice houses."

"I expect we'll get a council house one day, Tom."

"But when?" said Tom gloomily. "This'll fall down while we're waiting."

But Maggie was thinking of Ginger, the Christmas party and all the little ragged boys, perfectly happy, singing out there on the back yard wall. They had so little and asked for still less. They were so different to this present generation of boys. That was what was missing from the old house: the noise and laughter of the young. She knew she would have to leave one day but hoped it would not be too soon. These memories were warm and comfortable, she would miss them if she lived elsewhere. She yawned sleepily. "I think I'll go to bed."

Tom, lost in his own thoughts, never answered, so Maggie went next door to the front parlor where she still slept. Not much change in here either, she thought as she brushed her black, shiny hair. The old armchair that her lover Klause had fallen asleep in was still there. She had got rid of Liza's old bed and the bombs had smashed the vases. She slept on a settee bed now and very comfortable it was too. Yes, she certainly needed a change of scene. Perhaps the boys would settle down if they moved. Tomorrow she would go up to the council office and see what could be done. There was still Friday to look forward to. John Malloy was calling. Don't suppose he will come, was her last thought as she closed her eyes.

Friday came around very quickly. On the way home from work she bought herself a new dress. It was quite inexpensive but a very smart bright red, with white at the neck and the new length. She also bought red earrings to match. Furtively she dressed after tea hoping Tom would not notice the care she was taking and that he would soon move away from the fire and go out. I don't know what the hell's wrong with him, she thought, always indoors lately. There's Al who won't come in and Tom won't go out, you can't please them.

She made up her face and put her new dress on, combed her hair into soft curls and lacquered it. Now to face Tom.

"You're made up," was his comment. "Where you off to?"

She hesitated. "I might go to the pictures."

"What, on your own? You can't go on your own."

Maggie was beginning to lose patience. "Who's going to run away with me?" she joked.

Tom, as surly as ever, said, "You can't go running around the Mile End on your own. Why, Mum, you got lipstick on. Take it off. Makes you look like a tart."

At last her temper broke through. "Tom, go out and get drunk or something, you're getting on my nerves. I'll give you some money if you're broke."

Before he could answer there was a knock on the front door. Tom got up quickly to open it and Maggie with a sinking heart heard John's voice from the doorstep. Tom, his face very red, shouted, "There's someone for you, Mum."

"Well show him in," said Maggie. But Tom, uttering some four-letter words, pushed past John on the doorstep, shouting, "Let me out of here before I bash someone's bleeding face in," and went tearing up the street.

John Malloy stared up the street at the raging figure of Tom with amusement. Then he turned to little Maggie who stood looking ashamed. There were tears in her blue eyes.

"Well," he said to her, "let me in or someone's go-

ing to bash me flaming head in." Both of them started
to laugh.

In the kitchen he asked, "What the hell is it all
about?"

"I am not sure," said Maggie. "They're a funny lot
of sons."

"Well, if you say so, Maggie. So you've got four
now?"

"Yes," she said. "Jim and Joe are away and there's
only Tom and Al at home."

"Where's the other one?" he looked around expecting to be pounced on any moment.

"Oh, do be quiet," said Maggie. "It's no joke."

"I know, me old darling. Come and sit here and
we'll have a drink." He produced a bottle.

After that much needed glass of brandy, he said,
"Wipe those tears from your eyes, I am taking you to
see *My Fair Lady*."

"A real show? How lovely." Her eyes sparkled. "You
know, I have never been to a show up west."

"Well, Uncle John's going to take you. Come on,
Maggie, let's make up for those lost years." He drew
her toward him. Over her shoulder Jim's eyes stared
reproachfully at her from his photograph on the mantelpiece. But Maggie, throwing her bonnet to the wind,
with her arms round John's neck, closed her eyes so as
not to notice, and said to herself: I'm sorry, mate, but
I've got to go on living. And John, as he held her, said,
"I knew you were my woman, Maggie. I've always
known it."

Tom in Trouble

It was the noise in the street outside that woke her next
morning. It was remarkable that even the sounds had
changed. At one time when she lay in bed Saturday
mornings, the rattle of the milk float and the crunch of
footsteps were all that disturbed her rest. But now,
since the two huge twenty-story blocks of flats had

sprung up over the road it was quite impossible to lie in. Hundreds of children played on the green where there were swings and various amusements; and heavy lorries found their way through the widened street and shook and rattled the foundations of the old house. At night those tall gigantic towers lit up like huge crossword puzzles and the squares slowly came to life. The thought of all these little boxes frightened her.

This morning the noise and confusion outside worried her less than usual; her body stretched out luxuriously, she felt at peace with the world. She had had such a wonderful time out with John last night. Getting out of bed and slipping on a faded dressing gown, she sang a tune to herself: "Oh, so lovely sitting absolutely blooming still, I would never budge till spring crept over me windowsill."

Her voice rose high in a bad imitation of Eliza Doolittle. The songs and the music had been lovely; she never remembered being so happy. Her mind drifted to the supper and the visit to his flat. She sighed. Suppose it would have been more sensible to have come home. I knew I'd give in, I always do. I must be one of those women who can't say no. She smiled dreamily as she poured herself a cup of tea. It was nice though, better than I've ever known. Still, he had his money's worth. Don't suppose you will ever see him again. She stared miserably into the fire. Then suddenly a sweet sense of possession came over her. Silly fool, she told herself, you know he loves you. He always has.

Getting up, she began to busy about, still singing. Seems very quiet. Wonder why? Better go and see if the boys are in bed.

The beds, still neatly made, were empty. Neither Tom nor Al had been home all night. Oh dear, wonder what those two blighters have been up to. Back came the world of worry to destroy her happiness.

At midday the boys both came home. Al came in first, sickly and white with a peculiar look in his eyes.

"Where the hell have you been all night?" she yelled at him.

He opened his mouth and words just slurred out. "A party," he said.

"Some party! What a bloody state to come home in!" she nagged. Al just staggered up the stairs and fell into bed.

Then in came Tom all bright and breezy. "Hello, our Mum." He put his arm around her and rubbed the bristles of his unshaven chin on her face. Tears came into her eyes. Big Jim had always done the same when he had been out boozing and wanted to soften her up. Strange the way they still lived on in their sons.

"Don't try to soft soap me. Where you been all night?" she demanded.

"Was only round me mate's, playing cards," he protested.

"Well, don't do it again. I worry when you're not at home," she went on complaining.

"Give over, Mum, I'm a big boy now," he said. "Sorry I upset your boyfriend. You never went out with that poof, did you?" he asked.

"Don't be common," said his mum. Then with fingers crossed behind her back she said, "No, of course I didn't go out with him. He's a gentleman. What's he want to be bothered with me for?" she lied.

Tom gave her the same suspicious squint that Jim had had. "He better not start hanging around," he threatened. "I'll take care of our mum."

This is not going to be easy, she told herself.

Tom had returned to his usual seat in big Jim's armchair by the fire. He seemed very serious as he said, "Might be away for a few days. Going to drive a lorry up north."

His mum looked surprised. Not like Tom to find unnecessary hard work.

"If anyone comes asking for me, say you ain't seen me for weeks."

"Why? Are you in trouble, Tom?" she asked anxiously.

"No, just a bit of business to do. Don't want the whole bloody district to know." He pinched her cheek affectionately. "Don't worry, love, I'll be all right. Think I'll have a kip. Wake me about five." His heavy figure, so like his dad's, lumbered up the narrow wooden stairs.

She went around the house tidying up. There was an uneasy feeling inside her. Something was up with Tom and God only knows what.

She gave Tom a call at five. He came down dressed in a dark, roll-necked sweater and wearing plimsolls. He ate a good meal but seemed very preoccupied. Then he went upstairs and brought down a canvas bag he used at the gym.

"What's that in aid of?" she asked.

"It's my shaving gear and a clean shirt and a pair of shoes," he answered. Putting the bag behind the street door he said, "I'll call back for them."

Her brow creased in a worried frown as she watched his preparations. "Tell me where you're really going, Tom?" she pleaded.

His small deep-set eyes looked straight at her. "Smile before I go, Mum. Next year we'll make that holiday, I'm sure of that."

"I can't smile, Tom. I must know where you're going."

He sighed. "To do a bit of sparring up country. That suit you?" He grinned as she nodded. "It's a secret, don't tell anyone," he warned her. His old charming smile returned.

"Cross my heart," she said.

With a chuckle, Tom went out into the noisy street.

Still feeling a little disturbed even after Tom had left, she went upstairs and beat Al about the head with a slipper to make him get up for his supper. He lay like a log but after much persuasive whacking he came down, took one look at his plate piled high with food, and dashed out into the back yard and vomited.

"What the hell is wrong with you?" demanded his mother.

But Al, too ill to answer, slumped toward the fire where he sat shivering, his head in his hands.

"Better go up the bloody quack's," she groused. "Sitting there won't get you over the flu."

"For Christ's sake, give over," wailed Al.

"That's nice language as well. It's all that beer and Chinese slosh you get down your neck. Always was a greedy sod."

But Al had passed out again and was lying back with his eyes closed. Irritably she washed the dishes and decided that she would make him go up the doctor that evening. "I'll boot your backside all the way there," she called out from the scullery.

There was no reply, Al seemed to have pulled himself together and sneaked out the front door. Furiously she gave vent to her temper banging the plates until she broke one of her best ones. "All a bloody nuisance. Not worth the trouble, bringing up a family."

There was not much on the television that evening. On the nine o'clock news it was reported that there had just been a raid on a post office van on the other side of London. It did not interest Maggie much, so she turned it off.

Then came the sound of a car speeding down the street. It screeched to a standstill and out of it jumped Tom. He ran straight in and up the stairs. In no time he was galloping down again, snatching up his bag from behind the street door, calling out: "So long, Mum, don't forget what I told you," and was gone again.

Maggie could not believe her eyes. Well, that was short and sweet, she thought, and went to the front door to look down the deserted street. In her mind's eye she saw young Ginger belting breathlessly in through the front door and straight upstairs, with the copper only a step behind. He was a proper rogue, old Ginger. She thought of him fondly, for he had been a great help to her in the old days. Why did Tom run upstairs? His bag was down here. Ginger used to rush up the stairs to hide his loot, Maggie was sure of that. But Tom, not Tom! He would not be such a fool as that. No harm in seeing what was there.

So up to the boys' bedroom she went. Maggie did not know exactly what she was looking for but when she turned back the mattress on Tom's bed something crackled. There was a newly-made split in the material. Puting in her hand she brought out a parcel wrapped in brown paper. She opened it and her knees went from under her, she collapsed down onto Al's bed. The parcel contained four bundles of notes—some fives and some tens—all neatly packed together.

Sweat broke out on her brow. Her hands trembled as she held the parcel. "Oh gawd! you fool, young Tom, you bloody fool," she said over and over again. That was why he was so clinging, staying away from his old haunts; this was planned. On the telly they had said something about a raid on a post office van. The police might come here to search the house.

A sick feeling rose inside her. She had to hide it. But where? She sat for a while with the money on her lap. Then, out of the past, came a voice: "Take it Maggie, put it away for a rainy day." Of course! Ginger's "hidey hole" where she had once hidden the money Mick had given her.

She got up, weak legged, and automatically walked out to the small landing at the top of the stairs. It was dark on the landing. She felt for the hole. Yes, it was still there. She lifted the torn wallpaper and pushed the parcel in as far as it would go. Then she rammed newspaper into the hole and put the loose plaster back. She sat on the top of the stairs and stared in fascination at the hole. Perhaps she had better stick the wallpaper down, it would not be noticeable.

Going down to the kitchen to mix some flour-and-water paste, she saw in the hall cupboard a roll of wallpaper, a bucket and a brush. At some time or other Jim had been going to repaper the kitchen but it had never got done. She hesitated for a moment, then off came her dress and on went her overall. In no time she was dragging the steps upstairs and busily cutting wallpaper.

It had just gone ten o'clock when she began and by

the time she finished her back was aching, but she felt a tremendous sense of satisfaction. Now they can all come, she thought, as she sat on the stairs and admired the new interior decorating. The nice bright, clean paper went all the way up the stairs and looked very nice.

At two o'clock she made some tea and then went to bed. She lay awake staring at the shadows on the wall, waiting anxiously for news. She heard Al come slowly in and creep up the stairs but there was no news from Tom. Perhaps I should have left it there, she worried. Tom said he would be back. Still, if the coppers come, they won't find it easily. Then tiredness came over her and she drifted off to sleep not waking until the daylight crept in the windows.

At eight o'clock they came. She knew they would. She answered the door and pretended to be surprised at the sight of the two plainclothes men who stood on the step.

"Good morning, Mrs. Burns. May we come in?"

Maggie opened the door wider. "Certainly, Sergeant Murphy. It's a long time since I've seen you."

Sergeant Murphy, recently promoted to a detective sergeant, looked a bit sheepish. Maggie put on her sweetest smile. "Like a cup of tea?" she asked.

"No thanks, Maggie," he said quickly with a sidelong glance at his companion, a young chap with a thin face.

"We've got bad news, Maggie," the old sergeant said.

"What is it?" said Maggie showing great alarm. "An accident to one of the boys?"

"Not quite, he's been arrested."

"Who?" she said.

"Tom," said the sergeant.

"Oh, Tom," said Maggie calmly. "Not surprised. Been fighting I suppose. Gets more like big Jim every day. Don't live at home now, you know. I could not stand him sparring with the other two boys. Sure you won't have a cup?" asked Maggie in her best party manner.

The two policemen looked at each other and back at

Maggie. The foxy-faced one spoke up: "Mrs. Burns, your son Tom has been arrested for robbery. We have a warrant here to search your house."

"Oh!" She put on a great act. "It's not true. Tell me it isn't true, Sergeant."

Sergeant Murphy patted her shoulder. "It is, my dear," he said. "Let's look around, love. You say he's not been here, so I don't see the need to look but it's orders."

They went all over the house, looking behind pictures and cupboards. Upstairs, Al lay in bed like a statue.

"That's my young son. Come in late. You know what the boys of today are. I'll turn him out," said Maggie.

"Don't worry," said the sergeant. "Leave him there."

He turned Tom's mattress over and then banged the pillows, got down and looked under the bed. Then they took their departure. As they left Maggie stared up at Sergeant Murphy.

"What is it you're looking for?" Her eyes were full of affected innocence.

"About three thousand pounds, Maggie. That's all," he said.

"You're joking! Shall I come round and bail Tom out?"

"Waste of time, Maggie. They won't let him go till he talks."

As she closed the door the tears came. So, poor old Tom, they had caught him. But they never got the loot. If they put him away he was going to need it when he came out.

Later on, dressed in her best suit and a smart hat, Maggie marched off to the police station, her lips set in a tight line and the light of battle in her eyes.

Poor old Tom sat looking sorry for himself in a cold bare room. He seemed so tired and Maggie longed to comfort him. He made a grimace of a smile when he saw her. His mum was not weeping for him; she was just fighting fit, ready to defend him.

She sat next to him for a while very silent, knowing that a copper at the door was listening. Then she said, "Been down to your dad's grave yesterday, Tom."

He nodded, biting his lip, wondering what was coming next.

"Planted some lovely flowers on it. Don't know what they were called. I think it's primulas."

All this she said chattily. Tom was wondering what the hell she would go all the way over there for on a Saturday night. She had never been since big Jim died.

"Nice bright red they was, with dark green leaves."

Tom looked up. He had got the message. She had planted the money. Well, good old Mum. He'd do his time. Now they could all go to hell. He squeezed her hand and the policeman gave a warning glance.

"Well, I'll be going, Tom," she said. "Anything you want? Tell the old sarge, he's a mate of mine."

At this Tom really laughed. "So long, old lady. Take care of yourself," he said as they took him down again.

Outside in the reception, Maggie had plenty to say. As a matter of fact the young copper at the desk tried not to smile as her tongue whipped into the detective sergeant. He had been hanging around in the hope Tom's mum would have second thoughts and change her son's attitude.

"I want him bailed out," said Maggie defiantly.

"Well . . ." he put his hands in his pockets and began walking up and down.

"Stand still!" said Maggie, poking him in the back. "Do I get my son out or not?"

"Well, that's for the magistrate to decide in the morning," he said.

"Yes, and you got to prove it," she argued. "My Tom ain't never been in trouble before and he ain't done anything now."

"I am sorry, Mrs. Burns," he said. "But we have plenty of evidence. If you want to help him, persuade Tom to say what he did with the money. It might lighten his sentence."

"Do what?" yelled Maggie. "Do your bloody job for

you? That's right. Pity you ain't got nothing better to do, picking on innocent young boys."

After this very conflicting statement, with her head held high, she marched out.

Aimless Al

She entered the house quietly. Memories of years before overwhelmed her: her return from the courthouse with the two tiny babes after her husband had been sentenced, and the struggle for existence during those two years, ending in the death of her little girl. She looked up the stairs to the neat wallpaper, red and blue flowers, with the parcel beneath it. For a moment she faltered. No, she would not part with it. Big Jim did two years for nothing and came out with still less. Tom would have that money, she was going to make sure of that.

Al was up and sitting by the fire. He looked a little livelier than usual.

"Tom's got nicked," said Maggie.

His mouth gaped open. "What for?"

"Dunno. Been fighting, I suppose."

"Blimey," said Al. "What a show up. Hope it don't get in the paper."

"What's it to you if it does?" she picked him up sharply. He always aggravated her.

"Well, I've got my friends to think of," said Al. "Bad enough living in a dump like this without getting showed up by your brother getting nicked."

Maggie's face flamed scarlet. "Why, you selfish little sod," she said. "Not a word of sympathy for me or Tom."

"Not my doing," grumbled Al. "I mix with very posh people. Can't afford to be let down."

Maggie was in such a temper that she gasped for breath. "Well, I'm blowed, little Lord Fauntleroy and his society friends. Don't know what you get up to with them, but you look awful, like death warmed up," she yelled at him.

After that little set-to with Al, she felt exhausted and sat in the armchair to rest. Al very sulkily proceeded to get ready to go out. She watched him, thinking that as he got older he was becoming the best looking of all the boys. He was very fair with Maggie's straight line features. Wonder who these hoity-toity friends of his were. He was so deep and the only way to get information out of him was to beat him with a stick. She was beginning to feel that he was getting too big for a beating—might start hitting back, he had been a bit cantankerous lately. He came out of the washhouse looking very smart in the bright colored shirt she had got from work for him.

"Who said you can wear that shirt?" said Maggie. He never answered. He just went out and slammed the front door.

What a life, thought Maggie. Sometimes I think I'd sooner have been an old maid than have the worry of this lot. I'll go to see Joe next week. My little Joe, perhaps he'll turn out better than the others; after all, there's no Burns blood in him. Better write to Jim. He ought to come up for Tom's trial.

With a deep sigh she sat down and wrote to Jim in Bridgnorth. Then she went up the road to post it.

As she came back there was a dark shadow on the doorstep. Oh dear, they're back again, she thought, thinking of the police. But a breezy voice called out to her.

"Step on it a bit lively, Maggie Burns, I've not got all night." It was John Malloy. She ran breathless into his arms.

"Oh, I am so glad to see you," she whispered in between kisses.

"Who was chasing you?" he asked jokingly.

"Well, this will surprise you. I thought the police were."

He looked at her in amazement, then she realized they were still on the doorstep.

"Crikey, let's go in," said Maggie. "We ain't 'alf giving the neighbors a treat."

Over a bottle of cognac, they discussed Maggie's latest ordeal.

"Well, seeing Tom last week, it doesn't surprise me," said John.

"He's not such a bad boy," Maggie defended her son. "He's very fond of me. In fact I think that's why he did it."

"Well, don't get despondent, love," said John, "we will get him a good solicitor. They say in the papers that the money's still missing, well, most of it."

Maggie sat stiff and silent. Not even to John would she admit she had hidden the money.

"Did he come back here?" he asked, looking all around.

"Of course he didn't, I told you," said Maggie angrily. "Anyway, the damned police came and turned the place over."

"All right, my love, don't get shirty. It was only a passing thought. Let's go up town. Get ready, we might still catch a film."

The Junkies

Once out with John, Maggie's worries soon left her. He had a quality that Maggie had never known before: dependableness. She had felt a kind of responsibility for Jim with the same blind loyalty that she gave her sons. But with John she relaxed and felt young and gay again. You are a fool, she told herself repeatedly, at your age you should have more sense. He won't stick with you. Probably got some toffee-nosed wife somewhere. But when he put his arms around her she lost all sense of proportion and only wanted to be made love to. She did not understand herself. Jim had been very sexy and often brutal, and Maggie often tried to fight him off but it was useless. But with John she was as eager as he was. He came behind her and whispered in her ear as she made up her face. "Always time for love, Maggie," he said.

She turned and held her body close to him. "Oh gawd," she whispered. "I think you must be the lover I waited for."

John replied in a soft husky voice, "I'm glad I waited for you, Maggie. I think you must be a better woman now than you were at seventeen."

Later they strolled through the West End, hand in hand, passed the brightly-lit neon signs of Piccadilly down to the Embankment. It was a clear, crisp, cold night, a half moon shone down on the river. They looked at the Thames flowing still and silent. Young people strolled past and there was laughter and giggles from a hot-dog stall up the road.

"It's funny," said Maggie, "I never had time to stand and stare before."

"You sound like the poet," he said. "What do you mean, no time to stand and stare?"

"Don't laugh at me, John, but it's true. There was always someone who needed me. I never, until now, did anything to please myself, that's why it's all so wonderful."

He put his arm around her. "You're a strange little thing, Maggie. Let's get married."

She looked amazed. "Don't be silly, John, it's no good you marrying me. Tell me you were joking."

"Can't see why. I'm divorced and you're a widow," he persisted.

"I've still got the boys to consider," said Maggie.

"To hell with the boys. Will you or won't you?"

"I won't," said Maggie.

"Come on, then, let's go and drown our sorrows."

They went from pub to pub and then to a restaurant.

"Come home with me for a while," said John. "I'll send you home in a cab."

John's flat was in Earls Court, in a street of very tall houses where every other one was occupied by a foreigner. It was a self-contained flat with a lift, warm and very comfortable.

As they walked down the street to the end of the row, from a big house opposite there was a lot of noise.

"What's going on over there?" asked Maggie.

"Students' party," he said. "Got plenty of them here."

Just then several cars rushed up the road and a big, black police van drew up. The police poured out and ran up the steps of the big, brightly-lit house.

"Crumbs! A raid!" she exclaimed.

Down the steps they came, shouting and struggling. Young boys and girls, hanging on to each other were bundled unceremoniously into the police van.

One young girl Maggie noticed because of her lovely corn-colored hair hanging down to her waist. She shouted out four-letter words by the dozen and kicked and punched at the police escorting her. The reason for her distress was that her boyfriend was being frog-marched, not very gently, down the steps by three policemen. From among the little knot of spectators that had gathered, Maggie could see a tall, fair boy. He was quite unconscious and his long hair was over his face. But what struck her was the colored shirt. No, it wasn't possible. How could it be Al? She must be going barmy. Did look like him though, and those shirts were not in the shops yet. He had disappeared into the van and the doors were slammed shut and, amid the boos and the cheers of the spectators, the van moved off.

"Come on, Maggie," said John. "Wake up, it's all over."

"What they taking them in for?" said Maggie. "Because they were drunk? I thought you could drink as much as you liked indoors."

"They were not drunk, my love, just stoned up to the eyebrows."

"Stoned?" said Maggie. "What's that?"

"Drugs, my little angel. I doubt if you would know much about that but it's what the young generation do on their nights off. They smoke pot and shoot God only knows what into themselves."

Maggie could not forget that shirt. She recalled Al talking of his influential friends and she remembered how ill he had begun to look.

"Where are they taking them?" asked Maggie.

"Bow Street, I suppose," said John. "What's worrying you now?"

"Call a taxi," said Maggie. "Bow Street is where we're going."

"Whatever for?" asked John.

"Because I'm almost sure that that lad they carried out was my son Al."

"Oh no, Maggie," said John. "Not another one in trouble." But he put his fingers to his mouth and whistled a passing cab.

Bow Street had had a busy night and they were not in the best of moods at the desk. John made inquiries to the sergeant at the desk.

"Yes, we got 'em," he said, "and a damn nuisance they are too. What did you say his name was?"

"Allan," said Maggie. "Allan Burns."

"Some of 'em don't even know their own names," he muttered.

Soon a very whoozy-looking Al was brought in. He looked startled when he saw Maggie.

"How did you get here?" he said.

"Never you mind," said Maggie. "What have you been up to? Very nice, I must say, seeing you carted off like that."

"You can bail him if you like," said the tired policeman. "Bring him up in the morning."

While John was seeing to the arrangements for bail, and Maggie sat beside Al on the bench, she noticed that another disturbance seemed to have started up. The young blonde was being taken home by her father. He looked like her, very fair and tall with close-cropped hair and a military bearing. She was still protesting and they argued in a strange language.

Maggie was very amused. "Well," she said, "she's a spitfire. They've got a funny accent."

"Maybe South African," said the knowledgeable John.

But Al offered no comment. He just sat staring down at the ground.

"Better get him home, Maggie," said John "You have to be back here at eleven in the morning. I'll see you then."

All the way home Al never spoke, neither did Maggie. Both seemed wrapped up in their own thoughts.

3

Anne-Marie and Allan

Before they left in the morning Maggie did try to approach Al. "Listen, Al," she said. "If there's something on your mind why don't you say?" Still no answer.

"Whatever possessed you to get mixed up with those crazy drug addicts? They're as bad as the meth drinkers you see down the highway. Don't want to get like that, do you?"

"Don't be foolish, Mum. I doubt if you know the slightest thing about it."

"Perhaps I don't," said Maggie, losing her temper, "but I'll still have to pay the bloody fine, I suppose."

John and Maggie sat at the back of the court. The magistrate dealt with the whole procession of youngsters. Some were fined heavily and some got off lighter and, because they were so young, were put in the hands of the probation officer. Maggie paid the twenty pounds fine.

"Got enough?" asked John. She smiled at him gratefully; he was so good to her.

The probation officer explained to Maggie that Allan had told him about his brother being arrested, and that according to the medical reports he was not officially an addict.

"He's only been on soft drugs and he's only been taking them for a short time, so there's no need to worry. But he needs a firm hand and, if I may say so, he does not seem to be very happy at home."

Flaming little liar, thought Maggie.

"He talks of Aunt Dolly in the country. We wondered if he might settle down better away from disturbing influences."

So now I'm a disturbing influence, said Maggie to herself. A good beating is what he wants and what he's going to get.

"He has a girlfriend, he tells me, and I know her family would like him to stay with them. Perhaps you would like to meet her?"

Well, what next? But she said, "Do you mean the young lady that was brought in with him? I not only saw her, I also heard her."

"Now, now, Mrs. Burns," said this very patient probation officer. "Anne-Marie is quite a nice girl. She's a bit highly strung, that's all. She's here with her father."

Soon Maggie was being introduced to the young blonde and her father. They seemed to have recovered from last night. Both were smiling and very serene.

"So you're Al's mum," said the tall man. "I'm Ann-Marie's father. I have heard of you from Al's foster mother, Dolly. She's my housekeeper."

Oh! So it has all begun to fall into shape, thought Maggie. That's what's up with Al. Still pining for Aunt Dolly. She might have known it. And of course, this was Morris Bloom's niece—the little vixen that rode rough-shod over them all in the school holidays. It's a small world.

Maggie was polite and said, "Let's go for a cup of tea and talk things over." But she felt as if she would like to wipe the silly grin off Al's face as he looked at Anne-Marie.

So that's how they all came to be sitting in the nearest teashop, John, Maggie and Anne-Marie, Al and Lamert

de-Jager of the American Air Force, Anne-Marie's
father. Once the ice was broken they all got on well
together and Anne-Marie was a vivacious and amusing
child, but thoroughly spoiled.

"I remember Al as a lad," Lamert de-Jager explained to Maggie. "We had many fishing days with
Morris when I was on leave. Jante is my sister. You
see, my wife died in childbirth, so Anne-Marie has had
a lonely life and I was in America for years."

Maggie looked at Anne-Marie who was whispering
and giggling with Al. She did not look deprived.

"Strange you should meet again," said Maggie.

"Well, we did it for Dolly. She's always asking after
Al. So we found out where he lived."

"Oh, so that was it," said Maggie. "I suppose it
takes time to forget a boy who was with you all that
time."

"Will you let him stay with us, Mrs. Burns? Between
ourselves I am intending to keep Anne-Marie out of
London for a while and Al would be great company
for me as I am on six months' sick leave."

John looked at her and nodded his head.

It's all right for them to say but he's my own son
thought Maggie. Then her good sense prevailed. "All
right. As long as he don't start taking them drugs, he
can go where he likes."

"Now don't worry, I intend to keep those two in
order," he said.

"Can I go tonight, Mum?" said Al. "I'll come back
next week for the rest of my things."

"Please yourself," said Maggie.

She stood outside the teashop with John and watched
the smart red sportscar speed away, taking her son out
of her life. John put his arm round her shoulder.
"Home to rest, my love, we're now going to live our
own lives." That's what he thinks, thought Maggie.
But there's still three others. They still need me.

Maggie went back home on the tube. She refused
John's offer of a cab. "Waste of money in the daytime,"
she said. "Buses are still running."

At the last minute she decided on the underground. She found it a bit confusing having to change and the escalator worried her. When she at last walked down Witton Street, she felt exhausted. As she put the key in the lock, the door opened, and young Jim stood there.

"Hello, Mum." He picked her up bodily and hugged her. A good-looking Jim now had a big mustache which decorated his upper lip and his hair grew down the sides of his face in a most attractive manner. Her eldest son, Jim, was home.

"Pour out a cup of tea for Mum, Babs," he called out. "She's all in." Maggie looked out towards the scullery and saw a short, dumpy girl making tea out there.

"Meet my fiancée, Mum," said Jim. "This is Blodwen, but I call her Babs."

Babs came forward to meet Maggie. She was a bit shy but had a charming smile. Maggie liked her right away.

"Here's a nice cup of tea," Babs said. "You sit down and drink that."

Maggie sipped the hot tea. It was most refreshing. Maggie took a good look at her future daughter-in-law. She was a plain girl. This was a surprise, for Jim was such a perfectionist. She was wearing a fairly old-fashioned tweed skirt and a rust-colored home-knitted jumper. She was not even a smart dresser. Her straight black hair was twisted into a little bun, and she seemed quite at home in Maggie's funny little kitchen. A nice girl, thought Maggie, not a bit stuck up. She caught a glimpse of her eyes behind the thick, horn-rimmed spectacles. They were a deep green and shone like emeralds. All her beauty was in her eyes, deep, sea-green pools they reminded Maggie of. And she knew there was great hidden depth in Blodwen and that Jim had chosen well.

"We heard about Tom and we thought we had better come up for his trial," Jim was saying. "We can stay a few weeks, Babs is on holiday."

"That will be nice," said Maggie and began to tell Jim all.

"Don't worry," he said finally. "He'll think more of you after he's been away a while. Look at me." he said.

Maggie began to feel her old self again. They talked until very late. Babs was an ardent Communist and Jim was the same as ever, out to change the world, only in a more refined manner now. Maggie watched Babs's lovely eyes light up as she listened to Jim. More like "Jimmism" than "Communism," that she's got.

It was quite amusing when it was time for bed. Maggie yawned and said: "Shall Babs come in with me, Jim?"

Babs held grimly on to Jim's hand. "It's all right, Mum, we'll both sleep upstairs. We always sleep together." He looked Maggie straight in the eye, daring her to comment on this.

"It's all the same to me," said Maggie. "But getting married ain't going to be much of a change for you two."

"We don't believe in marriage," said Babs. "It's everyone's right to be unruled by the church."

Maggie looked at the small breasts that stuck out of her jumper and the dark rings under her lovely eyes. She won't be feeling the same next month, thought Maggie. Be more than anxious to get the ring. Looks like she's already copped. Fancy me a granny.

Life was pretty hectic in the next few weeks and Maggie gave up her job for a while. Jim and Babs went with her to Tom's trial. That dragged on for several days. Newspapers made headlines of the event and the court was crowded. Tom, solemn and quite unconcerned, sat with the three companions that had been with him. They both had previous sentences and got two years each but Tom was lucky and only got one year.

John sat in the back of the court watching Maggie's pale face as the judge sentenced Tom. His heart ached for her. He saw Jim beside her and wondered if he stood a chance against this family of hers.

He had not seen Maggie since the night Al went away. He had called the day after. A strange young man had opened the door and said abruptly, "My mother's out."

Disappointed, John had gone away.

Maggie had taken her future daughter-in-law shopping. And when she came back, Jim said, "Some toffee-nosed git called. A tall bloke. Told him you were out."

"Oh dear," said Maggie. "That's John."

"Who's John?"

"Just a friend."

"Well then, he'll keep."

I certainly hope so, prayed Maggie.

Maggie saw John in court and made up her mind to speak to him, but once it was over reporters came asking questions and taking photographs. Jim hurried Maggie into his car and they were gone by the time John had fought his way through the crowd. So once again the elusive Maggie was wrapped in the bosom of her family. "Hell," he said. "It seems a waste of time."

It was the beginning of November, the week after Tom's trial. The days had become cold and foggy and poor old Tom was now on his way to Parkhurst. Jim and Babs were still with Maggie. She found Babs very stimulating, bursting with good spirits and energy. She watched her take down shorthand notes for Jim, neat, quick and precise. Jim strolled up and down practicing speeches and they seemed to be rushing everywhere and to know everyone, visiting this club and that school. Maggie admired her and knew they were well suited. When they were not working they were making love and it became embarrassing some days, when she came in and found them stretched out on the rug.

One Sunday afternoon after dinner they were together in the armchair, and Babs's little short legs were curled around Jim's long ones. Maggie focused her eyes on the television, but the wriggles and the heavy breathing that came from the chair disturbed her. She was not sorry when they sneaked out up to bed. But she could not settle. She felt strangely disturbed, and she got up and looked at herself in the mirror. Her hair hung loose and uncombed. Not so bad for the wrong side of forty, she said to herself, and she began to pile up her hair on top of her head, placing a big comb at the back: little wisps of curls escaped from it and hung about her face. Wonder why John never wrote, she thought. Upstairs the bed creaked and her face grew hot.

Then, as quick as lightning, out came the big handbag and she carefully made up her eyes, put on a dress and a hat trimmed with fur and in no time was on her way towards the tube.

As she came out at Earls Court the fog that had hung overhead all day, began to descend but she found her way slowly to John's flat. It was quiet in the corridor, no one was about. She rang the bell. No reply. Then she tried the door handle. It swung open so she crept in.

There was no sign of John. She switched on the lamp over the shelf that held a fascinating tank filled with tropical fish. She watched them for a while, making little noises to them. Then looking around she saw bottles and glasses and plates of half-eaten food. Looks like he's had a party, she thought. Then she looked into the bedroom. John lay fully dressed on the bed, a bottle of whisky on the floor. He lay on his back with his mouth wide open. A lovely feeling came over her, she picked up the eiderdown that was on the floor and covered him up, smoothed back his hair and kissed him. He still snored. Then after a moment's hesitation, off came her dress and shoes and she got into the bed next to him. With a deep sigh she lay close to him. The evening was almost night when John put out his hand and felt her long hair on the pillow.

"My Maggie," he whispered. "My lovely little Maggie." Thinking it was some kind of dream, his arms closed around her. It was no dream to Maggie.

The Green Nightie

It was Monday midday when she woke. John still slept beside her. Oh dear, I'm a brazen hussy. Whatever will he think of me? She looked around the room. There were two wardrobes. She thought she would find a dressing gown and make some coffee.

The first one she opened was empty but for a pale-green nightie and negligee. Maggie took it out and held it against her. It was so long it trailed the floor. Blimey, I wonder who owns this. She's lanky; must be six foot! Then her face changed as she thrust it quickly back into the wardrobe. It can't be helped, it's no good me worrying, I ain't got no claim on him. But her happiness had gone. She made coffee and perched on the bed beside him.

"I am sorry, John, don't know what possessed me to do what I did."

"Why, you little devil, don't you dare say that. Why the hell do you think I was so drunk? Because I missed you, my darling." He pulled her towards him, but Maggie, with the green nightdress in her mind, pulled away.

"It's Monday," she said. "If you are going to work, you ain't 'alf going to be late."

"To hell with the office," he said. "I'm staying in bed today. I'm on my honeymoon."

"Well, I'm not," she said, getting busy clearing up the glasses and plates.

"I'm going to wash this lot up for you. Then, if you don't mind, I'll take a bath and after that I'm going home."

Home? Oh dear, whatever must Jim be thinking. She had never said where she was going. John lay sulkily in bed.

"That's just like you, Maggie Burns, leading me on, then letting me down flat. You haven't changed a bit. Don't forget what you did to me on our first date."

Trying not to smile Maggie said, "Shut up. How old are you? Eighteen or fifty?"

He rushed out of bed and chased her. They laughed and romped like two kids.

They never heard the bell, so when the door swung open and a tall, fair woman stood staring at them, Maggie was being chased around the room by John who was swinging a cushion and uttering horrible threats. They both stopped still like two kids caught by the teacher.

The woman stared haughtily at Maggie in a crumpled white slip and her hair hanging on her shoulders.

"Come in, Pat," called John, "and meet Mrs. Malloy."

He was full of beans this morning and one sour-faced secretary was not going to disturb him. Maggie darted into the bedroom to find her dress. The tall golden girl in a voice that crackled like ice said, "The office is all in, Mr. Malloy. We are snowed under with calls and nobody could find you."

"All right, darling," he said, "keep your hair on. I'll be with you in no time."

Maggie tidied herself in the bedroom and in the mirror she saw the long, slim, silk-clad legs of this girl, her short, cropped, dyed hair and the determined square chin and hard blue eyes. That's the one who owns the nightie, all right. A hard nut to crack that one. I suppose she's his secretary. They say that sort of thing goes with the job. You're no competition for her at your age, Maggie, girl.

Before John left he came and kissed her on the neck. "Don't leave me, Mrs. Malloy," he whispered. "Be here when I come home, or else."

Pat was rummaging in his desk for some papers he had lost. She never looked in Maggie's direction.

Maggie watched from the window as they got into the car. They made a handsome couple, both were tall and smart. Jealousy, a feeling she seldom had, nagged at her. Don't be a fool, Maggie, what chance do you stand against a young modern girl like that? Go home. Little Joe will be back for the school holidays soon and he'll need you now.

In John's bathroom she was in heaven. Hot water came straight out of the tap and there were lots of bottles containing powder and perfume. Why should she give it all up? Life never gave her much before, only a lot of worry. She knew he would marry her if she gave him the chance, but would he be faithful to her? You want your bloody cake and eat it, she thought. Old Jim was often off with a bird, you never really let it worry you. But this was different. To John she gave herself whole-heartedly. "Oh my God, I could not stand it." Her voice choked and her eyes filled with tears. It's not for you, Maggie Burns. The boys still need you, go home.

At two o'clock she handed the key to the janitor and left a note pinned to the door of the wardrobe that held the green nightie. "Goodbye, darling. Maggie."

There was merry hell to pay when Maggie got home. A white-faced Jim opened the door. "Good God! Mother, where have you been? I've been worried stiff. I was just going down the station to report you missing."

"And like a bad penny I turned up," joked Maggie.

"It's no joke," he said angrily. "It's upset Babs. She's been crying all the morning."

Maggie looked over to Babs. Her eyes were all swollen and without her glasses she looked very unattractive. She ran to her.

"Don't cry, love, I've been having a smashing time. I stayed up London with a friend."

"A man friend?" asked Jim, his eyebrows raised in disgust.

"Yes," said Maggie defiantly.

"Well, we will be leaving tomorrow so you can live as you please," he said, very sourly.

"Give over, young Jim," said Maggie. "You should be the last one to condemn."

Red Roses

Maggie was not sorry when Jim and his lady love departed. She saw them off. Jim was still a bit surly but Babs was very affectionate.

"Get that ring on your finger, my love," said Maggie as she kissed her goodbye. "All men are a bit selfish and that's the only weapon a woman has against them, especially when the little ones come along."

Little Babs held tightly onto Maggie. "I wish my mother was like you," she said. "I'd never have left her if she had been."

"Come back, darling," said Maggie. "And we'll have a wedding. That'll cheer us all up."

Babs smiled shyly as she got in the car. "Give my love to Tuck," called Maggie as they drove off.

She cleaned up the little house and thought of Joe. She dusted the kitchen mantelpiece and Jim's photograph. Sorry, old mate, she said to him. I've come back, haven't I? As she looked at him, she thought of Tom. Poor old Tom, so much like you even to look at. I won't leave here till he gets his money. No one's going to do him out of that. Joe will be home soon for his Christmas holidays, and I'll have plenty to do then.

There was a knock at the street door. She jumped. Her nerves were on edge, and she was in two minds about whether to answer it. But looking through the window she saw a boy on the step with a big box, so she opened the door.

"Mrs. Burns?"

She nodded.

"Sign here please."

Inside the box were two dozen beautiful red roses and on the note it said: Love you, John. x x x. He was not going to let her go. Well, what a surprise.

She put the roses in water. In the little drab room their color glowed deep red and their petals were like velvet. She could not help looking at them, and burying her nose in the deep fragrance of the blossoms. No one had ever given her flowers before. All day she prowled restlessly round the house, thinking of John. Whatever's wrong with you, Maggie? You're acting like a bloody love-sick schoolgirl.

At last in desperation, she pulled out the old-fashioned gas copper and the scrubbing board, and singing, she worked amidst clouds of steam. She was hot, and scrubbed the linen until after midnight. Then she tidied and polished everything until she was practically exhausted. She made a cup of tea. That's better. You're back to normal. Tomorrow Joe will be home, she said to herself as she fell into bed.

Joe arrived in the morning on the school bus. He stood, shy and reserved, on the doorstep. Maggie rushed to kiss him but he evaded her embrace and looked to see if the bus had gone.

"Don't want the chaps to see you kissing me, Mum," he said. "I'd never live it down."

Maggie, flustered and excited, said, "Sorry, Joe. I forgot." But once inside he held out his arms to her.

"Come on," he said, "no one's looking now. Give us a cuddle."

Dear Joe. He was taller and his voice was deeper but he was the same lovable boy, with his dark curls and deep brown eyes. Maggie, who now only reached just above his shoulder, looked up at him so proudly. She noticed his skin had darkened and there was a definite look of his father about him.

"How nice the house looks, Mum," he said. "And these lovely roses really brighten it up."

"I treated myself," lied Maggie.

Later, after they had eaten, they sat watching television.

"How you getting on at school?"

"Wait till you see my report. They are sending it on. Why didn't you come to the prizegiving?" There was a sad look in those dark eyes.

"Well, you know why, Joe. I thought I might let you down."

"Why should you do that?" he asked in surprise.

"It's hard for me to say, Joe, but you know I never go to Mass."

"That doesn't matter. It's a public school, Mum. Some of the boys' parents are divorced and some never had any religious beliefs, only plenty of money to pay the fees."

"I'm sorry, Joe, I didn't know that," said Maggie apologetically.

"Seems like I've got to educate you, Madam," said Joe in a soft superior tone.

"You do that, darling," said Maggie smiling and holding his hand as though he was a small boy.

"It's like this, Mother, dear. I get my education free. Some the government supplies and the rest the church. It's those that pay privately for their education that provide me with one, otherwise it could not survive, a big school like that."

"Do you mind, Joe," Maggie asked, "being a free scholar?"

"Of course not, Mother. I'd do anything to get this training. Without it I would never get into medical school."

"Does that mean that you want to be a doctor, not a priest?"

"That's it, Mum."

"Oh, Joe," said Maggie, "you don't know how happy you have made me."

They cuddled up close together, the fire blazing on them, and Maggie rested her head on his young shoulder.

A Moment of Truth

"I am glad I let you go off to school," Maggie said the next morning. "It's been so good for you."

"I've accepted myself for what I am, Mum. That is most of life's battle."

"What do you mean, Joe?"

"I mean I've decided that I am colored."

Maggie sat up, a knife thrust in her heart.

"Wait, Mum. Don't lose your temper, let me talk and then perhaps you will also accept it. When I lived here, ever since I could remember, I was called a black bastard by my brothers and by the kids at school. At first it was funny, I did not realize the color of your skin made so much difference. I loved you, little white Mum, but I knew that Jim Burns could not possibly be my father. I ran to you in my distress but you fussed and protected me and only made it harder."

Maggie had begun to cry silently. She wiped a tear away furtively.

"Don't let me upset you," he said. "Now, go on, it's better out than in. Well, I read books on the subject and discovered to my horror this terrible thing in God's children called a color bar. When the color of my skin was so important, I even considered that I might be a genetic throwback. But after thinking it over I realized that I was a product of an evil thing called war, and I swore that I would tear down this race hatred and no man would ever make me go to war."

"Oh Joe," sobbed Maggie. "What can I say? My little Joe talking like a grown man."

"Now hush, Mum, don't cry. Listen, I don't want you to tell me anything, it's your secret. I'll never mention it again."

Maggie cried on his thin young shouders and he held her until she stopped.

"That's better. Now let's go out to the pictures like we used to."

Maggie could not get the sadness from her heart that little Joe, unthinking, had put there. She had no defense, he knew it all and had wrapped it all into a neat little parcel and lived with it. She thought of her fears before he was born and the worry when she had had to face Jim. Yes! she had been wrong to sweep the dirt under the carpet, it still had to be faced. Then there was John. No, he would not understand about John. She remembered how Joe looked at her and said: "Is it because of me you don't go to Mass, Mum?"

"No, darling," said Maggie, "it's because I'm too lazy."

"But God welcomes sinners," said Joe, "as long as they want to be forgiven."

Maggie stared desolately at him. It was all getting complicated and she felt unable to face all these interrogations.

"Don't worry over it, darling, expect I'll get there one Sunday," she said.

Maggie began to get depressed and was glad when Joe took up with his friend Father O'Mally and disappeared each day to a place where soup was dished out to the down-and-outs.

Perhaps I'd better write to John in case he comes down when Joe is here. I never want him to know about Joe. She sat with the pen and paper, not knowing how to put into words what she wanted to say. Joe is right, I need to educate myself, she thought. I can't even write a proper letter.

She was still sitting staring at the paper when her other visitor arrived. It was Al, accompanied by Anne-Marie who was like a ray of sunshine in the gloom of Maggie's world. Her corn-colored hair hung to her waist and she wore a bright suit. She burst in, overwhelming Maggie with her vivacity.

Maggie had not seen Al since he had driven off with Anne-Marie and her father four weeks before. Here he was, very smart in a dark, tailored suit and a patterned tie, a faint line across his lip. Apparently he was endeavoring to grow a mustache.

There was nothing shy or restrained about Anne-

Marie. In spite of her upbringing, she settled in Maggie's poor little house as though she was quite used to it. Waving her hand, she said, "Like my ring? We are engaged."

Maggie looked at the expensive ring and wished her luck, knowing too well that Al, who had nothing, never bought it.

"We want you to come for Christmas," Anne-Marie said. "In fact, Dad insists on it."

"What?" said Maggie dubiously, "all that way? Besides, Joe's home."

"Joe as well, of course. And your boyfriend," she said mischievously looking at the roses.

Maggie pretended to be shocked. "What, at my age? An old woman like me? A boyfriend?" Her mouth dimpled and her eyes flashed a knowing smile.

"I hope I look like you when I'm your age," Anne-Marie said. "I'll probably be as fat as a pig."

Her light-hearted gaiety was infectious. Soon Joe came in, and over a cup of coffee they all went into stitches as Anne-Marie described the lurid details of her capture of Al, starting from when she put him up on her pony and it ran away with him.

"How's Tom?" she asked brightly. Maggie looked embarrassed.

"It's all right," Anne-Marie said, "I know he's in the nick."

She was so candid and so gay. Maggie could not understand Al allowing himself to be taken over lock, stock and barrel. But she hoped he would make her happy. It was just as well Anne-Marie had money for she doubted if he would ever earn any. The suit that Anne-Marie wore was green suede with smart tailored pants. Joe and Maggie looked admiringly at her. It was late as they said goodbye.

"Are you driving all the way back tonight?" said Maggie.

"It doesn't take long," said Anne-Marie. "We can drive faster through the night."

"Be careful, dear," Maggie said as she kissed her goodbye.

"Only good people die young," retorted Anne-Marie. "See you Christmas Eve." The red car zoomed off into the night.

4

A Spend Up

"That was a lively evening wasn't it Joe?" said Maggie as she cleared the table.

"She's lovely," said Joe staring dreamily into the fire. "I think Al's very lucky."

"That remains to be seen," said Maggie. "Do you want to go to Edgeley for Christmas, Joe?"

"Very much," he said. "I often heard the boys talking about the time when they were evacuated. I'd like to go. I bet it's really beautiful there."

"It's not quite the same now. Morris Bloom got killed and his wife went home to South Africa. I believe the abbey was sold. Anne-Marie lives in a cottage in the village with Dolly who used to be Morris's housekeeper."

Joe listened intently. "Let's go, Mum. There's nothing to stay here for."

Thinking of John, Maggie thought there could have been. She pushed the idea from her mind. She would go with Joe to Edgeley.

"Tell you what, we'll need to buy Christmas presents to take. They'll have to be nice ones. Can't show ourselves up, Joe."

"Can we afford it, Mum?" asked Joe anxiously.

Maggie went to a drawer in the dresser and produced a book. "Look, Joe," she said. "Count how much we got."

He opened the bank book and saw there was exactly two hundred and sixty pounds in there. "Crikey!" he said. "That all yours?"

"Yes," said Maggie and showed him another little book. "That's a check book. I can go shopping and just write in this and it pays for it. But I never had the nerve to do it."

"Where did you get it?" asked Joe.

"Every week I worked I put five pounds away out of my wages."

He looked at her in admiration. Little Joe, when he had money, was a shocking spendthrift.

"Tomorrow we'll go up town to one of those big shops. Do you remember when we went to Selfridges to get your school outfit? Well, we'll go and have a spend up, it will do us good. It's time I started thinking of myself."

Maggie looked up the stairs towards the place in the wallpaper. Behind there was enough. So why keep scrimping and scraping?

"Come on, little Joe, off to bed. Got an idea this is going to be a good Christmas."

It was a happy day when Joe and his mother went shopping up west. They always loved being together. Joe had a lovely unselfish manner; he never demanded anything from her and was so pleased when she gave to him. Tall and slim in a school blazer, he proudly escorted his mum, being careful how they crossed the road, holding her arm as the impatient Maggie went tearing across. "Careful, Mum," he said. "Wait for the lights to change."

"What lights?" said Maggie looking up at the traffic lights. "Can't wait all day for them." Joe laughed gaily but still held firmly on to her arm until the road cleared. They went to C & A and Joe stood looking while Maggie tried on fifty hats and then decided not to buy one.

"Let's go to Regent Street," he said. "I bet Anne-Marie buys her clothes there. She looked smashing."

They looked in the windows of the classy shops and Maggie uttered all sorts of sounds when she saw the lovely things in the window, and more still when she saw the prices.

A long green evening dress took her eye. "Isn't it lovely, Joe? Fifteen pounds. Crikey! that's a fortune. Can't afford that."

"But you can, Mum, and you'll look lovely in it."

He persuaded her into the shop and, with the air of a lord, waited while she tried it on and came out to show him how it looked.

"Gosh, Mum, you look like a duchess in that."

The long, slimline, emerald green material clung to her figure and the low neckline and sequin straps showed up her white skin and black hair. Joe's dark eyes gleamed with pride as he looked at her.

Before they left the shop a pair of velvet trousers and a high neck sweater had been bought for casual wear. "Now, that's enough, Joe," said Maggie. "I ain't never worn trousers before. I hope I look all right in them."

Joe reassured her.

"Come on, we'll buy you a nice suit and tie, Joe. Can't spend it all on myself."

They went home loaded and with only ten pounds left from the hundred Maggie had got from the bank. She felt so guilty spending all that money.

"Fancy me spending all that, Joe, we might need it later if you still want to be a doctor."

"Don't worry, Mum. You deserve it."

On Christmas Eve Maggie was thinking of John. A sad feeling came over her as she thought of him, and then of her big Jim, and even Dah.

"Funny leaving the house empty," she said to Joe. "Don't seem like Christmas with no decorations up."

"The house won't run away, Mum," said Joe. "And we won't be here to see the decorations. Get ready, they're sending a car for us at eleven."

"I suppose you're right, Joe," she said gloomily. "But I've always been at home for Christmas."

"Well, now's the time for a change," he replied. "Come on, let's put your suitcase in the hall."

Maggie stared up the stairs to where the money was hidden. I suppose it would be all right. Wish I wasn't going, she thought.

Soon a big car driven by an American Air Force captain came. He was a nice, chatty fellow and Joe sat next to him talking all the time. Maggie, wrapped up in the fur coat Tom had bought her once when he won the boxing tournament, sat like Queen Mary in the back.

As she relaxed back in the heavily upholstered seat she realized that there were not many inhabited houses left in the old street now, they were nearly all empty awaiting demolition. As they drove away she looked back. There were no eyes peering, no coarse voices jeering; just dingy windows and a few colored children playing on the pavement. Here I am all dressed up, in a posh car and no one to see and no one to care. The warmth and familiarity of the street had disappeared with the building of the tall blocks of flats. Deep down she wished she was not going, for no reason she could think of—unless it was because of John.

I wonder what he will be doing for Christmas, she thought. But the green nightgown and the tall blonde flashed through her mind. Don't suppose he'll be lonely. Got plenty of friends. I'm blowed if I'll let myself be sorry for him.

They were soon out of London and on the road to Reading. The green fields flashed past and snow flakes floated around. "I think it's going to be a white Christmas, Joe," she called out.

"Hope we get there before it gets too bad," said the driver. "Don't want to spend Christmas stuck in a snow drift."

As they drove, fluffy white flakes floated down more thickly and began to lay a white carpet at the roadside. Maggie looked intently at the station, trying to visualize the night when, with a little crowd of Londoners, she had stood watching the red glow in the sky as Hitler's bombs destroyed the dockland.

"That was the night when the street was bombed, Joe," she said. "Might never have been traveling in this posh car. Could have been shooting up daisies."

"Oh do stop reminiscing, Mother," said Joe. "We're going to a party not a funeral."

With a giggle Maggie cheered up. "You're right, Joe, I'm not very good company."

The countryside lay white and beautiful before them as they crested the hill and went down into the valley to the little village of Edgeley. The trees covered with snow, stood out white and magnificent, the leafless branches starkly outlined on the horizon, black and silver against a sky as gray as lead. It was most impressive to Maggie who had never seen the countryside in snow before. She held her breath as her eye took in the view.

"Lovely, isn't it, Joe," she said repeatedly.

Dolly's cottage was at the end of the village where the great woodland estate began. It was called Keeper's Cottage, having originally belonged to the gamekeeper. It was on a corner surrounded by an orchard and had tiny mullioned windows and a tall, brick chimney.

Al and Anne-Marie came down the path to greet them and a staid-looking Dolly stood in the doorway. Maggie was a bit shy of Dolly. As she shook hands with her, she noticed how white her hair was but that the same sweet serene smile was on her face.

"You don't look any older," she said to Maggie. "And all those lovely sons are grown men," she said putting her arm around Al. Strange, I never fussed Al, thought Maggie, he always aggravated me. Watching Al with Dolly and Anne-Marie Maggie wondered why she never fussed him. He seemed to thrive on it. He seemed shy with her, but so at home here in this cottage. Well, I failed him somewhere, but no good worrying over it. I suppose I whacked him too often or maybe it was him coming so soon after I lost that little girl.

Anyway, he seems to have found his own niche in life, and I suppose I should thank God for that.

"I hope you won't mind sharing a bedroom with me, Mrs. Burns," said Dolly, "only we are a bit pushed for space in the cottage."

"It's lovely," said Maggie, admiring the wide brick fireplace that burned huge sweet-smelling logs. Two rooms had been converted into a large sitting room, and there were big armchairs with bright cretonne covers and an old highly-polished oak sideboard. There was lots of shining brass everywhere. Dolly poured tea on a heavily laden trolley and Maggie toasted her toes by the red glowing fire.

"Call me Maggie," she said to Dolly. "It's not so formal as Mrs. Burns. I'm a widow now, anyway."

"I lost my Fred. Did you know?" asked Dolly.

"No, but I am sorry," replied Maggie.

"No need," said Dolly. "No one was more pleased than I was to see him at peace. He never got over what those Jap devils did to him."

This was said with such intense feeling that Maggie was a trifle shocked, never realizing that the calm Dolly could show so much feeling. She squeezed her hand. "We're both in the same boat now. Old Jim was never the same after the war. Seems a pity, they didn't get much of a life. Jim was only forty-eight."

"So was Fred," said Dolly. Together they sipped their tea and stared silently into the fire with the memories of their late husbands around them.

"You okay in there?" Anne-Marie came dashing in, full of beans. "Excuse us, Maggie," she said, "we're getting ready to switch on the tree. We've made the punch."

"So that's what all the laughing and chattering is about."

"I'll tell you the plans we made," she said breathless with excitement. "At six o'clock we switch on and all have some punch. Then we have dinner, and then the kids start coming. Tonight we have a teenage party, tomorrow a family party. The night after that is best of all; we go out to a dinner dance."

"Sounds hectic," said Maggie. "Hope my old bones can stand up to it."

Dolly stood up with her merry tinkle of a laugh that seemed to ripple around the room. "Get away," she said, "I bet you're worse than I am when you've had a couple."

Soon they "switched on" as Anne-Marie had predicted. In a very solemn manner they all stood around the tree with a glass of punch each, all the candles were lit and the Christmas tree blazed in its colored lights and silver trimmings. Then all sang "Silent Night." It was all new to Maggie and when she saw the three young ones—tall Al and dark little Joe with lovely golden-haired Anne-Marie between them—singing in the flickering candlelight, it went straight to her heart. It reminded her of lovely angels on Christmas cards, although she knew there was very little angelic about any of them except, perhaps, Joe.

The ceremony ended with the knocking back of the glasses of punch, which Maggie did with such gusto that she nearly choked, not expecting it to be so hot and spicy. After much back-slapping and laughter, order was eventually restored, and a starry-eyed Joe tied their presents on to the tree to be given out on Christmas Day, and Al and Anne-Marie put records on. Maggie insisted on helping Dolly prepare the meal and out in the kitchen they talked as they prepared goodies for the party. While the dinner cooked they put endless sausages on sticks and sliced cucumbers, laying out trays of this and that.

"You ought not to be doing this," said Dolly. "After all, you are a guest."

"Nonsense," said Maggie. "what else would I do? Sooner be out here with you, Dolly."

Dolly gave Maggie a generous smile. "To think I used to be a little bit uneasy with you," she said.

"I was scared stiff of you," Maggie replied. "Al never

forgot you. In fact, I doubt if you will ever get rid of him again."

As she swiftly sliced the bread Dolly smiled. "I don't mind. I've decided to go back to South Africa with them in the spring. I hope Al's coming."

"Is that so?" said Maggie. "Well, he can make his own decisions about that. What worries me is that Anne-Marie could have her choice of boyfriends, yet she picked a gormless oaf like Al."

"Don't say that, Maggie," said kind Dolly. "I am so fond of that boy. Ah, there's Bert," she said as the door bell went. To Maggie's surprise, Bert was Anne-Marie's father—he was known as Bert, or Uncle Bert to all Anne-Marie's friends.

"Lay the table in here," said Dolly. "We'll have dinner in here in case the guests come early."

Maggie laid the white cloth on the square kitchen table and marveled at the way the household was run. It was so easy-going and comfortable and what a kitchen—all white and shining, a fridge and a modern electric range. Maggie thought of her own dingy kitchen and the gloomy washhouse. It must be splendid to live like this.

They ate delicious soup made by Dolly from the turkey giblets and crisp, fresh-baked rolls, followed by cold ham and French fried potatoes and asparagus tips. It was a delightful meal. Maggie noticed that Joe was enjoying himself, watching Anne-Marie as words poured out of her well-reddened lips. But Maggie had seen the other side of the sweet Anne-Marie on the night they got Al from the station.

Soon the guests began to arrive—youngsters in all sorts of strange get-ups. They packed into the sitting room until Maggie began to wonder if it had elastic sides. All brought bottles with them and they danced a wild sort of war dance, where they stood still and wiggled and waved their arms and legs. Maggie and Bert went round with the drinks and Aunt Dolly offered tasty trays of food, until they sank exhausted in the kitchen.

"What will you have?" said Bert. "It's time we had a drink and let those kids get on with it."

The party ended in a snowball fight out in the orchard. Maggie and Bert joined in getting rolled in the snow by the young ones. The sky was clear and frosty and a lovely moon shone down on them as they pelted each other. It really was a happy Christmas. At two o'clock all the kids had gone and Joe, sleepy-eyed, had gone to bed. Al and Anne-Marie snuggled close together on the settee. Maggie, with her new jersey and pants on and snow in her hair, warmed her toes to the fire. "Oh dear," she said. "I've never laughed so much."

Bert patted her on the hand. "You're a great little sport, Maggie," he said.

Dolly said, "Come on, let's go up. Another big day tomorrow."

Maggie was so glad she had come. They were so warm and generous to her, and little Joe was happy.

She slept like a baby until Dolly's fresh face bent over her. "Like a nice cup of tea, dear?" It was Christmas morning.

Together Maggie and Dolly waded in clearing up the debris from the party. Bert was going to drive the young ones over to the camp for the service so Maggie said she would stay to help Dolly.

"You don't have to," said Dolly. "I'm used to it, I can manage."

"I never go to church," said Maggie.

"I thought you were a Catholic," remarked Dolly.

"I was, but don't know what I am now," she replied.

"Never mind," said Dolly. "Women don't get a lot of time to go trotting off to church. I say my prayers at home and they suffice."

But Maggie was silent thinking how lovely it was at midnight Mass with Dah at her side.

With a bottle of sherry between them and chatting all the time, they prepared the dinner. Most of it was ready cooked and needed only to be heated.

"Seems such a lot of food to me," said Maggie. "I

don't suppose you have ever known what it was to be hungry."

"I have, and I always think of it at Christmas. Why do you think I was in service at thirteen? There were too many of us in my father's tiny cottage."

"I never think of country people being poor," exclaimed Maggie.

"In some ways we are a lot poorer. There were lots of things we did without, like shoes and toys at Christmas. I was a poor little devil in my first job, hands red and raw and smothered in chilblains. I'd have to be up at five to light the fires and out on freezing cold mornings scrubbing the doorsteps."

Maggie remembered how she went round with the bucket to do the doorstep, cleaning for her mother-in-law. She felt suddenly close to Dolly. "It's funny how you think people are different from you and find out it's all the same."

"Of course," said Dolly. "We are the working people, the salt of the earth." She raised her glass of sherry. "Here's to us, a very merry Christmas." So they both proceeded to get tipsy.

In spite of the amount of sherry consumed, the dinner was a great success. They had turkey, crisp and brown, cranberry sauce, and Christmas pudding lit up with brandy. Bert had brought back two fellows from the camp and two old friends of Dolly's had also come from the village. Afterwards they played Monopoly and then taught Maggie how to play dice. Then they all got up and danced to records. Maggie kissed all the men under the mistletoe, and danced a wiggly dance, something in between the jitterbug and a modern dance.

The highlight of the evening was the show. Everyone dressed up and did a turn. Maggie, dressed in Anne-Marie's ballet outfit with a silver star on her forehead, sang in a high-pitched, out-of-tune voice, "No One Loves a Fairy When She's Forty," and wiggled and cocked up her legs like a young girl. Al had his face blacked to the same color as Joe and a great white line around his mouth and eyes, and white gloves. He and Joe danced together, singing Dixieland songs, while Anne-Marie in tights, twisted herself into acrobatic knots. Dolly asked to be excused. Her face was brilliant red with the effect of the sherry and she could not remember the words of the song she usually sang. So Bert and his pals sang suggestive songs at the piano.

"Good enough for the West End," he commented when the show was over and the guests were drifting home.

Maggie was having difficulty in dislodging the grip Bert's friend had on her and, when he insisted that she walk to the gate with him, Joe came to her rescue and piloted him to the car.

It was never to be forgotten that Christmas.

Boxing Day

It snowed heavily in the night. There was a silence when Maggie awoke as though the world outside stood still. Dolly was already up. But Maggie's head felt as though a sledgehammer was pounding it.

"Too much booze, I suppose," she said when Bert brought up the black coffee.

He said, "Dolly's all in too. Never mind, I'll take you for a walk. It'll do you good."

After a bath and more coffee she felt better, but Dolly still wandered zombie-like around the kitchen clearing up after the young ones. They had made their own breakfast and gone off over the hill with skis and a toboggan.

"I'll help you, Dolly," Maggie volunteered.

"No, love, go for a walk. I'll soon come round," replied Dolly.

So off they went, a little dark-haired figure in a white raincoat and red wellington boots beside the tall, smart figure of Bert, through the snow-covered village, up to the top of the hill where they could see the kids having a good time. Then they went back down the hill to the local for a special pick-me-up recommended by the landlord. As they sat by the roaring fire, Maggie said, "I'd like to thank you for this lovely Christmas."

He looked at her kindly and grinned. "It's not over yet," he said. "God knows what Anne-Marie's got laid on for tonight. A ball, I think. I leave it all to her."

"She's a lovely girl," said Maggie.

"Only when it suits her," replied Bert. "I've always given in to her. I did to her mother too—I can't help myself."

"Well, she's none the worse for it," said Maggie. "You know, I've never enjoyed myself so much."

"Well, we might be related soon, so perhaps we will have a few more Christmases together," he joked.

"Do you think they'll marry?" asked Maggie doubtfully. "They're a bit young. I know I was married at fifteen . . ."

"Weren't you happy, Maggie?" he asked.

"In a way I was, but I had no choice. I got into trouble and that's a bad start. You never get to know yourself, too busy with kids and making ends meet."

Bert looked thoughtful. "Did you know I was leaving the forces in the spring?" he asked.

"Yes," she replied. "Dolly told me you are going to South Africa."

"Anne-Marie won't come without Al, and I can't leave her here, not since that trouble with the drugs. Will you let Al go?" he pleaded. "I promise you if they decide not to marry, I'll send him back home. I have already told Anne-Marie that she can marry Al if she still wants to when she's twenty-one. I trust Al. After all, I knew him as a boy and the devil you know is always better than the devil you don't."

After this long speech, he put his hand to his head and sat looking into the fire. Maggie put her hand on his arm. "Stop worrying," she said. "Al is much happier with you than he was with me. I wouldn't be much of a mum to spoil it would I."

They sat silent for a while after that long discussion.

"Well," Maggie exclaimed, "I feel much better now."

And she looked it, the color had come back into her cheeks and her eyes were brighter. Bert stared at her curiously. "You know for your age you are a very good-looking woman."

She giggled. "Beauty is as beauty does," she quoted.

"No, I am not after anything," he protested. "I was thinking of John Malloy and whether you'll marry him."

Her face lost some of its color again.

"How did you know?" she asked very astonished.

"I saw you together at the court, the night the kids were arrested," replied Bert.

She thought for a moment, then she said, "Of course I remember, but how did you know who it was?"

"Everyone knows him, and in the States more so," exclaimed Bert.

"Why?" gasped Maggie. "What's he done?"

"Done? Nothing. He's famous. Didn't you know? He's a scientist, an authority on rock structure. I've worked with him in connection with the air force. You mean to say you didn't know?"

She shook her head dumbly, feeling very ashamed.

"When we get home I'll show you some old magazines with pictures and write-ups of him."

But there were tears in her eyes. To think she who loved him knew so little about him. She felt suddenly crushed and very humble.

"What's the matter, Maggie? Have I upset you?" inquired the kindly Bert. "I'm sorry, I never knew it was like that. You see, I was beginning to fancy you myself."

He put an arm about her and laughed boisterously. "Now it seems I don't stand a dog's chance. Come on, darling, let's go home."

"Don't mention John in front of Joe," she requested as they went up the path.

Dolly had recovered and there were plates of cold turkey, pickles and salad laid out for lunch. The young ones had already eaten and lay around the fire, fresh and glowing from their antics in the snow.

After lunch Bert found the old magazines and put

them in Maggie's lap. There were photographs of John in a boat and John at a very highbrow dinner. They made her feel very small and insignificant. She, who could not even write a proper letter and had never read a book, did this man such a favor as to sleep with him. He could not have been serious about marrying her. But she had swallowed it all. She thrust the magazine away impatiently.

Bert watched her with amusement from the other side of the room. "We should all have a nap to be fresh for the evening," he suggested. So they all separated, each to lie down. In Dolly's room Maggie wept into the pillow.

The Big Do

Dolly insisted on dressing Maggie's hair in preparation for the evening's "big do." She did it very well, piling the black curls high on Maggie's head, giving her height, and holding it in place with a pretty jade clip.

"I used to be a lady's maid," she said as her nimble fingers twisted the little curls. "That was before I married Fred."

"Aren't you coming?" asked Maggie.

"Good gracious," replied Dolly, "of course not. We're a bit informal here but, after all, I'm still a paid servant."

"I'll stay with you," said Maggie.

"No, you won't," said Dolly. "Get that nice dress on. Makes a change for Bert to have a lady to escort."

Maggie rubbed her chin on Dolly's hand like a cat that gives a gesture of affection. "You are all so kind to me," she murmured.

"Kind?" declared Dolly. "Why, we love having you. Your son's brightened my life and gave me something to live for when I lost Fred."

Anne-Marie had been supervising Joe's dressing. She had borrowed a dress suit for him. Now she came to see how Maggie was getting on. "You look super," she said. "Wait. I'll get you something to wear with that lovely dress."

She returned with a long pair of jade earrings and a necklace to match. "Borrow these," she said. "They were my mother's, Dad won't mind."

Al was ready and waiting down in the sitting room when Maggie went down. Bert had a tray of drinks already poured for them and Anne-Marie looked as smart and sophisticated as ever in a black velvet dress trimmed with white fur.

"Oh dear, I feel half undressed," said Maggie.

All together they said, "You look super."

"Where are we going?" asked Maggie as the car sped swiftly along the dark country lanes.

"To a house a few miles away," said Bert. "It belongs to a very old English family, but now they live abroad, so it's leased to an American, my commanding officer, in fact."

Maggie felt very excited at the prospect of dining out but was terribly nervous in case she did anything wrong.

"Oh dear, I hope I won't let you down," she cried.

Bert laughed. "Be your own charming self," he said, "and you will be belle of the ball."

They walked up a flight of white marble steps and entered the big house; the bright lights and the chatter of voices confused her. She gripped Joe's arm for a second. "Don't go far away, Joe," she whispered. "I am ever so nervous."

"Don't be silly, Mum," he said. "Relax and enjoy yourself." Anne-Marie whisked Joe off to introduce him to his partner for dinner, a stout young girl in a pink dress. Maggie managed to find the cloakroom, handed in her coat and sat at a little dressing table to powder her nose while all around her ladies talked very loudly and plastered lots of make-up on their eyes. In the mirror she saw her pale face and dark hair and the lovely necklace and earrings. Don't worry, you look as good as any of them, she told herself. She got up and sailed down the stairs to where the others were waiting.

The spacious room with great chandeliers and long tables shining with silverware and gay with candles and flowers, was so splendid that she held her breath for a moment. Then, head held high and her arm through Bert's, who patted it reassuringly, they went in to dine. The array of knives, forks and spoons bewildered her but she watched carefully to see what Bert did, and somehow she survived. All around, conversations were being held. A fat middle-aged man kept filling Maggie's glass from a bottle on the table. "Drink up, old girl," he said. "Keeps the cold out."

Maggie did so rather rapidly and in no time was listening to him talking about dogs. At first she thought of "the dogs," known in the East End—the greyhound track—but listening carefully she realized that these dogs he referred to retrieved animals and birds after they had been shot at, and had very soft mouths. She agreed with all he said and was not sorry when he lost interest and began to talk to a gawky female with a feather in her hair on the other side of him.

Bert leaned over and said, "Soon be over, honey. It's a bit of a bore, but look at the kids enjoying themselves down there." The young ones were all together at the end of the table and the wine had begun to take effect.

Maggie wondered whether she ought to talk about dogs but the only dog she had known was one called Pie Shop.

"Called what?" roared Bert, who went off into one of his fits of loud laughter. "Tell me, Maggie," he said, "about this Pie Shop."

So Maggie explained how Pie Shop had never let Jim get into bed when he came home on leave and described the battles that he and Jim had had. Not only Bert listened but gradually most of the others at the table joined him, and all thought Maggie charming and amusing. The ice was broken and Maggie began to enjoy herself.

After dinner the guests retired to an even more magnificent room with a highly polished floor for dancing. It was like a dream. A long gallery surrounded it and huge portraits hung on the walls. Maggie marveled at the lovely colors of the ladies' dresses as they danced under the spotlights. She herself had natural grace and, in spite of never having had any dancing lessons, she was able to follow her partners.

As she sat for a while to rest her aching feet, she noticed that Al stood on the stairs pointing to a big portrait. Around him were several men. He seemed to be drawing their attention to this big picture of a crinolined lady and everyone was laughing.

"Come here, Joe," she called as he went past. "Go and see what Al's up to."

Joe's white teeth showed in a merry grin. "He's showing off as usual," he replied.

"What's the joke?" Maggie asked.

"That's the same portrait that he and Tom cut out of its frame and ran off with. The owner had it restored."

"Oh dear, trust Al to show us up." Maggie was truly dismayed.

"Shouldn't worry too much, Mum. The Yanks love that sort of thing. Al's very popular with them."

But still Maggie sat looking very forlorn—she was thinking of poor old Tom spending Christmas in a lonely prison cell. Bert came and found her and dragged her to her feet. "Come on, Maggie, you can do this."

The band was playing jigs and reels. Maggie's Irish blood could not resist the excitement of it all. She danced until dawn, and they drove home through the snow-covered lanes as the cock crowed to herald the light of day.

Bert and Maggie had breakfast alone the next day. Anne-Marie and the boys had gone to the town with Dolly.

"This has been a wonderful holiday," she told Bert gratefully.

"Come back in the spring," he urged. "It's lovely here then."

"You go home in the spring?" she asked.

"I'd like to stay. To me there is no place like this English village."

"Must you go?"

He shrugged his shoulders. "Money reasons mostly," he said.

"I thought you had plenty," she replied.

"Well, I'm not hard up, but I will be when I leave the forces, unless I find another occupation."

"I never think of you as working class like myself."

"We're all working class," replied Bert. "My folks were farmers. Boers they called them. Tracked hundreds of miles in a wagon to seek new land. I belong to that land, that's why I am returning to South Africa."

Maggie sat in the window seat and stared out into the big orchard behind the house. The sky hung heavy with more snow and the branches of the cherry tree traced a pattern on the gray sky. There is something about life in the country, a feeling I never had before, Maggie thought, a kind of stillness inside. Bert smiled a trifle sadly as he looked at her.

"I am so pleased you like it here, Maggie. It is probably just what you needed."

"I've never seen Joe so happy." She paused reflectively. "Up here he's been treated the same as everyone else."

Bert looked puzzled. "Why not?" he asked.

Then, without hesitation, Maggie began to talk about Joe and Bert listened very sympathetically.

"I've never been able to make close friends, not since I had Joe. I never wanted to be questioned about him. Can you understand that, Bert?" She looked at him pleadingly and her blue eyes seemed to bore into Bert's very soul. He felt a queer sense of emotion as this little woman tore down all barriers of restraint. What answer was she seeking? It was obvious that Joe was colored. He must be careful, it seemed very important to her.

"Come let us sit by the fire," said Bert, "and I'll tell

you about my country. Perhaps it will answer your question.

"My land is beautiful," he began proudly. "There are great mountains and rivers, and it covers an area so immense that there are parts of it where no white man has ever trod. It belongs to the black man and the beat of the black heart is there all the time—a warning drum that calls out that this is their land. The white men brought money with them. Black and white killed each other for gold and the diamonds buried deep in the rich earth." He stopped for a moment. "Am I boring you, Maggie?"

"No," she said. "Go on, it's like a story."

"I am trying to explain how the black man is the white man's servant now. They do all the rough jobs, look after the children. Civilization brought them slavery. If a black man is stupid enough to love a white girl he will be hounded to death. If a white man wants a black woman he takes her. Any children are her responsibility. It's called a color bar and there's going to be bloody murder out there one day."

"Sounds terrible," said Maggie looking scared. "Don't go back there, Bert."

He began to laugh, realizing that Maggie had only taken half of it in. He cuddled her. "Look after your son, love. Give him a good education. The barrier is greatest where there is nothing to offer."

"You know, Bert, I never told my old man the truth about Joe."

"No joke. How did you get away with it?"

When she told him how Jim had said he had never seen a black Irishman, Bert laughed until he burst. "You know, Maggie, that husband of yours must have loved you a great deal."

"I know," she replied. "In his rough way I was everything to him, that's why I don't want to leave my little house."

He looked astonished. "But he's dead, isn't he?"

"Yes," she replied. "It might sound foolish, but I feel he's still there."

He took her hand. "I know the feeling. My wife is still in our home in South Africa. That's another reason for going home."

They sat silent for a while until Anne-Marie burst in. "What have you two been up to?" The house came to life once again.

5

The Aftermath of Christmas

Loaded with Christmas presents and pots of chutney from Dolly, Maggie glanced back at Al's long, lanky figure and Anne-Marie's golden head as they waved goodbye from the gate. She thought how lucky they were not to have to leave that warm cozy home. As the last glimpse of the red chimneys faded from sight, Maggie had already decided that when Tom came home she would buy a cottage in the country. To hell with the council and their twenty-story flats.

The journey home did not seem to take so long. The same pleasant man drove them back, and he and Joe chatted about Christmas and Joe leaned back like a real man of the world smoking a long American cigarette. As they passed London airport the jets zoomed overhead and Maggie ducked her head. "I never knew they made all that noise. Won't catch me up in one of them."

Joe said, "Mum won't go up a block of flats let alone in an airplane."

"Well, what's she going to do when we get to the moon?" quizzed their chauffeur.

"Stop kidding," replied Maggie. "I'll keep my feet on the ground till I get to heaven and that's rather doubtful."

"Do you think we will ever conquer space?" asked Joe in a very serious tone.

"Ten years from now we Yanks will," the man replied with confidence.

But Maggie was lost to the rest. She was looking at a car as it waited at the crossroads. It looked like John inside. In fact, she was almost sure, but with that soft felt hat obscuring his features, it was hard to tell. Then, in the back seat she saw the efficient Pat, whose short polished hair shone as her head bent over the paper in her lap. The car sped on and Maggie looked the other way. Going to the airport to meet someone, she thought. Think I'll go and see him tomorrow.

It was not long before the East End street came into view and Maggie was home again. As soon as the luggage was dumped in the passage, Joe said, "I'm going out, Mum. Won't be long."

She knew he was off to find his friend Father O'Mally to tell him of the wonderful Christmas he had had. The house felt cold and deserted. It reminded her of the day she came home after the blitz had ended.

On the mat were three letters. She picked them up. One from Tom with Her Majesty's stamp on it; one from Jim at Bridgnorth, and the third one, just a plain buff business envelope, bore no stamp. She turned it over and over in her hand, then slowly opened it.

It was her first love letter from John, there were two envelopes inside, it read:

Maggie darling,

I have waited anxiously for you to come to me and many times during Christmas I have waited outside your house in the cold and dark, wondering where you were, my love. You came to me of your own free will and I called you Mrs. Malloy because I felt that you belonged to me at last. What did I do that you should leave me again? I have grown too fond of the bottle since I lost you so I must get back to some real work. I cannot let even you destroy all I've worked so hard for so I am going back to Canada. Inside there is money for your passage and expenses to join me out here. Come to me, darling. I swear before God I will be good to you. Break from that dreary life that should never have been yours and come to this beautiful country and let us spend the remainder of our lives together. Please Maggie, darling, this is the last time I will ever ask you. Don't let me down, darling, you know we belong together.

All my love for ever,
John

P.S. Name of solicitors in Quebec in other envelope. Wire when you are coming.

The letter crumpled in her hand and, laying her head on the table, she cried her heart out. In her mind the image of that blonde head in the back of the car cut like a knife. "I've lost him, I've lost him," she repeated over and over.

Joe was rather surprised when he returned to see the lights still out and no fire in the grate and Maggie with her head on the table, her eyes red with crying.

"Who's upset you?" asked Joe. "What's the matter, Mum?"

Maggie got up quickly shoving the letter into her pocket. "Got a headache, that's all," she replied crossly. "Don't stand there like an idiot. Put a match to the fire." She went out to put the kettle on and Joe called out: "You haven't opened Tom's or Jim's letter, Mum. Shall I read them to you?"

"If you like," she answered.

Over a hot cup of tea, Joe read out Tom's pathetic little letter. It was not much, just briefly thanking his mum for the extras they had been allowed at Christmas, and said how he missed her. He also sent her a pass to visit him in the New Year.

"Poor old Tom," said Maggie. "I must go and see him."

They read Jim's. Bright and breezy, Jim informed them that he had got married by special license on

Boxing Day and, not to her surprise, that Maggie was to be a granny in the spring.

"Thought she would change her mind, once he got her in the pudding club," said Maggie gloomily.

"Done what?" Joe looked very puzzled.

"She didn't believe in getting married. Those Communists don't."

Joe was looking more surprised than ever.

"Who's a Communist?" he asked.

"Jim and his bird. What's up with you, Joe? Can't you even take a simple thing like that in?" she said irritably.

Joe looked offended. "I was not aware, Mother, that any of my family were Communists, apart from the fact that Jim's marrying one."

"So what?" argued his mother. "It's only politics, nothing to do with religion."

Joe had gone unusually pale. "Not according to Father O'Mally. He tells me they are heathens. They don't believe in Jesus Christ."

"Oh dear, no they don't. I forgot that. Don't let it upset you, little Joe."

Joe sat very haughtily with arms folded, staring at the blank television screen.

"Don't take any notice of me," pleaded Maggie. "I always get hold of the wrong end of the stick. Don't understand a lot what goes on." At all costs she must get back in Joe's favor.

Joe gave her his charming smile, "No, I don't think you do, little Mother."

Maggie lay tossing and turning, she could not sleep, there was too much on her mind. A moving pattern of lights reflected on the ceiling from the flats over the road. Someone was having a party. The sound of the music came drifting through the window. It must be nice to live in the country. She remembered the deep silence of the night at Edgeley. How easy it would be to open that other envelope and get a passport to a new life. She could not leave Joe, not now that he was making so good at school. Then there was Tom's money tucked away behind the wallpaper. How often she had regretted that impulse to hide it. She would probably be sent to prison if anyone found out. A kind of panic assailed her. She got up and wandered about. John would never understand her loyalty to her family. He could not, he had never wanted for anything. The years were flying past. What right had she to try and turn the clock back? No, her duty as a mother must come first. Suppose she never ever saw or heard from him again? A black despair descended, obscuring all her reasoning powers. She threw herself on the bed and wept till sleep released her temporarily from her troubles.

Joe went back to school the next week. "Take my library books back, will you, Mum?" was his last request.

She took the heavy books on science and chemistry, put them in her shopping bag and set out for the library. I suppose I'd better get a job now, she thought. I'm going to miss Joe. And I ought to write to John and explain. When she thought of writing that letter, it made her head spin.

Once in the library her eyes scanned the shelves of books. All that knowledge up there and what do you know, Maggie Burns? Nothing. Can't even write a letter, she told herself. She picked up books and put them down. Don't even know where to start. Then her eyes caught the familiar title of a book she had seen at school: *Little Women* by Louisa May Alcott.

So began her self-education. In several weeks she mastered the simple elements of the English grammar. She was very pleased with herself. She bought a good pen and paper and first tried out a letter on Tom. She picked out all the big words from the dictionary and was quite proud of herself when she posted the final result.

"What's up, Mum? You swallowed a bleeding dictionary?" was the reply she got from Tom. Then, starting off with a book for reference, Maggie wrote her first love letter—to John:

> John darling,
> I want to come to you, my dear. You will never know how much I love you but my life has always been like this, used up. I never get a say, it makes decisions for me. Perhaps it's because I am not a good woman and this is my own special kind of hell, but you will always be within my heart. If you ever return I'll be here when you want me.
>   All my love,
>   Maggie.

Taking the buff envelope with the money inside she went straight to the post office and registered it back to John, immediately feeling better.

Well, that's off me chest. Now I had better do something about a job seeing as I'm not going to be a kept woman after all.

Along the Mile End Road a new kind of shop had sprung up. They were called supermarkets and instead of standing in a queue waiting to be served, you just walked in with a basket and helped yourself. It really amazed her; knowing how the East Enders had sticky fingers she wondered how they managed to get paid for the goods. Something like old Sarah's in-and-out shop, and God knows they nicked more from her than she ever sold. Recently Maggie had mastered the intricacies of one of these new shops and realized that they kept you waiting at a little gate until the money was handed over and woe betide anyone who tried to dodge out. The local papers were full of those cases.

"Looks like they are trying to reform us East-enders," was her wisecrack to the manager.

He liked her jolly comments and each morning he greeted her pleasantly. "Want a job, Maggie?" he inquired.

"Job?" she answered. "What would I do in here?"

"Cashier," he answered.

"Get away, I can't count," she retorted. "You're having me on."

"No, it's easy. Watch." He showed how they added it all up.

"Well, I'm blowed. Do you think I could manage that?"

"I am sure you could, and a bright little person like you will bring in plenty of customers."

So Maggie was installed in the new supermarket. She sat upright in her cubicle with her hair tied back and wearing a smart blue overall. She loved the flow of people in and out, all the gossip that went on, and the wages cheered her up. It took years off her. The local people liked her, she was always smiling and laughing.

Months flew by and then Maggie received a strange letter from Tom. It worried her. He wrote to say that Terry was out of the nick and back in Stepney. He added: Be very careful, Mum. Don't forget about Terry. He's the one that plays the drums. Well, what did it mean? Terry was the brother of the boy who had gone inside with Tom. He came from a family of local criminals. One of them was always going in or coming out. But why should it worry her? Plays the drums? What's wrong with Tom? Going crazy or something? Perhaps I'll go and see him, she told herself as the register clicked and the customers streamed past.

Two women were talking in loud voices as they waited with their huge baskets of shopping; she caught scraps of their conversations.

"Always this time of the year. After me electric money they was, turned me flaming drum over, the bastards. Got away with sixty quid."

The drum! Why, the burglars had been in. That was it. The old East-ender's slang: "turned the drum over" meant your house was to be ransacked. Why didn't she remember? Oh God, was it too late? Tom's mates were going to look for the loot. What could she do?

At six o'clock she was on her way home. There was a kind of murky gray dusk and the street looked desolate and empty, the old houses empty and boarded up. Only her own little house still stood untouched. Its shiny windows and flowered curtains were the only bright spots in this desolation. Recently, down-and-outs had moved into the empty houses and lurked furtively in dark corners. Blimey, she muttered, what a dump. It's time I moved. A strange apprehensive feeling went through her as she put the key in the lock.

Instantly she knew she was too late. The door swung open with a protesting squeak. The lock had been forced. She stood perfectly still. Suppose someone was in there? What should she do? Run for the police? No, not that. Negotiate? Wonder if I'm brave enough. Screwing up all her available courage, she called out: "All right, I know you're in there. Come out."

There was no reply. Drawing a deep breath she went marching in. Chaos met her startled eyes. There were drawers pulled out, pictures off the wall, lino ripped up and everywhere things were thrown and broken. So incensed was she at the sight of the shambles that she forgot they might be waiting with a cosh. She ran around picking up articles from the floor. "The flaming so-and-sos!" Her language got worse with her temper. Then, looking up the stairs, she saw the wallpaper was still intact and burst out laughing. Well, they never found it, that's a good joke. Wait till I tell Tom about this.

She tried to tidy it up a bit, picking up papers that had been thrown down from the mantelpiece. She found several letters from the council that she had not bothered to read, telling her that her house was to be demolished in the slum-clearance scheme. They had offered her a flat.

"They can stuff their bloody flats," she grumbled. But I ought to get out of here now, she thought, they might come back. This thought really frightened her. She put on her coat again and went hurrying to the police station.

"I want to see Detective Sergeant Murphy," she demanded.

Out came her old friend, stouter than when she had last seen him.

"Sitting up here on your fat backside," declared Maggie, "and in broad daylight me house is broken into."

"Is that so, Maggie?" he said mildly. "I'll send someone down. What did they take?"

"Nothing," she said aggressively. "What could they flaming well take? Ten bob is all I get on widow's pension and I ain't saved much on that."

"Look here, Maggie. Don't get alarmed, but it could be one of Tom's friends. They never found that money you know."

"Well, it's not in my house." Her face blazed red and angry. "They turned my bloody house upside down, the bleeders. I want police protection, that's what I pay rates for."

"All right, Maggie, calm down," he begged. "We will see to it. It's a pity it never turned up, that money." He gave her a sideways look. "Might have been able to appeal against Tom's sentence if it had."

She stared straight at him, her eyes like blue fire.

"Look here, Sergeant, Tom didn't live at home when he got into trouble. You know I would never have allowed him to consort with those villains."

"Perhaps you're right," sighed the sergeant. Maggie always flummoxed him. She always had, even when he was a bobby on the beat and chasing young Ginger.

"I'll put a constable on watch," he said. "Go home, love, and get a good night's sleep."

She came home very pleased with herself. That will fox Terry. He can't afford to be nicked again. Looking up the stairs she said, "Won't be long now, Tom. I'll see they don't get your loot."

This was the obstinate streak in her that made her refuse to admit to either Joe's illegitimacy or the whereabouts of Tom's money. A law-abiding person might not approve of this strange instinct for survival, it was almost primitive. She had her own code of honor and no one would move her.

The Prodigal Son

In the morning Maggie looked out of the window. The police car was still there. Can't go to work until I get a new lock for the front door, she thought. I think I'll go up the council offices, see if I can get a house out of them. Don't fancy those flats.

She was about to slip on her coat when a taxi drew up outside; Jim and his new wife had returned home. Babs, tearful and very heavy with her pregnancy, hung on to Maggie. Jim looked travel-weary and slightly anxious.

"Hello, Mum, we thought we'd surprise you."

Maggie, eyeing the amount of luggage in the passage, was almost ready for the surprise.

"We've come to stay," announced Jim. "I thought of you on your own and decided that Babs would be company for you."

"That's nice," replied Maggie wondering what the real reason was. "Sit down, darling," she said to Babs, who was blinking owl-like at her through her thick lenses, her lips quivering nervously.

"Crikey!" exclaimed Maggie. "You got a big lump there. When's it due?"

"Four weeks," whispered Babs, "and the doctor says it's twins." She began to howl and it took quite a while to pacify her.

"We were in furnished rooms and the old cow of a landlady made Babs's nerves bad, kept complaining," said Jim.

"Just like bloody foreigners," said Maggie. "Never mind, love, plenty of kids been born in this house, don't suppose a couple more will hurt it."

Jim was looking at the torn lino and the broken locks. Maggie put a warning finger to her lips and he understood that she did not want to scare Babs.

Soon they were unpacked, they all sat around the old familiar kitchen table for breakfast.

"It's nice to have the family around the table," said Maggie.

"You're a good old mum," declared Jim. "I was at my wit's end. It was Tuck who suggested it."

"Oh, did he?" returned Maggie.

"Yes," went on Jim. "If this is going to be pulled down, we'll get a flat if you say we live here."

So that's it. They know where to come when it suits them, she thought a little bitterly.

"Old Tuck's got another idea."

"He seems to be full of them," said Maggie dryly.

"He's going to put up the deposit and sponsor me for a seat," burst out Jim excitedly.

"A seat?" She opened her eyes wide. "What sort of seat?"

"To be a member of parliament, Mum, to represent the district."

Maggie had always been a bit suspicious of Tuck ever since the old days when he had led her big Jim into politics. She eyed her son very shrewdly. "How can he help you?" she asked.

"It's easy enough, Mum," replied Jim.

"Jim, stay here and work hard, but stay out of politics. It only brought your father into trouble. Be careful," she warned.

"But, Mother, Dad only had ideas. I've got the practical knowledge and influence to back me up."

"Well, I suppose you know what you're about. But don't say I didn't warn you."

"Tuck's not feeling so well this year. He wants to retire," explained Jim, "so he's helping me to achieve his life-long ambition to gain a seat for the East End, the original home of Communism."

Maggie looked dismayed. "Oh no, Jim, not those heathens who don't believe in God?"

He looked in amusement at her. "Don't be silly, Mum, it's politics, nothing to do with religion."

"Well," returned his mum defiantly, "the church doesn't like it, so Joe tells me."

Jim's fiery temper began to rise. "Oh! so what bible-punching little brother says is the gospel I suppose," he replied sarcastically.

Their eyes blazed and they stood challenging one another. Babs stepped in as the peacemaker. "Mum," she said, "we fight for the rights of the workers. You don't want your grandchildren to live like this, do you?"

This only heaped more coals on the fire. Maggie got up, banging the plates as she cleared the table. "I've got no time for these 'isms' and 'asms,'" she declared. "They won't do a bit of good here."

Babs and Jim looked at each other anxiously. "You won't let us stay then?" Jim called out.

"Course I will," she called back, "and I'll help with the babies. But don't drive me mad with those bloody politics. I had enough of your dad and old Tuck years ago getting themselves knocked off every Saturday night."

Babs smiled at Jim in relief. He took her hand. "Mum's bark is worse than her bite," he told her.

6

More Boys

For the next month Maggie kept her job at the supermarket. Babs helped in the house but things were done rather haphazardly because her nose was always stuck in a book. Jim got a job as a checker at the docks. "Following in the old man's footsteps," said his mum. "Hope you don't get as fond of the booze as he did."

"That's the last thing to worry me," said Jim. "I want a good life for my kids. Don't see them toddling off to school in second-hand gear and all the other kids taking the mickey."

"Shouldn't count your chickens too soon if I was you. It's not all that easy to feed and clothe a family. But I wish you luck because you're sincere. That's more than your old man was."

Each evening Jim went off to his meetings, and Maggie would sit in keeping Babs company, rapidly knitting little baby clothes for Babs who was going to need two of everything. Before Jim left, Babs would hang about his neck, kissing him as though he were leaving to join the army. Then she would sit facing Maggie, her eyes downcast, and her face white and sad.

"Cheer up, he'll be back in an hour," Maggie would tell her.

"I don't like him going anywhere without me," Babs would reply tearfully.

"Better get used to it," retorted her mother-in-law. "When the kids come, it's us who stay home, not the men."

"Well, I won't," said Babs firmly. "Where Jim goes, I go. He needs me."

Maggie shrugged her shoulders. "Well, if you say so. I hope you get away with it."

Then out would come the big book of speeches and, with deep concentration, Babs would take down in her neat shorthand what Jim was to say on his next platform performance.

"Funny pair," Maggie would mutter, "but they're both of the same mind. Perhaps that's the secret of true love. I never found it."

Then came the night when Jim staggered in. He was not drunk like his father used to be, but he had a deep cut on his face and he was spitting out his front teeth.

"It don't surprise me," said Maggie as she bathed his face. "Cost a bomb for a new set of pearlies," she joked.

But little Babs, her face as white as death, went mad with rage.

"Oh! the beasts," she cried. "The villains!" She paced up and down dramatically. "Why wasn't I there with you?"

"Lot of good you would be with that fat belly," scoffed Maggie. "Calm down," she urged. "This is a rough area and the micks go round breaking up the Communist meetings. It was bound to happen in the end."

Babs stood rooted to the spot staring at the blood in the sink.

"Oh, go to bed will you!" said Maggie impatiently. "I'll see to Jim."

Maggie was not surprised to hear Jim running down the stairs in the middle of the night to phone for the ambulance. Maggie went upstairs and packed Babs's case.

"I am ever so scared," whispered Babs.

"Nothing to be afraid of, love," Maggie consoled her. "Blimey, I had old Jim on the same bed you're sitting on with no one there except old Granny Goring and her carpet bag."

Jim returned at midday looking worn out. "Two fine boys, Mum," he announced proudly.

"Oh, good!" exclaimed Maggie, but in the back of her mind echoed her own mother-in-law's words: "Boys, more bleeding boys."

"Must go and write old Tuck," announced the proud father and he went racing off up the street again.

Plenty of go in young Jim, she thought, probably knock out a football team before he's finished. Well, Maggie, so now you're a grandma. Makes me feel old somehow.

Jamie and Jason they named the twins and when Grandma saw them she went wild with delight. She dashed up the road to buy a twin pram and a cot. Must have a new pram. Can't help remembering that old pram I used to have to cart my kids about in. "No, my little darlings. Granny's going to see you get all the nice things you need," she told the sleeping babes.

Jim was looking at her with unusual affection. "What's up old lady?" he inquired. "Did you become a bloated capitalist overnight?"

"I'll get by," retorted Maggie.

Soon the little house was taken over by the twins. Wet washing hung in the passage and nappies on the fireguard.

Maggie left the supermarket because she was so worried over the babies. Babs did try to cope but she was muddly, starting one job and then going on to another, never with any routine. She would have one baby on her lap and another half-dressed on the floor and be reading items of interest from the newspaper while the twins yelled their heads off. Slowly but surely Maggie took over. She washed them, fed them and put them to bed. She stood washing nappies at the sink until late at night when her back was breaking. Oh, but they're lovely! It's worth the hard labor, she told herself.

Sometimes she thought of John who had written to her from Canada. Just as well he went, she told herself, I'm lumbered now.

The union had sponsored Jim, and Tuck put up the deposit and Jim began his political career with a vengeance. Babs, installed in the front parlor with a second-hand typewriter, was in her element. In the window was a poster of Jim all smiling and sophisticated, staring down the street, offering to fight for all working classes, and Maggie spent more and more time with the babies as Babs simply had to attend the meetings. Most nights Maggie sat weary and worn out in the armchair in the kitchen, the parlor having been taken over by the party who drank coffee half the night, sitting on the settee bed that Maggie slept on. On Saturdays they marched, carrying posters. Wheeling the twins up the Mile End Road Maggie would see them and dash off down a back street to avoid them; for some reason, they embarrassed her.

Sitting in the park, she looked forward to the summer. It had been a long winter and a dismal spring; how lonely she would have been without the babies. She looked at them sleeping, fat, clean and well fed; Babs could take them after the election; she felt she needed a rest. It's funny, in this little square I said goodbye to John all those years ago. She wondered how different her life would have been if she had not sent him away, when they had been in their teens. Well, no good crying over spilled milk, I suppose. She got up and pushed the pram slowly toward home. God knows what time they will be back. Could never tell when they started marching.

Parking the pram, she went indoors to put the kettle on for the babies' bottles. Then both the twins woke up together. She stood slowly rocking the pram to quieten them until their feed was ready. Then a voice beside her said: "Good heavens, is that a two-headed one?"

John stood looking down at the two babies in the pram. He looked very fit and sun-tanned. He wore a soft felt hat on his head and a light traveling coat hung over his arm.

"Oh, John!" said Maggie and melted into his arms.

The twins screamed their heads off but behind the street door they never heard them.

"I must give them their bottles, poor little darlings," said Maggie at last. But John held her tight.

"Let me go, John," she pleaded. "They're hungry."

"So am I," replied John.

"Go and wait in the front room for me and they'll settle down after they've had a feed."

"Whose are they?" he demanded. "Not mine I hope."

She giggled. "Don't be daft, I am past that age."

He sat waiting in the little box-like front room, smoking incessantly, until she had fed the babies and settled them down for the night. She came back looking very white and tired.

"Maggie, darling!" he exclaimed when he saw her. "You're all in. What the hell have you lumbered yourself with those kids for?"

"I know," she replied. "But Jim and Babs need me, the election is in a few weeks."

"Oh, I see." He stared distastefully at the red poster in the window. "What a waste of time. Too much trouble with Russia, no one's going to take in that rubbish."

"I agree," returned Maggie. "But they're young and so conscientious that I feel I must help them."

"But what about me, Maggie?" he asked. "Am I always to be shoved aside for this damn family of yours?"

She snuggled close to him. "Don't say that John. You don't know how I've missed you."

"Maggie," he said, "I must be crazy to run after you the way I do."

They made love, hungry passionate love, like two teenagers, on the small settee.

"I love you, darling," John whispered. "Let me take you out of this damn box you call a house. I am here for six weeks, spend them with me, please Maggie," he pleaded.

Maggie, limp and tired but utterly happy, said, "I'd like to see someone try and stop me."

The Party Member

On leaving Maggie, John had delivered an ultimatum. "Six o'clock at the station tomorrow, or else."

"Or else what?" she inquired cheekily.

"I'll come and drag you out by the hair on your head, sons or no sons."

"My caveman," laughed Maggie. As they said goodbye, a fleeting memory of the night big Jim had dragged her from the pub by her hair, made her laugh merrily.

Shortly afterward Jim and Babs arrived home. She gave supper to the happy wanderers. They were tired and dusty but jubilant, and they brought home a few comrades with them. Maggie watched them closely, wondering all the time what on earth there was in this party that held them all so close, had them calling each other brother and sister and gave them a certain elation. It was not drink or drugs, she was sure of that. It was an inner glow that, for the life of her, she was unable to define.

She listened to the incessant chatter that went on. Her Jim, sitting there in his red roll-neck jumper, was so superior handing out cigarettes as though he were bestowing on them the Order of the Garter. Babs's shortsighted eyes gleamed and she looked really pretty. The red jersey she wore brought out the whiteness of her skin and the dark gloss of her hair. She talked and laughed with the notebook clutched tightly in her hand. Maggie began to observe the other guests. A tiny pale-faced girl and a big sturdy young man held on to each other's hands, scarcely letting go except to drink coffee.

She wondered whether they were in love with each other or the party.

It was then she noticed Ben. A tall, dark lad of about eighteen with a mop of frizzy, black hair that badly needed cutting. He wore an old gray jersey and he looked poor and shabby and stood alone, staring sad-eyed at the rest of them as they excitedly discussed the results of the march.

"Come and sit here," said Maggie to him, patting the arm of the chair she sat on. Shyly he came over and she drew him into conversation. He told her he had recently walked from Scotland, hitch-hiking part of the way, and had arrived in England, footsore, weary and hungry. He was full of praise for Jim who had found him a job and given him money to tide him over until he was paid. Maggie was amazed; she never thought of young Jim as a great humanitarian, he always seemed hard and ambitious to her. Still, you live and learn, she told herself. Might be something in this party business after all.

She wished she knew more so she could talk and belong as they all did. But she sat sleepy and tongue-tied, waiting for the visitors to go home. Then she tumbled into bed.

Next day being Sunday, Jim and Babs slept until midday. Maggie washed and fed the twins and put them outside and did the washing and cooked the dinner.

They came down at last, one behind the other, Babs never being far behind Jim in anything he did. Maggie handed them both a cup of tea, still unable to say what was on her mind. Eventually she said: "That little sister of yours, Babs? Does she still want to come up to London?"

"Oh, you mean Megan? She can't afford the fare. I think she's saving up for it."

Maggie opened her handbag. "Here you are. Send her this; she can come up and help you with the babies." She handed Babs a five-pound note.

Babs looked astonished. "Why, Mum, where are you going?"

"I'm having a holiday," declared Maggie.

"But when and where, Mum?" demanded Jim.

Maggie, losing her temper, replied, "This is your family, Jim. You take care of them. I am going away for a while and that's that."

"If we're in the way, we'll go," said Jim, getting high-and-mighty. "Don't want the others to say I drove you out."

For the first time since Maggie had known her, little Babs stepped forward, taking Maggie's side against Jim. "Shut up, Jim," she ordered. "If Mum's going on holiday, it's her own affair, she's not our servant."

Jim was so surprised, he opened his mouth but no words came. Babs put her arms about Maggie. "Thank you for everything, Mum. Go and have a good time. Megan will come up, she will love to."

"I won't be gone long, darlin'," said Maggie and went upstairs to start packing. She could hear them arguing. From the up-and-down lilt of Babs's voice and the nasal twang of Jim's she knew who was gaining most ground. It was Babs who ruled the roost. I wish I'd had as much guts as her when I was young. If I had stood up to Jim and old Liza I wouldn't have been such a poor little cow, she told herself. Wrapping up the green dress she bought at Christmas she thought, well, here goes, Maggie, off on your second honeymoon. Ought to be ashamed of yourself at your age, but I am not, I am really looking forward to it, John darling.

Another Honeymoon

The first night they spent in a hotel off Trafalgar Square. She looked out of the window and saw the tall column with the small figure of Lord Nelson perched on top.

"Poor little man, up there all alone," she remarked.

"Let's get married, Maggie," said John from the bed.

But Maggie was still busy studying Nelson. "Don't he look lonely up there," she said.

"Good God," shouted John. "You are the limit, Maggie. Here am I proposing to you and all you can say is, poor old Nelson. He's been dead a hundred years. I've got all my parts, half of his were missing, and you don't want me. Even his Emma never got a chance like that."

Maggie went over to the bed and put her arms around him. "How can I make you understand? That's one of the reasons why I won't marry you."

He burst out laughing. "What, old Nelson? Where does he come into it?"

"Don't be silly," she answered peevishly. "It's because I'm narrow and ignorant. I don't know anything."

"But, darling," he protested, "you're the most beautiful, intelligent woman alive and old Nelson would think so too. To hell with Emma, he would say."

But as John joked Maggie looked forlorn. "It's no good," she said. "You won't listen to me."

"No. I won't," he said, very dogmatic. "You're my woman, the one I've always wanted and that's all that's important to me."

"Don't let's quarrel," pleaded Maggie. "Let's go out and get drunk like we did last night."

"Why you desolate wretch," cried John, "and you're the one who's talking of self-improvement."

"Not in that way," she replied. "Sex and booze I'm very good at."

He held her closer. "My sunshine," he whispered. "Always a smile, never bitchy and never greedy. Maggie, if you only knew the other side of life, you would never yearn for it. When I compare you with that cold fish I married with her pots of money and greedy grasping, I can't believe that life has been so good to me since I found you again."

Maggie stared at him. He had never mentioned his wife before, but she knew he had been divorced. She was shocked at the angry hurt in his tone when he mentioned her.

"That's what I mean, John," she explained. "Marriage might spoil our happiness together."

"Perhaps you're right, darling, but I'll be away for a whole year and I'm terrified I might lose you."

"You won't lose me," she giggled. "No one's likely to run off with me, I am not a teenager."

He grinned, his good humor returning. "Let's go shopping," he said, "and I'll dress you up like one."

"What a waste of money," she argued.

"It's my money and I choose to spend it," he retorted.

Eventually they went out into the brightly-lit West End arm in arm, and as carefree as two middle-aged lovers had ever been. It was April and the shops were full of spring outfits—gay hats, smart suits and frilly underwear—all such a delight to the feminine eye. Maggie had good taste, but protested furiously at the high prices. They found plenty to amuse them. In one big store Maggie suddenly developed a slow drawl like John's. Convinced they were Americans, the assistants fell over themselves to serve them.

"Fooled them, didn't I," she said triumphantly.

"That Irish blarney would fool the Yanks themselves," laughed John. "What shall we do with ourselves for the next six weeks? We could stay here for a few weeks and then we could go abroad, to Italy or Paris?"

But Maggie was a little shocked. She had not bargained for such a long holiday. The boys would be worried if she was gone too long.

"I like England in the spring," John was saying. "Orchards in Kent and the cool green meadows near a river."

She came back down to earth at the mention of Kent.

"Joe's down in Kent," she said. "At school."

He looked at her in amazement, so rudely awakened from his daydream.

"Which one is Joe?" he asked, remembering Tom and Al with disfavor.

"Oh, he's different," replied Maggie. "Very clever. He's going to be a doctor."

"Very interesting. Where is he?" he quizzed.

"St. Egbert's, near Aylsford," replied Maggie proudly.

"Why, that's a public school, Maggie. How did he get there?"

"He won a scholarship and the church helped him. Joe's the only one that's been brought up Catholic."

He looked thoughtful. He had a feeling she was hiding something.

"Shall we go and see Joe?" asked Maggie suddenly. "I want you to see Joe."

"All right," said John, "we'll go tomorrow."

Maggie breathed a sigh of relief. Must get this worry off my mind.

Maggie dressed very carefully in the morning, putting on the new suit that John had bought her. It was navy with a touch of white and she wore a new white hat with a brim that emphasized her features.

"How do I look?" she asked.

"Like a duchess," replied John.

"I want to look nice today. I've never been to Joe's school before."

"Why not? Not even at prize giving?" he asked.

She shook her head, "I was afraid I'd show him up," she admitted.

"What have I got to do to drive this inferiority complex out? Take you to a psychiatrist?"

"It's not easy for me to live as you do," she excused herself.

"Well, then I'm determined to make you," he replied.

It was a long but lovely drive down to Kent. The sun dodged in and out of the clouds which sprayed the earth with sweet April showers. At the top of Dartford Heath they stopped to look at a rainbow. Its glorious colors combined from pink and purple and green; its perfect arch swung over the sky, with London lying down in the valley and the green fields of Kent ahead of them. Maggie breathed deeply.

"It's wonderful," she cried. "I've never seen a whole

rainbow before. In London the houses get in the way."

"I've always been fond of Kent and I've got a feeling you'll love it too, Maggie."

"It's strange, but years ago I sat on the windowsill and dreamed of a house in the country," she told him.

"Might even come true. I've got great plans for our future, darling, but I can't tell you just yet."

"Why? Is it crooked?" exclaimed Maggie.

He kissed her, laughing all the time. "You'll be the death of me, my Cockney friend," he said as they drove on.

Soon they were traveling alongside the Medway. The river wound through a wide plain dotted with cute little farmhouses. As the car crested the hills, the air was fresh and heavy like wine.

"It's beautiful," murmured Maggie. "It's really beautiful."

The tall white school building alarmed her. The boys playing in the green fields reminded her of the day she went with big Jim to visit Ginger and Lennie in the approved school. Pull yourself together, girl, she said to herself, life's different now. Accept it. You're out with a famous man and you're wearing a twenty-guinea suit.

The old days are over. Repeatedly she turned this over in her mind seeking the courage she needed to go into that posh school.

"Why so silent suddenly?" asked John. "Anything wrong, darling?"

"I'm scared," she whispered. "Terribly afraid."

He patted her hand. "Get it over, Maggie, and it'll never bother you again. You must face things. Go in and get Joe and I'll wait outside."

She held on to him. "Please come in with me. I'll never make it alone."

John got out of the car and stood looking down at her as if she were a naughty child. But there was no need for a decision; down the wide steps came Joe's slim figure.

"Oh, Mother, it *is* you. How wonderful to see you!"

Maggie rushed toward her little Joe delighted to see him again. John stood by, slightly embarrassed by this demonstration of affection.

But Joe saved the situation: "How do you do, Mr. Malloy," he said. "I was wondering when I was going to meet you."

This was Joe, a charming boy, so like Maggie in his ways, bursting with life and full of the same generosity. John was charmed by him.

With arms linked Joe piloted them around the big school, proudly presenting his smart little mother to his friends. At one time the school had been a monastery. There were lovely stained glass windows, painted ceilings, wide stairs and beautiful gardens. Maggie could not believe that such beauty existed. How must Joe feel when he comes home to that dreary little house.

Over tea Joe and John talked a lot about a thing called nuclear invasion. To Maggie it was incomprehensible. It was all about something known as the bomb. What the hell does Joe know about bombs? she thought. But it was so nice to see them get on so well together, her lover and her favorite son. It gave her a feeling of warmth; she wanted to hug and kiss them both.

As they walked from the school to the car, Joe introduced John to his science master, who kept John chatting on the steps. Joe took the opportunity to hug his mum.

"Thanks, Mum," he said in her ear. "Thank you for coming, also for bringing Mr. Malloy. Be happy. Don't let the family bother you."

"How did you know about him?" Maggie asked.

"Anne-Marie mentioned him in a letter."

"What did Al have to say?" she inquired.

"He thinks you'll be a fool not to marry him. He's on his way up, didn't you know?"

"What am I supposed to know?" retorted his mum. "Only that he is going off to some God-forsaken hole for a year."

Joe's dark eyes twinkled at her logic. So like his

mum, nothing moved her once she made up her mind.

John had now rejoined them and Maggie heard the crisp sound of a note being put into Joe's hand as they parted. It was a great day for Joe whom no one ever visited, let alone gave fivers to.

"He's a fine boy," said John as they drove away. "I wish he were mine."

Maggie felt despondent and was not sure why. Surely she was not jealous? John hummed a little tune as they went along. She looked sideways at him, wondering at how elated he was. He liked Joe. She supposed she should be pleased, but somehow it was not the effect she expected that fact to produce. He had not said one word about Joe being colored. She was back where she had started.

"Let's take the long way home," he said as the car sped through a narrow lane toward the river. They drove through miles of orchards all in bloom, the smell of the apple blossom filled the air. There was not a soul in sight and the only sound came from the birds. It had a strange effect on her, a sweet sadness, like being in a church.

Where the river ran inland and created a little bay, he pulled up the car and began kissing her. All her resistance melted in her love for him.

"Now, Maggie darling," he said. "Tell me."

She trembled close to him. "Oh God, I wish I didn't love you so much. I never felt like this before."

With a far-away look in his eyes he said, "You've never lived before; you only existed with your old man."

Then it came, in between the passionate kisses. "But what about Joe, Maggie?"

She had begun to cry. "I knew you'd want to know about Joe," she sobbed.

"You've no obligation to tell me, Maggie. That's part of your own life, nothing to do with me."

But Maggie wanted to explain to him about Joe, to tell him of that mad night when she fell for little Klause. Suddenly she knew he was not going to listen. He pushed the car seat flat and pressed his lips on hers.

She pushed him away in panic. "No, John, not here, what's the matter with you?" He rested his head down on the steering wheel.

"God, Maggie," his voice broke. "If I get a picture in my mind of another man making love to you, I'm like a bloody lunatic. I want you more than ever. All I can think of are those wasted years and what wonderful kids we would have produced."

Maggie's heart went out in sympathy. This talented man who could have any young pretty girl, loved and wanted her and only her.

"Let's go for a walk," she whispered.

In the shady bushes by the river they lay close together until he was calm again.

"Don't let us have any regrets, darling. Let's live while we're alive."

"Hope you realize you've made me ruin me new suit," she grumbled jokingly as they sat watching a small boat go down the river.

"Wonder what this place is called? Nice here, isn't it," he said.

But Maggie's attention had been taken by some little black-and-white birds.

"Look," she said. "Like they are in evening dress."

"They're called house-martins," he told her. "They must be nesting near here. They're collecting in all that dried grass."

They walked hand-in-hand down the shady path toward a great oak tree. Behind it was a cottage. It was here the house-martins nested. The eaves were full of them flitting in and out, busy with the big nest-building project they had on.

While Maggie watched the birds, John was admiring the cottage. It had real old-world style—low eaves and tiny, mullioned windows. An old gentleman came from the back garden.

"Have you come to view the cottage, Sir?" he asked. "What a moment and I'll get the key."

"It's for sale?" asked John.

"It's for sale, to let or to lease, as long as we get the

right type. It belongs to the church. The vicar has let it furnished for a few seasons."

They followed the old man inside where John examined the wide, brick fireplace and admired the cozy windowseat. The furniture was shabby and the carpet faded but there was certainly some atmosphere about it.

"Who's the agent?" asked John.

"In town, Sir." He gave him an address and John slipped him a coin.

"I'll be back. Don't show anyone else over it."

"All right, Sir," replied the old man.

At the gate John looked back. "Maggie," he said, "with a bit of luck I'm going to buy you a cottage of your own. We'll spend the rest of my leave here and when I come home I want to see you waiting at the gate for me."

"Don't be silly," she said. "You haven't got it yet."

"But I will," he promised and pushed his foot down hard on the accelerator. The car sped swiftly toward the town.

The agent was pleased to get Oak Tree Cottage off his hands and in no time the deal was made. It was not often that cash deals were made in that little town.

"You're now the joint owner of a cottage by the sea Maggie, or at least by the river. We will spend the next six weeks making it shipshape. You do like it, don't you Maggie?"

He was so excited about this purchase. But she was not so keen and kept thinking how on earth was she going to leave her family behind for such a long time.

"We'll go back to the hotel, pick up our gear and come back to stay tomorrow." John was like a kid with a new toy and full of plans and new ideas for refurnishing the cottage. He whistled gaily as he drove back to London. "You, my little devil," he joked, "will cook for me, feed me and love me, and when I leave you, you will belong to me body and soul, wedding or no wedding."

She was still rather uncertain about it all, but responded jokingly: "Bloody old Bluebeard! I expect

I'll poison you in a couple of days, and you'll go runnin'
back to that posh hotel."

"You vixen," he said, but was so gay and happy
that Maggie loved him more than ever.

John was up early next morning. "I'm going to the
bank. Stay here, love. We'll check out after lunch.
What's the date?" he asked.

"First of May," replied Maggie looking at a newspaper.

"I won't be long. This time tomorrow I'll have you
spud-bashing," he threatened as he left.

Once he had gone, she sat down and wrote to each
one of her sons; Joe at school, Tom in jail, and Al
miles away in Edgeley and Jim in the little house in
Stepney. She gave no explanation except that she was
taking a longer holiday and would let them know where
she was later on. She never mentioned John. For some
reason she could not bring herself to put all her eggs
in one basket.

There seemed to be rather a lot of noise in the square
below. Getting up, Maggie went to the window to look.
Down in Trafalgar Square crowds were gathering. She
moved onto the balcony to get a better look at the
demonstration that was going on down below. They
were waving banners and chanting, and more proces-
sions kept arriving. The police were down there too
and there was a great deal of pushing and shouting. She
ran and got John's binoculars and tried to read the
words on the banners they carried: Ban the Bomb.
What's all the fuss about a bomb?

She was still looking through the glasses when the
East End contingent arrived and there, marching right
at the front, were Jim and Babs. She spotted their red
jerseys as the long line of marchers turned into the
square. Maggie smiled as she watched. They would
never believe it if she told them their mum was looking
down at them from a capitalist hotel and all dressed
up, gained by very immoral means.

She was still laughing when John returned. He looked

irritable. Crowds and demonstrations really annoyed him. When Maggie wanted him to see Jim and Babs down there, he refused. "Come on, darling," he said. "Start packing. Let's get away from this madhouse."

Maggie, who had thought it was such a good joke was rather disappointed. She began putting their things in a suitcase. The noise below seemed to be getting worse—she would just have a little peep.

The sight that met her gaze nearly made her fall over the balcony. They were all fighting; mounted policemen charging the crowds, a long line of police with arms linked struggling to hold back the screaming, yelling crowds, and people everywhere. The demonstrators were being dragged away struggling by the police and were being loaded into the long line of black marias, waiting in a side street.

"Oh my gawd," yelled Maggie. "My Jim's down there." She went rushing toward the door. But John's hand detained her.

"Where are you going?" he demanded angrily.

"My Jim's out there," gasped Maggie, a trifle shocked that he should grab hold of her like that. His eyes like steel points bored into her soul.

"Don't you dare leave this room," he commanded, pushing her unceremoniously down into a chair. Maggie was too shocked to utter a word. John went forward, turned the key in the lock, and put it in his pocket.

"Maggie," he said very seriously. "Do you know what's going on down there?"

She shook her head. "They're fighting. I'm sorry, John, but I was worried over Babs and Jim."

"Not fighting," he returned coldly, "but demonstrating. Have you got any idea what it would do if I got mixed up in that schemozzle?"

Maggie was speechless. She could not believe her lovely gentle John could treat her like this.

"Maggie, I'm on the government commission, I'm going with a team of American scientists to Christmas Island to see the bomb in action."

"What bomb?" Maggie burst out crying. "The only

bloody bombs I know about are what Hitler chucked at us. I thought the war was over years ago."

He came and took her in his arms. "I'm sorry if I hurt you. You're so immature, Maggie, that you exasperate me sometimes."

"I'll go home then," she answered defiantly.

"Oh, come on, darling," he consoled. "Let's go to our country cottage." He kissed her tears away. But a very subdued lady sat beside him in the car as they drove toward Kent.

"You're very quiet. What are you thinking about?" John asked.

"I was thinking that I was right not to marry you. I would probably let you down like I almost did today."

"Nonsense," he replied. "Wait until I get you down there. I'll teach you to behave. I'll beat the daylights out of you, my girl," he warned.

She put her head on his shoulder and gave a little smile.

7

Oak Tree Cottage

Together they settled at the cottage. It was much easier than she had ever dreamed. To see John in an old pair of overalls inspecting the roof and climbing up the wide chimney, coming down covered in soot, really amused her. The smart clean sophisticated John, usually without a hair out of place was quite a different person when dressed in old clothes and busy with the general repairs.

She had discovered the joys of gardening, digging the sweet-smelling earth, making things grow. The old man from up the road came to mow the lawn and he pointed out the plants from the weeds for her. Roses and honeysuckle entwined to make a frame for this lovely garden. There were great bushy shrubs, lavender, wisteria and huge clumps of marguerite and more roses than she could remember. She was like a child with a new toy, and she knelt on the soft, damp grass that smelled heavenly. Tiny spring violets still grew in the hedges and the grass in the morning shone with a thousand diamonds. There was so much to see, to hear and feel. She would hold up her arms to the morning sun. No words could express this love of beauty that she had never felt before.

301

"Oh, John, what's happening to me? I feel that I've been reborn."

"It's good to feel that way," he explained. "This love of nature has been lying in you. You've been starved of beauty until now."

In the afternoons they would sit to watch the birds that came down to feed and bathe in an old, fantastically-shaped bird bath. Blue-and-yellow tits, like budgies, squabbled endlessly over the crumbs. Then the old cock robin would come and chase them away. "Naughty boy," she would say. "There's enough for all of you." And John would go into spasms of laughter.

Up at the eaves the black-and-white house-martins flew busily in and out. "Why don't they come down to feed?" she asked.

"They feed on the wing," John told her.

"Oh, isn't it all wonderful! Look at those brown speckled ones." She would squeak with glee as they hopped over the lawn.

John's interest was mainly with the property. "Got a real bargain here," he would say very proudly. "Would have had to pay a darn sight more for this next year. Land is rocketing sky high."

He sent to London for his books and some fine pieces of furniture that were in store.

"We're just like the little house-martins," Maggie said, "building our nests."

"I wish I were not going away now I've found this place."

"Time will soon pass," Maggie tried to console him but he looked sad and far away.

"What's the matter, darling? There's no danger, is there?" she asked anxiously.

"Safe as houses," he replied. "Come on, love, don't let's get morbid. Let's find the local."

In their old earth-stained clothes they walked hand in hand to find the village pub. It was a cozy little place, close to the river, and known by the strange name of We Anchor in Hope.

John and Maggie spent many pleasant evenings there,

the landlord would entertain them with stories of pre-war days when the hoppers came down once a year from London to pick the hops. He would exaggerate about the Cockneys. Maggie wanted very much to speak up and defend them, but sat silent. She thought of her youth when Granny Goring used to take all the family hopping, kids, dogs, uncles and aunts, mums and dads, all loaded in a van amid pots and pans, all well-boozed going and in a worse condition on their return. She remembered how she used to look at all this, the annual exodus from London, and used to wish with all her heart that someone would ask her to go with them. But listening to this old man, she was not so sure she had missed much after all.

They were never bored down at Oak Tree Cottage, there was always something to hold their interest, and the days flew by on butterfly wings. Even the weather was good to them. In the warm May sunshine John swam in the river and one day they hired a boat and sailed down the river, out to the North Foreland Lighthouse.

At the rudder, John watched her dark hair blowing in the breeze. So slim in slacks and a jumper, Maggie seemed to have grown younger; her cheeks were glowing and a soft light shone in her blue eyes. He would remember her at this moment how ever long he lived.

Wrapped in a downy blanket of love, the days went fleeting by. They squabbled like kids over the cooking.

"You have no imagination, Maggie," he would say. "It's either chips or boiled spuds. I'll show you how to grill chops and French fry potatoes."

"Nuts," was Maggie's rude comment. She could not see any difference if the chops were fried or grilled, so she went out to her garden while John put on an apron and prepared tasty dishes.

Down at the very bottom of their garden was a little wood. A rickety gate led to it and often they strolled down there in the evenings.

"I'd like to buy this piece of ground one day," John said. "It's lovely down here. Look at these fine oaks."

"It's funny," Maggie remarked, "when I come through that gate I get the same feelings as when I used to go into church, the same sort of strange silence."

They were sitting on a fallen log.

"It's not so funny," replied John. "It has a strange effect on me too. I feel like reciting out loud."

Maggie giggled but he said, "Listen, darling." With a soft Irish lilt to his voice he began to recite:

If you stand very still in the heart of a wood
You may hear many wonderful things,
A snap of a twig, the wind in the trees,
And the whirl of invisible wings.

If you stand very still and stick to your faith
And wait for a voice from within,
You'll be led down the highways and byways of life
In this mad world of chaos and din.

"It's lovely," said Maggie with tears in her eyes.

John had a far-away look in his eyes. "Wake up," she said.

He looked down at her steadily as though he could see into her heart. "I'm not keen on this job," he said suddenly. "If I were not committed to it, I'm hanged if I wouldn't rather stay here and rusticate with you, darling."

"What's so bad about this bomb?" Maggie asked anxiously. "There's not going to be another war is there?"

"I hope not," he replied. "All this beauty would be destroyed. It would be the end of human civilization."

Maggie shivered and drew close to him. "Why bother about it? Let's live while we can."

"It's not so easy," replied John. "There must be men of peace to weigh the balance against the men of war and I'm on a commission seeking to use atomic energy for peaceful industrial uses. But let's not talk about it now. We'll go home and light a nice log fire."

Hand in hand they walked through the twilight as

the evening shadows descended over the lovely garden. Tomorrow, early morning, he would be gone.

The day John left it rained for the first time in weeks. "Look, the sky weeps for us, darling," he said.

"The sun will shine again," Maggie told him, "don't be sad. You're not going away for ever."

"That's right, love, cheer me up like you always do," he said.

Taking off his favorite apron, the one he wore when he cooked up the continental dishes, he placed it about her waist.

"Now Maggie," he said, "I want to see you here with that apron on when I return."

"Going to be a bit mucky by then," she joked.

He drew his arms around her and rested his head on her shoulder. "Make me laugh, darling. I am not as brave as you are. Perhaps I never had anyone I cared so much about before."

Poor, lonely John. Maggie would not have believed that anyone could obtain success and money and still be lonely, but listening to him it seemed possible.

"I'll be waiting for you, darling. Don't be sad. We have lots of time to make up . . . and how happy we'll be in our little country cottage."

"Please God," murmured John as he gave her a final embrace. The old taxi was hooting at them down by the gate and soon John had gone out of her life.

Already the cottage felt empty, something was gone from it. Maggie picked up his slippers and put John's pipe back in the rack. All his treasures were here to take care of. There was a fine bookcase full of leather-bound books, and strange pictures on the wall that he told her were so valuable. He trusted her with all his possessions. Somehow it made her feel very unworthy. A lump came in her throat. She could not cry. She felt the way she had when Dah had died—so terribly alone.

The quiet of the country no longer thrilled her, instead it depressed her. How was she going to stay here all the dreary winter alone?

It had ceased to rain and a pale shaft of sun shone out. She went to sit in the garden and felt better out there. Mr. York's white cat came and sat upon her lap. He had become very attached to her. She talked to him stroking his long white fur. "Don't you chase my birds, there's a good boy." The white tail waved as he purred his reply into her ear. She always felt at home with animals, it seemed as though they acknowledged the faults in humans.

She looked up at the pale blue sky and the rain-washed clouds gliding along in the wind. He was probably up there now in a great plane—that vast emptiness seemed so frightening. Oh, I want so much to stay here with my lovely garden she sighed, but alone I am hopeless. I always was. You're too good for me, darling John, I can't compete with you.

Her thoughts were interrupted by the sound of a cycle bell. She looked toward the front gate and a voice called out. "Thank God I have found you, Mum, I was just about to give up."

There was Joe, dusty and disheveled, riding a bike. She ran toward him: "How wonderful to see you, Joe. However did you manage to find me?"

"Didn't think you wanted anyone to find you," he said as he limped saddle-sore up the path. "I've been riding around for hours, I had to find you. I have half a dozen letters for you."

"Is something wrong?" she asked anxiously.

"According to big brother Jim, everything has gone wrong," replied Joe as he sipped the glass of cool cider she had handed him. Then he dived into his pocket and produced a bundle of letters.

"Oh dear," Maggie looked worried. "All these? How did you find me?" she asked once more.

"You sent me a postcard with a picture of the village," replied Joe, "and I rode about making inquiries. They told me where to find you at the local. I thought you might be known there!"

Maggie started to laugh.

"It's not funny," said Joe. "Wait till you read Jim's letter, you won't laugh any longer," he warned her.

Maggie took Jim's letter and began to read:

Dear Mother,

I hope at long last I have managed to find you. I have no wish to pry into your affairs, but I am being constantly pestered by the council officials to vacate the house. It is their intention to pull it down next week. We have been given accommodation in the block of flats opposite. Will you please instruct me as to your intentions regarding the house and the furniture. I can't afford to dilly-dally. I have a wife and family I am responsible for.

Kindly oblige with a prompt reply.

Your son,
Jim

"Oh, my gawd," muttered Maggie relapsing back to her Cockney accent.

Joe, watching her in amusement, said, "Well, Mum, you see what I meant?"

"Yes, Joe," she replied. "Jim's really put out." For a moment Maggie bit her lip in thought. Then she said, "Listen, Joe, when you've had a rest, go down the post office, phone him, cable him, anything, but put him out of his misery."

"What shall I say?" asked Joe looking perplexed.

"Tell him," said Maggie, her cheeks flushing in anger, "to take the bloody lot. It's all his, because I ain't going to live in no flaming tower block."

Joe was not used to Maggie using bad language. He looked shocked.

"Sorry, love," she apologized, "but Jim always gets me mad. Go and get it over, then come back and stay with me. Ring the school and tell them."

Obediently Joe wheeled the bike out and rode down to the village while Maggie sat reading her other letters.

Fancy thinking you were going to be lonely, Maggie Burns, she said to herself. Here we go again.

There was rather a pathetic letter from Tom, who had been moved to Maidstone. That's not so far away. I'll visit him soon she thought.

Then the vision flashed over her of the packet of notes behind the wallpaper. Blimey, I must go to London. They ain't going to get old Tom's money if I can stop them.

There was another letter still unread, very neatly addressed and posted in West London. She turned it over in her hand, then opened it warily. To her surprise it was from Anne-Marie:

Dearest Mother,
I can call you Mother now, as Al and I were married last week by special license. We would have loved you to be present but were given to understand you were on tour with Mr. Malloy. By the time you get this, we will be in Cape Town. Aunt Dolly decided not to come with us after all. Sorry it was all such a rush, there were several reasons for it. One, that Dad went back into the forces, and the other, you will find out soon enough. Forgive me for stealing your son.
         Love from Anne-Marie and Allan.

"Bless your heart," Maggie said as she finished reading, "I hope you'll be happy, darlings."

Joe had returned, hot and tired. "Got all the news, then?" he said, looking at the letters.

"Wouldn't think so much could happen in so little time. Still, not to worry." She pushed it all aside. Lost home, new daughter-in-law and an angry son. It was all in the process of living.

"Let's eat, Joe," she said, "and I'll show you my lovely cottage."

While Maggie got busy in the kitchen, Joe inspected the books and pictures. He was thrilled.

"Marvelous pictures, Mum," he cried.

"No accounting for taste," replied Maggie. "They look like road accidents to me."

"Living like this has not changed you a bit, Mum," Joe remarked as he tucked into a plate stacked with food.

"Hasn't it, Joe?" Maggie was looking very concerned. "I was hoping I'd become a bit refined. I did try."

"Don't worry, Mum. John must like you as you are. Look at the lovely home he's given you. Did you say the cottage was yours?"

"Well, let's say it's ours," she answered, "until John comes home."

Joe's eyes lit up. "Do you really mean it, Mum? Gosh, it would be nice to ask Trevor over. There's a river here and everything."

"And a boat," she told him. "And who's Trevor? Your schoolpal?"

"Yes," was Joe's reply. "His home is in Nigeria. He doesn't go home often because it's so far."

"You're very welcome here, Joe. Bring him at the weekend. I gotta go up and see Jim this weekend, but you can manage on your own. I'll leave the key with Mr. York next door."

So it was settled. Maggie would go up to London on Saturday and Joe would mind the cottage. She missed John's warm body beside her that night, but with Joe in the spare room it was not so lonely.

Joe went back to school on Friday morning and arrived back with his friend the same evening. Joe was so happy, he had never brought a schoolfriend home before. He had always pretended his folks were abroad. To bring old Trevor to his mother's weekend retreat, as he called it, was really something.

Maggie did her best for them; she dressed very nicely and served the meal in the way that John had taught her. Trevor was a nice well-spoken boy, as fair as Joe was dark, and they seemed such good pals. Maggie was truly glad to be able to do this for Joe.

"Have a good weekend," she told them as they saw her off at the station, and boarded the train for London.

While the green fields of Kent whizzed past the train window, she closed her eyes and wondered what it would be like to see Stepney again. It was as if she had been away six years instead of six weeks. Jim had lost the election; Al had got married; and now they were going to break up the house she had lived in for so long. Jim would be very disappointed about the election after all the work they had done and she wondered what sort of mood he would be in. He was an impressionable boy and in some ways she was a little afraid of him. It was an abrupt end to a honeymoon but at least she had kept them out of the way while John was there. He would never understand them but, after all, they were her own flesh and blood and she was saddled with them.

Young Jim's New Home

Maggie got a taxi from London Bridge. It pulled up outside her house. She paid off the driver and turned and stared in dismay at the broken windows and the front door which was wide open. The little house cried out in its misery to her and Maggie stood rooted to the spot. All the other houses were gone, they were just piles of bricks and rubble, like the blitz all over again.

The effect on Maggie was disastrous. She began to cry, tears rained down as she crept slowly in. Most of the furniture had been taken, just a few odd bits remained. One piece left was Liza's famous oak dresser, looking very desolate without the crocks. Maggie's eyes went round the kitchen and on the wall was old Jim's picture. There he was looking down at her with the same cheery grin, big and broad in his able seaman's outfit. Gently, Maggie lifted it down. "They forgot about you, mate," she said. "Poor old Jim." She held the picture close, there was the same familiar smell of living about the kitchen, but something was gone. What was it? Then in a moment she knew; it was her Jim. He was not there anymore. His presence no longer dominated that little home. Oh, it was like a knife in her heart. "I'm sorry, Jim. I went away and left you and, like Dah, you've gone on." She knew that John had replaced Jim, the same way Jim had replaced Dah, and with tears she tried to erase this hurt.

"Sorry, old mate," she sobbed, "I never meant to."

Going upstairs she got a nail file out of her handbag and ripped off the wallpaper, put her hand in the hole and brought out Tom's loot. Quickly she put the parcel in her handbag. "Well, let's hope I've handled this all right. Seem to make a mess of most things."

"Goodbye, little house," said Maggie as she stood forlornly in the doorway, the echo of children's voices ringing in her ears. Then slowly, her face all swollen with crying, and Jim's photo under her arm, she went to find the family.

It did not take her long to find Jim's new flat. It was directly over the road, there was no need to ask the way. The big windows, brightly lit, shone out onto the street and with no curtains drawn Maggie could see her old-fashioned furniture looking lost in the great big room.

A young girl, of about sixteen, opened the door. She was a taller reproduction of Babs. Maggie said, "You must be Megan. I'm Mum."

But Megan, as Maggie discovered later, was completely different from Babs in every way but looks. She was as domesticated as Babs was studious, and as alert and frivolous as her sister was shy and awkward. It was a case of chalk and cheese, as Maggie said, but together they were a team and things got done.

"Hello Mum," Megan said, welcoming Maggie with a wide smile. Megan weighed the whole situation up, with one look. "You've been crying. Come on in dear, and I'll make you a nice cup of tea."

She helped Maggie off with her coat and on the rug in front of an electric fire sat a curly-haired youth, surrounded by books and pamphlets.

"That's Ben," said Megan.

"We've met before," said Maggie.

"Ben, get up and put the kettle on. Jim's mum could

do with a cup of tea," she said sharply. Ben jumped up immediately.

"Come on, love, I'll show you the twins while the kettle's boiling. That'll cheer you up."

In a fair-sized bedroom, the babies were asleep in their cots, looking just as Jim and Tom had done at their age.

"Better not wake them," said Megan. "I always get them down about five, gives us a longer evening."

After a hot cup of tea Maggie began to feel her old self. "Where's Babs?" she asked.

"She's got a job," said Megan. "It's only for a few months. No sense in us both mooching about here."

Maggie was a bit surprised and must have looked it.

"It's all right," said Megan, "I'm better than her at housework. She's the clever one. Be in soon."

Maggie liked this straight-talking girl. At sixteen Megan seemed as mature as an old married woman. The others had not missed Maggie much with this domestic Megan around. Still, it was just as well the babies looked well cared for.

Soon Babs came bustling in, her eyes looking very tired from typing all day. She was all kisses and cuddles for Maggie. "Enjoyed yourself, Mum? How do you like the flat?"

Maggie looked around. It looked bare but there was plenty of room for them all. Looking closer at Babs she thought, I'm sure she's pregnant again, so they're going to need it.

The next one to arrive was her Jim. It was strange how pleased she was to see him, her first-born son. But Maggie was shocked as she looked at him, he was different, he looked sad.

"So you found us, Mother," he said as he kissed her.

"Wasn't hard," said Maggie. "Only over the road."

Jim smiled. Same old mum, always ready to do battle. "I must say, you look great." He inspected her smart clothes. "Never thought you would go on the other side, Ma. Got yourself a bloated capitalist."

"That's not fair, Jim," protested Maggie in defense of her John. "He works hard to get where he is, that's all. It's not a matter of whose side I'm on."

"Never mind, love, let's not argue. I feel a bit down tonight."

The girls had gone to the kitchen and were busy getting the evening meal, while Jim sat beside her. "I've just been to see Tuck. He's in the hospital down here."

"Oh, I'm sorry," said Maggie.

"But that's not all, Mum. He's got lung cancer." Tears came into his dark blue eyes. "You've never seen such a difference in anyone, it really upset me."

Maggie held his hand. Jim needed her. He was as fond of old Tuck as his dad had been.

"You know he put up the deposit for me and we lost the election. Well, it was not so terrible because I intend to try again and it gave me some prestige with the party. But look at this." He took from his pocket a battered post office book. "This is his, he can hardly speak. 'For the party,' he said, 'try again.'"

He opened it. The entries started in 1925; five shillings here and ten shillings there, a lifetime of saving on very little. Jim's voice choked. "'Take it now, lad,' he said. I couldn't touch it, Mum. I'll keep it. We might live a long time yet and need it."

Maggie was upset too. Dapper little Tuck, Jim's boozing and fighting companion to end up like that.

"Don't worry, Jim," she said. "Pray he don't suffer too long."

"Come and get it," called Megan from the kitchen. The kitchen was big and brightly decorated, with a shining white sink and the latest in gas cookers, but in the middle, laid with a snow-white cloth, was the old square table that had belonged to Liza. Maggie's eyes twinkled when she saw it in its new surroundings. It had served Liza's great family and also Maggie's. It had served as a shelter when London was blitzed and yet here it stood in modern surroundings waiting to share another family's load.

The meal was good: boiled ham, tomatoes and plenty

of spuds and tinned peas. The company at the table was so lively, even Jim lost his depression, for with Megan and Maggie there was no lack of conversation. Ben, who had joined them at supper, seemed part of the family. The dishes and the plates they ate off had been on the old oak dresser for years. Maggie had hardly used them—she had always been afraid that they would get broken. Now, loaded with food, this merry table seemed the right place for them. This was Jim's home and Maggie was very pleased for him. It was a gay, lively home, the kind of home Maggie might have had if it had not been for the war and the poverty-stricken days before it. Thank God her grandchildren were going to get a good life.

Knock after knock on the door after dinner brought this neighbor or another, or some child with a message. Eventually, Jim and Babs went off to the tenants' meeting—some group they were interested in.

"Don't mind sharing with Megan, Mum, do you? Only Ben's got the other room."

So Ben was part of the family too. Megan sprawled on her little bed—the same one that Ginger had slept in. "How do you like Ben?" she asked Maggie.

"Nice boy," she said. "You two courting?"

"We are practically engaged," she announced loftily.

Maggie was about to say that Megan was a bit young but she suddenly remembered that she had been the same age when Jim was born. Instead she murmured, "Congratulations."

"That's why Ben's staying here," said Megan. "Six quid they charged for them moldy old lodgings he had. If he stays here he can save up to buy me a ring."

"Very nice," said Maggie, thinking that Jim was going to get rich quick with all the free lodgers.

"I'd like a fish-and-chip shop when I get married," said Megan.

"Well," said Maggie, "I thought Ben was a budding politician."

"He can pack all that up," said Megan, "if he wants to marry me. Had enough of that down in Wales, all bloody strikes and no grub. Ten of us kids there was, all half starved."

"Well love, hope you make it," said Maggie. Seems they turn them out a bit more cute these days, she thought as she got into bed.

The next day was Sunday and Maggie took the babies out. They sat up now and gave her toothless smiles. She was quite sure they said, "Nan." She knew it was only the babies that could hold her. Stepney was no longer her home. She wondered if she would regret giving all her things up, but then she had no worries now. John gave her a good housekeeping allowance and there was Tom's money still in her handbag. No, she could return to Oak Tree Cottage with an easy conscience.

"You don't mind if I go home in the morning, Jim?" she said on Sunday evening.

"Home?" said Jim, very shocked. "This is your home."

"No, love," she shook her head. "This is your home. I'm all right. Here's some money to buy some curtains."

Those huge windows with no curtains worried her.

"But I can't let you do this. How do I know what will happen to you?"

Babs came to the rescue as usual. "Don't be silly, Jim," she said, "Mum's got herself a fancy man with plenty of money. Leave her alone. She's still good-looking and young enough to enjoy it."

Maggie flashed her a grateful smile.

"Here's my address, Jim. I'm near to Joe, he'll be staying weekends. Bring the babies down for a holiday."

Maggie was glad to get on her train, that brown paper parcel in her handbag was worrying her. That was another problem to straighten out. She had looked back as the taxi pulled out of the street. I never want to go back again to Stepney, she thought. Her last act had been to wrap Jim's photo up and put it in her bag. That was all she was going to take with her.

Getting off the train as it came in at the little country station, was an unusual experience for Maggie. For the first time she saw the name of the village in large letters: Hystead. This is my home now, she thought, I'd better find out all about it.

As she walked from the platform, the young man at the barrier said, "Good afternoon, Mrs. Malloy."

Maggie stood still. Then with a little grin and her head held high, she acknowledged his greeting.

The little village was pretty rural: a red-bricked school, lots of old cottages and the all-purpose store that held the post office and sold everything that the population needed. It was run by a chatty woman called Beryl. She was very nice, never a hair out of place; Maggie often wondered if all those red curls were her own.

On her way home Maggie stopped off at the shop to buy some stationery and stamps. "Pleased to see you home again," said Beryl.

Maggie was astounded, she did not think anyone knew she was there. Seems they don't miss much in the country.

"If you get lonely up there, now your husband's abroad, you can always come down for a cup of tea with me," said Beryl.

"Thanks," said Maggie, "but I read a lot."

"We've got a library here," said Beryl, "down the back. Go and have a look. I can get you all the new books from town if you let me know."

She went to the little butcher's next to buy something for tea. In his straw hat and a striped apron, he was really dressed for the part and also full of chat. "Just let us know what you need and I'll send the boy up with it Mrs. Malloy. Like a nice chick for the weekend?"

"Might as well," said Maggie, remembering that Joe would be home. As she neared the cottage, the tall oak stood out on the skyline, and little swifts dodged in and out of the branches. It was lovely. How lucky she was. This was that dream she used to have about a place in the country as she sat on the windowsill in Stepney when the boys were babies. She should be very happy, a dream come true. But without John it was not the same.

Mr. York came out to give her the key. He was a nice, courteous old man.

"The boys had a fine time," he said. "I took them down the creek. Plenty of fish there, they liked that."

"Thanks, Mr. York," she said. Down the path rushed Timothy the white cat. He had heard Maggie's voice. She picked him up. "Coming home with me, Timothy? I got something nice for you." Timothy purred his acceptance and followed her home, his tail waving proudly. Don't think I am going to be lonely here after all, she thought. She opened the little garden gate and her flowers smiled a welcome.

In the hall was a letter from John. The cottage looked neat and clean, and smelled of pine wood.

It's lovely. I know I'll settle down she thought as she sat to read John's letter.

Darling,
I am writing this as I wait for the plane. There was so much I wanted to say to you before I left, to thank you for the lovely weeks we have been through together. I'll never forget our dream cottage. It is the happiest home I have ever had. So try and settle, Maggie. I know it won't be easy. Be there when I come home and I promise I'll never leave you again.

I meant to tell you that there is money in the bank for you. Go into Rochester and see Mr. Benson at the Provincial Bank. He will handle any problems you may have. By the way, Maggie, they think you are Mrs. Malloy. Just a form of protection, darling, until I can make it real.

Take care of yourself, love, John. xxxxxx

So it was John who had established her respectability with the community. Dear, thoughtful John. He needn't have bothered because I don't care two hoots about any of them.

With the white cat on her lap she spent the evening reading. It was a silly love story and it was no good, she could not get interested. Outside it was dark and still. She got up and went to the window and looked out. The thick black night frightened her. She put the curtain down quickly. "Let's go to bed, Timothy," she said and picked up the cat and carried him up with her.

Timothy slept in John's place, spread out and purring his head off. Better than being alone, thought Maggie. I wonder what to do with Tom's money. I had better go and see him next week. She took the parcel from her handbag and placed it in the dressing table drawer. "No need to hide it. Ain't no one but me and you to nick it here," she whispered to Timothy as she cuddled him.

During the day she managed to keep occupied by cleaning the cottage and tending the garden. She was really proud of her garden. It was now the beginning of July and all the roses were blooming. John had explained to her that every rose had a name, then added humorously that "they all smell sweet." So Maggie in her innocence took it very seriously and proceeded to name every rose in the garden.

In the middle of the lawn were four beautiful standards, all in one bed. "My sons," Maggie had said. "The tall bright red one is Jim, that sturdy yellow one is Tom, and that beautiful dark red is my little Joe. Al can be the pink one that starts off pink and goes white."

John had been really amused at the childish games she played. Still, Maggie was so young in some ways.

Thus her family garden had begun. From the town she obtained two young trees, one red and one deep pink.

"Who are they in aid of?" John had inquired.

"Why, those are our little twins, Jamie and Jason."

In spite of haphazard planting and weeding her garden grew well. Plants thrived and the roses flourished.

"I have never had any place that I feel so carefree in as that garden," she would say.

The weeks were drifting past. Most evenings she would stay outside until dusk, but inside the cottage, in spite of Timothy's constant affection, she dreaded the black silent night that descended like a velvet blanket when the sun went down. Walking to the riverside followed by Timothy one evening she stopped for a chat with Mr. York who was busy digging up potatoes.

"Hello, Mr. York," she said.

He paused from his work to come to the gate, his old red setter walking with him. Timothy arched his back at Nep, the old dog.

"The cat's got fond of you," Mr. York said. "'Twas my wife's cat really. He was always jealous of the old dog.

"Wait a bit and I'll dig up some of these Michaelmas daisies for you. Make a nice show later on in the year."

"Thanks," said Maggie, "you're very kind."

"It's a pleasure," he said gallantly.

"Whatever do you do in the evening?" Maggie asked as she watched him dig the plants.

"Well, this weather I stay out here as late as I can, then I go in and watch the telly and off to bed."

Maggie looked dismal. "Haven't got a telly, never bothered much, always been too busy."

"You get used to living alone," he said. "As a matter of fact, I prefer it. I play chess with the vicar in the winter and do a bit of part-time work for the church."

"It's the night I don't like," said Maggie. "It seems so quiet outside, it frightens me."

"Nothing to be afraid of, my dear," he said kindly. "Old Nep and I have a good look around every night before we turn in and I got an old gun if there's any trouble."

Maggie smiled at this grand old man of seventy who was so anxious to protect her.

"You're a darling," she said, taking the armful of plants he gave her. "I'll go back and put these in."

A mist came up off the river and floated eerily around the great oak tree and tiny birds rustled about in their nests in the eaves. Maggie was glad to get inside and shoot the bolt on the door. Don't like it here at night time, she thought. Never mind, Joe will be here tomorrow and Tom's home soon.

8

Poor Old Tom

The recent visit to Tom in prison had not been a very great success. He had seemed moody and awkward. Nearing the end of his sentence he was allowed to walk about in the grounds. Tom did not seem happy at this open prison. Life was much easier but Maggie had a feeling he missed his mates. She sat with Tom on a bench in the grounds, surly and morose, having little to say.

"You heard from Jim? They pulled the house down," she said brightly.

"No, I didn't. Where we going to flaming well live then?"

"That's all right, Tom, we're going to live in the country. I won't say where. You never know if someone is listening."

"Don't think I want to live in the bleeding country," he said. "Had enough of the flaming country out on them bloody fields all day." Tom was sent out to work on the farms now.

"Breaks your heart," said Tom. "We all sit in the lorry after a hard day's work, hot and tired, and the bloody driver stops outside the pub and swigs down a cool foaming pint of beer, with us poor sods looking

321

on, our tongues stuck to the roof of our mouths. It's not bloody fair. I'll murder someone if I stay here. All ponces and queers they are. Be glad to get out."

Maggie sat quietly listening to his grousing. He had changed quite a bit. It was to be expected, a young man in his twenties to be cooped up like that.

"Don't worry," she said. "You'll soon be home, Tom."

"What home?" said Tom. "Ain't got no bloody home."

She came away feeling very depressed. It was certain that Tom would not settle at Oak Tree Cottage and John would find him an embarrassment. He was so much like poor old big Jim. Then there was this business of the money. How often she had regretted her impulse to hide it. Money was not important to her now she had John but it really belonged to Tom. He had paid his debt to society.

"Good mind to go home and burn the bloody stuff," she muttered. But knew she would not. Instead she wrote to Ginger asking him to take Tom into business with him and to send back a letter asking Tom to visit him. At least out there Tom would be away from the bright boys of Stepney.

Joe was home at the weekend. "Soon be breaking up for holidays, Mum," he said. "This will be the last year. I'll have to start swotting like hell for the exams in the spring."

"It will be nice and quiet here, Joe," said Maggie. "Nothing to stop you studying here."

"I know Mum, but . . ." he hesitated as though he were not sure.

"But what?" said Maggie.

"Well, Trevor did ask me to go home with him for the summer."

"He lives abroad, doesn't he?"

"Yes. Nigeria. It's in Africa, same place as Al is, only this is one end of Africa and Cape Town the other."

Maggie still did not look very interested, but Joe seemed determined to prolong the conversation.

"Father O'Mally's going to West Africa on a mission, I could have gone with him."

Maggie looked up. "You don't still want to be a priest, do you, Joe?"

He shook his head. "But I'd love to travel," he said. "It's so good for the mind. I am sure I would learn more that way than swotting over these damn books all the hols."

"Well, what is it Joe? Come to the point," said Maggie sharply.

He came closer to her and sat at her feet. "Forget I asked, Mum," he said. "You need me. I won't leave you here all alone."

"Give over, Joe," said Maggie. "What's stopping you? Come out with it."

"Well," he said looking shame-faced. "It's money."

"That all?" said Maggie. "How much?"

"I am not sure," said Joe. "But you couldn't afford it, Mum, and if I pass my exams I'll need more money for the medical school."

"Let's cross our bridges when we come to them," she said. "How much?"

"I need a couple of hundred for the fare and equipment," said Joe.

"All right, Joe," she said sadly. "You can have it." So little Joe was not anxious to stay with her after all.

He was so excited he hugged her. "Wait till old Trevor knows I'm coming," he said. "Think I'll go down the post office and phone him.

"What a journey, Mum! Right through Africa! Gee whizz!" Twisting his school scarf around his neck he dashed out to phone his mate.

Maggie sat very still. Teach me not to count me chickens, that will, she thought.

Joe went back to school in the morning and Maggie dressed up in her best suit. She was off to see this Mr. Benson at the bank, who John had said would look after her affairs. Before leaving she had unwrapped the parcel containing the money and taken out five hundred pounds. Got to chance it, she thought, I can't leave it to Tom, he'll only mess it up.

The Bank Manager

Maggie liked Rochester with its very old castle and the wide bridge that crossed the river. In the narrow, winding high street she found the Provincial Bank. Her knees went a bit weak as she went in; a bank manager was someone that she never tackled before. Keep your fingers crossed, thought Maggie.

Mr. Benson was kindness itself. She was invited into his thick carpeted office. "I am so glad you called, Mrs. Malloy. Your husband left instructions for your affairs to be kept in order. I wondered if you'd had the telephone connected yet, I was about to give you a ring."

It was then Maggie remembered that John had told her to contact the telephone exchange, but she had forgotten. "Perhaps you will see to it for me, if you don't mind," Maggie asked him. He seemed a very nice man.

"Yes, I'll do that. Is everything satisfactory otherwise? Do you want us to send your monthly housekeeping checks, or would you prefer to call on us?"

"It's all right," she said. "I'll come in if I want anything. I wanted to ask your advice about something." She licked her lips, her throat was dry, but she was determined to see it through.

"I sold my old house in London and the people were foreigners and insisted on paying in cash. I'd like to put it in my account."

"By all means." He looked surprised that she had come to pay in, not take out. She handed over the notes to him.

"Yes, I'll see to that, Mrs. Malloy. Also the telephone for you. Perhaps you would like to invest it in some stocks and shares. I'll drop you a line and we can arrange to meet and discuss it." With much bowing, he showed her out.

Well you have done it now, Maggie, girl. But who's going to suspect the respectable Mrs. Malloy of handling stolen money? I'll wait a week, see what happens and then I'll get rid of some more.

Within a few weeks Maggie had salted away more than half of it; two hundred in a savings bank for Joe; five hundred in a building society in her own name. The parcel was getting smaller. How could they find it once it got mixed in with all that other money that's floating about? A visit to another town, Maidstone; a post office book for another two hundred; a solitaire ring and a heavy gold bracelet set her back a few more hundred. It's becoming a work of art, she told herself, never thought I was such a good spender, only five hundred pounds left. She would take a chance on that! Give Tom a start in Australia, but how to get it there?

She brought down her suitcase and carefully cut away the lining and pasted all the notes inside. Then she placed newspaper over them. She sewed the lining neatly back and surveyed her handiwork. She felt very pleased with herself. She had managed to dispose of the parcel that had worried her for so long.

Little Joe would be off on his travels in a few weeks and all she had to do was to get old Tom off to Australia and then she could wait patiently for John.

She paid another visit to Mr. Benson's office to hear how he had invested her money, and then while waiting for the bus home she wandered round the shops. It was not one bit like London, plenty of shops but not crowded and no one in a hurry; it was rather pleasant. Going into the biggest store she wandered from counter to counter in the fabric department, fingering the beautiful curtain materials in soft glowing colors. Her eyes opened wide as she asked the price: "two pounds ten a yard." Well, a family in Stepney would live for a week on that much. It seemed wicked somehow.

"Can I show you something cheaper?" asked the assistant.

"No," she said. "I'm not sure that I'm going to buy any."

The girl shrugged and walked away. For some reason Maggie felt she'd been snubbed. She walked on to admire the lovely glassware.

You're a fool, she said to herself, you can buy this lot. Why don't you get used to the idea? The days are gone when every penny mattered, get wise to yourself. In a sudden flash she remembered that morning when baby Jim had wanted a twopenny rattle and she had not been able to afford to buy it for him. Old Ginger had nicked it because he could not bear to see the baby's tears.

She stood very still staring at the glass display cabinet with tears in her eyes. People passing looked at her curiously. Suddenly she turned, went back and called the assistant.

"I want twenty yards of that material," she said in a very superior voice. "I want it made up into loose covers and drapes and I'll let you have the measurements. I'll phone."

The girl began to measure the material. She looked surprised.

"Where's the coat department?" asked Maggie very briskly. "Get my bill together and I'll hand the particulars into the manager's office."

Maggie tried on endless fur coats and was really enjoying herself now. She went through the big store like a tornado. She bought a television, presents for the babies, expensive suits for the winter, a new coat (the latest in suede and fur) for traveling, shirts for Joe and Tom, in fact, anything that caught her eye. Her face was alight as though to do battle with someone, but it was poverty she fought. The demon that had haunted her for so many years, she took by the throat and disposed of him. She felt really wonderful. Assistants fawned on her and the manager hovered about, escorting her to the door, after she had signed a check for two hundred and fifty pounds. Not bad going in one afternoon. "Send it all to this address," she told them.

"Mrs. Malloy, Oak Tree Cottage, Hystead." Sounded lovely.

"That will teach them," she muttered as she got on the bus for home. I feel terribly wicked, but wasn't it fun? Wait till I tell John. It was then she realized there would be nobody at home to tell, only Timothy, and that lazy so-and-so slept most of the time.

The Return of Tom

August had gradually disappeared and most of the roses had gone, though multi-colored hollyhocks and golden marigolds still bloomed in Maggie's garden. Mr. York's Michaelmas daisies had just come out, and a pale, mauve clump of them waved a welcome each morning.

Little Joe had now been gone several weeks—she had received postcards from the different places hc had visited—and in the hall was a bright red telephone. When it was first installed she had stared in horror, wondering what on earth she would do if it rang. Suddenly it did. She held the receiver far from her ear and yelled very loudly into it. "Hello." It was the exchange checking to see if the number was correct.

The next evening another voice said: "Hold the line, madam, I have a long distance call for you."

John's soft voice said, "Hello, darling."

Maggie called out loud and clear into the receiver, breathless with excitement, but he said: "Now calm down, Maggie, hold the receiver near to your ear and speak normally."

"Sorry John, I thought you wouldn't hear me, you being all those miles away."

She heard him choking with laughter.

"Wait till I get home, Maggie, I'll punish you for that crack. Take care, darling. I'll ring every week. By the way I am sending you a present, it'll be there soon."

From then on Maggie loved that little red telephone.

She would ask the time, order her shopping and spend long evenings gossiping to Beryl in the post office. It is strange, she thought, how you get used to having things. I suppose I should thank my lucky stars really. Don't think my life would have been much after poor old Jim died if I had not met John, that's why I feel I can never do enough to repay him.

She lay back in her chair, dreaming of the first time they had made love, in his flat in Earls Court, and how jealous she was of the girl who owned the green nightie.

Then out of the blue a dark spot appeared on the horizon. Friday today, Saturday tomorrow. Crikey! that's the day when Tom comes home. How could she be so selfish to sit there planning her life, and poor old Tom had been shut up for a whole year?

Maggie had the queerest feeling as she stood outside the jail waiting for Tom to come out. It was as though there were two people waiting there, one that wanted to run back to the security of Oak Tree Cottage and the other one that yearned for the sight of her son, and wanted only to repay him for the lost time inside.

She saw him come out of the gates and stand still as if unable to grasp the fact that he was free. He was so tall and ungainly and had large feet that turned outwards as he walked. She went over to him and held out her arms. But he squinted at her through little narrow deep-set eyes.

"Got a cab?" he asked. "Let's get away from here for Christ's sake."

"We'll go into town and get a bus from there," she told him.

"Where is this bloody place?" he grumbled. "Come to something, when I don't know where I live."

"We'll be there soon, Tom," she soothed him. "I know you'll like it. Besides, it's nice and quiet there."

"I've had enough bloody peace and quiet to last me," moaned Tom. "What the hell did you have to leave Stepney for? I don't know," he snarled.

Maggie's patience was slowly leaving her. "They pulled the damned place down," she replied, "so I couldn't stay in it."

"You could have got a council flat," he said. "But no, gave it all to big brother Jim. Don't matter about me."

"Give over, Tom," she begged. "You've got plenty of money to make a new start, don't keep grumbling."

He looked keenly at her and was suddenly repentant like a small boy.

"Got any money, Mum?" he said. "I'd better have a drink, that will cheer me up. That bloody hole got me down."

They went into a pub near the bus station and Maggie slipped a fiver into his pocket. And Tom held that foaming pint up to the light as though he was paying homage to it. In two goes he had finished it and ordered another. She sat sipping her drink, then he was on to the third one. She began to get alarmed, after not drinking for so long it might affect him.

"Come on, Tom, we'll miss the bus," she said anxiously.

"All right, my love," he replied quite amicably. He seemed to have changed considerably after his drink of beer. He straightened his shoulders, and Maggie could see how thin around the neck he was. I'd better get him some new suits.

He had cheered up a lot by the time the bus was tearing along the green lanes to Hystead. Tom looked out of the window, and in his loud gruff voice he said, "Blimey, ain't this a gawd-forsaken 'ole. Nothing but grass and bloody cows."

Maggie looked about the bus nervously hoping that there was no one on board who knew her. Oh dear, don't tell me I'm ashamed of my own son. But she knew she had out-grown Tom. Every word he uttered and every move he made, grated on her nerves. It was just as if big Jim had come back to spoil her happiness. She had a fleeting memory of his mean face and she seemed to hear him say, "I'll get you and your fancy man as well." She grew cold with apprehension as though fate had decided for her.

Oak Tree Cottage beamed its usual welcome to her, it seemed to say: don't worry, it will all turn out all right. But Tom's attitude had depressed her and she was beginning to wonder.

"Not bad," said Tom as he looked around. "Who's it belong to?"

"He's a scientist, working abroad at the moment, and I'm taking care of the cottage for him."

"And then what are you going to do, old girl?" said Tom nastily. "Tower block or the workhouse."

"Behave yourself, Tom," said Maggie. "I'll not ask any help of you and that's for sure."

"By the way," said Tom, "where's all that dough you got hid?"

"In a safe place," she replied quietly.

"Well, here's a fine thing," said Tom. "I nicked it and you copped it."

"Now be sensible, Tom," pleaded Maggie. "I couldn't leave it here, now could I."

"All right," he said, "don't get upset, I'm only kidding."

But her eyes were full of tears. She had almost had enough of Tom. "I'll get something to eat," she said going out to the kitchen.

Tom turned on the telly, put his feet up on John's highly-polished antique table and smoked one cigarette after another, throwing the butts into the fireplace and scattering ash everywhere. After dinner they began to talk of the future.

"I thought it would be a good idea for you to take your money and go out to Australia. Ginger did very well out there."

"You can get that idea out of your head," said Tom.

"Why, Tom?" She was flabbergasted.

"Because I ain't going to no foreign place. I like it here."

"Well, suppose they come looking for the money?" she cried.

"I've done my time, and now I'll take my chance on the outside." Tom's reply was gruff. "Better get some of that dough ready. I'm going up to London tomorrow."

A Trip to Stepney

It was cool and misty in Maggie's garden that day. She wandered aimlessly about, picking a weed out here and there and a bowl of the last few blackberries. Her mind was very disturbed, she could not settle.

Early that morning Tom had got up after a good breakfast and said: "Come on Ma, cough up. I'm going up to London on the spree."

"But, Tom," she said, "stay here for a while. Don't go getting mixed up with those Stepney boys again."

"Turn it up, Ma, you don't think I'm going to be cooped up in this dump. Might as well be in the nick. Give us some money, then."

Maggie produced a fiver from a purse. He laughed with a cackle.

"What do you expect me to do with that?" he asked. "There was more than three thousand quid in that loot. What you done with it?"

Maggie got really mad then. "Look here, Tom," she said, "I kept that for you so as to give you a start, I don't want you to be a criminal all your life. I thought it would be better to go abroad and start a business or something."

"Do me a favor, Ma," he shouted. "I'm not a kid anymore. I'll say what I'll do with my life."

Her face and neck flamed red, not for a long time had she been in such a temper. She went to the desk and took out the bank book.

"It's here, most of it. Do what you like. I don't care." Then she threw the ring and the bracelet at him. "Here, these are yours, too. I don't want them."

He picked them up. "Good," he said. "Fetch a few quid quick these will. Can't draw it out with that book, it's in your name."

"I'll write a check," she said. "How much do you want?"

"Make it a couple of hundred," he said. "Going down the Mile End to get measured for some suits and might look around for a car."

He soon got ready, whistling away like nothing was wrong. But Maggie was hurt, not one word of thanks to her. He was so much like Jim that it was like having salt rubbed in an open wound. He would get rid of all that money in no time up in London. She had to think of some way of stopping him.

Before he left he threw the ring and bracelet on the table. "Take care of them, Mum," he said quite pleasantly. "Some bastard might nick them up there. So long, love. See you tonight."

Maggie was so mad she never answered him.

All day she prowled in and out, trying to sort out the problem. He was not going to go to Australia, that was for sure. Perhaps he might like to go out to Al in Cape Town—she'd ask him tonight.

The day dragged slowly by and at six o'clock John rang. Maggie was so pleased to hear his voice, it gave her that safe feeling that had disappeared since the moody Tom came into the house.

"You all right, darling?" he asked.

"Of course I am," she said cheerfully.

"Listen, darling, I may not be able to phone you for a few weeks, I have to go into the interior for a while and it won't be easy. Don't worry, the sooner I get this job over, the sooner I'll be home."

"What's the interior, John?" asked Maggie.

"Nothing to worry over, just somewhere where communications are difficult. You will still get my letters, darling."

"All right, dear, just take care of yourself," she said as his voice faded away.

The tears that had been building up all day fell down onto Timothy's white fur coat.

She lay in bed trying not to sleep, listening for Tom, but he did not come home. At about midnight she went off, unable to keep her eyes open any longer.

Tom arrived at about ten o'clock the next morning. He drove up in a long red sports car, very pleased with himself. His eyes were red-rimmed from lack of sleep and too much drink.

"Hello, little old lady," he said. "Like me car? Smashing ain't it?"

"How much?" said Maggie looking at the long, red monstrosity outside her gate.

"Got it cheap, bought it off me mate. Gave him fifty, got another £250 to give him tomorrow. Like me suit? This one's off the peg. Getting another couple made up. Bought some nice shirts too."

Maggie was thinking that there would not be much change from the money he took with him.

"I've had me breakfast," he said. "I'm going to kip now. Wake me about five, Mum, I'm going up London again."

For the next two weeks Tom spent the nights up in London and the days in bed. Maggie would lie awake waiting for the sound of that fast car as he drove up in the early mornings. In that time Tom got rid of another three hundred pounds. He had begun to look very washed out. Sometimes as she passed his room in the day time, she heard the sound of hard dry sobs as Tom cried in his sleep. The lonely days in prison had left this mark. She wondered how it would all end. Tom went about the cottage like a bull in a china shop when he was awake, leaving dog-ends everywhere, getting out John's precious books, leaving them on the floor and spilling tea on them. Maggie was not sure whether she preferred him at home or out all night. Something had to happen.

That night it did. He came home earlier than usual, it must have been about two o'clock. She watched the car lights as they shone on the wall of the bedroom. He seemed to be taking a long time to get out of the car. She waited for the crunch of his footsteps down the path. No sound! Why the hell was he still sitting out there? Must be drunk. Let him stay there, serve him right. She waited a while, then, feeling uneasy she got up and called out, "Tom! why don't you come in?" No reply.

Putting on her dressing gown she went out to the car. A terrible shock awaited her. There was Tom sprawled out on the seat completely unconscious. Blood was everywhere, streaming down his face from a deep cut in his head. His shirt had a deep dark patch of blood and his hands, still hanging onto the wheel, were unrecognizable for the masses of heavy, congealed blood on them. Maggie took one look, then darted back again. She wanted to stand and scream. Tom was dead. But she pulled herself together. Must have been in an accident, she thought. She ran quickly into the house and came back with a towel and a jug of water, then back again for a glass of brandy. She climbed in beside him. There was dark sticky blood everywhere and slowly she forced the brandy between his lips and wiped him down to find out where the wounds were.

Slowly Tom came round and Maggie helped him up the path with his tall body leaning heavily on her. She helped him into a chair in the sitting room, then ran upstairs for blankets and a pillow. The blood still poured from the wounds on his head.

"What happened, Tom?" she asked. "Was it a car accident?"

He shook his head. "No, some bloke duffed me up. Hit me with a chopper."

A cold shiver went down her spine. So it had all begun again.

"Put him through a plate-glass window, I did," he was muttering.

She knelt beside him on the floor trying to stem the flow of blood from the wound in his head. Every now and again he sank into unconsciousness. She bound

up his hands and when the cold, gray light of dawn
entered the room she was still kneeling with the bowls
and towels all around. Tom now rocked from side to
side muttering light-headedly. It's no good, I must get
the doctor. I do hope that the police aren't looking for
him.

She telephoned the village doctor. "My son's had a
car accident, please will you come to him?"

"Certainly," a sleepy doctor replied, "I'll be along
soon."

Maggie sat nervously chewing her fingers. Suddenly
she got up, taking the brass poker from the fireplace.
She went down to the gate and struck the windscreen
of the red car till it splintered and the sound of falling
glass filled the misty morning air.

The old village doctor was not long in coming. He
cleaned and stitched the wound in Tom's head.

"Got a bit of concussion. I'll help you get him to
bed," he said.

Once Tom was under sedation and his wounds attended to, Maggie relaxed. "Have a cup of coffee,
doctor," she said.

"Yes please, Mrs. Malloy," he replied. "How did it
happen?" he asked.

"Parking the car," said Maggie. "He ran into that
big oak tree down there, went right through the windscreen he did."

The doctor thought he saw signs of fighting but decided to mind his own business.

As he went down the path he looked at the car with
its cracked windscreen and was still puzzled as to how
neither the front nor back of the car was harmed. It
did not look as though he hit that tree. Funny business,
he thought, a strange patient too—not the type one
would expect at Mrs. Malloy's. Ah well! nought to do
with me. And he went on his way.

All day Maggie sat by Tom's bed as he tossed and
turned. Poor old Tom, she was so sorry to have been
down on him, his mind must be terribly disturbed. Hope
that other boy's all right. Oh God, if Tom's got to go

back inside, whatever will he do? I must get him away, even if I go with him myself. Once this idea occurred to her, she began to think about it more.

Perhaps the reason he would not go alone, was that he felt insecure and was clinging to her as a sort of last support. Prison had taken more from him than either he or she had realized. That's it! She would go with him to Ginger, get him settled and be back in time for John's return. John would not like it, he had no patience with her devotion to her sons. Needn't tell him. Could be out there in six weeks and home again before the spring. I wonder if I can get away with it.

In a few days Tom began to get better. The backs of Maggie's legs ached with the constant running up and down stairs with trays. He now sat up in bed reading the American magazines she had found for him.

"This bloke," said Tom, "John Malloy, who writes these articles about rock creation, is he the one who owns this place?"

"That's right," said Maggie wondering what was coming next.

"Must be great to have a life like that," said Tom, his voice showing admiration. "Look at me. I ain't been nowhere since I left school. The back streets of Stepney was all I got."

"There's still time, Tom. It's up to you now," said Maggie.

She sat on the bed looking at him, her blue eyes soft and loving. In bed he was her own son again, not the tough rough jailbird of the previous weeks. Tom put up his hand and stroked her curly hair back from her eyes.

"Do you know why I wouldn't go away to Australia, Mum?" he said.

Maggie silently shook her head. "Not all the reasons, Tom," she said.

"I don't want to be alone. I know I don't treat you right, but you're all I got. I'd like to be popular and make people like me but something in me won't let me. I never had much of me own. Jim took all the glory wherever we was. But Mum, I always loved you and I need you now more than ever."

Maggie did not really know what to say to this confession. "I'll never leave you till some girl who loves you takes my place," she said. "But Tom, how you going to find a decent wife in them gambling dives? Let's do some traveling. We can afford it."

"Would you come, Mum?" His rugged face lit up like a beacon.

"That's settled, we'll go then."

While Tom lay in bed—he had not a care in the world now he was secure in his mum's affections—Maggie paced up and down her garden. She watched a little squirrel frantically collecting the last few hazel nuts before retiring to his nice warm nest for the winter. Golden leaves floated gracefully down, laying a yellow carpet under the tree, and out of the mist the rose hips glowed scarlet. They were all going to sleep for the winter, thought Maggie. She gently touched a rose bush. So you won't really miss me. I'll be back in the spring. She looked around. Somehow the answer to it all was in this garden. Just out of her reach, she felt the air of mystery. How peacefully they settled down. We're not dead, they whispered, only asleep. We'll be awake in the spring. Please God, let it be all right. Let me be here in the spring, with John beside me. I know I'm bad but please forgive me. My son needs me, I must go.

It was first time she prayed in that garden, but not the last. She stopped dreaming and went inside.

First she wrote to Jim, sending him the bills for the suits Tom had ordered and the balance to pay. She asked him to collect them and to find out what happened to the other boy involved in the fight, and would he mind coming down at the weekend? She would pay all expenses. Then she got ready to go out. "I won't be long, Tom, I have to go to town. Don't get up will you?"

"Mind how you go," he said.

"That knock on the head seems to have done him

good," she remarked to Timothy, taking a bath on the lawn.

She called on Mr. York. He was eating a lonely breakfast of porridge, with the old dog close to his knee. He was a grand old man and she had grown very fond of him and he of her.

"I am going away, Mr. York," she said.

He looked dismayed.

"Only on a visit, I'll be back in the spring. I wondered if you'd take care of the cottage and my garden. Will twenty pounds a month be enough?"

"I don't want money, Mrs. Malloy, you're my most respected neighbor. It will be my pleasure to take care of things."

"Now, don't be silly," said Maggie. "You've only got your old-age pension. I can afford it. The bank will send it to you. If I have any letters you can post them back to Mr. Benson at the Provincial Bank, Rochester."

"I'll do that gladly," he said. "You're going out to Mr. Malloy?"

"No, I'm going to visit my son in South Africa, his wife is expecting a baby soon."

"Well, have a nice time. I'm going to miss you."

Maggie smiled, then looked sad. "Take care of Timothy, he'll miss me, too," she said. "I'm not going yet, in a week or two, so don't say goodbye."

As she went off to catch the town bus, she wondered why she had not told him it was Australia, but always in her mind was the fear that they might come looking for Tom. It was better to be safe than sorry.

Mr. Benson was as gracious and helpful as ever. Maggie amused him and in some way appealed to him.

"I want to go abroad," said Maggie. "Will you arrange things for me?"

"Certainly, my dear," he said.

"I want you to book a passage for two of us, first to Cape Town and then on to Australia. Perth, the place is called."

"Do you want to go by air?" he asked.

"No fear," said Maggie. "Won't get me up in one of those planes."

He was trying not to smile.

"Do you know," she said, "if they crashed you get roasted alive. No thanks! I'll take my chance on the water."

This was too much for Mr. Benson, he burst into loud laughter. "Wait a moment," he said, "I'll get some coffee."

He ordered a tray of coffee and biscuits and produced some travel brochures and spent an hour of his busy time with Maggie, and thoroughly enjoyed it.

When she left his office her arrangements were almost completed. "A second-class passage, don't want no first class," said Maggie. "I want to be comfortable!"

"It was quite easy really, Tom," she said later. "I never knew how to start. He's a nice man, that Mr. Benson."

But Tom was very quiet. He was not sure now if he wanted to leave England at all. But Maggie was. Her mind was made up. "Better off out there, than in the nick here," she told him.

Jim came down alone on Saturday. Babs was not feeling very well. She was so heavy they had reckoned on twins again. Poor old Jim seemed a bit harassed.

"Never mind," said Maggie, "the more the merrier. I'll help Babs get the things together."

"You've been good to the children, Mum. We're going to miss you."

"I'll be back in the spring to meet my new grandchildren, I want a little girl this time." She was happy today as she sat and talked with her son. "What's the news in Stepney?" she asked.

"Well," said Jim, "this fellow Tom did in is still in the hospital. So far the cops aren't involved, but his mates are looking for Tom and, believe me, Mum, they're right tearaways, razors and all."

She looked serious. "I thought he was in trouble. It's a good job I've got him to agree to go away. I know what it's like down there, I have seen it all my life.

Get on the wrong side of those crooked fellows and they never leave you be."

Tom scowled at them. "Not much good everybody running. I'd like to see them try and get me."

"It's all right for you, Tom," said the upright Jim, "but I can't afford to be involved. I've got my family to think of."

Oh dear, thought Maggie, they're going to start.

"Don't argue," she said. "Come on Jim, I'll take you to see Mr. York. Tom, you're not fit enough to go out yet."

They strolled down the lane to visit Mr. York and then they went on to the pub where Jim was welcomed by the locals. He played darts and Maggie sat and silently said goodbye to the little pub.

"John will be home in the spring," she told the landlord. Later she said goodbye to Jim. She wondered when they would meet again. Maggie had never left England before and it was no easy task for her to make this journey.

9

Aboard Ship

The *Transvaal Queen* sailed from Tilbury in the first week in November. The weather was bad; as soon as they got into the open sea, the ship rolled from side to side and so did Maggie's stomach. She took to her cabin, too ashamed to let anyone see her being sick, and lay looking and feeling like death warmed up.

Tom came to see her, looking very spruce in a light suit. He seemed to be having a good time; the bar was always open and there were plenty of people to play cards with. Maggie, wishing fervently she had never come, just lay there afraid to move in case she started being sick again.

The cabin next door was shared by a mother and daughter. The girl, called Anna, was about sixteen and a real beauty. Maggie had admired the way she strolled gracefully up the gangplank, not looking to either side. But her mother, who was as wide as she was tall, clambered up nervously, talking all the time. The reason Maggie noticed them was because they were dressed alike. This amused her—the big wide mother and the tall slim girl in paisley windcheaters, blue scarves on their heads and heavy skirts and boots. To little petite

341

Maggie in her silk stockings and well-fitting suit, they had seemed funny.

On the second night out, when Maggie still stayed in her cabin there was a tap at the door.

"Come in," she called and the two tall shapes stood in the small doorway.

"Me Hester," said the Mother. "This is Anna, my daughter."

"Come inside," said Maggie. "I'm pleased to meet you."

"We came, as you were not at dinner. You sick. I bring drink and biscuits for you." Her tone was stilted, as though each word must be carefully thought out. "Come, Anna, give lady drink."

Anna, who held a tray with a glass of whisky, a dry ginger and some biscuits, came forward shyly.

"That's nice of you," said Maggie sitting up, "but I honestly don't think I could."

"Yes! Yes!" Hester said. "You must eat, whisky settle stomach."

She was so persistent that Maggie rose and sat in the armchair. She liked the old mother, she was fun. In no time, in a low, halting English, Hester had told the story of her life. The whisky did Maggie good and she nibbled a biscuit. Hester talked nineteen to the dozen, but her daughter sat pale, almost never speaking or moving unless her mother requested her to do so. "Anna, pick up that ashtray for the lady. Anna, put the glass on the table."

Anna automatically obeyed every word with zombie-like indifference, her lovely face showing very little expression and her thick dark lashes veiling strange dark green eyes. Maggie, who always wanted a daughter, really admired this lovely girl. She tried to say how beautiful she thought Anna was, but Hester was so wrapped up in the injustice of her life, she did not want to listen to Maggie's praise.

"Tomorrow, it will be nice weather," she said. "We will sit up on the deck. It'll do you good."

Eventually she did retire to bed. "Come, Anna," she said and Anna trailed after her like a young puppy dog.

"What a funny pair," said Maggie to Tom, when he came to say goodnight. "Did you see them?"

"Saw the young bird," said Tom. "Smashing ain't she?"

"Not much chance there, Tom," said Maggie. "That old gel won't let her out of her sight."

"We'll see about that," said Tom.

Maggie felt better already, it was strange how a bit of company livened her up.

As Hester had prophesied, the weather was lovely in the morning. The sky was blue and white-flecked waves gently rocked the ship. Maggie and her new-found friend Hester sat on the sundeck. Beside them was Anna looking far away. Tom sauntered about the deck dressed up in a tee-shirt and lightweight slacks. He was really having a good time, Maggie was glad.

"Why don't you go and walk with Tom?" Maggie asked Anna who looked down waiting for her mother to make the decision. To this Hester replied in Polish. It must have been "No," for Anna never moved. This irritated Maggie who ignored the mother and leaned over and said sweetly to Anna, "Be a dear, and ask Tom if he's got any cigarettes."

She got up, cast a defiant look at her mother and went toward Tom who leaned nonchalantly on the rail.

Old Hester's lips set in a grim line.

"What's the matter?" asked Maggie. "Why do you keep that young girl at your side? Let her enjoy herself."

The performance old Hester put up! Tears poured down. "If you only knew how I worry over that girl. What can I do? I, poor woman alone, have to bring her up. Her father, the old devil, he deserted me, left me miles away from home. That's what he did mine devil."

Maggie was sorry "mine devil" did what he did, but could not see the reason for Hester taking it out on her daughter. So she tried to divert the conversation.

"Going to Australia, are you? I will be going once I've visited my son in Cape Town."

"Me a poor refugee. The Germans take me from my home in the night. Never see my poor mother again. I work, I dig. Look at hands." She produced two great horny hands for Maggie's inspection. Maggie showed great interest because Anna and Tom had now disappeared below deck and she knew she had better keep the old girl talking.

Once out of sight, Tom said, "Blimey, can't your old girl jaw. Thought I was never going to get a chance to know you."

They were as tall as each other and Anna turned and looked Tom straight in the face, her green eyes opened and whatever Tom saw there, he liked it. He put his hand through her arm. "No hurry, is there? Let's go for a drink."

"She won't miss me," said the dutiful daughter, "too busy telling your mother I am a bastard."

Tom roared with laughter. "Bit of a mean bastard meself," he said. "Let's make the most of it." They disappeared for the morning.

Anna was dead right. Hester was telling Maggie how "mine devil" got her pregnant and then could not marry her. She discovered a wife he had forgotten. Did not seem fair to tell a stranger, thought Maggie, but these foreigners were different. You could never tell what they were thinking. Tom was taking his time and Maggie was pleased about that.

They returned at lunch time. Their cheeks were glowing and there was a sort of a Mona Lisa smile on Anna's face. Old Hester nagged and moaned in Polish and Anna helped her from the chair and collected her belongings.

"She's a nice girl," said Maggie later.

"Smashing," said Tom, almost licking his lips.

Well, thought Maggie, seems there's more in Anna than meets the eye.

*   *   *

The weather remained calm and beautiful and the sea like a millpond. Maggie found her way around the ship once she had acquired her sea legs. The immense amount of space, the movies and the swimming pool really amazed her. She simply could not believe all this was going on in the middle of a vast ocean. Hester now stuck to her like glue. Maggie did not mind as it gave Anna a spot of freedom which Tom made good use of.

In Tangiers, they went ashore for a few hours. In a big, flamboyant, bright-colored kimono and a huge straw hat Hester haggled in the Arab market, dragging Maggie here and there. Maggie felt very confused. The heat and the smell got on her nerves so she was not sorry to get back on board with a pot of tea.

Tom and Anna had gone to the market with them, but they managed to disappear and did not arrive back until very late. Like a raging bull, Hester had been marching up and down the deck for hours. Maggie laughed outright at the expression on Anna's face when she saw her mother waiting. The girl took to her heels and ran to her cabin, half tipsy and loaded with all sorts of rubbishy presents that Tom had bought her. He was very drunk and very happy.

"Hello, Ma," he called out boisterously. "What the hell is wrong with that old battle axe? We had a marvelous time."

On the last night there was a very special celebration dance. Hester buzzed in and out of Maggie's cabin trying to find out what Maggie was going to wear.

"I make beautiful dress," she told her. "Come, I'll show you."

In the cabin next door, Anna was putting the finishing touches to a lovely white dress. Her supple fingers stitched quickly, her face was pale and tear-stained from a recent battle with her mother. Maggie touched the soft, white material and looked at the handmade, pink rose buds that went all the way down the front and trimmed the hem.

"Why Anna, that's lovely!" Maggie burst out.

Anna's pale face lit up. "I made it," she said. "I'm glad you like it."

She held the white dress up to her as she stood up. Her chestnut-burnished hair hung in two long braids. With its straight classic lines, the dress suited her to perfection. It did look homemade, but that made no difference to her poise. Maggie looked at her unable to explain her admiration of this lovely young girl.

Suddenly a heavy hand descended on her shoulder. "Come now, I show you mine dress." It was Hester. From a suitcase she produced a dress that was identical to Anna's. It was the same in every aspect, except there were yards of it. It was like a tent. Maggie could not believe that this foolish woman was going to wear the same dress as her daughter and spoil the young girl's pleasure. To her common sense it did not seem possible. Anna had left the cabin as soon as her mother produced her dress.

"This, I make," boasted Hester holding up the flowing dress.

"Isn't it the same as Anna's?" asked Maggie rather lamely. She was feeling uncomfortable.

"This is better," replied Hester. "More material. Cost more."

Maggie was sure of that. "But perhaps it would be better not to both look alike," she urged.

"Not look same." The round, marble-like blue eyes almost popped from her large Teuton head. "I look much better. I got good figure," she added proudly.

"But young girls like to find partners," protested Maggie timidly.

"Me too," replied Hester defiantly. "I get man. I look for rich husband in Australia. What you think? I be nun? I want man."

Eventually Maggie retreated from the battle. There did not seem much good arguing with this stupid, puffed-up woman. But she ceased to look forward to the dance. She hung about a bit, trying not to get ready too early.

Tom had already taken Anna who looked sweet and lovely beside the big ugly Tom. It was like beauty and the beast. He looked nice but was not sober, and seldom had been since they had come on the ship. Maggie repeated to Tom that Hester intended to find a husband in Australia. He was amused and so was she when he replied, "She's more than likely going to mate with a bloody kangaroo."

At last the big white apparition appeared in the doorway. Hester in full war cry, white evening dress, earrings, beads—the flaming lot. "A walking Woolworths," was how Maggie described her.

"Let's have a drink first."

Maggie poured herself and Hester a couple of stiff brandies.

"You look very nice, Maggie," said Hester.

"So do you," replied Maggie praying fervently for forgiveness for the lies she told.

"Your Tom," asked Hester as she sipped her drink. "Is he in business?"

"Oh yes," she lied. "He's off to Australia to take over his uncle's sheep farm. Had a nice business in London but he fancied a change. You know how it is with these youngsters."

"Oh yes," grinned Hester looking very pleased with herself. "How long will you be in Cape Town?" she inquired.

"Not more than two weeks," replied Maggie.

"Let's go to the dance, it's getting late."

Hester sailed in like a ship in full sail. All eyes turned toward her, including the sad ones of her daughter who was dancing very close up to Tom.

Maggie tried hard to suppress her mirth as Hester dragged a mild little man out on to the dance floor and whirled him round and round. From the corner of her eye Maggie saw Tom and Anna slip quietly out of the door.

At Home with Anne-Marie

It was cold and rainy and a fine mist hung over the harbor as the *Transvaal Queen* entered Cape Town Harbor.

Maggie leaned over the rail looking toward Table Mountain. "Can't see a thing," she exclaimed. "Is this supposed to be a hot climate? I feel darned cold."

"It will brighten up later, it's the early morning mist," a ship's officer informed her.

On the quayside she spotted Anne-Marie and Al. She waved excitedly. Anne-Marie was as smart as always in a dusty pink suit and a wide-brimmed hat. The lanky Al stood beside her in a bright shirt and Panama hat.

Tom had been looking for Anna and now came up to Maggie.

"Hester won't let her out," he said gloomily.

"I should think not after your goings on last night," was his mum's unsympathetic reply.

"Oh, nuts," said Tom. "She wasn't a bad little bird. Would have liked to say goodbye."

Then he saw Al and began calling to him. Anna was forgotten.

Soon they were driving through the wide streets of Cape Town. Maggie, sitting in the back seat of the car with her daughter-in-law, thought the couple looked very prosperous but not exceptionally happy. Anne-Marie's face was pale and her lips were set in a grim line. She was eight months pregnant, but did not show much.

"What's the matter, darling?" Maggie asked softly.

"It's my dad," whispered Anne-Marie putting her head on Maggie's shoulder. She did not cry, but there was a dreadful sadness in her little white face. It tore at Maggie's heart. "What's happened to him, love?" she asked.

"He's missing, Maggie. In a reconnaissance plane over North Korea."

MAGGIE 349

Maggie held the trembling little body close to her. "Stop worrying," she said, "Bert's like a bad penny, he'll turn up."

"I hope and pray each day that he will. He's all I've got," burst out Anne-Marie.

"Don't say that, my love, you have Al and the baby to live for."

But Anne-Marie only stared in scornful silence at Al's back, then in a hard voice said, "I wish I wasn't having this baby."

"You don't mean that, it's because you're upset," replied Maggie. But Anne-Marie just sat sad and silent for the rest of the journey. Oh dear, thought Maggie, what have I landed in this time? She stared out of the car windows. The sun was now up. A bright scorching glare beat down on the white pavements and the crowds hurrying to work. These were mostly made up of black men and women with a strange pattern of movement, something different to anything she had ever seen.

The mountain showed up clearly now, it seemed to hang over the town—a square tabletop laid with a snow-white cloth.

It was the house that surprised her most of all. There were great white stone columns at the entrance, huge ornamental pots that held long trailing ferns. Inside there was a cool half-darkness as though the blinds were drawn and, across the big marble-paved hall, black servants floated silently about. Tom stood staring, open-mouthed, up at the high-domed ceiling and when he spoke, he whispered as though the house overawed him.

"What a lovely house!" exclaimed Maggie.

"It's not mine," replied Anne-Marie sharply. "Uncle Morris's family built it. They were Dutch settlers. Better come upstairs, Maggie, we'll rest until lunchtime."

As Maggie followed Anne-Marie up the wide, soft, carpeted stairs, her eyes could not believe the luxury she saw. Heavy gilt-framed portraits lined the walls; in the bedroom the big four-poster with silk drapes almost frightened her. But Anne-Marie, bored and weary, took very little notice of her mother-in-law's exclamations as she admired her surroundings. She sat small and fragile in the big winged armchair, a drink at her side.

"Gin, isn't it?" inquired Maggie, picking up the glass.

Anne-Marie nodded. "Help yourself," she answered.

"No thanks," replied Maggie, "seen too many drunkards in my lifetime, and I'm bloody sure I wouldn't touch the stuff if I was pregnant."

For a moment Anne-Marie looked angry. Then suddenly she smiled. "Doesn't harm you. Just gives you a lift, that's all."

"Seen babies born with soft brains over that gin," continued Maggie. "You don't want to give birth to an imbecile, do you?"

"Oh, shut up! Don't you start on me."

Tears leaped into Anne-Marie's eyes as Maggie had expected them to. She caught hold of the girl and held her tight.

"Come on, my love, let the tears come, you'll feel better for it."

Her head on her mother-in-law's breast, Anne-Marie cried out the delayed tears. Maggie laid her on the silken bed. "Now tell Mum, what's that Al been doing to upset you?"

"Oh, Mum, he's driven all the love out of me. I swear I'll get my own back on him one day."

She sobbed bitterly into the pillows and Maggie tried to comfort her. She stayed with her until the long golden lashes closed on the blue eyes. Then covering her gently, she went downstairs to sit out in the garden.

"This is nice," exclaimed Maggie as she sat to admire the white mountain that shone a myriad of colors in the blazing heat of the sun. Her thoughts strayed to little Joe. Hope he's taking care of himself. Then her mind wandered from Joe to John. It's three weeks since I wrote to him. Better let him know where I am.

She was roused from her thoughts by a soft-footed,

white-coated servant, with his inscrutable, coal-black face, inquiring politely if she would like some lunch.

"No thanks," replied Maggie. "Where's the kitchen? I'll go and make myself a cup of tea."

He looked very alarmed. "I'll bring you refreshments, Madam," he said.

"No you won't," replied the strange guest. "Tell me where the kitchen is. I'll wait on myself."

With an amused shrug, he led the way to the kitchen. Then he disappeared. The shining rows of copper pots and the array of stainless steel confused her for a moment. Then she spied a familiar object—a kettle. She pounced on it, filled it up and then began to look for a gas stove. She opened and shut doors muttering all the time. A big, black woman stood in the doorway, the white of her eyes standing out from her shiny black face. "Does you want something, Mam?" she asked.

"I can't find the stove," said Maggie. "I'm dying for a cup of tea."

The woman's mouth slowly opened in a grin that stretched from ear to ear. "Dat der cooker, Mam." She pointed to an electric stove.

"Gawd," exclaimed Maggie, "it's as big as a bloody piano."

Two black hands took the kettle and switched on the stove. Then the servant opened the fridge to show Maggie where the food was kept. Maggie cut some chicken sandwiches, then sat on a high stool enjoying her meal, while Lottie, as the maid was called, continued her job, down on her hands and knees scrubbing the floor.

"Have a cup of tea, love," offered Maggie.

"No thanks, I only drink cold drink. It get hot afternoons."

"Go on, love," persisted Maggie.

But Lottie went on with her scrubbing, just laughing at her.

"Well, have some sandwiches then."

But Lottie looked shy. "If you don't eat them, I'll take them home for the children," she said.

"How many kids you got?" inquired Maggie.

"Five," replied Lottie.

"Blimey, that's enough to feed. Don't seem long ago to me that I was scrubbing floors with two kids screaming around me."

But Lottie would not be drawn into a conversation. She finished her job, fetched a paper bag and put in the remainder of the sandwiches. Then, with a short "Good day, Mam," she was gone again. Funny lot, was Maggie's thought, ain't got much to say for themselves.

Anne-Marie rose for dinner. She looked much better. "No good waiting for them, Mum, Al's always late."

"Why, what's he up to?" inquired Maggie. Knowing Al she was very suspicious.

"He prowls about the town taking photos," Anne-Marie told her.

So Al had taken up a hobby. "Morris had some good equipment, including a dark room, and Al is teaching himself the art of photography, and spends his time in the town looking for subjects, young ladies in bikinis and such like."

"Well, I never," declared Maggie as she listened to Anne-Marie. She looked so sweet, her fair hair on top of her head in an artistic knot and dressed in a well-cut maternity dress. What a fool Al is not to take better care of her.

"I never minded him always being out," her voice rose plaintively. "But, Mum, it's those models always ringing up, to have their photos taken in the nude."

Maggie started to laugh. "No, not Al, surely, taking pictures of girls with no clothes on."

Anne-Marie nodded her blonde head. "And one little bitch, he stayed out all night with. I went downtown and punched her on the nose."

"Now that's more like it, my love," giggled Maggie. "Didn't think you'd take it lying down."

Her sons had arrived. She could hear them dashing upstairs to change.

After dinner they all sat out in the conservatory. The outside was deep and dark, strange bird cries drifted in. The house was on the side of a hill so they could see the lights of the city lying in the valley. It was very pleasant out there after the heat of the day and, over iced drinks, they talked of family matters, of the much-loved Uncle Morris and the good times with him when they were evacuated. Anne-Marie was more relaxed but there was still an air of restraint between her and her husband.

At midnight Anne-Marie went up to bed and Tom followed soon after. For the first time Al and his mother were alone. He had grown up quite a bit since their previous meeting. He brought his photographs and camera out to show her. Maggie had never known him to be so keen on anything before.

"Look, Mum," he produced a shot of a beautiful girl in a bikini. "I got money from a magazine for this one," he said proudly.

"Is that the one who caused all the trouble?" inquired his mum.

"No, not her, that was the kid trying to get on the films. Used to pester me to take photos of her, but Anne-Marie beat her up. Came in the bar and broke my best camera over my head," he added dolefully.

"Can't you find something else to do?" suggested Maggie. He stood looking very forlorn, as though he were a little boy again, still with that lock of fair hair hanging over his eyes.

"I've never been any good at anything before. I'm fond of her, mum, but she treats me like a pauper. I want to earn money of my own and support my wife. I don't want to scrounge off her relations all my life."

Well, this was a surprise! Al standing on his own two feet.

"Try and make it up," urged Maggie. "This worry over her father hasn't helped."

"Don't you think I miss Bert too?" said Al brokenly. "He was like a father to me."

Poor little devils, all this luxury and nothing of their own.

"Listen, Al. Don't tell the others," she said to him,

"but I'll give you a stake to get started. You can pay me back when you've made a million. Get yourself a studio, and for gawd's sake make it up with your wife."

"Thanks, Mum, but how can you afford it?" Al asked.

"Don't you worry over me," said Maggie.

She wrote a check for £200. "Be careful with it," she warned.

Al kissed her. "I won't forget, Mum, and I will pay you back," he said.

The two weeks with Al and Anne-Marie soon passed. Maggie was not sorry; she did not like Africa. The heat made her head bad and there was something there she felt she never could understand. Many of the black people smiled, but they were not over-friendly. The streets were so busy and there was an air of prosperity for the whites and poverty for the blacks. She felt it like a gathering storm.

Tom was fed up too. He had always been in trouble for taking Al out boozing. First with Anne-Marie and then with his ma and then there were all those bloody wogs. "Can't stand them," said Tom. "Don't even like the bloody smell of them."

Maggie, thinking of little Joe who was his brother, was very shocked, but she never bothered to argue with Tom.

By now they were in a plane to go to Australia. Maggie had not wanted to go that way, but Anne-Marie managed to persuade her. "It's fine, Mum," she had said. "Look at the time you'll save. And you do want to get back to John by the spring."

As they boarded the plane, she was terrified. Across the tarmac was Al with his arm around his wife. Maggie closed her eyes and waited to leave the world behind.

It was Tom who brought her back to earth. "Better have a drink, old girl, you look ghastly."

She realized they were in the air and nothing very terrible had happened. It was just like traveling in a bus. As the plane droned through the night over mountains and oceans, she dozed fitfully, dreaming of Oak Tree Cottage, wondering if it was snowing in England. In two weeks it would be Christmas. How nice it would have been to be with John by a blazing log fire, with Timothy on her lap. Yet here she was halfway across the world and no idea where John was. Tom snored beside her, his mouth wide open. Tomorrow he will be safe in Australia, she thought. She hoped he would settle down. At least Ginger would do his best for him.

She opened her eyes and looked out of the window. Dawn was just breaking over the mountains, the plane was flying low before going in to land for re-fueling and before her was a sight she remembered all her life. A pale golden sun rose over the horizon, painting the mountain top a deep glowing pink. Some dark rain clouds bounced their way to the left and seemed to stand still as the sun, a supreme artist, painted the sky a thousand colors. She held her breath at the beauty of it all.

At midday they landed in the lovely city of Perth and Ginger, middle-aged, big and boisterous as ever, embraced her in a great bear hug, shouting, "Maggie! My lovely little Maggie. Welcome to Downunder."

10

Briggs Place

At first sight she liked Australia and the gaiety of the people in the hotel where they stayed overnight. The cleanness of the city and the fresh wind that blew in from the sea was bracing after the heat of Cape Town. Ginger had changed very little. His hair was still bright red and very plentiful. He was loud and cheerful and seemed to know everyone. Tom liked him, she knew he would. The only thing they had in common was their capacity for drink.

"Hope you won't mind," Ginger told Maggie. "Lorna, my wife, has gone to Sydney to stay with her parents."

"That's all right, Ginger," she replied. "I'm not staying long, only till Tom settles down."

Ginger gave Tom a hearty thump on the back. "Just the boy for the old outback, he'll settle down all right."

Maggie had her doubts. Tom seemed very good at doing nothing, and even better at getting rid of his money.

In the morning they started out for Briggs Place, where Ginger lived. They traveled in his old jeep for hours and hours, the countryside changing from cool green slopes to sparse, rocky plains. The wind still

blew but it was hot and dry and carried with it clouds
of dust. There were some magnificent views in the distance, blue mountains soared up into the sky and the
ground changed to red and often looked purple, and
all this time they saw very few people. They did see a
few shacks on the roadside and a few cars on the road.
A strange, desolate land, thought Maggie. Why is everyone so anxious to leave our beautiful green England?

Late afternoon they reached their destination. "We're
entering Briggs Place," yelled Ginger. "Named after
some bloody old ex-con."

There were a few nicely built bungalows, a row of
shops and plenty of old wooden shacks. The land had
become green since they crossed a big river and thou-
sands of white woolly sheep roamed the pasture land.

They drove down the drive to Ginger's house. It was
a very nice, low white dwelling, and tall lime trees grew
in front of the house. It was then she realized how few
trees she had seen on the journey.

"Chopped them down to build their shacks, them
damn fools did," Ginger informed her. "That's why it's
so dusty. Not so good for sheep anymore, don't get
enough rain."

Tom looked at the landscape with lack of interest,
until he saw the fine horses in the paddock. "Now
that's what I'd like to do," he said. "Always fancied
myself on horseback."

"So you shall, my lad," joked Ginger. "Can't get far
without a mount out here."

It was homely inside the house, plenty of room and
comfortably furnished. Maggie looked around. Something was missing, the room had a neglected air about
it. There was dust on the ledges and the curtains and
covers were slightly grubby. They sat in the shade of
the living room and a dried-up little yellow man brought
them cool drinks. It was then it came to her: the room
lacked a woman's touch. How long did he say she had
been gone? A week? A bit longer than that, she decided.

The yellow man was called Tong Lun. But Maggie
called him Long Tongue and he never liked it at all.

He cast evil looks from his slit eyes at her and muttered curses in several dialects. The dislike became mutual; Maggie could not stand him. It appeared that Long Tongue was in charge of the domestic arrangements in Ginger's house. When Maggie ran her finger along the top of the dingy chairs and showed him all the dust, he was most put out.

"Woman come to clean. I busy cooking. I not see if she work."

"Well, you all get wages, don't you? Fetch me a flaming duster, and send that old gal to me. The bathroom's filthy."

From then on it was a war between Long Tongue and Maggie. She put Ginger's home into ship-shape condition, with the aid of an old, faded woman, Ada, who had originally come from Ireland.

Tom was learning to ride and he and Ginger were out all day riding and half the night drinking. In ten days, not one visitor came. Maggie did not hear the sound of another woman's voice, except that of old Ada.

"How long has Mrs. Burns been away?" Maggie asked her.

"Will now," she slurred, her brogue was still very thick. "Oi never seen her much this year. That twin's poorly. She's gone to town to take her to the hospital. 'Tis the dust you know. Makes me cough shocking." She proceeded to cough with great racking sounds, until Maggie produced a tumbler of whisky.

All day Maggie pondered on this news. Things are not what they seem. I wonder why Ginger doesn't tell me? His twin girls must be about twelve now. A family for twins, this one.

Late evenings they sat out after dinner on the verandah. A great moon floated in a clear sky and she had never seen so many stars. It was the best time out here in the evenings, away from the dust and that hot wind, that made her so irritable. "I wouldn't mind it here but for the wind and that bloody Chinese devil in the kitchen," she informed her host.

"Maggie, darling, you're homesick for Stepney." Ginger treated most things as a joke. He would stir up Long Tongue against Maggie and vice versa. Still, it was a lazy sort of life, nothing much else going on.

That evening there had been the usual set-to. On their plates had been a strange, chopped-up mess—bits of chicken floating in white worms. Tom and Ginger, who ate only for the sake of eating, were scoffing it up. But Maggie pushed her plate aside. "What's all this?" she asked.

"It's chow," said Tom with his mouth full. "It's smashing. Try it."

She shook her head, going rather pale. "Take it away, Long Tongue," she said. "I don't like the smell of it."

With a lot of muttering, he did so. His little black eyes flickered wickedly. "Lady not like chow? Nice, good chicken chow."

"Take it away, I don't like it," she said. Two spots of color appeared on her cheeks.

"What lady like then?" asked Long Tongue as he waddled off.

His sarcastic tone annoyed her. She got up and walked out onto the verandah, trying not to lose her temper. Once alone out there under the starry sky, the homesick feeling welled up inside her. She could never live in this place. No wonder Ginger's wife has left him. There was no reason for her to stay for as long as she had planned. She would try to get home for Christmas. It will be nice to see Babs and the babies. In this frame of mind, she watched the silver moon sail over the sky. Little white clouds chased it, looking like white birds. What were they called? She screwed up her eyes to look at the sky, tears were very near, but she must not cry. White doves! That's what those clouds look like, soft white doves! Gentle, like her John. She must go home, she could bear it no longer. Then another good thought occurred to her. That beautiful, strange, silver moon, there was only one so wherever he was, John could see it too. It gave her comfort and a little smile began to hover about her lips.

She was rudely awakened by a big hand that slapped her on the back. "Cheer up, Maggie," said the incorrigible Ginger. "I just gave that old Chinese devil such a beating, he won't sit down for a week."

She burst into a laugh. The same old Ginger. As a little lad he had chased the tears from her eyes with his funny jokes. She linked her arm through his and they stood close together.

"Do you still remember the old days in Stepney?" she asked.

"All of it," cried Ginger. "Many's the time I've sat out here and been so bloody homesick for those bloody old slums, I could have packed up and gone straight home."

"That's how I feel at this moment," she said.

"Don't leave me yet, love," he begged. "It's Christmas next week. We will go down and stay at the beach club. I expect I've left you alone too much."

"It is a bit lonely," she replied.

"Sorry, Maggie, I am afraid it's a habit of mine." His blue eyes looked sad and she knew he was missing his wife. Her heart went out to him.

"All right, Ginger, I'll stay till after Christmas."

"Good!" He jumped up clapping his hands. "Drinks! you old Chinese bastard," he yelled. Old Ginger was back in action.

They sat talking of old times and drank till sun up.

In the morning the long-awaited mail arrived. There was a long letter from Jim. Babs had had twin boys again. They were to be called Tom and Terry, keeping up with the family tradition. There was also a large buff, official-looking envelope from Mr. Benson at the bank. It contained two letters from John; one telling her of a trip he expected to make, which might bring him home early; the other complained of a lack of correspondence from her and informed her that he was going to America for the New Year. I was wondering, if you would like to join me, it read. I'm going to Connecticut and I thought you might like to visit your old pal Sarah. I'll cable you to let you know. Happy Christmas, darling, if I am not with you, love and kisses, John.

The words danced before her eyes, and a cold shiver went down her spine. New Year, possible Christmas! God! What was she going to do? She must go, he might be on his way home. Her head ached. She felt jaded. This climate did not agree with her and it was a good excuse for leaving. She must talk to Tom.

But Tom was very preoccupied. He had received a letter and there was a somber expression on his face as he read it. He put the letter in his pocket when he saw his mother looking at him.

"Tom," said Maggie timidly, "I must go home tomorrow."

"Why? You ain't got nothing to rush home for," insisted Tom.

"I want to be home for Christmas," she explained.

"Might go me bleeding self," muttered Tom. "Ain't sure I want to be stuck out here in the wilds all me life."

She did not feel like an argument. So she took herself off to her room to re-read her letters. If she was going, she had better get a move on. A thousand problems cropped up. The money in the suitcase belonged to Tom, but she had no intention of parting with it, until he made some decision with regard to his future. I must go to town and book up a seat on the plane.

"Tom," she pleaded later that day, "take me into town."

"I can't," returned Tom. "Ginger's out with the jeep."

He seemed very bad tempered; she began to wonder who the letter was from.

Another day dragged by and nothing was done. Seeing her worried face, Ginger asked, "What's up, Maggie?"

She handed him John's letter.

"This that bloke you live with?" he asked.

She nodded miserably.

"Didn't you tell him you were coming?" he asked incredulously.

She shook her head.

"Blimey!" cried Ginger. "He'll think you've hopped it. Do you love him, Maggie?"

"Might sound crazy for a woman of my age, but I'm mad about him. I suppose he's the one I should have married."

"I have a faint recollection," said Ginger, "of you running down the street and him chasing you."

"And I remember how you blackmailed him, you little swine," returned Maggie with affection.

Ginger immediately became very kind and considerate. "Get ready, my love, I'll take you into town and fix up your plane ticket."

It was Thursday when they drove into Perth. The first business was with the bank, where she deposited the rest of Tom's money.

"Put it into a deposit account," Ginger advised. "No questions will be asked. They all know me, and as soon as I see a little place going I'll get Tom set up. But between you and me, Maggie, Tom's a real townee. Can't see him settling to a sheep farmer's life after all."

"I know," she replied somewhat forlorn, "I only hope he won't get into trouble out here."

"He's a big lad, Maggie, leave him be," advised Ginger. "Funny, don't recall anyone bothering over me and young Lennie. Chucked straight from school we was into a bloody war."

He was sad when he spoke of his brother Lennie.

"Don't look back. It'll do no good," Maggie told him. "And you're quite right about Tom, I'm going to forget about him as soon as I get back home."

It was a great relief once the rest of that stolen money had gone into the bank. Then they tried all the travel agents. No bookings, all full. Everyone was traveling home for Christmas. The disappointment showed in her face.

"Looks like you'll be spending Christmas with me, after all," said Ginger. "Don't want you to get stuck halfway, might be some Godforsaken hole, all alone on Christmas Day."

She could see his point, he was probably right. So she took a chance and booked a flight for the twenty-ninth, four days after Christmas. Then they went to a hotel for dinner and a drink.

There were very few women in the brightly lit bar. Maggie wondered what the married women did with their leisure time. She watched Ginger as he hung over the bar and whispered to a lovely young girl who served the drinks. Maggie's bright eyes took everything in. He seemed to know that girl very well. She was pretty but had deep coffee-colored skin and strange eyes that gleamed yellow like cats' eyes. Gold rings dangled from her ears and her neckline was very low. But as she smiled the whole of her face changed. She had a wide, warm, white-toothed smile, a love of the joys of life. Ginger came back flushed and slightly embarrassed.

"She's a very striking girl," Maggie remarked.

"Who? Mai? Yes, she's lovely. Used to live out at Briggs Place."

That's why Lorna left home. The thought flashed quickly through her mind, but he seemed to read her thoughts.

"She's half Aborigine. I have known and loved her since she was a child."

Maggie remained silent, not knowing what to say.

They arrived back late that night. Tom was very surly and morose. "Blimey," he said, "I wondered where you was."

"I went to book a seat on the plane. I'm going home, Tom."

"Please yourself," replied Tom, "but leave me dough behind. Might go to Sydney myself for Christmas."

"There's not a lot to spare now, Tom. I've put the rest in the bank for you."

"What the bloody hell did you do that for? They might trace it."

"Well, that's a chance you got to take, better than wasting it."

"Whose bloody lolly is it?" yelled Tom.

"I want you to buy a place of your own," pleaded his mother.

"Don't know what I'm doing yet," growled Tom. He left the house and was not seen any more that night.

The night was hot and Maggie was restless, she tossed and turned and at one time a shadowy figure stood beside her bed. She must be dreaming, it was big Jim. Strange, she never dreamed of him now. The figure bent down and kissed her forehead. "Goodnight Jim," she murmured sleepily.

She heard a car drive out just before dawn—Ginger going out already?—then she went off into a deep sleep, not waking until the bright sun shone in her eyes. Oh dear, I've overslept. Yawning and putting on her robe, she saw the note on the dressing table, written in Tom's childish hand.

Dear Mum,
I am sorry I did not say goodbye. I must go to Sydney, something is worrying me. I took my bank book, also the ring and bracelet, in case I need any ready cash. Take care of yourself.
Love Tom.

Maggie went as pale as death. So it had not been a dream, it was Tom in here getting his money, and he had taken her jewelry as well. He had not left her much. Might have waited till she had gone. They were all a bit selfish these boys of hers. She wanted to cry. A lump like a large piece of apple was in her throat and would not disperse.

She dressed and went down to where Ginger sat, head bent over the breakfast table. As soon as she looked at him, she knew that he knew Tom had gone.

"Why such a dark secret?" she protested.

Ginger looked sheepish: "It's that bird," he said, "the one he met on the boat. He told me all about it. But honest to God, Maggie, I never made up his mind, he did that himself."

This time she was in a blazing temper. "What a fool I am. Came all the way here with him and he hops off. Took all his money and my jewelry as well."

"I didn't know he took your ring and bracelet, Maggie, but he said the money was his. I lent him the jeep to get to the bus station."

"Thanks for nothing," she yelled at him.

He stared at her. He loved Maggie in a temper. "Don't let him bother you, love, it's Christmas Eve. Let's enjoy ourselves. Tom will make it okay."

"I damn well hope so." She stormed up and down. "No good running to me when he's broke, I'll never lift a finger to help him again."

Ginger produced a glass of brandy, hoping to calm her down, but it seemed to excite her more. Her eyes like blue fire, her hair hanging down, she clenched her fists as though bursting with a desire to strangle someone.

"Keep that bloody yellow devil out of my sight today," she said.

"Did you hear that, Long Tongue?" called out Ginger who knew he was eavesdropping.

But the storm was over and they both burst out laughing as they heard the flip of the Chinaman's slippers as he ran off back to the kitchen. So they sat close up on the settee while they finished the brandy.

"She's only a kid, that girl of Tom's. He told me she was a virgin till he had her and she's got a battle-axe of a mother."

"I know," said Maggie. "Well, if he's facing the music, got a lot to worry over, there. All right, Ginger, let's have some fun, take me to that beach club you were talking about."

A Very Merry Christmas

They sat up very late on Christmas Eve, talking of the old days in Stepney and of Liza.

"What a tough old gal she was," said Ginger. "I never remember her showing even the slightest hint of affection, only to Jim. She loved Jim, he took the place of the old man. She must have loved him, never got over him being killed."

"It's a strange world," said Maggie. "I don't know how anyone can live with a man in the grave. I couldn't, yet I was fond of my Jim."

"He was not very good to you, Maggie. Often kids see more than they should."

"I know he was unfaithful to me. Saw him with a woman once, never hurt so much. They say where there's no sense, there's no feeling."

"I dispute that, Maggie, you had plenty of love and feeling. What would us poor little kids have done without your loving care?"

She smiled at him. The brandy had loosened her tongue. She wanted to explain how she had suddenly grown up and how different her love for John was.

"Perhaps there are two kinds of love," she suggested. "If I think about John sleeping with another woman, I could do a murder, I'm so jealous."

"It's true. The reason Lorna left me was over Mai."

So the truth was out. "Tell me, if it makes you feel better," said Maggie.

"That kid used to help with the children. She was only twelve when she came, a poor unwanted kid of mixed blood. Lorna was hard on her, so she always came to me with her troubles. Lorna took long trips in the summer, she can't stand the heat up here. Well, you can guess the rest. At fifteen she was ready for a man, almost hanging about my neck. One hot night, full of booze, I took her. I have no regrets. I entered a world unknown to me and I have never wanted any other woman. At sixteen she was having my child. The news went around the village and Lorna found out. I paid for Mai to get an abortion and, when she was well, I got her a flat and a job. She's still my woman.

"When Lorna left it was not so important, but I miss the kids. I've let her know that if she does not return in the spring, I'll sell up and move into town, but I won't give up Mai. I've no time for cold-fish white women anymore."

"Well," said Maggie dryly, "I'm quite safe with you then."

He grinned. "Now that's another story. As a matter of fact, you are the warmest, most lovable woman I know, next to Mai."

"Thanks a lot," said Maggie. "But I'd think twice if I was you before you let your wife go. You're well over forty and Mai's still a young girl in her teens."

"Don't you think I ain't thought of that, darling?" replied Ginger. "Come on, finish the bottle and give me a kiss, it's Christmas Day."

Later as she lay in bed, she thought of little Joe. She had not heard any news from him. He should have gone back to school at the end of November. She would be glad to get home to find out what had happened. She drowsed, going over the conversation with Ginger. She had understood what he meant, having recalled that night out with Joe's father. But it was better not to, white people did not belong. I wonder who my little Joe will marry. Her head was swimming with the extra amount of brandy, but it was a nice sensation, worries seemed so far away.

It was a strange sort of Christmas morning, a blazing hot day. First of all, there was no breakfast. Long Tongue was missing. Maggie made coffee and omelettes in the sacred kitchen that Long Tongue would not normally allow her to enter.

"Where's the old devil gone?" she inquired. "Home to China for Christmas?"

"He doesn't miss a trick," declared Ginger. "He knows we're going out, he has been listening. So he buzzed off last night on an opium binge with another old heathen down in the village."

Over breakfast they talked of home, the snow and the Christmas cards on the mantelpiece. "I can't believe it's Christmas Day," she said. "Nothing to remind me."

"You will, it's all laid on down at the club, Christmas pud and turkey and all the trimmings."

"What will I wear?" she asked.

"Make yourself look nice, love, and I'll be proud of you. It will knock some of them dowdy old hens over when they see you in all your smart gear. Got a swimsuit? We'll have a bathe—got a cracking beach—and bring a nice dress for dinner. We'll hit the ceiling tonight, Maggie, my love."

Dear old Ginger, she was glad she stayed, he would have had a lonely Christmas.

"I'll go and borrow a posh car." He was off like a shot, his red hair gleaming in the sun as he jumped his horse over the fence and went tearing down the road.

Soon they were heading for the country club. There was a suitcase in the boot, and brandy and cigars in the car which they had borrowed for the occasion. They skirted the town and drove to the beach. The great expanse of blue sea and the frothy lines of surf as they came dashing inshore was a grand sight. Surf boats and surf riders, Maggie had never seen before. "Look at all the people. I was wondering where all the young Australian girls were."

"On the beach, Maggie. That's where you find the glamor in the summer," explained Ginger.

Lovely, young, tanned bodies frolicked in the water. Beautiful girls walked gracefully along the promenade, showing off the latest thing in swimsuits.

"Oh, this really cheers me up," she cried taking deep breaths of the fresh salt air. "It's so nice to get away from that hot, dry wind. Why don't you live down here, Ginger?"

"Bloody sheep won't eat sand," laughed Ginger.

They drove along the front to where the club lay, back off the road, with its own private beach in front. It was very smart and there were plenty of people here too, but mostly with their clothes on. They sat in the dining room where the long windows gave an excellent view of the sea, palms in pots and soft-footed waiters.

"Let's have a light lunch and then we'll go down for a swim," Ginger suggested.

Maggie had a glass of wine and a sandwich but Ginger had several beers and a couple of whiskys, together with a big dish of oysters. It did not stop there. He knew everyone, and they all wanted to buy him drinks. So he drank, shouted and cracked jokes, he was really enjoying himself.

By the time they got to the beach, his face was very red and she was sure he was intoxicated. It was nice lying in the sun watching the sea, she was beginning to feel that it was not so bad in Australia. That was until Ginger insisted that she joined him for a bathe. It was not a success, for he was a strong swimmer while she could only just manage to keep afloat. And he was so boisterous. He grabbed hold of her and pulled her under the waves which scared her to death. She was not sorry when he went surfing and left her to sunbathe. She lay there thinking of her kind, gentle John, of when they went for a swim in the cool, green river and how they lay close together in the shade of the trees, not a soul or sound to disturb them.

The dinner that night was a grand affair. There was a big Christmas tree, and the table was laid in the traditional manner with candles, holly and mistletoe.

"You look cracking, old gel," Ginger said as they went in to dinner. Maggie had bought the dress in Cape Town and it was the first time she had worn it. Anne-Marie had helped her to choose it and she had impeccable taste. It was white, very low cut and exquisitely beaded. It contrasted with her dark hair, and her slim neat figure stood out among the more hefty Australian matrons.

Halfway through the evening she began to think that

a suit of armor would have been more suitable for the occasion, after being whirled round and round by large farmers who did not take no for an answer. Beer and wine was sloshed over her and the heat of the ballroom was terrific. Ginger, who had guzzled endless brandies, was now engaged in a shouting match with a crowd of men at the bar. She went to the ladies room to cool off, gazing at her disheveled appearance in the mirror. I must be getting old, this is all a bit strenuous for me. Still, must be over soon.

But it had only just begun. On the beach a barbecue was in progress, a fire had been lit and fairy lights were strung across the lawn. Those still able to come out to dance, did. This included Ginger who staggered about, with a bottle in one hand. He wanted to dance with Maggie and held her so tight that she could not breathe. His hands slid familiarly up and down her bare back. She began to get worried. He's drunk, doesn't know it's me.

Afterward they sat out in the shade of the trees, in every corner young couples made love. He poured out a big glass of champagne for her and his big hands fondled her breasts.

"Let's go home," said Maggie.

"Not yet, darling, it's Christmas."

She considered getting up and leaving him but, hoping for the best, she just drank some more and let him fondle her. Soon his rough mouth was kissing her and a strange kind of excitement swept through her. It was big Jim, he lived again.

"Oh God, Maggie," cried Ginger, "I've always fancied you." Then sobering up suddenly, he said, "Let's go home."

She was glad he was sane once more, but she suspected his sudden desire to go home. She crossed her fingers. Let's hope I can hold him off till we get home.

The big car tore through the dark deserted roads, taking most of the bends on two wheels. Ginger was very happy taking swigs from his brandy bottle and his free hand went up and down her silk-stockinged leg.

"Lovely legs you have got, Mai."

Crikey, he thinks I'm his girlfriend! This is the last time I'll celebrate with you, my lad.

After a while he calmed down and she felt awfully sleepy with all the drink and the excitement of the day. She felt her eyes closing as the car slowed down.

"Are we home?" she asked sleepily.

"Not yet, darling," said the slurred voice. "There's a place I must show you."

He opened the car door and took her hand. She could hear the sound of drums beating and in the distance she saw the light of a fire. "Where the devil are we?" she asked.

"Shush!" He put a finger to his lips and crept forward. In the light of a fire black men and women danced to the weird beat of a drum. Breasts hung down and bodies glistened with sweat. Eyes glazed, they twisted and twirled, their bodies close together, a mass of arms and legs. It was like a dream, a terrible frightening dream.

"Oh, my God!" Maggie turned to run, but Ginger held her tight forcing her to watch.

Strange emotions urged within. In a moment she wanted to throw off her clothes and dance naked with them. But instead she turned and pressed herself close to the virile body that whispered, "Relax, my darling, they know how to." She forgot everything. They slid close together down onto the grass, no identity, just a man and a woman locked in a passionate embrace. His rough hands tore at her beautiful dress.

Sanity returned suddenly, and turning her head sideways, she saw a little way to the left, two black bodies writhing like snakes in the grass. With all her might she pushed his heavy body off her and ran for the car, feeling as though she wanted to be sick.

He seemed quite sober when he got in the car. "Smashing, wasn't it?" he said. "Thank you, darlin'."

She never replied, her dress all covered in mud and her hair hanging loose, she shivered and hung her head.

He put his jacket about her shoulders. "Don't get upset, Maggie. We never did anything."

Never in her life had she felt as degraded as she did at that moment. Reaching home, she dashed up to her room and put the bolt on the door.

She was up with the lark in the morning. She took a bath and washed her hair and started to pack her clothes. She looked at the lovely dress she had worn last night, it was ruined—stained with mud and wine and the neckline ripped by Ginger's rough lovemaking. Her cheeks flamed red at the memory of last night. How was she going to face him this morning? There was no noise downstairs. He must still be sleeping it off.

Soft footsteps padded past her door, she opened it, and Long Tongue was out there, with a smug expression on his wrinkled face.

"Oh, so you've come back," she greeted him. He gave her no direct answer but instead he said, "Master, he sleep. Master, he pretty sick." His eyes gleamed wickedly at her. "You want coffee, nice black coffee?" he urged.

"It's nice master what was drunk, not me," she snapped. "I'll have white coffee."

He padded off and when he came back with the coffee she had put her suitcase outside the door. With folded hands he watched her drink the hot coffee. It went down well, she felt so cold and shivery this morning.

"Lady go home?" asked Long Tongue.

"In three days' time I do, and won't you be pleased," she said spitefully.

He bowed low. "Now no more called Long Tongue, but my name honorable father gave me, Tong Lun," and with much dignity he walked away.

She watched his funny little shape go plodding down the passage and her conscience pricked her. "I want you," she called after him. He turned and came back immediately, his yellow wrinkled face inscrutable.

"Here you are." She pushed a note into his pocket.

"Go and buy yourself some more of that bloody dope you are always sucking up."

He opened his mouth and showed a line of black-and-yellow teeth and a strange noise came out, almost a cackle. "Tank you, lady, most kind." He went off again, his shoulder shaking with some sort of a spasm. Laughter or tears, Maggie was not quite sure.

At midday she sat ready and waiting for Ginger to appear. She heard him get up and take a shower. Then he came down the stairs in a clean, very white, freshly laundered shirt, tucking it into the top of his trousers as he came in, his red hair plastered down flat. He looked so young and boyish that she wanted to laugh. He was just like that little boy who used to be the terror of Stepney. But she would not look at him. Ginger was full of beans, showing no remorse whatever.

"Had a smashing Christmas," he said. "The best in years. Thank you, Maggie."

She was amazed, surely he had not forgotten that he almost raped her and also ruined her thirty-guinea dress? Inside she felt very angry but decided not to remind him. He tucked into a good meal, a large steak and potatoes.

Long Tongue, as he served the lunch, placed beside her a plate of crisp fried chips. "Here Lady, I make you slips." Tears came to her eyes. Poor old Long Tongue, after the way she treated him, he had presented her with a gift.

A Long Way Home

The next few days went slowly and Ginger never mentioned the incident on Christmas Day. Finally the day of her departure came. At the airport, Ginger loaded her with books and candy.

"Don't worry love, I'll see to Tom when he gets back. I'll come over the next year," he promised. "We'll have a binge. What about a pub crawl all around the old places in Stepney?"

Maggie wanted to remind him that the London he knew had disappeared with the blitz. Suddenly he bent over and kissed her, whispering in her ear as he did so. "It was nice the other night, wasn't it, Maggie my love?"

She pulled away. That damned rogue Ginger, he had not forgotten after all.

A terrible fear overcame her as the plane took off; her face was like death as she fumbled with the seat belt. The passenger next to her leaned over to assist her and he patted her hand. "Nothing to be afraid of, Madam. Is this your first flight?"

She shook her head. "No! It's the second time. I flew out."

She felt grateful to the young man for pulling her together, she had thought she was going to pass out.

Maggie thought back over the places she had been and the things she had seen. To think that she might never have left Stepney, might have been born, lived and died there. Lots of people did and no one knew or even cared. She looked at her hands. How different they were since she had done so little housework, very white, and they seemed smaller. She missed the ring that Tom had taken. Perhaps John would buy her another. At the very thought of him, she felt sick and faint. Dear God, she prayed, don't let him come home and find Oak Tree Cottage empty, he'll be so hurt.

The plane was delayed at Aden and as she waited in the airport lounge an airport official announced a further delay. This time a change of planes at Paris. She had been waiting ages, she wondered if she should wire someone to let them know, but sat feeling too tired and exhausted to bother. The noise about her confused her, the gabble of unknown languages made her head ache.

Eventually, the plane took off for Paris but there was another long wait, because of fog this time. It was ten o'clock and the New Year revelers drifted in and out. Young ones in paper hats sang and drank. She sat hunched up in the airport lounge feeling most peculiar.

She pulled her coat tighter about her and wished she had remembered to wear her boots—her feet felt perished with the cold. Must have a touch of the flu coming on, she shivered. Should never have gone off to Australia with Tom, he went his own way in the end.

She sat commiserating with herself until it was time to board the last plane and at the stroke of twelve they were over the coast of England and another year had begun.

A coach took her to London, the deserted streets were carpeted with a blanket of snow. She thought of booking in at a hotel, but changed her mind and with grim determination went on. She must get there before John. Cold and miserable, she waited for a fast train to Kent. The snow-covered fields flying past the train window looked cool and white, different from the heat and dust of Australia. It's lovely to be going home. She imagined warming her feet by the big log fire.

Outside the station she hailed the one and only taxi. By then it was nearly three o'clock and she was travel sick and weary. She looked to see if Mr. York was in his cottage, but it was empty and forlorn.

"Is Mr. York all right?" she inquired of Bill the taxi driver.

"He's okay," was his reply. "Gone to his sister's for Christmas."

"But the dog and the cat?" she asked anxiously.

"The dog's gone with him," said Bill, "and the cat's down the post office. Don't 'alf look fed up."

"Poor old Timothy," said Maggie. "Tell Beryl I'll call for him tomorrow."

She walked up the snow-covered path. The oak tree, stripped bare of leaves, stood out stark and black against the skyline. No one was there. Thank God, she had made it in time.

Once inside, she kicked off her wet shoes. Better have a hot drink, I feel terrible. I'll soon get the fire going. Going into the small kitchen, her face changed. On the cabinet was a cup and saucer carefully washed and turned upside down, and propped against it was a note. In large letters it said: "HAPPY CHRISTMAS, MY ELUSIVE MAGGIE. BEEN AND GONE. YOUR JOHN XXXXX" An arrow pointing downward indicated that there was further information in the cupboard.

She sank down on the stool. Oh dear, I've just missed him. All that traveling for nothing, tears of self-pity flowed down her cheeks. Inside the cupboard was a parcel and a letter.

Maggie darling,
I don't know where you are, I cannot find you. You will never know how disappointed I was. I sent a cable asking you to be ready, as I was only making an overnight stop. I wanted to take you with me, as I have a special commission in the States until the end of January. Here is your Christmas present, write to this address.
Love John xxxx.

Inside the parcel was a lovely handbag.

Oh, I'm sorry, John. She sat weeping and getting colder every minute. Her hand shook as she made a cup of tea. Oh dear, now I've caught the bloody flu, she told herself.

I wonder why little Joe hasn't been home. Upstairs his room was just as he had left it. Something has happened to him. She grew panicky with worry. Her hat and coat still on and her head was swimming, what should she do? I must see Jim. I have to talk to Jim. He'll know where little Joe is. Picking up the phone she rang for a taxi again. "Sorry, Bill," she said, "but I must go back to London."

"All right, Mrs. Malloy, I'll be there in five minutes," replied Bill. It was five o'clock when she got on the train. She remembered very little of the journey, everything was far away. At eight o'clock, lugging the heavy suitcase, she dragged herself to the door of Jim's flat. All the lights were on and from within came the sound of music. Jim was having a New Year's party. Bright and breezy, he came to the door and into his arms fell his limp, weary mother. The lights went into one big ring. Maggie knew no more. She had passed right out.

The Party's Over

There had been a lot of parties in the new flat, but none that broke up so rapidly, as when Jim carried his mum into the sitting room and laid her on the settee.

"Babs," he called. "It's Mum. She's passed out."

Babs, her face as pale as Maggie's, knelt beside her. "Oh, Mum," she sobbed, "what happened to you?"

It was the tall capable Megan that kept her head. "Run quickly for the doctor," she ordered Ben and she held brandy to Maggie's lips, telling Jim to take off her shoes and stockings and Babs to get blankets.

The guests drifted out. The doctor diagnosed nervous exhaustion. "Put her to bed," he said. "She'll come round soon."

When Maggie did come to she thought she was back in the house in Witton Street. Why was she lying in bed? Better get the kids up for school. She tried to sit up and found she was unable to. Then slowly her memory returned. Why was she coming to Jim's? She tried hard to remember but felt so tired. Babs came in soon and sat beside her, looking very scared. Then Jim, her lovely, tall Jim. She caught hold of his hand and gave him her sweet smile.

"Lie very quiet, Mum," he said. "You've had a bad turn."

"Sorry to worry you, Jim. Must have got a chill."

"You're no trouble to me, Mum," replied Jim in his most solemn manner. "Who else would you go to? Your home is with me."

"I'll be all right tomorrow," said Maggie. "There are presents in the suitcase for the children."

Outside the door they held a conference. "We can't tell her about Joe," worried Jim. "What shall I say when she asks me?"

"Don't worry, dear," cried gentle little Babs.

Later on Jim came in very soberly. He could never hide his feelings, he was as open as the blue sea.

She came straight to the point. "Where's Joe?"

"Don't get upset, Mum," he replied, "but Joe's still in Africa."

She was becoming agitated. "What's the matter with him, for God's sake, Jim? Get on and tell me."

"He got delayed. He joined Father O'Mally's mission and never came back to school. He's with Al at the moment. I expect there'll be a letter in the post."

"Oh dear," sighed Maggie. "I should never have gone with Tom. Everything's gone wrong. Now he won't be able to take his exams."

"Try not to worry, Mum," said Jim; his own brow was furrowed. But Maggie reached up and smoothed out the wrinkles.

"I'll tan Joe's backside when I catch up with him," she grinned.

"That's more like our Maggie Burns," Jim said as he cuddled her.

Jim had not told the truth about Joe who had almost died of fever out in Africa and was now convalescing with Al until strong enough to travel home. But his mum seemed brighter and that was a load off his mind.

"I want to get up," she told the doctor when he returned.

"Just a few questions, then you can," was his reply.

"Get it over then," said Maggie, "I'm not an invalid."

"You were forty-eight this year?" he asked.

"Don't tell everyone. I am not going past forty, if I can help it."

"I want you to go to the local hospital, just for a check-up." He used his best bedside manner.

"Whatever for?" She was most annoyed. "I'm going home tomorrow. You're not getting me in no hospital."

"Just as you wish, Madam." He smiled at this strange character.

Babs said, "Mum will be fine, she's got plenty of spirit."

"Doctor don't think so, wants her to go to the hospital," replied Jim gloomily.

"Oh no. Why? What's wrong?"

"He's not sure, but thinks there's a reason for her passing out like that."

"Poor Maggie, she hates being ill."

Jim sat full of gloom, his wife close beside him. "Wait till I get my hands on Tom, he's behind all this."

"Don't blame anyone till you know, Jim," begged the prudent Babs. "I believe she came back to see John Malloy."

"That's another swine I'll have a go at," said Jim, his anger rising at the thought of his lively little mum being ill. Someone was responsible. Maggie would have been proud to hear her impatient Jim, so ready to defend and protect her. Loyal and generous, he was at his best when he was most needed and for the first time in his life his independent little mother needed him.

By morning Maggie was sitting up and was her usual chirpy self. Megan washed her face and brushed her long, black, waving hair and Babs brought in a lightly boiled egg and a pot of tea, all laid out daintily on the best tray.

"What's all the fuss about?" declared Maggie.

Jim hovered about looking unhappy. Maggie's mind was clear this morning. Something was wrong, what was it? Megan was gossiping in her usual way, telling her she was getting married, having got herself in the pudding club.

"Ben's got a regular job now," she announced. Maggie smiled and squeezed her hand, she liked this outspoken girl.

The doctor had spoken to Jim. "I've done my best to persuade her. It's up to you now."

"Is it anything dangerous?" inquired Jim.

"Can't tell without X-rays. She's a funny age, could be life blood that she's losing."

Jim stood for a while, his face in his hands. How

was he going to make her see reason? He went slowly into her room and she lay looking silently up at the ceiling. He sat beside her, wondering how to approach her.

But Maggie with a wry smile said, "Don't sit there like a bloody fool, Jim, I've made my decision. I know there's something wrong with me and I'll try to get well, but if I don't, I've had a good life and the hospital is the best place for me."

Jim's head went down on the bed. That was his mum. She had made her decision, he was so relieved. Had it been in the negative, he knew he could never have beaten that strong will.

"I want Megan to come with me," Maggie said. "I don't want you gloomy pair."

She and the vivacious young Megan chatted and laughed all the time while they waited for the results of the X-rays and the various tests. She told Megan of Anne-Marie and Long Tongue the Chinaman, and Megan talked of her Ben and the forthcoming wedding.

The results were positive. Maggie was to be admitted immediately.

"I am scared," Maggie confessed.

"Get away," retorted Megan. "A nice long rest in bed you'll be having."

She did not leave until Maggie was tucked up in the white hospital bed. Kissing her, she said: "I want you out of here in time for my wedding. Can't hang about, you know." She placed her hand on her tummy and winked knowingly. Maggie's laugh echoed behind her as she went out of the ward trying to hold back her tears.

11

In the Hospital

Maggie had been in the same hospital when Joe was born, and when little Marie was born. It was all a long time ago, but this place still had sad memories for her.

It was a bright pleasant ward, flowered curtains adorned the cubicles. She was glad she was next to the window; looking out she could see the old, gray, stone walls of the tower, high up on the hill. Pigeons strutted and cooed on the wide stone window ledge. There was one with a fuzzy pink head, fussing and pecking at the male birds all the time. It reminded Maggie of Beryl at the post office. In the beds all around her were old ladies, lying very silent, poor old dears. Fancy ending up like that. Don't think I want to get that old.

A fresh-faced, white-clad nurse brought her lunch. "Sit up, Mrs. Burns, mustn't lie moping," she said in her brisk, kindly manner.

Maggie sat up and began to look about her.

By the time tea was being served, she had managed a long conversation with three old ladies nearest to her. One was very deaf and the other could not see, but the conversation was translated to the deaf one by the blind one by movements of hands and sometimes by shouting loudly into her ear. Maggie's spirits gradually revived and soon she was beginning to enjoy herself.

In the bed next door was a little old lady. Her name was Miss Stiles, a real old maiden lady. She became Maggie's pet right away. She was lovely, so tiny that she looked lost in the hospital bed. Her dainty hands, just like a doll's, hovered on the white quilt. She had a small, very wrinkled face, but wonderful, very expressive dark eyes, which stared out scornfully at the rest of the patients. She told Maggie that she had been a concert pianist. She sat propped on two white pillows, her back very rounded, as though it were a kind of permanent hump and, with a lace handkerchief from the pocket of her nightie, she sniffed and patted her nose in a most lady-like manner. Maggie wanted to pick her up, take her home and look after her.

Many visitors came that evening to see Miss Stiles. They brought beautiful flowers, fruit and other expensive presents. But Miss Stiles gave them all a very bad time; she seemed to revel in the fact that she made them all most unwelcome. Maggie sat up and watched as Miss Stiles, lying there in her frilly nightgown, looking like a duchess, kept her visitors running in and out, changing flower water, taking complaints to sister, until red-faced and somewhat embarrassed they went home.

"You've got a big family," Maggie remarked after they had all left. Miss Stiles folded her lace handkerchief carefully, and her sad eyes shot a strange look at Maggie.

"They are all my nieces and nephews," she said.

"How nice," returned Maggie.

"Nice?" snapped Miss Stiles. "Do you know what they are trying to do?" Maggie shook her head.

The dark eyes blazed with anger. "They're trying to sell my home and put me in an old ladies' home. But I won't let them get away with it. I'm not dead yet," she declared.

Maggie grinned. At eighty-eight, this old lady was quite a character and from that first day they became firm friends, not just sympathetic but real, warm companions. Maggie admired her, she was very understanding and had traveled the world and read many books. In spite of her demanding cantankerous ways Maggie found her a very entertaining bedside acquaintance.

"Do you know, they had my cat put to sleep," Miss Stiles confided to Maggie. "See that fat one? She's after my television table. What a sauce, come and asked me, she did."

Maggie could see no reason why the fat one shouldn't have the television table.

"Surely out of all those relations one will offer you a home," she suggested.

"Wouldn't go to any of them," declared Miss Stiles vehemently. "They can all stay away. The only one I want to see never comes," she added a trifle sadly.

"Who's that, darling? Your boyfriend?" asked Maggie.

The old lady tittered. "No," she answered. "It's my nephew, the cartoon artist."

"You don't mean that one in the evening paper? Why he's famous." Maggie was most surprised.

"That's him. My twin sister's boy. She married very late in life. Cost her her life, having that boy."

Maggie stared at Miss Stiles. She realized where the cartoonist got his inspiration from, his cartoons were always of little hunched-up women. Miss Stiles worshiped him and sat pining each day and he never came.

Next day she wheeled Miss Stiles up and down the ward in a bathchair and got to know the rest of the patients. She met some women years younger than herself, who had lain for six months bedridden, crippled with arthritis. Never before had she valued her life of good health. She cracked jokes and gossiped with them and was very popular.

Mornings were spent in bed, until after the doctor's visit. The pink pigeon had become very tame and waited patiently for her breakfast. Miss Stiles would hand a piece of bread and say, "Give this to Beryl."

Beryl would strut and coo and preen her feathers. Both Miss Stiles and Maggie loved birds and all animals. Miss Stiles still fretted over her cat.

"Never mind, darling, I'll get you another one," Maggie would try to console her.

"Wouldn't be the same. Had him twelve years, I did."

Then Maggie would think of Timothy with affection, and wonder how things were down at the cottage.

It was never dull next to Miss Stiles. A raging battle had just abated, involving nurses, sisters and eventually the doctor. It concerned her breakfast. She insisted on a certain cereal which the hospital did not provide. But after endless arguments, she got her All Bran and sat up triumphantly eating it.

Maggie used to feel sorry for the student nurses, who got a rough time from the strict ward sister. She was instilled with admiration for them, remembering the girls she worked with in the blitz.

Tomorrow was her big day; she was to go down for that operation. The big, burly, good-humored surgeon had visited her with his team of assistants and a bevy of students, who stood by the bed catching each word like gold dust as it rolled from the lips of the great master. Clever young boys and girls. Her Joe might have been one of them. She felt sad when she thought of Joe. She wondered why he had not written to her.

"See you in the morning, Mrs. Burns," said the surgeon cheerfully as he moved on to the next patient.

A hysterectomy they told her. She would no longer be a woman, probably have to live the rest of her life on pills. It would be better if she died.

All sorts of conflicting emotions passed over her, and her fear must have shown in her face. A little student nurse named Eileen came to her, with a pale freckled face and deep-set eyes that surveyed her closely.

"What's the matter, Mrs. Burns?"

"I'm terrified," confessed Maggie.

"It's nothing, dear. You don't feel anything. You must trust in the Lord," she whispered. "Look." She put her hand up to the tiny silver crucifix that she wore about her neck. "Death is nothing to be afraid of. It's life we must learn to face. Have faith, my dear, it will help you a lot. It's always helped me."

Maggie smiled at the wisdom of this fanatic little Eileen with her elf-like face and deep sincerity. "I wish I was like you, darling," she told her. "But too much has happened in my life, I can't pick up the threads anymore."

"Please, stop worrying. Having an op. is nothing," pleaded Eileen.

"All right, love, I'll try." But self-pity overwhelmed her. She wanted to scream and sob, do something. But instead, she lay like a log trying to come to terms with leaving John and her family behind.

A thin wavering voice came through to her. "Hi, Maggie." It brought her to earth again.

Miss Stiles was most put out. "I've been calling you for ages," she complained. "What's up with you? Get up and bring your glass over, we'll have some lemonade and biscuits."

So Maggie put on her dressing gown and went to join Miss Stiles. Her companion was very smart in her frilly gown; her tiny hands, like tremulous butterflies, hovered over the plate as she passed the biscuits, as dainty and self-possessed as any society hostess.

"You're in a most depressing mood, Maggie," she declared, slightly nettled, because her friend was not her usual charming self.

"I can't help worrying about the morning," Maggie told her.

"That won't make any difference, be out and about tomorrow," said Miss Stiles.

But Maggie was looking for sympathy and, finding it lacking, wanted to cry. "I've got this feeling I won't come through it," she said miserably. But the tough old lady only cackled. "Been half a dozen in that bed since I've been here and they all came through," Miss Stiles said in a tone that implied it was a pity that they did.

"Oh, have a heart, Miss Stiles," pleaded Maggie. "I'm scared stiff."

"Well, forget about it then," replied the tough old lady. "No sense in dwelling on it. Have another biscuit."

Maggie sighed. Must be the secret of old age, she thought, not thinking of tomorrow. So they began to talk of more mundane things.

"Why didn't you get married?" she asked Miss Stiles suddenly.

"See that hump?" returned the old lady. "I've always had that. Was born with it, so no one fancied me. Still, I got by, had a good life, wouldn't want to change it."

Maggie stared at her in admiration. "I was thinking of marrying again, but I've changed my mind now," she told her.

"Why?" demanded Miss Stiles munching her biscuit, her dark eyes looking shrewdly at her.

"Won't be much good to a man, time they have finished with me," she confessed gloomily.

"Don't be such a fool, you might even be better at it," Miss Stiles declared.

"Why, Miss Stiles!" Maggie's blue eyes opened wide and her white teeth showed in a grin. "I'm shocked. You never done it, how would you know so much?"

"I never said that I hadn't done it," returned the old lady. "What I did say is, that it's all in the mind. You can be as much of a woman at fifty as you are at twenty, it's entirely up to you."

Maggie looked very astonished, but Miss Stiles gave no indication of prolonging the conversation and began putting her bits and pieces in her locker ready to settle down for the night.

Maggie lay in the dim light still thinking of the morning. It was that unmentionable word that frightened her: cancer. She had heard it whispered by nurses and other patients and although she laughed and giggled and was the life and soul of the ward, that word burned like a hot cinder in her brain. Several times she picked up her pen to write to John, but words and explanations refused to come. Better wait and see what they do to me, she told herself.

Babs and Jim had brought the children in for a while that afternoon. The twins were lovely, but not so much alike as the first two had been. James and Jason were not yet two, they had stood solemnly by the bed looking up at her, silver blonde heads and china-blue eyes. How lovely that little family was. She had everything to live for.

"Cheer up, Mum," Babs had said. "We are all going to live in the country. Jim's put our name down for a big council house, so we can all be together."

Good-hearted, loyal Jim, he was already planning to take care of her. But better to die under the op. Poor old Jim had enough on his plate. This depression would not lift.

"Any news of Joe?" she asked.

"He's on his way home, Mum, and Anne-Marie and Al might come too."

Babs gave her a reassuring smile. "They discovered her father was being held prisoner in Red China. He's coming home too, got news from the American Embassy."

"Teach him not to go spying," muttered Jim. "Bloody warmongers, those Yanks."

But they ignored this remark, Babs and Maggie. Neither of them felt in the mood for Jim and his politics. Babs continued to tell all the news.

"Anne-Marie had a little girl. She was a bit premature, but they said she is making good progress."

"How lovely, the first little girl!" Perhaps she would never see her. Tears welled up. The twins began to play up; Jamie having spotted the tea trolley had decided it was an ice-cream cart.

"Wanna lolly," he screamed, his brother joining in.

Jim collected his family, kissed his mum and left.

With sad eyes she watched them leave. There was plenty to think about, a new granddaughter and little Joe on his way home. I wonder where poor old Tom is tonight, she pondered.

Maggie lay awake until the gray light of a new dawn rose over the dome of St. Paul's and came shyly through the window. The pigeons rustled their feathers and began to coo. A strange peace came over her. It came and went just like the dawn, it was nothing to do with us, it was all in the hands of some higher person. She closed her eyes and lay still, and the very efficient theater sister, pushed the pre-med needle into her thigh. All her cares had left her, she was in a strange misty world.

The Return of Joe

As Maggie watched the London dawn come up, so did a little middle-aged lady sitting in the arrival lounge of London Airport.

They were coming home to her and bringing that long-awaited addition to the family with them. Aunt Dolly had been there since last night, her hands clasped patiently on her lap, a little felt hat pulled over her ears, and wearing a warm tweed coat. There was an anxious light in her pale gray eyes as she looked up at the sky. All that she held dear was up there. Please, God, bring them down safe, she prayed. How often she had wished she had gone with them, it had been very lonely at Edgeley without them. Now they had a baby, the cottage was sold and she had some savings. Surely they would not turn her away, they would need her now. So with furrowed brow, Dolly sat waiting for Al and his wife Anne-Marie and, above all, the new baby.

The plane was in and they came through the barrier. Dolly ran to them, arms outstretched, this smart young couple with a tiny baby in a carry-cot. Dolly kissed and hugged them, her eyes devouring the lovely baby with its wealth of red-gold hair.

"Oh, I am glad to see you," sighed Anne-Marie as she handed her the child. Behind them was Joe, tall and thin, long dark side-whiskers and a hint of a mustache.

"My, you have grown up, Joe," declared Dolly. "Maggie will be pleased to see you home."

Joe's face was sad. "How is my mother, Aunt Dolly?" he inquired.

"I am not sure, but you'll see her today, Joe, don't look so unhappy." That kind, motherly Dolly wanted to take them all under her wing, like a warm, clucking, fussing hen.

Together they drove out to Haverstock Hill, where a house belonging to an old relation was available. It had been let furnished for a few years and Jante was about to dispose of it, but then offered it to Anne-Marie when she heard they were returning to London. It was at the top of the hill, very large and very tall and somewhat gloomy; a big front garden and an untidy laurel hedge hid the exterior from the main road. The bottom part of it was still let and only the top was available.

As they entered, the worn linoleum in the hall stood out against the rich, old, faded wallpaper and it all smelled of foreign cooking. Anne-Marie wrinkled her nose distastefully and Al looked around, hands in pockets.

"It's a change from the Cape," he told Joe, "but still, this is ours. It's nice and big too, make a lovely studio."

He surveyed the long, half-empty lounge that had a huge bay window and looked directly out on to the vast green expanse of Hampstead Heath.

Joe looked soberly out of the window across the heath. "Nice and open," he said. "It'll do the baby good." Joe's voice had a deeper tone, sad and serious. "Think I'll shoot off now, Al, I'll go over to Jim and see how Mum is."

Dolly had found the kitchen and bustled about taking care of the baby and making a cup of tea. Anne-Marie plonked down wearily, kicking off her smart shoes, and the old battered wickerwork armchair creaked protestingly. "Oh, dear," she moaned, "what a dump. Why didn't we go to an hotel?"

"Stop grousing," said Al. "We can't afford hotels.

You wanted a house of your own, now you got it, so pipe down."

Dolly's mild eyes looked a little shocked. "Now don't quarrel," she said. "We'll soon make it comfortable."

She handed them hot tea and cradled the little one in her arms as she gave her her bottle. Aunt Dolly was content. They'll settle down. It's a fine house, thought Dolly.

"Thank God for Dolly," said Anne-Marie. "I would never have coped, what with the baby and that nit of a husband I've landed myself with."

Joe took the tube over to Jim's—no taxis for him. He had very little money in his pocket, just the remains of a fiver that Al had scrounged off Anne-Marie and what a fuss she made about it. He certainly had missed his mum, always on hand with pocket money. Lying sick out there in the jungle he thought he would never see her again. He could not understand what had happened to his independent, happy-go-lucky mum and why had John Malloy left her to end up back in the East End in hospital.

Joe arrived at Jim's in the evening, just as the babies were being washed for bed. Jamie was at one end of the bath and Jason at the other and Babs was up to her elbows in water. Jim was trying to pacify the other babies who yelled, kicked and screamed in the cot, and the whole area was littered with baby toys and washing. Jim grasped Joe warmly by the hand. He had never shown his younger brother a lot of affection, but this time he was real pleased to see him. Joe's sad eyes wandered about the room. The familiar pieces of furniture that had been Maggie's caught his eye; these things he had lived with all his life. There was a tightness in his throat.

"How is she?" he asked huskily.

"She's bad, Joe," replied Jim. "It's a major op."

They relapsed into silence and Babs trotted in with the usual cuppa. "She hadn't come to when I was there an hour ago," she said.

Joe's knuckles glowed white as he clenched his fists. "Whatever happened to Mum?" he cried brokenly.

"She traveled all the way out to Australia with that bloody swine Tom," returned Jim.

"But John Malloy, where is he?" asked Joe who was still rather puzzled.

"Don't talk to me about that capitalist bastard," retorted Jim. "He doesn't care, off on one of his bloody war-mongering schemes out in the States."

"Doesn't he know Mum is ill?" asked Joe.

"Not that I know of," replied Jim. "Nor is he likely to. She's better off without the likes of him."

Joe's lips set in a grim line. "I'll pop over to the hospital," he said and walked out.

He sat for some time beside Maggie in the curtained cubicle that separated them from the rest of the ward. He sat very still, but upright, afraid almost to breathe as he watched her sleeping off the effects of the anesthetic. She looked so small and pathetic as she lay there, her hands outstretched on the white sheet. He took one small hand and held it gently; she stirred slightly.

"It's me, Mum," he whispered. "Little Joe."

But Maggie's mind had gone way down the past to Witton Street. It was old Granny Goring sitting there and her Jim had just been born. She was so tired she could not open her eyes.

A Nigerian nurse came in around the screen, her black face shining, and there was sympathy in her wide smile.

"You go home, honey," she said to Joe. "Your mum will be fine in the morning."

Tears shone in the corners of Joe's deep brown eyes. "She's all right, isn't she?" he asked anxiously.

"Right as ninepence," replied the nurse. "She's just tired after all she's been through. Come back tomorrow, love."

"Will you find her handbag for me?" he asked. "I want an address of someone she will want to see when she comes round."

"Sure, honey." She groped in the locker for Maggie's handbag.

Joe found John's letter with the address of a New York hotel at the top. He replaced the bag, kissed his mum and crept out again into the night.

It was past midnight and the streets of London were deserted. Joe turned and went walking toward Clerkenwell, where the post office stayed open all night. With his last two pounds he sent a cable to John Malloy: MAGGIE VERY ILL IN LONDON HOSPITAL STOP JOE STOP.

Then, feeling very tired but much more content, he began to walk back toward Hampstead, away from the lonely city streets of the West End. He sat for a while on the steps of Eros in Piccadilly to watch the night life that revolved about it. A very young prostitute approached him. In his charming way Joe said, "Sorry, love, I'm broke."

Surprisingly, the plump young blonde replied, "Don't matter, I am turning it in now. You can go home with me for some food and a kip if you like."

Joe laughingly declined. "Some other time, darling."

She went limping away on her high heels, her hips swaying. Probably got a heart of gold under that tight jumper, thought Joe as he watched her.

The neon lights flickered and an old man nearby was scratching himself vigorously and two young boys full of dope sat very close together. The pattern of life about him interested Joe. How much he would have liked to have been a doctor, then he would have life in the palm of his hand. All kinds and all creeds made no difference in the medical profession. But it was too late, he would never pass the exam now. Besides, money was short and he would have to get a job to take care of his mother.

Never had much success with girls either; white ones used him and black ones were afraid of him. He thought of the first time he had slept with a woman, the blonde and lovely Sister Cora at the mission, her stiff starched white headdress and the commanding way she had with

the natives. Under her white mosquito net in the heat
of an African night—he had thought it was love. But
he soon learned to his regret how fickle she was, when
a new G.P. arrived from her home town in Scotland.
You get over these knocks, he told himself.

Then a cold sweat broke out on him, Oh God, what
would he do if he lost his mum? He shivered, better
get going, didn't want to bring the fever back.

He got up and set off in the direction of Regent's
Park and Hampstead. It was still a long way and it
would soon be daylight. Oh God, was there no place
where there were arms as warm and loving as his
mum's to hold and protect him from this terrible
despondency? Hanging his head he walked slower and
slower. Then suddenly a face swung in front of him,
a black, shining, laughing face. That's it! He knew
where he would go. The first bus came slowly past, he
ran and jumped aboard. "Camden Town, please," he
said, and sank down into the seat exhausted.

Joe's Woman

A cold bitter wind blew and it was six o'clock in the
morning, when a strangely excited man ran up the stone
steps of a tall tenement house in Camden Town. There
was no knocker on the front door, it stood wide open,
and inside was a long, dark passageway; it smelled of
spices. On each side were doors, and a flight of un-
carpeted stairs led upwards. He hesitated for a moment
but a woolly head poked out of a door. "Is dat der
postman?" a husky voice inquired.

"Excuse me, will you direct me to Miss Eva Delo's
flat?" he asked politely. Out came more woolly heads.
A bright turbaned one appeared on the stairs and half
a dozen voices in several dialects called out.

At the top of the stairs stood Eva in a long, flowered,
red dressing-gown. Her flat African face beamed with
pleasure at the sight of Joe. He ran lightly up the stairs.
She took his hand and closed the door on her inquisitive

neighbors. Two soft warm arms went around him and Joe, his head pressed to her ample bosom, cried like a baby.

"Hush, hush, honey," whispered the soft gentle voice of Eva. "Don't cry."

Later they lay very close together on her little trestle bed. Joe had come home. He had found a place he belonged, one he had sought for so long.

It had been Eva who nursed him at the mission hospital before she had returned home to her job in a London hospital. But Joe had never forgotten her, nor the sweet patient, tireless energy she possessed, and now she comforted him with the warm generosity of her love. He was sure that he would never go away from her again.

They had first met under a star-studded African sky. While he had sweated and shivered with jungle fever in the medical tent, she had bathed his heated body with cool water. The intonation in her voice had drawn his attention. She uttered little quips of humor. Some of the things she said and did were so much like his mother Maggie, and through the burning fever he lay wondering why this shiny, black, African face should remind him of his own lovely white mother.

As he slowly recovered he realized that Eva had a strong Cockney accent.

"Me, love?" she giggled at him. "Like your ma, and she's from the Mile End? Well, that's all right, I'm a Cockney girl too. I only came out here to work my vacation. I was curious about Africa, but shan't be sorry to see the old smoke again. I've got a job at St. Thomas's. I'll be swotting for exams when I get back."

She was gay and friendly and under her expert care Joe soon recovered. He had promised to visit her in London. He remembered how one day, as she washed his slim, coffee-colored body, Eva had said, "What's your pa? West Indian?"

Joe confessed he did not know. He began to tell her of the fears that were always dormant in his mind, how his white mother always insisted he was not colored, but he knew he was not completely white. Eva's dark eyes gazed admiringly down at him. "You're a colored boy all right," she said and Joe shyly covered himself with a towel.

"But you mustn't let it worry you," said Eva. "Gawd knows who my father was and I'm damn sure he wasn't white." Her laugh rang out gaily. Joe laughed with her. Her personality kept the mission hospital alive; it was dead when she had gone home.

Now as he lay in her arms, it was a moment of truth for Joe—his world was black, that was where he belonged.

On the other side of London the early morning bustle had begun on the wards—bedpans collected, bowls dished out and breakfast trays brought round. It was the noise and the rattle of the trays that roused Maggie.

Funny, she was still in the ward, must have changed their minds and not operated after all. At the window was Beryl, tapping with her beak, the little, pink-crested feathers standing indignantly. It was time to open the window, she was waiting for her breakfast. Maggie smiled at her and tried to reach out a hand toward her, but found to her astonishment it would not move; her arm was attached to a board with a long pipe hanging from it.

"Nurse," she yelled. "Come and take this flaming thing off my arm."

The sister came around the screen. "Oh! so you're back with us, Mrs. Burns."

She pulled down the sheet to examine the dressing. Then Maggie realized it was all over; she had had her operation. She was all bound up down below and could not move her legs. Strange that she never remembered anything. And she was still alive. Beryl cooed impatiently.

"Let me give her her breakfast," said Maggie. The sister indulgently opened the window and placed some breadcrumbs on the sill for Maggie's pet, when a thin voice, like a crackle of newspaper, came from alongside her.

"Is that you, Maggie? It's about time you came to." It was Miss Stiles expressing her pleasure at Maggie's recovery in her own inimitable way. The news spread like a bush fire. "Maggie's awake," the blind old lady informed the deaf one. The arthritic ladies called out, "How are you, Maggie?"

"Bloody awful," she called back. They all smiled, she was okay. It had been unsettling to see that bright little woman lying so pale and still.

After lunch two nurses washed her, sat her up and tied a blue bow on her hair. "What's this?" asked Maggie, "Guy Fawkes Day?"

"For the visitors," they told her. Young sweet faces and not a hair out of place. Maggie loved looking at them, as they went about the damn rotten job, not complaining as factory girls did all the time, just keeping busy with an eye on the sister, who would pounce like a hawk on these young trainees. There was tall, dark, lovely Francoise from Belgium; fat, rosy Bridie from Cork and little Eileen, her funny freckled face full of religious fervor. With gentle hands they made her comfortable:

"Who's coming?" inquired Maggie. "The Duke of Edinburgh?"

"You'll be surprised," they said as they picked up the bowls and drew the curtains back. Maggie looked around the ward; at Miss Stiles who sat anxiously waiting; at the old ladies who stared over at her.

"Hello, girls," she called. Oh! it was good to be alive. That feeling inside her, like the smell of the fresh spring flowers in the ward, it lingered, like being reborn.

At two o'clock it was time for visitors. The first one in was a very tall man, erect and most distinguished looking. In his hand a soft felt hat, he stood hesitating at the door, then with long strides he was at her bedside.

"John, darling," she whispered.

"Maggie, my foolish little love, what have you been up to?"

He stroked her hair, tears not far from his eyes and Maggie, her eyes bright with unshed ones, just looked at him and could not believe her John was home again. His face tanned brown from the heat of the sun, his eyes a clearer gray than ever.

"How did you know?" she asked.

"Not from you, my love." He sounded a trifle sarcastic. But that was John; she knew when he was hurt.

"Joe cabled me," he told her. "I came straight away."

"Joe's here?" Her eyes searched the doorway. "Where is he?"

"He's outside, I'll get him. But, darling, I had to take a look at you first." He went to get Joe.

Maggie was so happy as she held each one by the hand, her John and her baby Joe. Was it her imagination or was there something different about Joe? Her deep blue eyes looked intently at him, but he, unable to stand the scrutiny, looked away. Something's wrong and it's serious. Wonder what it is.

The rest of the family were waiting to come in, so Joe and John left together. Jim, standing out in the corridor, ignored them. Joe made as if to stay, changed his mind and went with John.

Babs came in so pleased and tearful to see Maggie sitting up, behind was her Jim looking very serious. Then the tall, graceful Anne-Marie, well-dressed with her golden hair a shining halo about her head, and Al, tall, smart and good looking. All eyes popped as they came in. The old ladies whispered and nodded. There was a weariness in Anne-Marie's face but Al was his usual gormless, nonchalant self.

It was nice to see them all, but after they left, Maggie asked the nurse to lay her down, she felt exhausted. Then she closed her eyes and slept, dreaming of Oak Tree Cottage, herself beside a big log fire and Timothy asleep on her lap.

A Family Conference

At Jim's flat a family debate was in progress. They had all gone back there after visiting the hospital.

Aunt Dolly was there with them with her charge, the new-born, red-haired Marguerita, named after Maggie whose real name was Marguerita. She was to be called Rita, and she was a beautiful child even at six weeks old. Creamy skin and lots of curly red hair. There was another young girl helping Dolly with the children, aged about thirteen and fair as a lily, with silky bobbed hair, that hung in a fringe over two deep brown eyes. This was Jenny; Babs had produced yet another sister from Wales. The children were well taken care of and Aunt Dolly was in her element in the world of young children.

The adults sat at the table discussing the future of their mum. "Of course," spoke Jim with great pomposity. "I consider that mother is my responsibility, and I have never shirked my duty yet, nor am I likely to."

Al looked rather puzzled. "But Mum will be her old self in a few weeks. Both you and I know she won't let us tell her what to do."

"Oh, I agree," replied Jim, "that Mother is very independent, but there comes a time in life when one has to give in."

Anne-Marie started to giggle. "Maggie give in? Why, she won't give in."

Jim started at her coldly. "I suppose you do realize the extent of Mother's illness," he said.

"It was cancer," Babs joined in, her eyes wide with fright.

"Yes, I know," replied Anne-Marie. "But lots of women have it in the womb at her age—that's why they take everything away—and they get over it."

"Nonsense," retorted Jim. "I lost my best friend last year. God forbid my mother should suffer like he did.

I intend to see that she has every comfort while she is with us."

Dolly broke in: "My goodness, Jim, don't bury your mother before she is dead. It's not as serious as all that, she will be as good as new in a month or so."

"What about John Malloy?" Anne-Marie asked. "She might get married again."

Jim began to get angry. "I will not allow her to be swayed by that swine."

"Don't seem such a bad bloke to me," said Al. "Must have cost a bomb to get home as quick as he did."

"Thanks to dear little Joe," snarled Jim aggressively. Babs put a restraining hand on Jim's arm.

"If Maggie wants to marry him she will," declared Anne-Marie. "I can't see what all the argument is about."

But it went on all through tea and in the evening over beer and sandwiches. Nothing was settled, except that Jim was determined to get rid of John Malloy.

Having said goodbye outside the hospital to John, Joe went straight back to Camden Town. Eva cooked some eggs on her small gas ring and they sat on the rickety bed talking of the future.

Eva was wearing a bright red housecoat. Joe examined it and asked what the pattern was—flowers, birds or bees. Eva was sitting cross-legged, munching an apple. "I don't know what pattern it is, I washed it so many times, I forgot." She laughed good humoredly. Being poor was something Eva was quite used to, she made no secret of the fact. This little room was the only home she knew, unless she chose to live in the nurses' hostel. "No sir," said Eva, "like it here better."

The reason for the dressing-gown off duty was to save the wear of her uniform. She could not buy many dresses on the poor pay she got while training. Joe slid his hand up and down her slim, shiny leg.

"I wish I could be like you, Eva," he said. "You

seem to take life in its stride, nothing seems to worry you."

She leaned forward and planted her full lips on to his. "Oh! I get worried all right," she answered. "When I think how bothered I was when I thought I'd never see you again."

He drew closer to her, little Joe a real man now, hands and eyes seeking his girl, involved in a deep passionate love affair. Afterward they lay quite still and Joe said, "Let's get married, Eva."

She sat up, her eyes rolled until they showed the whites. "Oh boy, oh boy! Do you mean that Joe?"

"Yes I mean it, let's get married as soon as possible."

"Where we gonna live?" asked Eva with slight doubt in her tone.

"I don't care," replied Joe. "I want to marry you. I'll stay here."

"Well, I suppose we could get a bigger bed," suggested Eva. "Ain't a lot of room in this one, Joe," she grinned.

"It's served its purpose," declared Joe and together they began to laugh as though they never had a care in the world.

"I've got no job and no money," said Joe. "Still want me?"

Eva swung her slim legs down to the floor and sat looking thoughtful. "Listen, Joe," she said. "Why are you in such a hurry? Don't have to buy me no legal ticket to love. I'm your woman and you're my man. I chose you, boy."

"It's rather more complicated, Eva. I wonder if I can make you understand." He thought for a moment before going on. "All my life I was brought up to believe I was white. My brothers showed me very little affection, but my mother tried to make up for it, she loved and fussed me so much that I lack confidence. She wanted so much for me to be a doctor, she helped me to study, created ambition in me. But I let her down, I never finished my last term at school and now she's ill and I might lose her. And I want to go to her and say, 'Mother, I have found happiness. This is my way of life. Be happy for me.'"

Eva looked sad. It was not like Eva to be sad. Joe stopped talking and gazed at her with a question in his eyes. Had he said the wrong things? "Poor little Joe, you sure need someone to take care of you."

He breathed a sigh of relief, Eva understood.

"You know, boy, I had ten different families in my life," Eva solemnly informed him. "Some white, some black, but it was for money they fostered me, not love. I want to marry a steady boy. I don't want no kids of mine to grow up in the orphanage."

Their arms went about each other.

"I'll see Father O'Mally tomorrow. He will marry us. Then we will go and see my mum."

12

V.I.P. Treatment

It was a fine January morning, the winter sun
dodged in and out of little black rain clouds and Maggie lay watching them from her bed. Having enjoyed
her breakfast Beryl had retired to a warm corner and
was contentedly pruning her feathers. Maggie felt more
alert this morning, a bit stiff and sore but able to cope
with the problems on her mind. It had been so nice to
see John again, she felt she loved him more than ever,
the soft touch of his well-manicured hands and the
pleasant smell of exclusive after-shave. He still looked
ten years younger than her, and how would she look
after all this? She felt lazy somehow, she did not want
to strive to live up to him. She could not fathom it out,
but the glamor had gone. Then there was Oak Tree
Cottage and he had been talking of taking her back to
the States. There was some new project he had become
interested in. Something about getting in on the ground
floor. She wanted to go back to Oak Tree Cottage, to
Timothy and her lovely garden; it would be awakened
in the spring, crying out for her.

Two nurses came in and started to move her things,
all her cards and the red roses that John had sent that
morning.

"What's up?" asked Maggie.

"We are moving you, Mrs. Burns," said one of the nurses.

"Moving me? I don't want to be moved." Her face got very red.

"Where they taking you, Maggie?" inquired Miss Stiles looking rather shocked.

"They ain't flaming well taking me anywhere," declared Maggie. "I'm staying here. Sister! What's going on?"

The white-clad sister came up smiling, cool and smooth. "Calm down," she said. "You are going up in the world. Off to a private patient's ward."

"No, I am not," declared Maggie. "If anyone moves me I'll get up and go home."

The sister motioned for the nurses to go and then sat on the bed. "That young man of yours has been pulling strings. He's got you some V.I.P. treatment."

"Well, he can mind his own bloody business," replied Maggie. "I'm staying here with Beryl and Miss Stiles."

The battle was soon over and Maggie stayed in her corner. The news went around the ward and everyone was curious and very amused. When John came at two o'clock loaded with parcels, Maggie met him with a surly look.

"What's the matter, darling? Don't you feel so well?" he asked solicitously.

"I'm all right," muttered Maggie. "But what the hell did you have to go poking your nose in for?"

He looked shocked. This was not his sweet little Maggie. It must be some reaction from the pills. "Do what?" he said. "Poke my nose?" His eyes twitched; it sounded rather funny.

"It's not a joke," snapped Maggie. "They nearly moved me into some toffee-nosed ward away from Beryl and Miss Stiles."

He started to laugh. That was it. He glanced at Miss Stiles who was straining her ears to listen. She shot a most malevolent glance at him.

"I seem to be unpopular," he added dryly.

"Yes, you are," retorted Maggie.

"All right, darling, I only wanted to take care of you. After all, I am responsible for you."

"Don't see as you are," argued Maggie.

"Don't quarrel with me, darling," he pleaded. But she was in a very obstinate mood.

"Get a lot of time to think things over lying here," she said. "And I still think you will be better off without an old crock like me."

"Maggie, be quiet!" he demanded. He was beginning to lose his temper.

"No," she replied. "I am still free to pick and choose and so are you."

John went very pale, but remained silent. He handed her a card. "Ring me if you need me. I'm going to be busy. I'll come in at the weekend." With a cold peck at her cheek, he had gone.

Once alone, she started to weep, she was not sure why but the tears rained down. Miss Stiles handed her a tissue. "Don't cry, love, no man's worth crying over."

"I am not crying over him," sniffed Maggie. "It's my lovely garden and my cottage in the country. I keep thinking that I'll never see them again."

"Whose name is it in?" asked the old lady very shrewdly.

"I'm not sure," replied Maggie, "but if I don't stay with John, I'll not take anything off him."

"Well, then you're a damned fool," retorted Miss Stiles. "Take what they want, don't they?" Her head nodded and her wrinkled mouth looked vicious. "They ain't so keen when the bloom goes off the apple. Make them pay, that's what I say. Hit 'em in their pockets."

Maggie gave a little giggle. "Oh, Miss Stiles," she said, "you are a caution."

After a few more days Maggie was allowed to get up and sit near her bed. The doctors were very pleased with her progress. She had got used to the hospital routine and was never bored or fed up, there was always someone to listen to and something to make her smile.

The welfare officer had been up to see Miss Stiles this morning. Her relations had made an application for her to enter an old ladies' home. There had been such a set-to. Miss Stiles simply would not listen to anyone.

"Maybe we could get someone to share your home with you," suggested the harassed welfare officer.

"You let me go home," demanded Miss Stiles. "I'll be all right. Don't want no nosey parkers in my house."

"But we can't do that, dear, you're not able to take care of yourself."

"Who's not?" said Miss Stiles. "I'll get right up out of this bed. Get my clothes. I'm going home."

She struggled frantically to get up and had to be given a sedative to calm her down. Maggie sat beside her bed and held her hand. It seemed useless to live so long; no one wanted you. That shriveled little body contained such an alert active mind. This was a cruel world, poor little old lady.

Still weeping, Miss Stiles said suddenly to her, "If you decide not to go and live with that bloke, Maggie, why don't you come home with me? They would let me alone then."

Maggie squeezed the frail hand. "I might even do that, love."

But in her mind was that host of formidable relations.

She had not seen John for a few days; he had sent her more flowers and a message to say he was busy. And where was little Joe? He had not been for two days. She must try not to worry; as soon as she was better she would probably be up to the neck in troubles again. Better relax while she had the chance.

So the days passed quickly and Maggie trailed about the ward with a stick, doing a little dance to make the patients laugh, and helping with the hot drinks at night. She noticed that Miss Stiles was not her usual perky self this night. Before she settled in bed she asked, "You all right, love?"

The old lady looked with those magnificent eyes,

wide brown pools in a small white face. "Give us a kiss, Maggie," she said.

"Why, you fast old thing," Maggie joked with her as she leaned over and kissed the wrinkled brow. Miss Stiles closed her eyes contentedly and went off to sleep.

Early in the morning something disturbed her, the screens were around Miss Stiles's bed, something was wrong. The doctor came, nurses and Sister trotted in and out.

"Isn't Miss Stiles well?" she inquired.

"Go to sleep, Mrs. Burns," ordered the night sister.

There was a cold fear in her heart. She had to know. She leaned forward and pulled the screen slightly to one side. Miss Stiles lay still and peaceful in her last sleep, the sleep of death.

In the full light of day the death of the old lady shed a gloom over the rest of the ward. The empty bed next door haunted Maggie. At least there was one consolation; Miss Stiles would never have to go to the old ladies' home she dreaded so much. But there was an empty void in her heart at losing her.

"Can I walk in the corridor?" she asked the sister. "Anywhere to get away from that empty white bed."

"Don't go far," replied the sister.

Maggie slowly walked down the shining corridor looking out of the long window at the end, over a forest of smoky chimneys. It was not a very impressive view. There was a small door. She pushed it open and discovered another long passageway that led to a beautiful little chapel. It was silent and empty. Some unknown force drew her in, down the aisle to the altar rails, and weakly she sank to her knees. A sweet feeling of peace and beauty overwhelmed her. She repeated a prayer of her school days. It was the first time since her Dah had passed on that Maggie had said the simple prayer that she had learned at his knee.

"If you are in heaven, Miss Stiles," she pleaded, "think of me, dear, I am really going to miss you."

She gazed up at the hand-painted screen over the altar

which had been created by an over-zealous art student. The Holy Trinity was portrayed in very bright colors. What caught her eye was the gaudy silver dove with a pink head that represented the Holy Ghost.

"Why, it's Beryl," cried Maggie out loud. "It's just like her. I wish you could see it, Miss Stiles."

A cold breeze wafted about her as though a door had opened and she had the strangest feeling that someone entered and knelt beside her.

"I believe you can see that picture of Beryl, Miss Stiles," said Maggie.

She left the chapel filled with a peaceful sanctity. God had not forsaken her in spite of all her wicked ways.

Maggie Goes Home to Jim's

Jim came to see her during his lunch break.

"Ask the doctor if I can go home," she pleaded to him. Losing Miss Stiles had triggered her off. Suddenly she wanted to get outside. Jim was pleased. He felt he had won the tug of war between John Malloy and himself.

The resident surgeon came. "You want to leave us, Maggie?" he asked fondly. Her personality had made her popular with the hospital staff.

"I'll go to my son's house," she told him. "He only lives up the road."

"You must take it very easy and attend every morning for treatment," he told her.

"I promise, doctor," said Maggie.

"All right. I'll get your discharge for the morning. You seem to be in good hands. He's a very nice lad, that son of yours. Take care of yourself, Maggie."

The next morning, when she said goodbye to the staff and patients, she worried about Beryl who came to the window to have her head stroked.

"I'll see you in the park," said Maggie. "Now be a good girl."

"Make sure someone feeds her," she instructed Eileen who stood looking sad at Maggie's departure.

"Can I come to visit you, Mrs. Burns?" Eileen asked.

"Of course you can, darling, but look after Beryl, won't you?"

"Well," declared Maggie, as she got into the lift with Jim, "I hope I never go back in there again."

"I thought you liked it, Mum," said Jim very astonished.

"No, I like being healthy better," she replied.

A big reception was waiting at Jim's to welcome her home. There were all the children, Babs and Megan. Also Aunt Dolly with the new baby was there. When Maggie saw this little girl, she went crazy over her sweet roguish face and masses of auburn curls. In fact, Dolly was a little jealous of the attention Maggie gave her charge.

Around the old familiar square table they all sat down to high tea. It was grand to have her family about her again and all the relics of the past, of the little house in Witton Street where it had all begun. The plate before her heaped up with salmon salad was one that had stared unwinkingly from Liza's oak dresser the first time she had entered that little house. How long ago? Over thirty years. It did not seem possible.

"We've got a surprise for you, Mum," Jim told her, "but don't get excited, it might not do you any good."

Maggie looked at them wondering what they were up to. At a given signal, in rushed the big clumsy Tom, nearly knocking the table over, and behind him the tall graceful Anna.

After Maggie got her breath back from Tom's rough hugging, she held out her hand to Anna who came forward shyly, but did not smile. She looked magnificent, and Maggie's diamond ring shone brightly from her finger, along with another ring, a band of plain gold. The heavy gold bracelet jangled on her wrist.

"Welcome home, Anna," said Maggie as she kissed her new daughter-in-law. They joined the rest of the family at the table and Maggie's eyes shone bright blue as she looked around at them all. Only little Joe was missing. I wonder where my little Joe is?

Jim and Tom seemed to be getting on reasonably well, she noted. She could hear Tom's gruff voice.

"Crummy place, Australia. Ended up in the nick out there I did. Old Ginger had to hook me out."

"What are you thinking of doing now?" There was a touch of sarcasm in Jim's voice as he quizzed Tom.

"Might get meself a pub," said Tom.

"Got plenty of money then?" said Jim dryly.

"Christ, I ain't," declared Tom. "Fined me a bloody bomb out there they did. But still, I can always flog her jewelry, get myself a stake."

Maggie watched Anna. She showed no change of expression, but slid her hand up and down her arm, as if to protect her lovely bracelet.

The only one of the family that was missing from Maggie's homecoming party was Joe. At that very moment Joe was attending a party of his own. Clad in a bright jazzy shirt and a pair of very tight slacks, he cavorted and wiggled his hips in unison with a very large brown lady who, in spite of her size, managed to move even faster than Joe. He was dancing at his own wedding.

The news had leaked out, so the generous West Indian family below had thrown a celebration party for the couple. With many spicy Jamaican drinks inside him and perspiration streaking on his brow, Joe danced to this crazy soul music, having the time of his life. Nearby danced Eva, in a new cotton dress. The large room contained very little except a few beds and some large bowls of fruit. They danced, black, white and brown, until the small hours, when Eva and Joe staggered upstairs to their small trestle bed amid loud cheers and showers of rice and confetti.

It was not until the next morning that Joe began to think clearly again. His head was still very heavy with the after-effects of the strong rum. Eva lay beside him, snoring loudly. He pushed her over slightly, his arm having cramp. There was not a great deal of room in this small bed. Joe suddenly had a feeling of shame. What about his mother? He wondered how she was. Supposing she had died? A kind of fear came over him. He was not sorry he had married Eva, he loved her and her gay approach to life. But what would his mother say, marrying in a registry office and not letting the family know? He knew it was unforgivable for him and now he had to face the music. It had been Eva who had persuaded him.

"Look, Joe, if we're going to get married, let's get it over with. That old priest will talk you out of it. I've got a month's pay, let's go and get a special license. I don't want no one up the hospital to know I'm getting married. I'll get my finals in a few weeks, then they can all go to the devil. I'm moving on anyway."

It seemed a good idea at the time, so he did as she asked. But now he had to face Maggie and he was scared stiff; he crept closer to Eva as though for protection. Eva said sleepily, "Give over, Joe boy, ain't you had enough loving. Let's get some sleep."

It might have been coincidence that caused Joe and Eva to meet up with John Malloy. Joe had tried all day to get Eva to go with him to see his mother but Eva was trying hard to dodge it.

"Can't," she said. "Got to go on night duty."

"We can go see my mother first," suggested Joe.

"Don't fancy being on parade for them pale-faced brothers of yours," she grumbled.

"Please, Eva," pleaded Joe. "I must get it off my mind."

"Okay. Have to wear my uniform and go straight on duty."

They stood at the bus stop in the pouring rain, Eva in a navy mac and the stiff white collar of her nurse's outfit showing at the neck.

A long gray car slowed down and tooted at them. "Want a lift?" a voice called out.

"Why, it's John Malloy. Come on, Eva," said Joe. "He's probably on his way to see Mum."

Seated in the back of the comfortable car, Joe in-

troduced John to his wife. John surveyed her through
the mirror and grinned, wondering what Maggie would
say to Joe. She seemed a pleasant girl, and it was time
Joe stood up for himself.

"Gave up the medical idea then, Joe?" he asked.

"Not sure how I stand. Left myself high and dry,"
replied Joe.

"Plenty of other fields for a bright boy like you, Joe.
Why don't you try a job in a research center. You could
still go on with your studies. There are plenty that come
up that way."

"I did think about it, but I'm not sure where to
start," confessed Joe.

John took out his book and with one hand on the
wheel wrote down an address. "Go and see this chap.
Tell him I recommended you."

"Thanks, John, it's very good of you."

"I'm getting a new job myself," said John, sounding
mighty pleased with himself. "I'm taking your mother
to the States when she is well enough."

Through Joe's mind went the thought, will Mum go?
But he made no comment.

"I'm joining a new project," continued John. "It's
only in the air at the moment but it will surely come,
just as the atom bomb did. I'm jolly lucky to get a
chance to be in it at my age."

"Is it very secret stuff?" inquired Joe.

"Not exactly. It might sound over-ambitious but the
Americans are planning to explore the moon."

"Sounds exciting," said Joe.

"Well, you never know your luck, lad. Work hard
and in ten years you might be one of the first scientists
up there."

"Up on the moon?" giggled Eva. "Oh boy, what will
they think of next?"

The conversation ended as they reached the hospital.
Eva held Joe's hand and he squeezed hers until it hurt.
They were both so nervous of facing Maggie. Joe
looked anxiously at John. "We'll wait. You go in first,"
he offered.

"No," replied John. "We'll all face the music together. Might give you a bit of Dutch courage," he grinned.

The sight of the empty bed, all neat and tidy with the sides tucked in, alarmed them. They stood in the doorway just staring. They were told she had gone home the previous day.

"Better go and see Jim," suggested Joe. Very depressed, they drove along the Mile End Road. John did not answer, he was too disturbed at the thought of Maggie leaving the hospital without informing him.

Outside Jim's flat, he refused to come up. "No, Joe, I'll wait here. Let me know what's happening."

The usual chit-chat was going on in Jim's flat. Friends were visiting from upstairs, the babies were all in bed and Maggie was watching the telly. She had been thinking of Joe, worrying why he had not been to see her. Then he walked in.

Maggie jumped up and held him close. "You naughty boy, little Joe, where have you been?"

Then she saw Eva standing looking at her, her white teeth showing in her friendly smile.

"Meet Eva, my wife," said Joe. "We got married yesterday."

The shock was too great for Maggie. She went deathly white and passed out. It was Eva who dashed forward, caught her in her strong black arms and laid her on the settee.

"You bloody fool," Jim was shouting at Joe. Babs was weeping. But in Eva's professional hands, Maggie soon opened her eyes again.

"Oh dear, I'm sorry. Whatever is wrong with me?" All apologetic, Maggie sat up while Eva's cool hands stroked her brow.

"Don't let my black face scare you, Maggie," she said. "I'm a Cockney girl like yourself." From that moment Maggie loved Eva.

Order was soon restored and cups of tea passed around. It was then Joe remembered poor old John waiting out there, but he had given up and gone.

"Forgive me, Mum, I forgot about him, with all the excitement in here."

"Don't worry," said Maggie trying hard to smile. "He'll turn up, he always does."

Inside she felt strangely hurt, as though nothing really mattered anymore. Joe would never know how much it had shocked her when he produced his black wife. Eva was a splendid girl and there was no doubt that she was going to be very popular with the family. But there was a deep hurt, so deep-set, that she had no strength left to wrestle with it. All through the years she fought, so determined to force her husband to accept Joe. To herself and the rest of the world Joe must be an ordinary, white, working-class lad, no one dared say anything otherwise. It had become an obsession. She would listen to no one's advice, convinced it was a battle she had to fight and would eventually win. But when defeat came so suddenly it was like a blow in the face from her loving son Joe. It was deep and it hurt. She knew she had to fight it.

Eva saw the sadness in her eyes, and she cuddled her. "Sorry we didn't tell you, Mum. I was scared someone would talk him out of marrying me. I've been in love with Joe since we met in that jungle tent."

"I know, dear. I'm all right now. Let's forget it," insisted Maggie.

Joe said very little. He knew Maggie was thinking of John Malloy and blamed himself for his stupidity.

Jim was gloating. "Never waited long, did he?" he said to Babs. "Different question now, isn't it? Not so keen is he?"

"Hush, Jim," gentle Babs restrained him. "Mum's in love with him, she's just too proud to show it."

"Not our mum," replied the dogmatic Jim. "She's happy to be with her family again. She'll pick up now, I bet you."

"Hope you're right," murmured Babs. "Can't bear to see Maggie get hurt."

But Maggie lay awake, restless and longing for John and the beauty of the Kent countryside. Can only blame myself. He asked me to ring him. Perhaps it is for the best; what will be will be, she sighed. But the sadness was there with her through the long night. She thought of big Jim and Miss Stiles, and prayed to God to give her courage if it was her turn next.

In all her troubles, this was the most depressing night she had ever spent. The previous day she had been to the clinic for her radium treatment, tomorrow it would be the same; it was to go on for another three weeks, and she dreaded it. To be put in a kind of machine and roasted each day, it was not painful, only frightening. It was the waiting along with the other patients that upset her, their faces like zombies, all with the same dread in their hearts. Many were well advanced in this terrible disease and they looked dreadful. Happy-go-lucky little Maggie, who could not believe that such a place existed, now sat in the line with them waiting her turn. She pressed her face to the pillow, dear God, give me courage, she prayed. She felt sure that if she was to go down to Oak Tree Cottage, she would get well. Now she stood a chance of losing John and her cottage. The world seemed a sad, lonely place without them. If I do ever get well, I'll probably end up scrubbing floors again. She commiserated with herself until the dawn light came through the window.

The next two weeks fled swiftly by; she visited the clinic each morning and returned hot and exhausted. Eva, her new daughter-in-law, would be waiting to give her a cool drink and help her to bed. Babs grew very fond of Eva. She could cook, clean and tend babies with such little effort. Babs admired that cool efficiency. Her own fear of illness made her nervous and she relied on Eva's judgment to take care of Maggie. When the children fell and got a bump, Eva was there, ready and willing to repair the damage.

Maggie lay most of the day in the spare room listening to her family, sometimes they argued and sometimes they laughed. She had such a mixture of daughter-in-laws—Babs from Wales, Anne-Marie from South

Africa, and the dull beautiful Anna of Polish extraction; and now gay, generous Eva who never knew who her parents were and never cared. Strange thing a family; it grew like that big oak tree in Kent. Lots of branches and leaves, all from that one stout trunk, something of that tough old Liza, and of heavy, muscular, hard-working Dah. Life was very puzzling, was this the end for her? She lay listening to the babies playing and to Eva singing. No, Maggie Burns, take hold of yourself, it can't be.

Heavy footsteps and a gruff-sounding voice told her that Tom had arrived. He opened the door calling, "How are we, Maggie old girl? Feeling better?"

"I am fine, Tom," she replied with a smile. "Leave the door open, I like to see you all."

Tom began to tell them how Anna and he had got rooms in a shocking dump in Aldgate.

"Ain't staying long. Bleeding niggers upstairs and Pakistanis all over the place."

Eva was peeling potatoes in the kitchen to help Babs with the dinner. "Oh, so you're one of those, are you, Tom?"

"One of what?" inquired Tom.

"Racialists they call them, don't they? They hate colored folk."

"No, I ain't," argued Tom. "How can I be when me own flaming brother is colored?"

"Oh, I am pleased about that," returned Eva cheerfully, "but personally I don't care who calls me a black bastard, 'cause I is one." Then she went off into peals of laughter that echoed all over the flat.

Tom gave Eva a bang on the backside and said, "You're a bit of a lad, you are, Eva."

Maggie, listening to them, was amused, but wondered how the cold far-away Anna was faring with the rough, tough Tom. It was good to have a family even if she did lose John, but this ever-growing tiredness worried her. Must be the treatment, she might feel better later on.

The End of the Road

One morning she had a letter from John. It hurt, but did not surprise her.

Dear Maggie,
I sincerely hope that you are now on the road to recovery, and being taken good care of by your devoted family. I always knew that I never stood a dog's chance while they were around, and you have them all at home with you now. I have grown rather tired of this cat-and-mouse game you play with me. For the sake of all the past happiness we have known, and the warm generous love you have given me, I want us to part friends. I begin to see your point about us not getting on together, so I have taken a new situation, one which is of great interest to me. Please, I ask you, to tell me for the last time, will you come with me? It is my intention never to return to this country. If you decide in the negative, you can keep the cottage and I will pay an allowance into the bank for you, but I want an immediate answer.

John Malloy.

So this was the real hard John, this cold man, that so far she had only a surface glimpse of. Well, he knew what he could do with his money and his cottage. Cats, mice and bloody dogs. Some love letter. She fumed in a white hot temper, and sat down and wrote back to him.

Dear John,
Many thanks for your kind, considerate letter. I wish you the best of luck with your new career. I'll take my things from Oak Tree Cottage next week. Keep your money, I don't need it.

Bon Voyage. Maggie.

While little Jenny went to post the letter for her, she looked out of the window. Her temper had now cooled, she saw the tall overpowering blocks of flats and the children playing on the debris of her old home. "Goodbye Oak Tree Cottage," she whispered. "Goodbye my lovely roses and Timothy." Then the tears began to fall. What now, Maggie Burns? she asked herself as she wiped the tears away. What are you going to do with your life now?

Her treatment at the hospital had finished and, in spite of her depression, she had begun to feel more like her old self. There had been no more news of John, but Joe had received a parcel of medical books through the post. On hearing of this she presumed that he had begun to dispose of the cottage.

She spent a lot of time just staring out of the window of Jim's flat. Lorries went tearing past, the children fought and screamed in the gardens in front of the flats. Then, like a soft perfume wafting on the breeze, her mind would go back to Oak Tree Cottage. The housemartins would be returning to their nests in the eaves. Primroses would be growing in the little wood. She wondered if the last two roses she had planted had taken. How she would have have loved to go and say goodbye to that cozy home, but pride forbade it. So she kept herself busy with the babies.

She went on a bus ride to Hampstead to visit Anne-Marie who was engaged in her own interior decorating and making a fine job of it too. Tom still loafed about, but Anna, majestic as ever, was a barmaid in the Red Lion. Tom had managed to wheedle her diamond ring from her, but she still clung to her bracelet.

Maggie was really surprised by Anna, but what Anna thought of them was a mystery, she never ever held a conversation with anyone. They are all settling down, and you, Maggie Burns are drifting with the tide. I ought to find something to do, to take my mind off things.

Jim had promised to go to Oak Tree Cottage to fetch her belongings at the weekend. Not much of value there, only her clothes and John had bought most of them. It was February, it would soon be spring. However was she going to stand it, being cooped up here all the summer?

"Give an eye to the babies, I am going down the road," Babs's voice broke into her thoughts.

"Yes," she replied vacantly and went to stare at herself in the mirror. What a mess; her hair needed cutting, her face was pale and drawn, and she seemed to live in this old dressing-gown these days. With a sudden burst of energy she turned on the bath, rummaged in her case for fancy underwear, took out a nice dress and put it on a hanger. "Got to pull yourself together!" she muttered. "You look about ninety."

She began to transform her appearance. On tip toes she peeped in the mirror. Don't look as though I ain't got long to live, they might have made a mistake. She tried hard to console herself while she painted her face and piled her hair in a new style. Not bad, she said admiringly. High heels, smart shoes, and neat stockings made all the difference. It suited her, that green dress. She painted her nails and squirted perfume on her hair. When all was complete, she sat down, her chin quivered: "All dressed up and nowhere to bloody go," she said. When Babs comes back, I'll go and get a job. Can't hang about all day, it will drive me mad. Full of determination and feeling more like her old self, she awaited the return of Babs.

She dashed in somewhat breathless and very excited. "Crikey, Mum! You look smashing," was her first comment. Then she asked, "Did you know?"

"Know what?" demanded Maggie.

Babs opened the front door wide. "Look who I found in the street," she said.

Standing on the doorstep was John. No hat, untidy hair, his shirt collar undone and smelling strongly of whisky. He dashed in and caught her up in his arms.

"To hell with the man in the moon," he cried. "I can't get along without you, Maggie darling."

Then Babs discreetly disappeared. Maggie did try to restrain him, but once his lips pressed on hers and the rough unshaven skin brushed her cheek, she was beaten, the battle was over. They clung like two limpets together.

Then they sat on the old settee that the kids played on. The springs were coming through and there was children's litter all around them. It might have been the Ritz for all they knew or cared. John half boozed and dumb with happiness and Maggie wondering however she had lived without her love. The world seemed a different place already.

"I saw him wandering down the street. Thought I'd better rescue him," explained Babs.

"I was in that pub on the corner," said John.

"That's the old Barley Mow. There's not much else left of the old days."

"This is what I came for, darling." From his pocket he drew a little box and he slipped a lovely emerald ring on her finger. "Tomorrow another ring will join it. I want no arguments, Maggie." He waved a piece of paper. "A special license, we are going to get spliced."

Maggie stared down at the gleaming stone in her ring. "Oh John, what can I say?"

"Tomorrow?" yelled Babs. "I must go and phone Anne-Marie and tell Anna."

It's a bit soon. I wonder if I can get ready in time, pondered Maggie.

"I have been riding round with your trousseau in the back of my car for weeks. If you had turned me down, I was going to give it to the first little woman I saw."

"A new suit?" said Maggie with interest.

"The whole bloody caboodle, and all the way from Paris."

"You are so good to me, I don't deserve you." Her

lips quivered. There were still doubts in her mind, flickerings of fear. Could she still be a wife to him? Had the operation spoiled that part of her life?

He seemed to read her mind: "Maggie, darling, we will go straight to Oak Tree Cottage after the wedding and you will be as good as new in a few weeks."

She knew he was right. Already somewhere inside her, the sap was rising and she began to feel like a woman once more.

After John left, Babs and little Jenny brought all the boxes up. The excitement and "oh's" and "ah's" as they opened them! A lovely beige suit in shiny material with a fur-trimmed collar and cuffs. In a round box the dearest little hat made of the same fur and lots of veiling. Maggie placed it on her dark hair. "Blimey!" she said. "What's this? A bird's nest?"

"It's lovely," said Babs in an awed whisper as she stroked the fur on the suit. "I believe it's *real* mink."

There were shoes and a handbag and a fabulous nightie.

"He thinks of you, Maggie," said Babs without envy. "I think you're ever so lucky."

Jim came home from work and stared in amazement at all the finery laid out. "What's that? Someone won the pools?" he asked.

"Mum's getting married tomorrow," Babs informed him.

Jim's face dropped a mile and Maggie picked up her parcels and left the room. From the sound of their voices they were arguing. Babs was on her side and Jim was being brought into line. Good, she thought, once Lord Jim was on her side, the others would follow. Not that she cared. Her mind was made up to marry John, but the love of her family she still held dear.

At midnight, Babs crept in to kiss her goodnight.

"It's all right, Mum, I've settled with Jim. We will all be at your wedding tomorrow."

"Thanks, darling," said Maggie and, reaching for her

handbag, she got out the last three five pound notes and said, "Go down the market in the morning and get yourself something nice and get that little sister of yours a pretty dress."

Babs cuddled her: "No one will ever be like you to me, Mum. I do hope you will be very happy."

The Wedding

The wedding was fixed for three o'clock at the local registry office. The girls helped her to dress, all happy and excited. They all looked very smart.

John was waiting in the lobby and was surprised to see all the family supporting her. He had waited so long for this day, he cared only to get it over with. As John slipped the gold band on Maggie's finger, he breathed a deep sigh of relief.

Outside, Al took many photos of them. Maggie looked very nice in her suit, and a spray of purple orchids brought out the blue in her eyes.

John wanted to drive straight down to Kent, but the others were persistent and they went back home to the party that had been laid on in a local hall. It was quite a do, swimming in beer with lots of food. It reminded Maggie of the night when she married her big Jim. But there was one big difference—a cool, calm John, who never left her side.

At six o'clock they left for Oak Tree Cottage, amid the cheers of the guests and the rattle of tin cans tied to their car. At eight o'clock they drove down the lane to the cottage, to see that the lights were on.

"Someone's in there," said Maggie rather startled.

"Only Mr. York," said John. "He's keeping the fire alight for us. I have been staying down here the last two weeks. I believe it was this place that made me decide to stay in England."

In the twilight, the garden looked strange and misty. A silver frost lay on the lawn, and the oak loomed tall and shadowy as they went up the path hand in hand.

"We're coming home, Maggie," whispered John. His strong arms picked her up and carried her over the threshold.

A log fire burned brightly in the red brick fireplace. The brasses shone and the floral curtains were drawn to keep out the dark night. Just a pink light glowed from the old-fashioned lamp standard in the corner casting a warm glow onto a bowl of white hyacinths and golden yellow daffodils in the middle of the table—a gift from Mr. York's garden.

"Oh! how lovely!" exclaimed Maggie as she buried her nose in them.

She saw Timothy sitting on the rug in front of the fire, taking a bath and sank down on the settee. "Oh John," she said. "It's lovely to come home again."

He put his arm around her. "Yes, darling and now it's forever."

Timothy jumped up onto Maggie's lap.

"Hey, hoppit, you old rogue," said John. "This is my girl."

"Let him stay," said Maggie. "Where did you find him?"

"Out in the woods. He looked like a scarecrow—as black as ink. But I promised him I'd bring you back and I did," he said triumphantly.

He fetched a bottle of brandy. "Let's celebrate our own wedding and get drunk together."

In the morning John still slept on, but Maggie was out in her garden. Little green shoots were appearing on the rose trees and pale primrose spikes showed above the ground. The grass, moist with dew, smelled fresh and heavenly. She took deep breaths of the clean air and felt she wanted to run and jump like the young lambs out there in the meadow. It's funny what this place does to me, she thought.

It was still cold but with a warm sweater on she went down the lane to greet the milkman, who said, "Good morning, Mrs. Malloy. How are you? Much better I hope."

Then along came the paperboy on his bike. She took

the milk and papers and feeling on top of the world, went back home, cooked breakfast, laid it all out on a tray and took it upstairs to John who loved breakfast in bed. She curled up on the end of the bed and opened the newspaper. Then suddenly she jumped up, spilling the coffee. "Why," she yelled, "that stupid nit Al! Look what he's done."

On the middle page was a photograph that had been taken outside the registry office.

"Calm down, Maggie," said John hanging grimly on to his coffee. "What the hell has that son of yours done?"

She was speechless. "This," she said thrusting the picture at him. John looked at it for a while, then burst out laughing. Maggie, very disgruntled, snatched the paper back.

"It's no joke," she said. "Now all the flaming village knows we only got married yesterday."

"Oh, you don't care all that much. And I'm sure I don't."

"But listen to this," she said and read out: "One of our most eminent scientists, John Malloy, was married today to an attractive widow, Mrs. Maggie Burns. The couple are pictured after the marriage surrounded by her family by her first husband."

In the picture was little Maggie and tall John all smart, and alongside them was Maggie's family. Jim and Babs holding the twins by the hand. Anne-Marie with her baby in her arms. On the other side were big Tom and Anna, and next to them, all smiles, were Eva and Joe. In the background was tall Megan and frizzy-haired Ben.

"How did they get in it?" declared Maggie. "I look like the old woman who lived in a shoe."

John was still looking at the picture. "Tell you what, Maggie, you look the youngest one there."

"Get away," said Maggie. "It's because I'm the smallest." But she smiled softly and said, "They're a lovely looking family. Don't you think so, John?"

John did not answer, he was still a bit jealous of them.

"That stupid Al," said Maggie. "He would sell his soul for a packet of fags."

"Forget it, Maggie darling. I must get up, I want to show you my new project."

What's he up to now? she thought.

Soon he was showing her the piece of woodland he had acquired at the bottom of the garden. "Got it cheaply," he said proudly.

She walked down with him to see it. The smell of burning wood met her nostrils and Mr. York was there. He had a fire going and had started to clear the land.

"You're not going to pull down all those nice trees?" she asked.

"Not all of them. I am going to build a tall tower to house a telescope."

"Whatever for?" she asked.

"To watch the space race," said John. "Can't stay out of it altogether. Great discovery, space."

Maggie shrugged her shoulders. She did not know what it was all about and did not care. Knowing John, he could not remain idle for long. As long as it was down the garden she did not mind, instead of far away in some Godforsaken hole. Oak Tree Cottage was all she wanted. She knew she was going to be happy there.

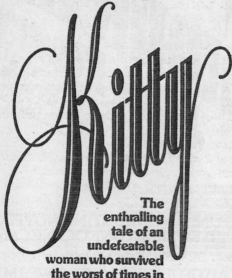